KINGDOM OF THE STRONG

TONY CAVANAUGH

hachette
AUSTRALIA

Published in Australia and New Zealand in 2015
by Hachette Australia
(an imprint of Hachette Australia Pty Limited)
Level 17, 207 Kent Street, Sydney NSW 2000
www.hachette.com.au

National Library of Australia
Cataloguing-in-Publication data:

Cavanaugh, Tony.
Kingdom of the strong/Tony Cavanaugh.

ISBN: 978 0 7336 3295 2 (paperback)

Cold cases (Criminal investigation) – Queensland – Fiction.
Ex-police officers – Queensland – Fiction.
Detective and mystery stories.

A823.4

Cover design by Luke Causby
Cover images courtesy of Arcangel Images
Author photograph courtesy of Jasin Boland
Text design by Kirby Jones
Typeset in Sabon by Kirby Jones
Printed and bound in Australia by Griffin Press, Adelaide, an accredited
ISO AS/NZS 14001:2009 Environmental Management System printer

For Matt Ford

PART I

SUSPECTS

'Evil brings men together.'

ARISTOTLE

THE MAN WHO WOULD BE KING

I AM SINKING.

All around me the press and swell of water. Above me a shimmering surface, a radiance of dappled sun. I can't get back up to it. I can't hear anything but the roar inside my ears. I'm sinking. Below me I can't see form or place, but it's dark. I'm on my way down to the ocean floor. If I make it there, still alive, I'll probably thud. My arms are waving, my legs are scrambling. I'm trying to find something firm, for my feet to touch, to springboard back up towards the surface, but there's nothing, only the crush of water. Drowning is supposed to be a pleasant way to die, that's what I've been told. Really? Better than falling asleep and not waking? If I open my mouth and inhale, a rush of cold water will fill my lungs and I'll sink even faster. Will it bring bliss, that rush of cold water? I don't think so; I think it will bring panic, an onslaught of panic, greater than the panic I'm feeling now.

Before I was sinking I was getting scared – scared that we were so far from the shore, like the old man and the sea, from the book Dad read me when I was in bed and he'd sworn off the grog, last time for sure, when I lay on the cool pillow that smelled of lemon and the breeze came in off the paddocks, fluttering the curtains, when he came in and sat on the end of my bed and said: Son, this is a great book.

My heart is being crushed. I'm not so good at science, but I think that's what happens when you sink in water: your insides get crushed.

Why aren't I floating? Why can't I float to the top? Why am I sinking? It's against the law of nature, isn't it? I'm messed up. An aberration.

I think I can see the bottom. Will I hear a thud? Maybe not. No sounds down here. It's really quiet. Getting darker too. I can't make out the outline of our little fishing boat. What happened at the end of *The Old Man and the Sea*? Did the man die? Did he bring that fish in to land? I might have been asleep by the last page.

—

I HATE WATER. Not the stuff that comes out of taps – that's okay. I hate being in it. Oceans. Lakes. Swimming pools. Rivers. I almost drowned when I was eleven. My father, in a riotous fit of spontaneous whatever, after too many beers and my worried looks, lifted me from the floor of our rental tin boat and tossed me into the sea. I sank. In what I guess was a sudden hit of the guilts, he then jumped in after me and scooped me up, mid-sink, and carried my limp body back up to the surface. He didn't apologise, didn't say anything, just plonked me into the boat, started the engine and steered back in the direction of home. Since that day, some thirty-five years ago, I've managed to avoid bodily contact with water, aside from taking showers and baths. People scoff when I tell them this. 'Oh but, Darian, swimming in the ocean is just the most exhilarating experience.' That sort of thing. No, it's not. Give me a footpath, give me concrete, give me a place where my feet are firm on the ground.

It certainly wasn't nostalgia then that led me to a cabin on the edge of a lake, a place of hibernation where I had been for almost a month, where I would sit on the balcony staring at the expanse of charcoal-grey water; where, most days, I'd drag a small wooden boat, which came with the hire of the cabin, into the water, jump in and chug towards the middle, casting a line, spending hours unsuccessfully fishing while I stared at the mountains in the distance, whose peaks were always shrouded in layers of winter mist.

I was the only tourist in the Great Lakes district on the coast of New South Wales. I'd turned off the highway in search of a motel and got lost while driving along twisted roads that clung to the forms and shapes of the jagged mountain range that hovered over a series of interlocking lakes close to the Pacific Ocean. I'd been driving hard and fast, away from failures. Rose, a woman I loved, and The Train Rider, a killer I'd hunted, their worlds coalescing into an increasingly dark spiral I was unable to control, were both now lost to me.

Rose I had left behind in Byron Bay, a day's drive from the lake, and The Train Rider, a man whose depraved serial killings had begun to define me, was in the wind. Would I connect with either of them again? I didn't know. I was in the wind too.

Sitting in a wooden boat in the middle of a lake in dark winter, I was doing an awesome job of not thinking about where to go to next. Back home, on the Noosa River, up in sunny Queensland, my land of sarongs and hammocks, a life of early retirement, didn't yet feel like an option. My house on the river – yes, more water, but I only look at it – was a brooding reminder of those failures. Not long ago Rose had moved in and her scent would still be in the walls even though she was no longer there. The Train Rider had followed me from Melbourne, had infiltrated the entire area, from Noosa to Nambour, Gympie, Tewantin, towns dotted across the hinterland and coastline; he had vanished just as I came close to finally catching him, but he had left a mark on that part of my life that wouldn't fade anytime soon.

I had tried not to think about him, which was as successful as not noticing that daylight followed the night. The Train Rider was a monstrous killer. He'd taken, if we were to believe his horrid ex-wife, hundreds of girls in a rampage that'd lasted decades. Snatched them off trains, raped then killed them. Then stuffed them using a state-of-the-art taxidermy process. It was beyond anything I had ever seen, and the house full of his victims, naked and preserved, was like a horror movie that I couldn't shake off. I'd failed to catch him. First in Melbourne, as a cop, then on the Sunshine Coast. I didn't like failure. I wasn't used to it and his survival ate at me like a decay inside my body. As far as we knew he had fled the country. The Train Rider, Kirk Thornhill, was also very wealthy and I couldn't help but see him sitting on a beach in a resort somewhere in Asia where the policing isn't what you'd call rigorous, rising from the sand and surf to ride another third world train, take a girl and add her to a growing tableau of real-life dolls.

I'd stay here, on the lake, until the tourists and the sun turned up; that was my plan. And after that, there was no plan. Maybe a trip to Thailand to visit some of my late father's greatest hits in an effort to get to know him, the bars and the brothels where he spent his last couple of decades in the absence of the son he'd tossed into the sea in a drunken burst of anger a week before he closed the front door behind him, walked across the paddocks to the highway and never returned home.

I dragged my boat out of the water, up onto the sand, and hurled the anchor back into the lake. I lassoed another rope around the base of a tree on the shoreline and then began to trudge up towards my cabin. Yet again without any fish. I pulled my thick black woollen jacket tight around me. Light was fading and the chill of the night was fast developing, blowing down from the mountains.

A white Toyota Camry, late model, was parked out the front of my cabin, next to my mid-sixties bright red Studebaker. Hire car written all over it. Maybe another tourist in search of some midwinter lake activity, I thought at first. Then I saw, as I drew closer, that the front door to my cabin was wide open. I had a visitor.

'Is that you, Darian?' I heard from inside, as I walked towards the steps leading up to the porch.

'Yeah, boss, it's me,' I said.

I stepped inside.

—

THERE ARE THREE very different breeds of Police Commissioner. One is the guy – always a guy – who went from wearing a school uniform to wearing a police uniform, no interruption, and began to pound the footpath, learning the ways and whys in the land of crime, from the hopelessly pathetic to premeditated savagery, from the skivs and popheads to the gangs and killers. This is the guy who works his way up from the street; who, by the time he's reached a desk on the top floor of HQ, has got to know every single person on the floors beneath him. Many are friends, some are enemies, but all of them have a job that he also did, once, so from his grand office of control he knows and understands the challenges of every working man and woman in the Force. When this type of Commissioner is a good guy, not corrupt or in dumb league with politicians, he earns a ferocious loyalty.

Then there's the guy – pretty much, again, always a guy – who works his way up the ranks, does the hard yards, understands the rigours of the job, earns the respect of his men and women, pledges to help and then, having got the top job, finds himself seduced by the power and influence and turns on his men and women, once loyal but now increasingly disillusioned as his decisions and behaviour become more about currying favour with politicians than active concern for the wellbeing of his troops. This is the guy who disconnects and, in the job, grows into another, unrecognisable person. This is the guy who usually goes down in a coup.

Then there's the Commissioner who went to university and studied up on criminology and psychology and business, and arrived at the Force wearing a suit and carrying a degree and a whipper-snip skill in Microsoft Excel spreadsheets and wowed the fuck out of the gangs of accountants and lawyers with PowerPoint presentations and felt the cool comfort of a desk while noting trends and talking the talk. These men and women were becoming increasingly popular with governments. The bull-headed old guys were being eased out; they weren't so hot at TV news conferences and they didn't do the latte thing with the rest of the media. They smelled of beer and chased skirt. They were old school, twentieth century.

Well, it wasn't really that black-and-white. The character of Commissioners was always much more nuanced, but cops live in a black-and-white world. Good guys, bad guys, them and us, the boss who understood and the one who had no clue, living in a world of data and politics.

Copeland Walsh, the man waiting for me inside the cabin, was from the old school. He became a cop in the late fifties. His term as Commissioner started in the nineties and crossed into the early twenty-first century, when he was replaced by a hot shot graduate from Sydney University who managed to alienate the men and women in uniform, the police union and finally a new government, who eventually decreed that the infighting and disgruntlement of the police department needed to remain out of the newspapers. He'd been fired and Copeland had been brought back, out of retirement, to take over as Commissioner. It was supposed to be an interim seat-warming type of thing but Copeland was good at his job and loved by all, a rare and true blend of the old school with a complete understanding of spreadsheets, data and how to drink a coffee without offending anyone. He was now close to seventy-five, the mandatory age of retirement for public servants having been blissfully ignored by him and the government he served.

Copeland, nicknamed Copland because he was a walking encyclopaedia of the land of cops, taught me pretty much everything I knew and was responsible for my own fast-tracked rise through the ranks to becoming Officer in Charge of Homicide at an unprecedentedly young age.

'Forgive the intrusion, but there's only so long an old man can stand outside in the cold. What say we light a fire?'

'Good to see you, boss.'

'And you, Darian. Haven't aged a wink.'

'Nor you.' Copeland was a tall man, at least six foot four. And he was big. He didn't walk. He lumbered. In his youth he had played cricket for Victoria. He was dressed in a dark-blue suit, blue and white striped shirt and a tie from one of the clubs he belonged to. This one today looked like the Melbourne Cricket Club tie. One of the most exclusive clubs in the country; took Copeland twenty-five years of waiting before he was granted membership.

'Liar. But kind words, old son, kind words.'

He had already set the fire. Manners, which he had in abundance, had prevented him from lighting it; that would have been an intrusion too far. Scrunched-up newspaper, kindling and small logs had come from a cane basket next to the stone fireplace. The cabin was all wood, old dark hardwood. It had that rustic North American cowboy feel to it, a sort of pioneer let's-be-men approach to walls and furnishings. There was an open-plan living and kitchen area with two bedrooms; everything I needed. Windows looked out to the lake and, on the other side, a forest of gum and tree ferns at the base of a mountain.

The flames took hold, crawled across the wood.

'How'd you find me?' I asked as I removed my coat and wet boots, sitting across from him.

'Credit card on your check-in,' he said.

I settled back in my chair and waited. Police Commissioners don't leave their offices on the top floor of HQ, let alone the building itself, let alone the city or the state, let alone hire a car and drive a couple of hours from the nearest airport to a remote cabin by a lake for a fireside chat with a former detective who abruptly resigned four years before. And if they *do* undertake any of the above, they don't do it alone. Whatever it was he needed from me it was important. To him.

'I understand that you read. To fill in the days,' he said.

'I do. But there hasn't been a day that felt it needed to be filled.'

'Embraced it totally? Good for you. Wish I could have said the same about my retirement. Bloody awful. Completely boring. I tried golf. That's what retirees are meant to do, that's the image on the sides of buses. Disaster. I felt as though I'd died and gone to hell. I tried to renovate the house but that was the same. And what was the point anyway? Renovations are for young couples, not an old man. Somebody suggested a cruise. I can't remember who but I remember thinking: Is this the end of the line? Sitting on a cruise ship, circling the world without point or meaning? Is this how it ends? You can imagine then how I felt when the Minister rang and asked if I'd go back, renew stability, keep the seat warm, a show of support for the troops until we found the right person to fill the post. No rushing the decision, that's what we agreed. Whoever was going to replace me needed to be thoroughly vetted. None of this postmodern psychobabble in the interview, either. A solid man. Or woman. Reliable. One of the troops. Someone they can look up to. None of this rancour and infighting. A leader. Someone with notches on his belt. Or hers. Know what I mean, Darian? Of course you do. Someone who's done the hard yards, walked the beats, worked in the tough divisions, successful conviction rate. But modern. New-media savvy. Might even have his own Twitter account. Or she might. No hint of corruption, of course. No scandal, or if there was, discounted. Thoroughly discounted. You know what the Force is like. *Service*, I should say. Rumours. Innuendo. Never escape that. But unless there's anything concrete, anything proven – you know what I mean, Darian? Of course you do – then it's just talk. Give me the facts. The evidence. That's our bread and butter.'

Copeland could be direct if he needed to but, in some instances, like this, the end point, the actual meaning of his speech, was arrived at via a circuitous route and, in some instances, again, like this, there wouldn't appear to be a meaning or end point at all. I'd played this game before. I was one of the few who knew how to play it; in fact, I was probably the only one in the police department. Most cops just stared at him blankly, waiting for clarity.

'You want me to resolve Isobel Vine's death,' I said. It wasn't a question.

He smiled, as a father would to his son upon the latter correctly divining a tangled challenge.

'That's my boy! Always on top of it. I knew I could count on you. Always get to the end of a conversation before we reach it.'

'Racine's been nominated to replace you,' I said. Again, it wasn't a question.

He leaned forward, nodding, grinning, eager, excited. Like a teacher with his best student.

Outside it had begun to rain. This was a regular pattern: clouds of mist in the morning, the pretence of fair weather in the early afternoon, icy squalls at night. Usually I'd be sitting by the fire reading my way through *Infinite Jest*, written by the linguistic genius David Foster Wallace, who had also been a junior tennis champion and killed himself at the age of forty-six. My age. Rain spattered the windows.

'The government wants him, you want him, the men and women in uniform want him and even the police union want him,' I said.

Nod, nod, nod, smile, smile, smile. That's right, Darian, keep going.

'And he wants him.'

Nod, smile. Almost there, Darian.

'But there's that small matter of twenty-five years ago.'

'Tragic incident,' Copeland said. 'Hell of a misunderstanding.'

'And even though everyone's forgotten about it …'

'Except you,' he interjected.

'… it's the sort of blemish that could derail him.'

'First thing the press will do upon his announcement. Look into his past service record.'

'But if there's been an independent inquiry, just completed ...'

'Which fully exonerates him.'

'... which fully exonerates him, then the blemish is gone. And Racine has a clear path to become the new popular, successful Police Commissioner.'

Go to the top of the class, Darian.

'You'll have your own office, staff of your choice, total independence, report only and directly to me, no interference. Excellent remuneration. One month, tops. Maybe two. Car and apartment, per diem, all provided.'

He was leaning closer, his hands clasped. By now, in this life I'd established in the cabin, I would normally not only be reading by the fire but I would have eaten. The owner of the cabin had taken pity on me and my inability to catch a fish in the entire time I'd been here and had given me a bundle of fresh trout and whiting to freeze; enhancing the tourist experience for me.

I also leaned forward. Copeland knew what was coming and edged even closer.

'But what if I couldn't exonerate him?'

'If he's guilty?'

'If he's guilty,' I said.

'It was suicide,' he said firmly.

'The Coroner gave an open finding. He was balancing suicide, self-inflicted accident *and* murder. He couldn't decide between them. And it wasn't just Racine implicated; there were other cops.'

Copeland held my look, spoke sternly, a righteous man. 'I don't, *cannot*, believe that Racine, or any of the others for that matter, did it. Killed that poor young woman. But if your investigation reveals that he did, or was somehow involved, even witnessing one of the others, he goes down. This is, as you understand, a matter driven by political expediency, but it has to be, at the end of the day, about justice. I wouldn't have it any other way. Find the truth, Darian. I know you won't let me down.'

For four years, since leaving police HQ in Melbourne, I had been sitting by the Noosa River in a generally successful attempt to capture a sane and tranquil life. River watching, reading in the hammock, pelican feeding, cooking and listening to the crash of the ocean and the swell of the river, the sounds of the birds and happy cries of tourists had become my new four walls of existence. Melbourne, which I had fled, and to which I had returned only once, briefly, while on the hunt for The Train Rider, was a city defined, for me, by murder. You know when you hear a song and it reminds you of a first kiss or a break-up maybe, or catch a fragrance and re-run a moment from the past, when those sensorial moments are flooded by distant memories, joyous or otherwise ... The grid, the suburbs, the streets, the beaches and parks were all imprinted upon me through a history and culture of rampage and blood. Bodies strewn across the landscape. A city of murder. That was Melbourne. That was where Copeland wanted me to return.

Since losing Rose and failing to catch The Train Rider, I'd come adrift, sitting in the middle of a lake, doing slow circles in the water. No direction home, that was me. Home, my new home on the Noosa River, was defined by a shimmering failure: the presence of a girl who left me and a serial killer who eluded me.

'Why not get Internal Affairs to do it?' I asked.

He leaned towards me, as if inviting me into a secret, and jabbed his finger at me.

'Too political. They're all driven by bias and innuendo. Active-duty cops investigating active-duty cops? No. *You*, Darian. You upped and left without a goodbye or a thanks-for-the-memories. Turned your back on us and left Victoria. No grudges, old son. No hard feelings, not on my account. I understood, when they told me. You're a rogue. A loner. True to the righteous values. Independent. No loyalties to sway you. Nothing but contempt, a back turned and a new life begun. There couldn't be a better choice for the job.'

What are you not telling me, boss? I wondered as I stood up.

'Let's cook up some trout,' I said. 'The rain will ease in an hour or so. Then you can grab your bag from the car. I'll make up the bed in the second room.'

He grinned, the grin of a happy father, it seemed to me.

WE LIVE FOR MURDER

I BLINKED. IT WAS TWO MINUTES PAST FOUR. STILL DARK. Deep silence but for the sounds of snoring from the next room. The old man wouldn't be up for a few hours. I rolled out of bed. It used to be that I would stagger out of bed, stumble, crash, knocking myself out in the process. Not now, not since I'd left the Force – now I welcomed being awake with a bright zap of hello.

The fire was long dead. I pushed away the ash, then built a new cathedral of kindling, added some small logs and lit it. The cabin was freezing, but not for long. The flames caught and the glow and warmth spread through the room. I made a coffee, then another and another.

I sat in the chair where the boss had sat last night. We'd eaten the fish and talked of the old days. Reminisced. Swapped war stories. He told me how, when he came to the big chair, second time around, he'd discovered that all the troops in the Crime Department had been screwed over with their overtime; they worked an eight-hour shift, then, if still on a case, they worked the next four hours for no pay, and then, to add glory to glamour, they would work on at half their hourly wage. This they did, working at half-pay until they knocked off, maybe up to thirty hours straight. The concept of 'knocking off' doesn't really apply when you're on a murder investigation. That was the brilliant cost-saving approach of the previous Commissioner. Copeland was demanding the government change the madness and insisted he wouldn't budge from the seat until they complied.

We do it for justice, we do it for righteousness, but we also do it to pay the rent and send the kids, if you've got 'em, to school. Without a fair dollar, you can't focus on the job. As Officer in Charge of Homicide, I got that – whenever there had been a financial injustice done against my crews I'd go ballistic.

I liked the sound of the boss's snoring. It felt reassuring.

I hadn't said I'd do the job but I was going to. We both knew it. I'd deflected, changed the subject to food, dinner, fish, my inability to catch them; he'd laughed and played along without comment, brought up the war stories, the guys who'd gone down or gone away, and, as always, he ended up in a retrospective crimson gallery of his wife's memory. Jan had died of cancer after a far-too-long battle against it. I'd gone to the funeral. It was a very private ceremony and, as is sometimes the case, full of inter-family politics and acrimony.

There had been a problem with the body. She had cancer and it wasn't a good cancer, not that any are, but this one ravaged her body, shutting it down week by week. There was time to prepare. Her death could be marked in a diary, not the exact date, of course, but within a certain time frame. Copeland wanted her buried, intact, in a grave. Her sister wanted her cremated. Jan didn't care and was unaware of this developing family dispute over how to inter the crumbling body of the woman they loved.

It has always struck me as a curious dispute, because, really, when you're dead, does it matter?

It mattered to Copeland and it mattered to his sister-in-law. He was steadfast and he won. I suppose they were arguing over something else below the surface, but it became intense and permeated the funeral service to the point where the sister refused to even look him in the eye.

I was the only other cop there, aside from his Chief of Staff. This was just before he retired as Commissioner, first time around. Afterwards, in the car park, away from the family and mourners, he'd fallen into my arms and wept. I've never been good with the expression of my own emotions but, funnily enough, I'm good at it when it comes to other guys. I held him tight in the flat gravel car park of the Malvern Catholic church, telling him not to worry, telling him that it wouldn't matter if we were late for the lowering of the casket at the cemetery, telling him to let it out.

'A beautiful woman,' he had said at the time. 'Wise, sharp, smarter than me,' he kept repeating.

—

COPELAND WAS OFFERING more than a job. I'd been trying to fight it but having a hard time. I was remembering the buzz and the thrill of an incoming murder announcement. We lived for murder. It was exciting. In Victoria we'd have about a hundred a year, but we always wanted more. Give me two hundred, three hundred, give me a city of killings. The swirl of the eighth floor, the crews working Homicide, the buzz and the thrill, the oxygen that gets us moving. Eventually, over time, I was poisoned and burned out, unable to break free of the victims and their wraith-like murmurs of anguish fingering out like tentacles, reaching into my increasingly vodka-soaked mind as I kept searching for the very few killers, most notably The Train Rider, who slipped the net, stayed in the shadows, killing again and again or maybe retiring after one or two successful shots at it, leaving behind the plaintive sounds of the victims, calling for justice. Or calling out for me, at least, the guy who wanted to be perfect, Mr Hundred-Per-Cent, that's how it seemed. I couldn't deny, not after seeing the boss and hearing the war stories, that old feeling of camaraderie within the ranks of the crews on the eighth. The idea of going back to HQ, to solve a twenty-five-year-old killing, was giving me flutters of excitement.

COPLAND

MY FEET WERE HURTING. I WAS WEARING LEATHER SHOES FOR the first time in four years. I was also wearing a suit, again for the first time in four years. Shirt tucked in and a tie squeezed around my neck. I was walking into St Kilda Road HQ, up the steps and into the foyer. It was my first day back on the job as a cop.

St Kilda Road HQ was built to intimidate. All police HQs are. It's all about intimidation. I was in my early twenties the first time I walked into this building, a kid with just a few years in uniform behind him. I'd been picked by an older, powerful cop with influence to join Homicide at a ridiculously early age. Copeland had been impressed by my investigative skills and fast-tracked me.

I was intimidated the first time I stepped inside the building. Not today.

—

THE FOYER IS large: a tall, open space full of light that blasts through the facade of windows that face the street. A white marble floor. A long reception desk to the left, a security gate nearby, leading to a corridor where the lifts whisk you up to one of the nine floors above. A guy in uniform sitting behind the reception desk, dreaming of better things. Sometimes it'll be a woman. They are cops, who are not noted for welcoming skills, but, on average, they exceed many of the hotel greeters I've encountered around the world. My footsteps carried to the guy behind the reception counter as I approached.

'Darian Richards,' I said.

'Seeing?' he asked.

'Detective Inspector Darian Richards. I've been assigned an office. If you could tell me which one and buzz me through.'

'Yes, sir,' he said and began both an online and hard-copy search for any record of my name and expected arrival details. Behind me I could hear the incoming traffic passing through the revolving doors and walking across the foyer, zapping themselves through security and heading towards the lifts. I kept my back to them. In four years there would have been a turnover of cops, but most of those who walked behind me, across the foyer, would have known me. Was it yet out, on the gossip cycle, that I had returned? Most likely. Would anyone care? Only the crews, up on the eighth: my crews, those I had abandoned without a farewell, let alone an explanation.

'Detective Inspector?'

The guy was smiling. He'd finally found me in the system.

'You're on the second floor. Office 26G.'

Guys in uniform love hierarchy. Hierarchy is everything. Rank, position, respect. Intimidation also.

'Put me through to the Commissioner,' I said.

He stared at me as if I'd just announced I was a suicide bomber.

'Excuse me, sir?'

'The Commissioner. Get him on the line for me.'

'He's in a meeting.'

'I don't care. Tell his PA to interrupt him. Tell her to tell him that I need to speak to him immediately.'

Who is this fuckin' guy? he must have wondered as he pursed his lips in a very non-cop way, punched in the numbers and then spoke softly into the phone. 'Jen, it's David at reception. I have a Detective Inspector Darian Richards here and he wants to speak to the Commissioner … Yes, I told him that …'

I leaned over the desk and took the phone from David. He looked as though he was going to arrest me – he was a cop, after all – as I spoke: 'Jen, Darian. Get the old man out of the meeting. Tell him I need thirty seconds. Tell him, "precedential ground rules".'

'I warned him you'd still be a troublemaker, Darian.'

I laughed.

David looked as though he might have a stroke. I turned around, for the first time, still holding the phone and leaned back on the counter, now eyeing the shufflers and the stragglers. It was well past nine. The swaggering and the drunk, the heroes and the losers, tough guys with too many abs and too much attitude, the geeks and the cowed – you can pick 'em all. Every division has its own physicality, look, attitude. As they walked in for the new day, I now held their gaze. Most I knew, though not necessarily their names, and some I didn't. No-one from Homicide. Not yet. That would come.

'Is that you, Darian?'

'Boss, you've put me on the second floor.' Hierarchy rules, perception is everything.

'Not me, old son. I told them: don't put him anywhere but the eighth. Even the ninth, up here next to your old boss, but you know what they said? No space. Recruitment drive since you left. Bursting at the seams. We'll be putting desks on the bloody rooftop soon. It's a good office, Darian. I went there myself, checked it out. It looks straight across at Melbourne Grammar. All that bluestone, eighteenth century, not to my liking, never been convinced by the concept of boarding school, but it's necessary I suppose if you live hundreds of miles away from Melbourne and want the best for your son – or daughter – but it *is* gracious, that view.'

'I'm on the eighth or the ninth or I'm not here at all,' I said.

There was a moment's pause, then: 'Still a black-coffee man? Or has the life of sarongs and hammocks got you drinking herbal tea?'

'Still a black-coffee man, boss.'

'There's an excellent cafe at the top of Toorak Road, just across from France-Soir. New. Best coffee this side of the Yarra. You'll be comfortable there while we sort this out.'

'I'll be waiting for your call,' I said.

It might have been petty-minded and childish of me, schoolyard behaviour, but it was also necessary. If I was to get cooperation and respect from other cops – and in order to conduct a cold case in which the suspects were cops, that was exactly what I needed – I had to be seen to be the top gun I once was, not a loser, not a wannabe, not a forgotten hero who'd lost touch, now rusty. They had to believe I was still the leading homicide investigator, the guy with the best solve rate, the guy people lived in fear of, the guy who ran the sexiest and most sought-after division. Even if I wasn't that guy and, after four years in a hammock by a river, I *knew* I wasn't that guy, not anymore. I had to pretend and hope like hell everyone bought it.

—

ON THE NIGHT of 21 December 1990, eighteen-year-old Isobel Vine was found dead in her house in Osborne Street, South Yarra. She was slumped, naked, on the back of her bedroom door, hanging by a man's tie that had been wrapped around her neck. She, or someone else, had secured the tie to a solid brass hook on the door. Because she was naked the immediate assumption was that she had died during a fling with auto-erotic asphyxiation that had gone terribly wrong.

I was sitting in the cafe, looking out across Toorak Road, a long boulevard that sweeps down from St Kilda Road, past swanky outdoor cafes, expensive designer-clothing shops, restaurants and hotels, down a hill through the suburb of South Yarra, one of the hippest and most expensive in the city, until it reaches a stately park on one side and a modern library on the other and begins to climb up another hill; over the other side is Toorak, the heart and soul of old money and tradition within Melbourne. Trams clattered along the street, which was, like all the old streets of Melbourne, originally built from bluestone cobbled blocks, many of which still remain. BMWs and Saabs jostled for space on the road, trying to slide past the trams, which paused to let on and disgorge passengers every few hundred metres. I was going through the original case file, which had been dragged out of the Archives building in North Melbourne and couriered across to my rented apartment, which happened to be just around the corner, off Toorak Road, in a street lined with oaks, Davis Avenue.

The file wasn't exactly thorough. The details of the case – a dead teenage girl in a South Yarra house – were pretty straightforward, albeit exotic in a weird sexual way, to the first responding officers. As they sealed off the house and waited for CIB, the Coroner and pathologists to arrive, they speculated that the death was her own fault. She had indulged in some masturbatory fantasy while going for the thrill of the choke and then lost control.

There were no signs of a struggle or of any violence, anywhere inside the house. No break-in at a window or door. Rape and murder were not only discounted, they weren't even considered.

Auto-erotic asphyxiation was, and remains, a very unusual death, and for a young woman to die in this way was extremely rare. More recently it has taken on a cultural relevance, with Michael Hutchence and David Carradine allegedly dying while experiencing the rush and thrill that the loss of oxygen can bring to a sexual experience. The problem with choking yourself, despite whatever fail-safe mechanisms you put in place to avoid a nasty accident, is that you flirt with the edge of consciousness, and it's a very narrow edge. One half-second too long and you've lost consciousness and you're dead. Choking during sex is definitely a two-person game.

Additionally, the responding cops considered suicide, presuming that Isobel had deliberately wrapped the tie around her neck and then slumped to choke herself to death. A little weird, but there was very little that they hadn't seen before.

What seemed like a Coronial toss-up between an auto-erotic asphyxiation gone horribly wrong or a suicide suddenly went awry when, some days later, Isobel's father, an elderly jeweller named Eli, loudly and angrily announced that it was in fact murder.

That was when the shit well and truly hit the fan, and that was why I was sitting in a cafe in South Yarra, waiting on an office in St Kilda Road, reading a crusty old file and wondering if any of the original responding officers were still in uniform.

Eli's story provoked questions not only about Isobel's death but also about police involvement in her life in the weeks leading up to it. Seven weeks before she died, Isobel had returned to Australia from an exchange program where she had spent a term in her final year at a high school in La Paz, Bolivia. When she stepped off the plane she'd been met by members of a Federal Police task force, who'd been tipped off about a small quantity of cocaine she was smuggling into the country. These Feds, according to Eli, had harassed Isobel right up until her death, with some hardcore threats of jail time, wanting to know whom she was bringing the cocaine back for.

The revelation that Isobel was being harassed by the cops and, no doubt, by the drug importers, placing her firmly in the middle of one gang wanting her to talk and the other wanting her to stay silent, added credibility, some suggested, to the suicide theory.

But old Eli kept screaming. It was murder. And, he added, the ones who killed her were the ones with the most to lose: cops who were in with the drug ring, Eli claimed. They were the ones Isobel was most scared of. They got her to bring in the cocaine and then they killed her when she was caught. Nobody paid a lot of attention to the old guy. Just a distraught father howling at the wind. Give us the evidence or shut the fuck up, was the general attitude.

The case then took a turn when it was revealed that four young cops *had* been at Isobel's house on the night she died. She'd hosted a party and they'd turned up. I checked the file. Isobel had died at approximately four in the morning. The party had begun at seven the previous night and, according to the very brief witness statements, the last person at the house left her alone, stoned, drunk and listlessly happy at about 2.45am.

The four cops were all young constables. They all said they'd met up with a friend, a girl with the improbable name of Ruby Jazz, at one of the city nightclubs, the Underground, and she'd told them about a party at a girl's house in South Yarra. Ruby was going there and suggested they tag along. Which they did. Their witness statements were also very brief. They'd arrived at about midnight and had left by one.

The first three names listed in the file were Boris Jones, Jacob Monahan and Aristotle Pappas.

The fourth was Nick Racine, the next in line to become Victorian Commissioner of Police.

Confounded by the lack of evidence amid the accusations, but having confirmed that Isobel was being hassled by Feds who were investigating a drug-importation ring, the Coroner gave an open finding. In other words, he couldn't make up his mind. Soon afterwards, Isobel was cremated.

All of this happened well before I joined Homicide.

Over the years the Isobel Vine case took on a mystique, largely because it had never been solved, but also because at its centre was the strikingly memorable image, conjured up in lurid reports by the media, of a dead naked girl tied to the back of her bedroom door. And because her father, Eli the jeweller, had raged at the injustice of her death ever since. Like one of those obsessive nutjobs you occasionally see hanging around outside the front of an embassy or an abortion clinic, old Eli took to mounting a lonely and ignored vigil by the front steps of the St Kilda Road police HQ on the anniversary of her death. Every year he came with two hand-scrawled placards that railed against the murder of his daughter and the ongoing cover-up from within the walls of the building, a cover-up orchestrated by the police who were guilty of Isobel's murder who now, year after year, determined to keep the truth silent, never to be exposed or revealed. *When will the true killers of my daughter – POLICEMEN! – be held to justice?* he asked in thick black texta. I remember seeing the old guy, dressed in a cheap plastic coat, shivering against the cold wind and ignoring the rain as it fell around him, parked by the steps leading up to the foyer, holding his signs, each one bearing a colour photograph of his daughter. He was there, out the front, every year on the day of her death. He didn't speak – he just glared at every one of the passing cops, especially 'the four', Jones, Monahan, Pappas and Racine, as they arrived for work. After a while nobody bothered to even notice him. He was mad, obsessed. As more time passed, 'the four' went on their way, slowly climbing the ranks, and, one assumed, began to forget about the fresh-faced, dimpled Isobel with her shortish dark bobbed hair, her high cheekbones and wide smile with one crooked tooth.

Until now. I knew that Racine had, according to the boss, welcomed my appointment to investigate Isobel's death, but I wondered about the others. I didn't know Boris Jones and had met Monahan only a few times in the past. Last I heard Monahan was high up in the Drug Squad. Pappas was a Homicide cop. I'd knocked his application back a few times while I ran the squad. My successor, Zach Reeve, had hired him. Pappas was okay but he seemed, to me, a little too prone to fits of anger and he did have something of a wild past. Girls and clubs. I wasn't surprised to read that he'd been involved with the others at the inner-city nightclub. Back in the eighties he was a booze-girls-and-coke boy. I'd always had a bad vibe about him.

Twenty-five years is a long time to completely forget about an embarrassing incident – at best – or a crime – at worst – that never caught up with you.

My phone buzzed. I put down the file and answered.

'You're on the eighth floor: 803, next to Homicide,' said Copeland.

'Be there soon.' I glanced down at the files. 'Hey, the files that were sent across to me, are they the only ones? They seem thin.'

'No idea, old son. I just put in the request and left it up to the archives people.'

Copeland signed off cheerily, leaving me to worry that the scant official records of her death were going to make the job, nearly three decades later, all the more difficult. And I couldn't get it out of my mind that some cops deliberately keep case notes at a bare minimum in order to deflect prying eyes. Was that what happened with Isobel's file? If so, a good job was done.

There's an old truism in policing: every moment beyond the actual crime is a bad moment lost. The killing is a hot zone and as the hours tick by the investigation becomes more challenging. Cold case work relies on recreating that hot zone and the case files are the first important element.

This was starting to feel icy.

ROADWORKS

Sitting inside a police cruiser watching a procession of cars crawl past her at the highway-roadworks regulation speed of forty kilometres per hour would have to be the most boring task on earth, thought Maria. For three weeks she had sat in the car, its red-and-blue lights circling to advise drivers that yes, roadworks speeds were enforced, staring at the construction guys as they poured asphalt and rolled backwards and forwards over the freshly made new lane in the highway. The two northbound lanes on the Bruce Highway, close to the Nambour turn-off, had narrowed into one and the traffic inched by as trucks and construction vehicles and men in yellow safety vests laboured on. Why the government had seen fit to place a manned police cruiser at every roadworks site along the highway she did not know. It seemed a huge waste of resources. Up and down the length of it there would have been at least a dozen other cops, like her, bored out of their brains, watching the cars, watching the road being built, wishing that something, anything, might happen. All she did was stare vacantly through her windscreen, hoping that a driver might go insane and smash out onto the dirt-and-gravel shoulder with a hundred-kilometre surge of dust and stone, endangering life, so she could fire up the siren and give chase. Maybe the driver had a pistol and he could fire at her, *The Fast and the Furious* style, and she'd fire back, hit their tyres and watch as the getaway car skidded off the road and, sailing through the air, crashed into a tree, whereupon it would burst into flames. Then maybe she could leap from her cruiser, gun at the ready, and run to the car and drag the bank robbers or drug dealers with a boot full of coke and cash out of the flames, just before a massive fireball engulfed the entire area.

Nobody did anything remotely illegal. They all drove at their stately forty and smiled, sometimes nodding or waving to her as they passed.

Occasionally she fantasised over some of the better-looking guys who drove the trucks and poured the asphalt, but that, too, was a short-gain trip. They were all too busy to talk to her except the occasional dumb-arse supervisor who would lean on the side of her parked car and chat inanely about black spots on the highway or how many fish he'd caught on the weekend. And anyway, none of the highway workers were her type. They all had the sunglasses-tatts-and-beard thing going on, and even though her lover Casey was as tattooed as Ray Bradbury's *The Illustrated Man*, the thick-beard look, which reminded her of the Kelly Gang or dirty pirates from three hundred years ago, gave her the creeps. She stared at their beards and wondered what insects and vermin and foodstuffs had gathered in them.

This was her punishment, she knew, from Fat Adam, her boss, the head of the Noosa Hill police station, a gift to her from his envious little heart, for having become high profile in a world where mediocrity reigned. Only recently she had been reassigned, by the Commissioner, no less, to a very high-profile task force to investigate The Train Rider, a Melbourne serial killer who had relocated. Maria had worked out of the salubrious Homicide offices in Roma Street HQ, down in Brisbane. The task force had exploded. She'd been fired out of it but, soon afterwards, almost caught the killer and, in doing so, saved the lives of three terrified girls. And Fat Adam didn't like any of it.

Another forty-three kilometres of roadwork to go. It was a big reno, and both the state and federal governments were proud of their nation-building in the form of added lanes to the existing highway system, which spanned the edge of the continent, connecting each of the capital cities in a vast, open, lonely, empty land. When she wasn't imagining fireballs in the paddock or staring at the groaning road-building machines, she'd sometimes try to do the calculations on how long it was taking them to construct the road on which she sat. She'd never been good at maths, but this was impossible. Some days they'd advance a metre. Some days, thirty metres. Some days it rained and nobody turned up. Except for her, of course, because even in the rain, when the trucks lay idle and the workers enjoyed a paid day off, she had to sit in the cruiser and enforce the speed limit. Occasionally Casey rode out to her on his Harley and kept her company in the passenger seat of the cruiser – breaching a number of cop regulations, but she didn't care; she was past caring – with a lunch of cooked noodles, Thai-style mostly, and her favourite: key lime pie. He'd regale her with stories and, like kids, they'd play I-spy, then, when that wearied, they'd make up fantasies about the people inside the cars that passed them so slowly that they could see in and get a snapshot impression of the driver and passengers. None of the stories were as good as the car chase and gunshots ending in flames as she heroically rescued the baddies from the burning car. Some days she listened to *The Hunters and Collectors Best Of* CD and chanted the chorus of 'Holy Grail'. Some days she jived to the indie band Machine Gun Fellatio, who Casey insisted had the best name band ever, with the possible exception of Les Négresses Vertes.

Cars on the highway, an endless stream. When she was a kid she'd loved being in the back seat in her parents' car on the highway, staring out through the rear window. Who are these people? she used to wonder. Where are they going and where have they come from and are they happy? Are they driving into the arms of a lover or a kid like me or are they driving to a place that will make them angry? Or sad. She'd often give them names. She would sit there, on the back seat, staring through the rear window and think: hello, your name is Ant. Or: hi, your name is Sissy. Or: hello, you don't have a name because you look mean and I think you should die.

Cars on the highway, an endless stream; this wasn't why she had become a cop. Sure, all cops did the drudge. Part of the gig. But if Fat Adam had his way, she'd be on road patrol for the rest of the year and well into the next. She'd been thinking about transferring out of Noosa. Even a one-dog town in the middle of the outback would be more fun than this. Casey had said he'd follow her – 'No dramas, babe' – just as long as she was happy.

Her mobile rang.

'Hello?'

'Chastain?' It was Fat Adam. Maybe he'd just got news that the roadworks were going to be extended for another two hundred k's.

—

How DOES SHE do it? thought Adam.

Is she fucking Darian Richards?

Is she fucking the Police Commissioner?

Before picking up the phone to call her, he'd been sitting in his office, staring, yet again, at the letter from the Commissioner that stated that his officer, Senior Constable Maria Chastain, had been seconded, at the request of the Victorian Commissioner, to Melbourne, to work on a short-term special investigation. I mean, really, come on, from one Commissioner to another ... about *her*?

Does this have anything to do with Darian Richards? It has to, thought Adam.

He stared out through the window of his office at the teams of detectives and investigators who worked the main open-plan room at Noosa Hill. They were under his control, all of them. The only wild card was Chastain. He wanted to hurt her.

He'd been staring at the letter for over a week. When he first read it he was astonished. Angry. Bitter. He ignored the letter for as long as he could, but now, after a week, he knew that he'd soon get a phone call, saying, 'Why isn't Chastain in Melbourne?' and there'd be no answer. You can't say, 'Because I'm pissed off she gets all these high-profile cases and no-one ever thinks about me.'

Adam came from Melbourne. He'd been on the Sunshine Coast, running Noosa Hill, for just over three years. He knew Melbourne and all its back streets and its bad guys, he knew the cops who owed him a favour and he knew it could be a tough town. If Chastain was going down there to work on a special investigation, at the request of the Commissioner himself, then maybe Adam might arrange for a bit of a welcoming party for her. Give her a bit of rumble, give her a bit of *Think you're so high and mighty? Take this, bitch.*

But as he picked up the phone, he knew he wouldn't follow through. He couldn't admit it to himself but he was scared of payback from either Richards or her crazed boyfriend, Casey Lack.

'Hello, Maria,' he said. 'You're going to Melbourne.'

TANTRUMS

I PACKED UP THE FILES AND WALKED ACROSS FAWKNER PARK, a large and gracious expanse that extends from Toorak Road down to Commercial Road, towards HQ. More oak trees. This part of Melbourne, like many parts of the inner city, was created back in the nineteenth century by wealthy Englishmen. These were the empire-building days. English-mansion-style houses were surrounded by cramped workers' cottages, wide boulevards by narrow side alleys and streets for the less important. Large parks had been designed and built by Englishmen who planted elms, poplars and oaks; they weren't just creating a park, they were advertising the glory of the British Empire. As winter fast approached, many of the trees in the park were losing their leaves. Melbourne is, really, the most European city in the country.

Fawkner Park is quite beautiful but, like pretty much every place in Melbourne, it was defined for me by crime. Many years ago the entire park was wired, all of its trees, for the surveillance of some guys bringing in drugs. I'd been in the park on three other criminal occasions. All murders. The Commercial Road end of the park was the wild part. The Alfred Hospital was across the road and its emergency department was the hotspot for ODs.

Halfway across the park my phone buzzed. It was Maria.

'Are you at the airport?' I asked. 'Jump in a cab and meet me at St Kilda Road. We have to get you sworn in as a special constable.'

'I'm not at the airport,' she said in what sounded like a very brusque tone. 'I'm sitting in a police cruiser on the Bruce Highway.

I've only just been told by Adam that the Victorian Police Commissioner has seconded me to work on some independent investigation.'

'Yeah. Adam just told you that? You were meant to be here yesterday.'

'What's it all about?'

'I'll tell you when you arrive. When can you leave? If you catch a flight this afternoon we can get together tonight and I'll brief you.'

'You're working for the Commissioner? Down in Melbourne?' She sounded completely taken aback.

'Yeah, I'll tell you about it tonight. Call me when you arrive. I might even be able to pick you up from the airport.'

'Hang on. Not so fast.' Now she sounded pissed off. 'I'm not going to simply drop everything and leave Casey and my home just because of you. You don't rule my life, Darian.'

Jesus H, I thought. She's a great detective but spare me the attitude. I gave her the hard sell:

'I need someone who's smart, disconnected from the history and politics of the Force down here, disconnected from the rumours and history of this particular case we're investigating. Someone I've worked with before, someone I can trust.'

'The shorthand thing?' she asked.

'Yeah, the shorthand thing. We know our way round one another.'

'We do. And you should be familiar with this piece of shorthand between us: get fucked.' And with that she signed off. I stared at the phone, shrugged and kept walking across the park. I was enjoying the oak trees, of which there are none up on the Noosa River.

———

MARIA STARED AT her phone. Then she stared at the highway traffic crawl. A blue Range Rover, driven by a teenage kid, with P-plates on the windows, was easing past. The kid smiled and

33

waved at her. He had, Maria assumed, his girlfriend next to him and three teenage friends jammed tightly in the back seat. They all waved and gave her a thumbs up. She wanted to pull them over and arrest them for being rich, attractive and happy.

She dialled Casey. 'Darian wants me to go to Melbourne.'

'Awesome. When are we leaving, babe?' She hadn't quite anticipated that response. Casey flirted with the edge of the law. He was a small-time crim and Melbourne was his old stomping ground; the idea of her lover rollicking the back streets and nudie bars and dodgy nightclubs, scamming deals down by the docks and in the shifty underworld with the Italians, Greeks and Lebanese, the old-fashioned, traditional gangsters in Melbourne, while she was an active member of the Victoria Police, filled her with significant unease. She'd already spent their past seven years together concerned about his, albeit small-time, crime – moving stolen goods, harbouring crims on the run and, for Darian three years ago, supplying him with an illegally gained pistol – worrying that one day, inevitably, it would come back to haunt her as a police officer. Up until now the cops at Noosa Hill had given Casey a wide berth because they were scared of him. He was unpredictable and happily open to the concept of running them down on his Harley if need be. But this was different.

'Well, maybe if I go … Do you think I should go?' she asked.

'Of course. Whatever the big man is up to down there it'll be a fuck ton more interesting than sitting on a highway.'

'Well, maybe I should settle in first and see what the lie of the land is.'

'Promise I won't do anything illegal, darlin',' he said, a promise that swept past her like a small gust of wind. 'But that's a sound idea anyway. You get yourself set up down there and just let me know when it'll be a good time for me to come. Relationships wither when lovers are separated by distance; I gotta be there for you, having the spag bol and Thai stir-fry ready for when you get home. Gotta be looking after you, babe.'

IT TOOK ME ten minutes to stroll across the park in a welcome burst of sunshine, over the six-lane St Kilda Road with its sweep of date palms, and back to HQ. That made twenty minutes since the boss had called with my new office details. I knew the room. It wasn't an office – it was an old boardroom formerly used by Homicide and Missing Persons, the latter unit disbanded in the mid-2000s.

As I approached the steps leading up to the building my phone buzzed again. I expected Maria but it was the third and most critical member of my team.

'I'm resigning,' said Isosceles before I could even say hello.

We were all getting off to a wonderful start.

'Why?'

'This is a ridiculous job. It's below me. I have better uses for my talents. Yes, it is true I was born in the last century, but aside from that fact, there is no connection, no interest and no desire to be a part of it. In any way. Find someone else. I'll recommend somebody. I hear there's a girl who's rather good. Not as good as I, of course, but Darian, that is how it is. I believe she's pretty, so no doubt you'll enjoy her company. As to her skills, well, I cannot say. Farewell, my friend. Remember me.'

And with that quaint and operatic tirade he signed off. I was left standing there, on the footpath out the front of HQ, staring at my phone. It had now started to rain lightly. Another of those Melbourne days where the weather took you across all climates within the space of an hour.

Isosceles was a computer geek upon whom I had relied heavily not only when I ran Homicide but in the past three private ventures when I reluctantly came out of retirement to clean up and dispose of some bad people. I needed him again now.

Isosceles lived in a large open-plan apartment on the top floor of one of Melbourne's tallest buildings, in the heart of the city, encased in floor-to-ceiling glass walls, through which, as he sat at his array of computers and screens – the pulse – he would stare out into the canyons below and imagine he was Batman, saving all of humanity. Utterly dysfunctional in the ordinary world, he rarely ventured out, ordering all his food in, and, rarely, sex with high-class ladies. He slept on a mattress covered in a sheet that had a life-size image of 1960s bombshell Hollywood actress Raquel Welch, and he dressed up in swathes of thick clothing so that he resembled a yak hunter, as his computers were so powerful he needed to keep the airconditioning at arctic levels. I had worked with him for many years and his navigational skills through cyberspace were vital for my investigation.

There was nowhere he could not get to. There was almost no information he could not access. There was no firewall he could not dismantle.

But there was a place that terrified him.

The past.

The pre-digital age.

When I had called him, on my drive down from the Lakes District, the day after Copeland had left me, I knew this one was going to be a challenge.

'This is a world of *paper*,' he had said to me. 'Typewriters. Ink. Was the fax machine even invented? Darian? This is when people had those clunky telephone things. Landlines. When you had to sit in one place to be on the phone, at home or in the office. This is back when people used to write with *pens*. There was no storage of information. No cloud. I mean, yes, I remember a few years ago, before the cloud, but how can one exist without it? What happened to all that paper? All that information stored in filing cabinets?'

'It was digitised,' I had answered, as I barrelled down the highway, the mist-covered mountains that encircled the lakes fast disappearing in my rear-vision mirror. 'Everything was digitised.'

'Are any of these people still alive? A quarter of a century later?'

'That's what I'm hoping you'll tell me. And where they are now living. As soon as I get to Melbourne and get a hold of the case file, I'll pass on the names of everyone involved.'

'Very well,' he had said, unenthusiastically, at the time.

Now I stood and waited for him to call me back. It wasn't unusual for him to act like this and these sorts of rants were most often followed by an apologetic call moments later.

It didn't come. The rain started to get heavier. I walked up the steps leading to the entrance of HQ and stood under the awning.

I dialled him back.

'No is no, Darian,' he said. 'I've decided I need a wife. I'm going to the Philippines. I am going to find a woman to take care of me.'

Jesus, where did that come from? I wondered but pressed on regardless, using my only weapon.

'Maria will be tremendously disappointed if you don't join us.'

'Maria is coming down to work on this case?'

Isosceles had a teenage-like crush on Maria. The last time we were in Melbourne he had danced and swooned around her and whenever we skyped he would stare at her with deep admiration. He especially liked it when she wore low cut T-shirts.

As to whether or not Maria was joining me, I still wasn't certain. But I wasn't going to tell him that.

'She wants you,' I added, piling it on, 'as much as I need you.'

'I'll do it for her,' he said, sounding like a martyr.

'She'll be thrilled. I'll have the case file copied and sent over to you. I'll call you this afternoon and we can go through our plan of attack.'

I signed off, stepped inside and headed up towards the eighth floor, where I was to be greeted by an unexpected visitor.

ICARUS ASCENDING

I STEPPED OUT OF THE LIFT AND WALKED PAST THE ENTRANCE to Homicide, which is a large open-plan area that takes up most of the floor up on the eighth.

My old office, now occupied by my successor, Zach Reeve, was sort of in the middle, a small room that was mostly open, where in my time I had looked out on the crews as they sat at the four-desks-put-into-one stations. The office had a door and blinds so a modicum of privacy could be afforded the Officer in Charge should he – there has never been a she in that role – desire it. Along one of the walls were the interview rooms, where we could talk to witnesses or suspects, and behind them was a narrow passageway for the cameras and digital video feeds to ensure that every interview was recorded and that, on tape, it was clear a suspect had been fed and watered, had been read their rights, told that anything they might say could be used against them in a court of law; to ensure that, unlike the bad old days, the process was clean and legal. The Victorian police force, like all police forces – sorry, it's called a police *service* now – has had its bad days. In 1982 a royal commission attempted to root out corruption and seriously unethical and rotten behaviour. This was revisited in 2007 in an extensive report by the Office of Police Integrity and, even more recently, some cops have been found guilty of murder.

Hence the process of interviewing a suspect in Homicide was taken very seriously; every cop had his or her eye on the impending trial and the defence lawyer's eager search for a break in protocol.

Homicide cops are walking experts on how a murder trial can and can't go and what lawyers will do to fuck up their brief to the Office of Public Prosecutions.

I was both looking forward to reconnecting with the crews of Homicide, the guys I'd worked with for years, and at the same time feeling a little anxious. I had, after all, turned my back on them and walked away without a farewell, without even a let's-get-drunk going-away party. Of course they were all tough Homicide guys, independent, resourceful and hardened to the vagaries of human nature; it wasn't like they wanted an apology or an explanation. Still, I felt they deserved an apology and an explanation.

Later. That would come later. Now, I had to get into the office, make sure the phones and internet were working, that I did indeed have all the original files, and then start a culture and history of the case on a whiteboard.

I walked inside to find a man dressed in a black Italian suit, impeccable in cut, sitting behind the desk, waiting for me.

'Hello, Darian,' said Nick Racine.

'Nick,' I said, closing the door behind me.

He stood, smiled and extended his arm. We shook. Racine was tall, thin and muscular with jet-black hair, combed back into a perfect narrow sweep across his long and handsome face. His eyes were green and he spent a lot of time smiling and nodding, as if in agreement with everything you said. He reminded me of a cross between Bill Clinton and Marcello Mastroianni. To look at, he was the perfect choice for Police Commissioner. Beneath the charm, away from the hint of Bulgari aftershave and the perfectly cut and polished fingernails, the six-hundred-dollar shoes, all black, Italian and sleek, lurked the guy who'd pounded the footpaths as a uniformed copper. As much as I could see him in a South Yarra house with a flawless wife sipping Moët, I could also see a tough guy knocking back the beers and good for a headbutt if things got out of hand.

I'd never disliked Racine. His orbit and mine had rarely connected, so I'd never had to think about it.

Now I did. Here he was, in my office, smiling and shaking my hand like we were old buddies and isn't life just super.

Of course he was on my list of people to interview but I hadn't intended to do that for some time, until I had a greater understanding of the case. And, additionally, I had no intention of seeing him in any way until that formal time came about. It was, we both knew, inappropriate for him to be in the office and for him to kick off the conversation with: 'I'm completely innocent.'

I didn't say anything.

He smiled. 'Just thought I'd put that on the record.'

'Duly noted,' I replied.

'So,' he said as if we were about to get cracking on the job as a team, 'you've read the case files? What next? Isobel's dad? He's still alive, but he's a complete loony. Still, I guess you have to interview him.'

'Nick,' I replied, 'I'm sure I'll want to interview you within the next few weeks and will send through a request, up to your office. Until then ...' I let it hang, waiting for him to get the message and get the fuck out of my office and stop interfering with my investigation.

He didn't move.

'Isobel was a sweet kid. Of course I only met her briefly, that night, at her house, during the party. But you can tell when you see a sweet kid. Innocent. Who would have known that beneath the dimples and that little sweet smile was a need to go right off the reservation and experiment with kinky sex? Check the boyfriend. He's still around. I never believed his story. Said he left her at two-thirty or three in the morning. Bullshit. He was part of it, the kinky sex stuff. He was the one who strung her up. Fucked her while she was choking, fucked her while she was hanging on the door to her bedroom. They'd done it in the past. It wasn't a first-time thing. Or maybe it was. Maybe it *was* the first time. And then, *bang*, she's dead, all choked out. He does a runner. Wouldn't you?'

He stopped and held his hands up, palms towards me, feigning apology. 'Hey, sorry, I shouldn't be telling you this stuff. You're the investigator and the homicide expert. I'll get out of your way.'

Another smile – reptilian – and then he was gone, leaving behind the waft of his expensive aftershave.

I revised my opinion of Racine. I disliked him.

CRUEL WORLD

LIKE MOST MODERN BUILDINGS, POLICE HQ IN ST KILDA
Road wouldn't allow you to open the windows. Had I been able
to, I would have, to let in a breeze to get rid of that faint, sickly
aftershave smell from Racine. It was worse than the lingering
smugness in the guy's smile and talk.

Sometimes it takes a little effort to suppress one's personal
feelings in a murder investigation.

But was it murder? On the face of it, Isobel appeared to have
either suicided because of the intense pressure she was under from
the cops or died as a result of a sexual encounter gone wrong.

If the latter was the case – and if I had to choose now, at the
beginning of the investigation, it was the most likely scenario –
then we'd have a very fucked-up ex-boyfriend and a rather tangled
moral conundrum about what to do with him some twenty-five
years later.

But in the back of my mind I couldn't ignore the voice tugging
at me, saying: this looks like the work of a killer.

—

I STARTED TO map out Isobel's life on the whiteboard.

I had always worked this way, examining the life of the victim
to try to find a killer within the details of their daily routines.

Part of this process is geography. Where people were at the time
of the death. Or said they were. And with whom. Then I'd check

these alibis, to ensure that people were indeed where they said they were, and find out who could confirm it. I wanted to track Isobel's last movements, a week, maybe the seven weeks, before she died. Who was at the party. Again, what each of those people had said in their original statements. What time each person left and confirmation, if possible, of that departure and arrival at their destination.

I needed a detailed breakdown of the night she died; then I would spread outwards, into her other worlds. I knew that Isobel worked part-time in her father's small jewellery store in Chapel Street, not far from where she lived alone in South Yarra. Her house had been purchased by her father, Eli, and I wondered if he still owned it, or if he'd sold it, unable to contemplate the existence of a place where his only child had died.

Eli was still alive. Or he had been six months ago, when the anniversary of Isobel's death rolled past. Copeland had told me that the old guy had yet again kept vigil out the front of HQ from before dawn until midnight, swaying in the cold, looking like a nut with tufts of hair sprouting around his neck and face, eyes ablaze, carrying his cardboard placards with the photo of his little girl.

Isobel had a boyfriend. His name was Tyrone. Isobel was eighteen when she died. Tyrone was nineteen. Some of this stuff I remembered from the newspapers, reporting on the death at the time. He was an alpine skier, wanted to compete in the Winter Olympics. I vaguely remembered seeing photos of him bereft, hiding behind sunglasses, being held by Eli, at the coronial inquest. I remembered the noise on the floors at HQ, ugly noise: *that kid must've got the fuck of his life* and *he'll be having trouble getting it up from now on* and *talk about a bad fuck*. Ha-ha funny stuff from morons in uniform who thought a naked girl dead from weird sex fell into the category of 'she deserved it'.

Tyrone's statement, like all the others, was brief:
Isobel rang me at six pm and she said she was going to have a party and she wanted me to come over then to help set it up.

She said she was going to call all her friends and that we were all going to rock the house. I went to the bottle shop and got some beer and some cheap flagon wine and some port and drove to her place in Osborne Street at about seven. Lots of our friends were there ... yeah, sure, I can give you their names ... and ... yeah, she did drink a lot, but, no, I didn't see her smoke any weed or do any coke; she couldn't afford coke ... And, so, after a while the party kicked in and she was having a great time. I left at about two-thirty ... yes, I did want to stay the night ... yes, I've already told you that Isobel and I had slept together, but not ... not a lot. So, I left the party and drove to my flat in Smith Street, Elwood. I woke up and called her as I was getting ready for work. There was no answer, so ... I don't know. I had this bad feeling. Anyway, about half an hour later I called again and still no answer. So, I got a bit concerned. So, I rang my supervisor at McDonald's and told him I was sick and went around to see if she was all right ...

... and the front door was open, like, it wasn't locked, but she always left it like that, which really pissed me off but, anyway, I walked in and ...

... and, well, there was no answer and ...

... and, well, so, you know, I walked into ...

... I walked into the bedroom ...

... and I had to, like, push the door because it was heavy and ... I remember thinking, 'What's wrong with the door?'

I had to, like, really push it, you know?

Sorry. I'm, I'm okay. Sorry, just ah ...

So, you know, I pushed the door, expecting to see her in bed and at the same time thinking how weird it was that the door was heavy and hard to open ...

She wasn't on the bed and ...

... I turned around ...

... and, ah ...

Yeah, thanks, if you could just give me a sec, thanks.

There she was. On the door. Hanging, you know? There was this tie – it wasn't hers, or at least I'd never seen it – around her neck and, ah …

Well, it was obvious … it was obvious that she was, you know, she was …

She was dead.

How could I tell? Are you serious? How could I fucking tell? Because she was fucking blue in the face and her tongue was stuck out of her mouth and there was … and it was … a huge red fucking welt around her neck. That's how I could tell, you fucking prick.

I think it was Ben Harper who penned the song, 'Welcome to the Cruel World'.

I'd interview Tyrone soon. I was sure that he, like most others involved in the case, would be freaked out by my turning up after so many years. This I would use to my advantage. Unexpected questions often lead to revelatory answers.

I thought back to Racine's assertion that Isobel had died while she and Tyrone were having sex, and that he then covered it up. The Coroner had determined that she'd had intercourse on the night of her death, but there was no semen inside her, so whoever he was wore a condom. Tyrone denied he and Isobel had sex that night. Either he was lying or she had sex with someone else, before or after the party finished and she was left alone in the house.

The Coroner found that Isobel had died due to asphyxiation. A ligature mark around her neck was an obvious sign, not only to him but to the constables who first attended the scene. I had learned that the Coroner had since died, but I wondered if the constables were still around. I wanted to interview them to get, as best as they could recall many years later, their thoughts and feelings about the crime scene. The stuff that doesn't get put in official reports.

According to the toxicology report, Isobel had significant amounts of alcohol, marijuana and cocaine in her system. Nothing that unusual for a party in 1990.

Which led me now, as I scribbled her life onto the whiteboard, to drugs and the accusation made by her father, Eli, that she was being hassled by the Feds to spill the beans after she'd been caught arriving back in Australia with a small amount of cocaine.

Of this there were many rumours at the time Isobel died. Back then four young cops were alleged to have hassled her on the night of the party because they were somehow involved in a drug ring, one that was being investigated by the Federal Police, one that Isobel was also somehow involved in.

Jacob Monahan, one of the four constables who went to her house on the night she died, was, like Racine, sitting in a large office on the floor above me. Now head of the Drug Squad, as I'd learned a while back.

This was what I knew about the drugs aspect of the case:

Upon arrival at Melbourne Airport, after having spent a term at a high school in La Paz, Bolivia, as part of an exchange program with her school, Isobel was detained by a customs official. She was then released into the custody of two agents with the Australian Federal Police. They had been waiting for her. They knew in advance that she was carrying a small amount of cocaine. The Feds weren't after a conviction – they were after information. They thought she could lead them to a suspected man about town, a wealthy, influential guy; a guy not normally associated with the importation of drugs; a guy who regularly graced the social pages, with models hanging off both arms; a guy who had a big house in Toorak and another at Portsea, a more exclusive version of Toorak but on a remote and beautiful beach. And they thought there were some crooked cops involved, helping out with the arrival and movement of the drugs and maybe the protection of the racket.

This was all I knew, and I knew it only through what I'd heard in the whispered conversations up and down the corridors of police stations at the time, over twenty years ago, when old man Eli went turbocharged on his allegations of murder and when the Coroner was determining Isobel's cause of death. Rumours. Innuendo. From over two decades ago.

There was nothing in the files. No reference to a Federal Police task force. None of the witness statements mentioned drugs, cops or wealthy Toorak guys with suntans and flashy sports cars. Maybe there was nothing to those rumours.

Or maybe there was.

THE SILENCE OF THE SIRENS

'HELLO?'

'Hi. Is that Isobel?'

'Speaking.'

'Hi, Isobel, it's Brian.'

Mr Dunn? What's he doing calling me? Shit, I hope nothing's wrong. 'Oh. Hi!'

'How's it going over there?'

'Amazing. Really, Bolivia is the most incredible country, like really beautiful, and La Paz is just totally fantastic.'

'How's the school?'

'Well, you know, it's a school, but great. Everyone's really nice. Very different to home. How's everything back there?'

'Same old, same old. Coming up to the end of term. Marking. Groan!'

'Ha ha.' *Why is he calling me? Is he checking up on me or something?* 'Everything's good here. I'm going to really miss it when I leave, even though I'm looking forward to coming home.'

'Great, Izzy, great.'

This is weird. There's something he wants to say but he's not saying it ... why? 'Is everything okay?'

'Yeah. Hey, Izzy?'

'Yeah?'

'You're my special girl, right?'

I am? Really?

'You are my special girl. You know you are.'

'You were really kind in sponsoring me for the exchange. I appreciate it, Mr Dunn.'

'Brian.'

'Sorry?'

'Brian. I'm Brian. You're Izzy. Remember. That Mr Dunn stuff is bullshit. Am I going to call you Ms Vine? No. Of course not. Don't go all formal on me, Izzy. Not after the fun times we've had. Okay?'

'Okay?'

'Say it: Brian.'

'Brian.'

'You still going to Melbourne Uni next year?'

What is he not saying? Why is he calling me? 'Yeah. I'm hoping to.'

'Whoo-hoo.'

'If I get accepted.'

'Of course you'll get in.'

Why is he calling me at nine o'clock at night, at my home-stay in La Paz, Bolivia? It's like, what time back home? What is he not saying? 'Thanks, here's hoping.'

'So, ah, hey, Izzy...'

Here it comes. Maybe there is some problem back home at school or maybe I've done something wrong while I've been over here in the exchange program ... have I? No. Surely not.

'Yeah?'

—

MR DUNN – BRIAN – rides a Harley to school. You can hear the rumble for about two minutes before he arrives. Sometimes I would stand and wait, listening to that growling noise approach. The Harley is all sleek and black and he wears big biker boots and a black leather jacket and one of those matt black helmets which are cool and sort of dangerous looking, like what real bikies would wear, and he has Ray-Bans which, for the most part, are so lame but not on him, and he's got long hair, which is blond but it's not too long because I guess he'd get into trouble with the school authorities, and he's tanned, like he spent a long time in Bali or Phuket. He doesn't have a wife and the girls at school think he's going out with a pole dancer at Players who has implants.

When I first saw him I thought: *come on*. Is this some sort of B-grade actor in an American daytime soap? But then, when he started to teach us English, wow, he was so inspiring. And when I got interested in applying for the student exchange program, for a term at a high school in La Paz, he was so helpful. And then one day, after an English class, he said to me: Hey, what are you doing this weekend?

And, totally freaked by the question, I said: I dunno.

And he said: You wanna hang?

And I said: Yeah. Okay. Great.

So we did. He took me to the Underground, the huge nightclub at the bottom of town, on Spencer Street, and we danced until the morning. Our secret. Nobody else knows.

—

'HEY, SO I WAS wondering if you'd do me a favour?'

'Yeah, sure, of course.'

'Say no if it's a problem.'

Why would there be a problem? 'No problem.'

'You don't know what it is yet, ha ha.'

Ha ha – it's okay, Brian. 'It's okay. Anything.'

'Really?'

'Of course.'

'Can you bring a little present back for me?'

'Sure.' *What sort of present?*

'It's something from a friend of mine, a friend of mine in La Paz.'

'Okay, sure.'

'Say no if it's a drama.'

'No, it's fine ...'

'I don't want to put you under any pressure. It's just something small, from a friend of mine, and it saves him the hassle of sending it through the mail.'

Drugs. No, impossible. He wouldn't do that to me. It'll be a book or something like that. 'No, it's fine.'

'Tell me what you see.'

'What do you mean?'

'From your window, where you're staying.'

'Mountains.'

'Describe them.'

'There's snow ... they're jagged, really beautiful. Really high and ... far away, like ...'

'Like what?'

'Like dreams. Chimeras.'

'What's a chimera, Isobel?'

She laughed and then got serious. 'Well, there are at least two definitions. Firstly, from Greek mythology, a chimera is a terrifying fire-breathing monster, made up of many different parts, almost like a Frankenstein. He might have a lion's head but the feet of a goat. Whatever, he is something to be avoided, blowing all that fire, causing destruction. Then a chimera can also mean something illusory. Something that's there but you can't see it. It's like a ghost of itself. Like a mirage.'

'Brilliant! Did I give you an A plus in English?'

You don't remember? I was the only one in class who got an A plus. 'Yeah.'

'Of course I did. Hey, so, when you get back, you and me ...'

What? You and me what? Will you kiss me and hold me?

'Are you there?'

'Yeah. Here.'

'When you get back, Isobel, you and me, we are going to –'

And then, as Isobel had discovered during her ten-week stay in La Paz, capital city of Bolivia, a country known especially for, among other things, its cocaine, the phone connection suddenly collapsed in on itself and the line went dead. Brian was no longer there.

IMPRESSIONS

I WAS STARING AT A GARGOYLE.

It was perched atop a portico out the front of an impressive two-storey dark brick mansion that, in another time, would have been home to a wealthy Melbourne family. The building looked as though it had been erected sometime during the 1800s and had a fake-Tudor gingerbread feel to it, though the gargoyle, appropriate to the occupants, I thought as I crossed the street, lent it more of a Gothic atmosphere.

I'd crossed the Yarra River, passed through Richmond and across the edge of the city to East Melbourne in my bright red Studebaker, which I'd driven down from the Great Lakes. Although I am tremendously bad with directions and can get lost walking to the corner shop, this was a destination I knew well.

All cops did.

I found a parking spot near the Fitzroy Gardens, another example of a gracious Victorian-era park, over sixty acres of lawn, sculptured gardens, English elms and Canary Island pines and other tree varieties in a neat massive square on the edge of the city, created out of swamp in the early twentieth century. About three kilometres up the road, on Hoddle Street, Victoria had its worst mass-murder shooting in 1987 when a nutzoid named Julian Knight took it upon himself to gun down random people, killing seven and injuring another nineteen. He was nineteen years old and was sentenced to seven consecutive life sentences. But because life doesn't mean life, even if it's times seven, Knight was originally due for parole in

2014. A special act of parliament was passed to keep him behind bars, where he will stay for the rest of his life.

I walked under the gargoyle and into the Police Association Victoria offices where, some twenty-five years after being one of the first attending officers to the crime scene in Osborne Street, one of the first cops to see Isobel naked and dead on the back of her bedroom door, one of the first people to walk in and feel the trauma in the house, Buff Townsend, then a young constable, now worked as head of the police union.

Townsend was arguably one of the most powerful men in the state of Victoria, alongside the Commissioner and the person who's meant to be the most powerful person in the state, the Premier.

When the police union is unhappy, the government is in trouble. This was first discovered, in glorious style, back in 1923 when a combination of bad pay – horses were getting a better deal than cops on the beat – and a very unpopular Police Commissioner coalesced into a massive police strike. For almost a week cops refused to work, causing chaos in the city: riots, looting, trams overturned, three people killed, gunfire in the streets and a desperate government asking for troops to be sent in to restore calm. Since then the strength and power of the police union has been unassailable. Sometimes for good, sometimes for, some would say, a more sinister use. Me, I didn't mind the union; it worked hard to support the men and women in the Force. Still, I'd seen, across the country, how a police union could blindly stay loyal to a cop who'd broken the law and needed to go down.

I hoped that if my investigation uncovered a cop's involvement in Isobel's death, I wouldn't have to feel the heat and weight of the union against me. As far as the union is concerned, its members are honourable and to be defended, at all costs, no matter what the circumstances are.

I try to avoid politics but it's impossible. It's there, like evil. Turn a blind eye, sure, but the machinations and backroom deals in the world of police are constantly chattering, like the cogs in an engine.

BUFF WAS IN his early fifties, a big guy, about seven feet tall and built in the shape of a hippo.

'We were a little taken by surprise when the old man told us you'd be running this investigation,' he said by way of introduction. I didn't reply. We were sitting in his office, a far cry from the beat he'd walked during almost thirty years of active duty.

'I mean, I think it's sensible that Racine is cleared by an investigator who's at arm's length from the Service. Nobody really trusts an internal inquiry. So, that's a plus.'

I ignored his not-so-subtle hint at the preferred outcome regarding Racine, clearly the union's favourite for the top job.

'Still. Can't complain. You're an honest guy, if a little rusty and … you might say, tarnished, what with that sudden departure, turning your back on the Force and all that. How is Noosa? I took the wife and kids there a few years ago. I prefer Bali myself but sometimes a man's got to bend with the wind and give in to the stronger forces.'

Time to change the subject and focus on the purpose of the visit; he could go on for as long as he wanted, making oblique threats and references, all of which would boil down to one basic message: exonerate Racine at all costs. 'Tell me about your impressions,' I said, 'when you first arrived at Osborne Street.'

'All right, then,' he said, leaning back in his chair and closing his eyes as if the memory were a movie being projected in his brain. 'Everything looked terribly normal. The kid had rung triple-O … and by "kid", I mean the boyfriend. Tyrone?'

I nodded. 'Tyrone.'

'Funny name for a kid. Yeah, so he reported a death to triple-O, they could hardly understand him, between the sobs and tears, and we were dispatched. We were just around the corner. We'd been told that the deceased was a young lady, not even in her twenties, living alone in South Yarra, so Al and I turned up expecting something resembling a student house, know what I mean? Not at all. Dishes done in the kitchen, floor and furniture spotless, no sign of mess, no sign of mayhem, no sign of violence, nothing at all. Like we were walking into the home of a little old lady who'd died in her sleep. Except we weren't. There was a girl hanging on the back of the door to her bedroom. Well, that was unusual. The kid, the boyfriend, we kept him in the lounge room while we went and looked. Al … remember Al Grant?'

'No,' I said.

'Alphonse Grant. Died in ninety-six of a brain haemorrhage. Anyway, he was a Baptist. Always trying to get me to come to church with him on Sundays. Kept a pocket-sized copy of the Bible in the car with him all the time. Good fella. Honest. Straight. Boring, though, I tell you. *You* try spending a year riding with a Baptist who wants to convert you. Anyway, Al wasn't kindly disposed to the image of the young naked woman hanging by a tie around her neck on the back of her bedroom door. He didn't say anything, of course. Not at first. Too professional for that, but I could see he was demonising the poor lady, Isobel, as we later found out her name was, for having gotten herself into this wanton display of nudity.'

'Are you kidding me?'

'As I said, nice fella. Straight and honest. But he saw life and the job through the prism of God. Not exactly suited to a lot of police work. So, he then turns to me and says, "This is a suicide, Buff," and I say, "How do you figure that one out, Al?" and he says words to the effect of, "Only a person willing to commit that sin would contemplate being found like this." After that I ignored everything else he ever said and helped get him transferred to the traffic branch. So, that's how the suicide theory originated: from Al the Baptist.'

'And what did *you* think, Buff?'

He leaned back in his chair, kept his eyes on me and thought for a moment.

'Well, I didn't think it was suicide. Seemed too …' He strained for the right word, '… *orchestrated* for suicide. I know this is going to sound odd, but my first thought was that she looked theatrically posed. Like something you'd see on the stage.'

'Like she'd been placed there?'

'Yeah. That's it.' He smiled. 'Hey, this was back in the day when the Force was still a force, not a service, and the diehards ruled. Way before we'd bring in a profiler, much less a psychologist.'

'So, you discounted suicide.'

'I did. Yeah.'

'And?'

'Well, Darian, you know that Al and I were just the attending officers. Within twenty minutes of us arriving there, CIB showed up and took over.'

'I know, Buff. It's those first impressions I'm wondering about.'

There was a mandarin on his desk. Morning tea, I suppose. He picked it up and began to squeeze it, then started to throw it from one hand to the other as he ruminated.

'We all come to view a death with what they teach us at the college and with what we know. Al knew about God and not a lot else. It so happened ...' He stopped and stared hard at me, with the merest hint of a smile. 'I grew up in a tough neighbourhood. My dad ran out on me before I even knew such a person existed, or was meant to exist, and my mother got by on the kindness of strangers, if you know what I mean.'

I nodded.

'So it happened that I knew something about auto-erotic asphyxiation. Days I care not to remember. Nonetheless, it seemed to me that the young lady was an unfortunate but willing victim of a fuck gone awry. There were no signs of struggle, in any way, and I'm talking the bedroom was neat and orderly, like this girl was in control, know what I mean?'

'You talked to the boyfriend?'

'At the time, yeah.'

'He was where?'

'I told you; he was in the lounge room. At first, when we arrived, he was waiting for us out in the front yard. Then he stood and waited for us in the house while we attended the scene in the bedroom.'

'I've read the interview, done later that day, but what did you feel about him?'

'At the time I thought it wasn't him. In fact I felt sorry for him.'

'At the time?'

'He seemed too innocent. But I've been thinking back, especially since we heard the case was being reopened and knowing that I'd be questioned. It was a long time ago but I remember it quite well. Back then, when we talked to him, I thought there was no way a kid – and he was no more than eighteen or nineteen, like her – could have created that sort of sexual scenario *and* no way he'd be able to hold in the truth. Something would have tumbled out; he was raw emotion; something would have given way. But I was naive, I think. Despite my upbringing, I'd not seen very much. I didn't know then what most people are capable of, how they can disguise their feelings. Their guilt. How survival kicks in. How people lie to you. I look back on it, Darian, and I think I was the innocent one, not the kid.'

'What did he say? Again, I've read the interview, but I was wondering if there was anything that he might have said to you as you arrived, as you went into the house, stuff that didn't get put down in the statement.'

'How long do you think this will take?' Buff asked, abruptly changing the subject.

'I should be done in about ten minutes,' I said.

'No, I didn't mean that. How long do you anticipate the inquiry will drag on?'

I knew exactly what he meant. A new enterprise bargaining agreement was stuck in negotiation with the government. Covering annual leave, work conditions and a proposed 2.2 per cent pay rise, the union needed it to go forward and be approved, or else the rank and file might become impatient, and guess what? Elections for the union executive were fast approaching. Impatient rank and file, sick of being told that better pay and conditions were coming, might toss them out, including Buff. As I have discovered, politics or not, everyone clings to survival above all else. Especially above ethics and justice.

'When *are* the elections?' I asked.

He leaned forward, hands clasped on the table, a man ready to do business. 'I know you're a rank-and-file man, Richards. I've heard the stories, how you went in to bat for the men and women if ever there was anything unfair, so I know you'll understand. We have a timetable.'

We do?

I didn't respond, just waited for him to continue.

'The elections are in thirteen weeks' time. I need to get that enterprise bargaining agreement pushed through, agreed to by the government. Then I need to get it ratified by the executive. Then I need the members to approve it, all before the election. My problem is … Let me rephrase that. The problem that the men and women of the Service have is that the current Commissioner, beloved by all, is old. Slow. Goes into a meeting with the government to negotiate, and these meetings aren't like you can just pick up the phone and say, "How's next Tuesday?" – these meetings take ages to even set up – so when your Commissioner goes in and starts to talk about the old days and crime rates and golfing conventions in Belfast, and nothing gets achieved, a certain desperate pressure comes into play. A pressure to have the new Commissioner appointed, a younger, dynamic officer, just sitting there, waiting in the wings, knowing that everything has been approved, everything signed off, all ready to go but for one little, tiny, fucked-up glitch.'

'I'm sure you can imagine, Buff, that after three years in a subtropical climate, you get acclimatised.' Which was my oblique way of saying I wanted to wrap up the case as quickly as possible, saying what he wanted to hear, without saying I wanted to wrap up the case as quickly as possible, because, frankly, I'd be on it for as long as it needed.

'Yeah. I can imagine you want to get back to the sunshine. Every day another day in paradise; that's Queensland, right?'

I put on a smile. Not big on being pressured.

Buff started to rip the skin off the mandarin. 'So, where were we? Oh yeah, the kid. Tyrone. I recall him saying, "It's all my fault."'

BAD MOON ON THE RISE

LIKE MOST PEOPLE WHO FLY INTO MELBOURNE FROM Queensland, Maria stepped out of the arrivals hall dressed in jeans and a T-shirt to be greeted by an instant blast of frozen air, whipped up from the Antarctic. She wasn't alone – all the arrivals on the flight from the Sunshine Coast stepped onto the concourse and reacted with shock at the sudden weather change; people reached into their carry-on bags, scrambling to retrieve a jacket or a coat, if they even *had* a jacket or a coat, since neither item is useful when you live in Queensland, where the sun shines every day and the temperature rarely falls below twenty degrees.

I was waiting out the front, double-parked in the Studebaker. Maria, I noted as I climbed out of the car to open up the boot, was travelling heavily. She dragged two massive suitcases on rollers across the road towards me and had slung a carry-on bag over each shoulder. She looked as though she were moving home and had packed enough clothes to last her ten years.

'Fuck, it's cold,' she said by way of greeting. And then, taking one shoulder bag and leaving me to heft her luggage into the boot, she ran to the passenger seat and firmly closed the door. 'I'm starving!' she shouted. It was close to 9pm. Of course she was starving. She eats like a herd of wild bison.

'I booked a table,' I shouted back at her, grabbing the last of the suitcases with both hands. It felt like it had rocks inside it.

'I want Thai!' she shouted back at me from inside the car.

'We're having French,' I said.

'I hate French food! Too many carbs in the sauces!'

Then don't eat the sauces, I felt like shouting back at her.

I closed the front door as I settled into the driver's seat. I'd left the engine running and the heater was doing a fine job of maintaining Queensland weather inside the car.

'We're having French,' I said.

She rummaged through her bag and, as I put the car into gear and headed out of the airport, dragged out an old, worn jacket, which she put on over the T-shirt. Now dressed for Melbourne, as we sped along the freeway towards the city, she leaned back in the seat and said: 'Hi.'

—

FRANCE-SOIR IS ONE of those hip Melbourne restaurants that make you feel you have entered another place, another city. In this instance, Paris. In the long, narrow, very noisy, bustling bistro with small tables covered by crisp white sheets of paper, waiters wearing the traditional Paris garb of a white smock over a black suit, looking as if they'd stepped out of Escoffier's world in 1915, grab you as you enter, as if the world were to end at midnight, and then pause, freeze-frame and smile slowly, as if suddenly the world won't end tonight, as they notice the lady by your side.

'Madame,' said the head waiter as he politely pushed me aside and, as if she were Princess Grace, escorted Maria, who seemed both enthralled and repulsed, to our table opposite the long bar that spanned one side of the restaurant.

'I like this place,' she said to me while the Jean-Paul Belmondo look-alike unfurled the freshly laundered white cloth napkin and gently placed it in her lap with the merest hint of a seductive smile, at the same time running through the specials du jour and would the lady like a glass of Perrier to start? Or perhaps an aperitif or even, perhaps, could he suggest a vin rouge from Burgundy? Not a vin ordinaire, non, non, a petit cru, still very good, very good indeed, made in fact in a village close to where he was born. He finished with a Maurice Chevalier smile.

'Great. Thanks. That would be awesome,' said Maria.

Normally in these types of restaurants that sort of Australian response would be met with a thin, sour smile. But Jean-Paul smiled, all teeth and graciousness, as if a princess had indeed spoken.

'Monsieur?' He turned to me.

'Perrier, thanks.'

'Oui,' he said and then, 'Voilà!', which I've come to understand means about a thousand things in French, from 'There you are!' to 'Oh, fuck, the cat's dead.'

—

'So, who was the wealthy guy?' asked Maria.

She had ordered coquilles St Jacques aux champignons (scallops with mushrooms) for an entree – inhaled, not eaten – then filet de boeuf et frites (steak and chips and hold the sauce) for the main course – not exactly inhaled but absorbed with gusto in less than five minutes – and was now, having forgotten that she hated French food, eyeing off the crêpes Suzette, thin pancakes cooked in Grand Marnier then set alight at the table by the waiter, Jean-Paul, who had congratulated her on every choice from the menu and Madame, are you from Melbourne? and Oh! Voilà! How long will you be staying here in South Yarra? To which she smiled at me across the small table, as if to say, isn't this French guy just so amusing? While we ate, I briefed her on the basics of the case.

'His name is Dominic Stone,' I said.

'Still alive?'

'Yeah.'

'Where is Isosceles?'

Our volatile computer-geek genius who had guided us through our past three investigations and was enthralled by Maria would normally have slain me like a superhero not to miss the chance to spend time in her gorgeous company.

'He wants to make an impression on you tomorrow. This is an incredibly difficult case for him. Everything happened at a time when people made phone calls on a telephone, in their house, and used paper to type documents on electronic typewriters. So he sends his apologies and looks forward to dazzling you with his brilliance when he has conquered this ancient world and found the current addresses and phone numbers of everyone involved.'

'When were mobile phones first used?' she asked, curious that I'd brought up the issue of technology, and the lack thereof, in our investigation.

'Late eighties, a couple of years before Isobel was killed. The first mobiles were like bricks. They became common in the early nineties.'

She nodded. 'So what do you know about Stone?'

'He's in his late sixties and living down the road, in Toorak. Not much else. He's rich and influential. Has been for years. The sort of guy you constantly see in the social pages, constantly hear about, but until Isosceles has cracked him open, hardly anything.'

Maria stared at me for a moment, then said, 'I know we have to eliminate suicide and accidental death – but it's murder, isn't it?'

I didn't reply.

'The Coroner was a man?'

I nodded.

'There is not a woman on earth who would commit suicide in such a blatantly sexual way, nor would a woman hang herself on the back of her bedroom door just for the thrill of it. Being choked while you're having sex, in bed with a guy, or a girl, yeah, sure, but hanging from a door? It's a male fantasy. The *killer's* male fantasy.'

She polished off the last of the crepes Suzette and was, I'm sure, thinking about some cheese to finish off the meal; three courses were not enough for a woman like Maria.

'You want some cheese?' I asked.

Her eyes lit up. 'Are you going to have some? That'd be great.'

I didn't want cheese. A steak and chips had filled me up. I was just intrigued at the depth of the well. I waved to Jean-Paul and he scampered across to us – to Maria.

'Oui?'

'Fromage?' asked Maria.

He almost swooned with delight at her wonderful use of the local language.

'Voilà!' he said.

The cat's dead, I thought.

And off he scurried as if Charles de Gaulle himself had just ordered food.

'This murder was a one-off, right?' Maria said, her line of thought mirroring my own.

I nodded.

'Because it has the signature of a serial offender, but it's not, because Isobel is the only woman to have been found dead in this way.'

'Yep,' I said.

'So, it was designed by someone, the killer, who clearly was incredibly arrogant. He was making a statement. Maybe he was sending a message, like one of those characters in *Game of Thrones* when they impale someone or shove their cut-off head on a stake, saying, Don't fuck with me, but in this case it was You talk to the Feds, you talk to *anyone*, then this will happen to you. And whoever this person, the killer, was – is – he feels bulletproof. Safe. Impenetrable.'

The fromage arrived with a bow and a *Madame* and an appreciation of her brilliance in choosing the very best off the menu that evening.

Maria was staring at me. She hadn't noticed the fromage nor the waiter's swooning.

'It's a cop.'

I didn't say anything.

'Isn't it?'

'The cheese looks good,' I said. 'I love this restaurant. Back in the early eighties it was a failed diner that had been decked out to look like the inside of a 747 jumbo. I can't remember what they called it. In fact, funnily enough, this room has been a restaurant for over sixty years – a lot of restaurants were here and none of them worked until these guys decided to turn the space into something you'd find on the Left Bank.'

She hadn't heard a word I'd said. She was, like I had been, rolling through the implications.

'Fuck, Darian. This isn't a good gig.'

—

WE STEPPED OUT of the restaurant onto the footpath. Toorak Road is even busier at night than it is during the day. Nightclubs, bars and restaurants come alive and people throng to this part of Melbourne. White fairy lights were strung around small pyramids of shrubbery lining either side of the street. The icy gale-force winds had eased and the night was still. Above us was a full moon. No clouds.

As we approached my car, parked a few doors down, Maria stopped and stared up at the moon and the clear sky.

'He's out there,' she said after a moment.

'Our killer?' I asked.

'The Train Rider,' she said and turned to look at me. 'I dream about him. Actually I don't. I have nightmares about him.'

She walked towards the car. 'Take me home, wherever it is that I'm staying.'

'You're across the street from me, in Davis Avenue, just around the corner. We've both got an apartment. Courtesy of Victoria Police.'

As she reached over to open the passenger door of the Studebaker she looked at me hard and maybe remorsefully as she said, 'I'm not used to failure. I don't like it.'

And she climbed into the car, closing the door behind her.

—

AT FOUR IN the morning I climbed out of bed and stood on the balcony of my apartment. Dawn was hours away. I looked up and down the empty street at the hundred-year-old oaks along both sides, listened to the faraway clatter of a solitary tram, at this time of day most likely rumbling to a transportation yard, screeching as it ran along the old tracks. There were some birds in the sky, a long way away it seemed to me, as I listened to their calls. It had rained overnight and the street, anvil blue, was wet and shining. It was, to quote Maria, fucking cold. I was about to go back inside and boil up a coffee when, from across the road, I noticed movement beyond the stark branches on one of the balconies in the apartment block opposite. I paused and stared. I'm not a voyeur; well, maybe I am, but in my job you need to scope out everything and everyone. What was somebody over there doing at four in the morning, outside?

She stepped forward on her balcony, out of the shadows, and she was looking directly at me.

'Hey,' whispered Maria, across the empty street. A word, floating, like a lost song in a dark alley.

'Hey,' I said back to her.

I couldn't see her clearly but I felt her smile.

THE SPECIAL CONSTABLE

THE TERM SPECIAL CONSTABLE, WHICH WAS WHAT MARIA was about to become, has been around since 1901, when a law was passed allowing judges and magistrates to appoint civilians to preserve the peace if there was a riot or the danger of one, to protect people and property; basically, if the cops of the day were outgunned and outmanned, in the opinion of the court, then ordinary people could be granted the powers of arrest and, indeed, any of a police officer's powers. Special Constables are rarely, if ever, used in this way. The role is, however, most valuable when travelling interstate or if you happen to work near a state border and you need to cross it while chasing after a low-life who's just committed a crime in Victoria and is screaming his vehicle for South Australia or New South Wales hoping to avoid capture. If you're a Special Constable you can cross the border in pursuit and arrest him there, in the other state; if you're not a Special Constable you'll have to pull over on the state line and watch the crim get away. To work with me in Melbourne – and I had been temporarily reinstated back to my old rank of Detective Inspector – Maria had to be granted that status so she had the same powers as any Victorian constable. It was a formality but one that made everyone, especially the pen-pushers, happy, and if this ever came to a murder trial in a court of law, something we needed to have done. Murder trials require the most pedantic and bureaucratic work done by cops in order to survive the high-octane adversarial duelling practised in court.

We found a parking spot on St Kilda Road, which has to be one of the widest streets in the country. It's two outside lanes are covered in a green canopy of elms and squat, old date palms that must have been imported from Egypt or somewhere nearby in the early 1900s, and then, across grass-covered, tree-lined islands is the boulevard itself, four wide lanes with two in the middle for trams to roll up and back. If the traffic's heavy and you're not relying on the lights, you might need to take a packed lunch just to cross the street.

Isosceles had rung me earlier confirming Eli's address. And with a complaint:

'Eli Vine does not have a mobile phone! How can I track these people if they do not belong to our world? Is everybody involved in this investigation going to be decrepit, disconnected? Really, Darian, it's too much.' But he hadn't resigned, knowing of course that he was to see Maria shortly.

Eli was our next destination. Isosceles had been sent the case files and had been going through each person named – the cops attending the crime scene after Buff and Al the Baptist, the guests at the party, Isabel's boyfriend and anyone he could squeeze from the clamp of darkness regarding the Federal Police task force into the drugs, both the investigating cops and their suspects.

David the receptionist looked as though he was strangling a burp as I walked towards him, Maria in tow.

'This is Senior Constable Chastain from Queensland. She's here to be sworn in as a Special Constable,' I said.

'Yes,' he said, clearly expecting us. 'Detective Inspector Reeve is handling that. Up on the eighth floor.'

Overseeing the simple signing of a formal document was not something that a cop of his position would even consider. Way below him. Maria gave me a look, expressing the same thought.

'Is this about intimidation?' she asked.

I nodded. 'Welcome to St Kilda Road HQ,' I said as we walked towards the lifts.

We rode up to the eighth and stepped into the large open-plan space of Homicide. If I was expecting a welcome back, all is forgiven, I didn't get one; if I was expecting a sweeping attitude of recrimination, I didn't get that either. There was, instead, studied indifference as we walked across the floor towards my old office, the one that Reeve now occupied.

Towards Maria, on the other hand, with her Victoria's Secret appearance, there was a big *Hello, babe* attitude, although they were all too sophisticated and professional to act like hungry boys on heat. But for one. One of the detectives leaned back in his chair, arms folded behind his neck, a big grin on his face and eyes that followed us. Prematurely grey with sparkling blue eyes, he looked like a silver fox. It was Pappas, one of the four who went to Isobel's party on the night she died, one of the four who were possibly working for Dominic Stone. I swear I heard him wolf-whistle, softly, as Maria and I entered Reeve's office.

'Maria Chastain,' said Reeve with a beaming smile, standing up from his desk, arm outstretched like he'd been eagerly waiting to meet her. 'Zach Reeve, Officer in Charge of Homicide. Come in, take a seat. You too, Darian.'

Bemused and wary, Maria smiled and shook his hand. She didn't sit. Nor did I.

Reeve had the blond surfer look going on. He was a big guy with thick arms and a round piggish face full of an innocent and charming smile. I'd employed him years ago. He was a good cop – but he had an issue with his ego. Or, to be more accurate, he didn't – *I* did.

'Great to have you in Melbourne,' he said. To Maria. With the beaming smile. He was ignoring me, all attention focused on her. 'So, you've come down to solve one of our famous cold cases. Fantastic. We have our own Cold Case Squad here – they're just around the corner – but they're very happy to have a couple of Queensland hot shots come in and do this one.'

'Where's the document for her to sign?' I asked.

He sat and leaned back in his chair, enjoying himself, casting a look up and down Maria's body. She hadn't said a word.

'I hear the Commissioner has put you up in a couple of apartments down in South Yarra. Nice. I heard, in fact I was told – or ordered you could say – that you will have all resources at your disposal, including any of my men. Nice. That's power, Maria. That's the good old Darian Richards power.'

Maria stepped forward and picked up a piece of paper that lay in front of him, on the desk.

'This it?' she asked.

'Got to love a girl who can read stuff upside down. Sharp eyes there, Maria,' he said.

She ignored him, took a pen from his desk and scribbled a signature, then dropped the document back onto the desk.

'Been a pleasure,' she said and we both turned to walk out.

'Comrades,' he shouted after us, 'one small point.'

We paused at the door, turned back to him. His smile was gone.

'No vigilante behaviour. Keep the tough-guy antics on the other side of the border. I don't want to hear about witnesses being punched in the nose, suspects vanishing, dangerous guys with a bullet in their head. Got me? The Commissioner might be ignorant of some of your past behaviour or maybe he's too old to fully appreciate it, but none of that Darian tough-guy shit is happening while I'm sitting in this office.'

'Have a nice day, Reeve, and keep smiling,' I said.

'Lovely to meet you,' added Maria in her sweetest voice, and we walked out.

—

Pappas, yet another fine example of the best of the best, was waiting for us at the lift.

'I'm Aristotle Pappas, but you can call me Stolly,' he said to Maria with his best, but not very successful impression of a George Clooney smile. He held out a business card.

'This is Tyrone Conway's current address. In case you haven't read the file yet, Tyrone was Isobel's boyfriend, the one who said he found her. At the time he managed to avoid serious questioning because everyone thought it was suicide, but he's your guy. It won't have been premeditated. Just an unexpected fatal turn of events in the middle of kinky sex. But maybe you can nail him for tampering with a dead body, withholding evidence, covering it up. Or maybe you can mount a case that it was manslaughter. That's what I'd be going for.'

Both Maria and I stared at him as he rattled off his theory. Two suspects approaching me within the walls of HQ in two days. First Racine, now Pappas. I was intrigued.

'And,' he added, flicking the card around and holding it up for Maria to read, 'on the other side, that's me. Call me anytime. Day or night. Especially if you're lonely down there in that apartment in Davis Avenue. I'm your man.'

And with that, he was gone. Maria stared at the card as the lift arrived. We stepped in.

'I'm your man?' she said, shaking her head. 'Well, that was fun.'

'Speaking on behalf of my old squad, those two are not representative of the species. In fact, they're aberrations.'

'Why *did* the Commissioner bring you in? Why not get Cold Case to handle it? Doesn't it seem a little weird?' asked Maria.

'He said he wanted an outsider. Someone without current links to the Force. But I'm sure we'll discover the real reason in due course.'

THE DAY BEFORE
YESTERDAY

As we drove down Commercial Road, about to turn up into Chapel Street, on our way to talk with Isobel's father, my phone buzzed.

'Darian Richards.'

'It's Sullivan.'

'Thanks for calling me back.'

'I heard you retired. Living in Noosa.'

'I am, but I'm back in town investigating an old case. It involves the Feds.'

'Okay. Fire away.'

I tucked the phone into my neck as I turned the wheel.

'About twenty-five years ago you had a task force going. Looking into a possible drug-importation ring that may have involved Dominic Stone.'

There was a pause.

'What are you investigating?' asked Sullivan.

'Isobel Vine.'

There was another pause.

'Yeah, let's not talk about this on the phone. Meet me at the Chow, six tonight.' And without waiting for a response he hung up.

'Who was that?' asked Maria.

'Our connection within the Feds. We've just landed our access into the secret dealings of that task force.'

'Move! It doesn't get any greener!' Maria shouted at the car in front of us, as the lights flicked from red to green. It did, and I turned into the bustling street.

Maria watched the shop numbers tick by out her window looking for our address, but she also managed to stare at the clothes shops that lined either side. Chapel Street is designer-clothing heaven for women. Famously, when she was as big as Madonna in the eighties, Cyndi Lauper used to buy clothes in this street. There is nothing like Chapel Street in Noosa or, indeed, the entire state of Queensland.

'It's just up here on my side,' said Maria. Chapel Street rises up from the Yarra River, cuts across Toorak Road and forms a straight, long line of boutique stores, extremely expensive clothes shops and masses of outdoor diners selling Indian, Turkish, Arabic, Ethiopian, Italian, Greek and everything-else food. Then, as it crosses over Malvern Road and High Street, everything becomes a little tattier, stores huddling closer together, retro-looking old clothes shops that haven't changed since the fifties, dank-looking sex shops and dodgy old pubs where desperados hang out for 10am opening time and are still sitting there staring out the windows, from the gloom inside, listening to the races on the TV, midafternoon. The glamour and glitz are slowly making their crawl along Chapel Street and one day the entire length of it on both sides will be hip and cool, but for now, there was a clear divide. Eli's jewellery store was at the sad, impoverished end of Chapel Street, wedged between a kosher butcher and a framing store, both empty of customers, as was, we could see as I parked out the front, the jeweller's.

—

ELI KNEW THEY were cops; he saw it as he stood at the counter, staring out through the front windows as he did every day. He unlocked the door at five to nine every morning, stepping in, turning on the lights, bringing out the rings and bracelets, the brooches and silver chains that sold the most, from inside the old safe. Then, having laid them out, he stood over them at the counter, waiting, staring out through the windows that needed a clean, at the passing life at the top end of Chapel Street where, fifty-five years ago, the stores had all been owned by old Jews and refugees from Yugoslavia.

He tried to control his feelings as he watched the tall man in an expensive suit climb out of the car and, like all cops do, quickly scan the street. Watching, seeing, observing; missing nothing. Then, following him, came an attractive young woman in that regulation casual wear of detectives, jeans and white T-shirt; instead of scoping out the area and people around her, she looked in, squinting, to see if she could spot the old man they'd come to talk to.

His left hand began to shake and he stared at it for a moment, then, as he did whenever his body betrayed him with an exhibit of emotion, he slammed his hand down onto the counter as hard as he could, hoping the sudden pain would extinguish the loss.

It never did. The pain was always there, on the other side of his eyes, every waking moment of every day, but now, not so often, thank God, throughout his sleep. Yesterday was the day she died, that's how it felt, and the day before that was the last time he had been happy.

Why now? he wondered. There hadn't been a flicker of curiosity from the police for over twenty years. In that time he had been made to look like a fool, an obsessive maniac hell-bent on an impossible and ridiculous revenge. He stared hard at the man and woman as they stepped onto the footpath and made their way to his front door. The man was strong, not just in body but in mind and attitude. He reminded Eli of his father, who had survived the ravages of war-torn Germany. The woman was tanned. She wasn't from Melbourne, he thought. She was from a warmer climate. Maybe Queensland. He looked back at the man. Although he was wearing a suit, he too was tanned, in the face. That made no sense to him. Why were two detectives from another place coming to see him? Or maybe his mind was playing games with him; how could he possibly tell they were not from Melbourne?

'What is it you want of me?' he asked as they walked inside.

'Mr Vine,' said the man, 'my name is Darian Richards and this is Maria Chastain. We would like to ask you some questions about Isobel.'

Eli stared at this Darian Richards and thought: he is dangerous, but he is also a good man, and now, finally, I think, my girl is in the hands of a man I can trust.

'You are not from Melbourne?' he asked.

'No, sir. I used to be in Homicide here in Melbourne, but Maria and I live on the Sunshine Coast in Queensland.'

Good: his mind was still as sharp as it had always been.

'Let me turn that sign from open to closed, so we can talk without interruption,' he said as he moved away from the counter. 'It won't matter. I haven't had a paying customer in here since 2012. In fact, my only visitors these days are the teenage girls on their way home after school, stopping in to see how cheap my chains are being sold for. They tell me they can get them cheaper on eBay and I tell them, Good, do that, bye-bye, and they go.'

—

'I AM NOT a madman,' said Eli.

'No, of course you're not,' said Maria.

I said nothing. This old guy, I thought, as I watched him, was whip-smart and had been through a life that had sharpened all the senses. He was in his seventies and was tall and a little stooped. It looked as though he cut his own hair. He reminded me of what I thought the old fisherman from *The Old Man and the Sea* looked like. His hands shook. His eyes wept. But not from crying, or maybe it was from crying. Years ago – many years ago – I discovered that the effect of tragedy doesn't have a use-by date.

'He's dead,' said the old guy. Which confused both Maria and me.

'Who's dead?' I asked.

'The monster. The man who killed her. There can be no other reason; twenty-five years I've been waiting, and nothing. Why? Because he had the power. He killed her, then had all those people around him cover it up.'

I knew, or thought I did, to whom he was referring, but it was better to play dumb and not ask leading questions.

'Who are you talking about?'

'Dominic Stone.' The old guy leaned in towards us and said, with gravity, 'I'm glad he's dead.'

'He's not dead,' said Maria.

'Then why … Why? For twenty-five years the police ignore me, ignore their duty to investigate Isobel's murder. So, why now? What has happened to make you two police officers, from another state, enter my shop?'

Yeah, I feel your pain, old guy, but we're the ones asking the questions.

'In the weeks leading up to Isobel's death, can you describe her state of mind?'

If he was annoyed about not having his question answered, he didn't show it. 'She was agitated. She was feeling pressure from all sides. The police were wanting her to talk about Stone and that evil viper, Brian Dunn …'

Dunn was her teacher. He'd organised her trip to Bolivia and there had been suggestions of impropriety between him and Isobel. Dunn was a shadowy character for us. There was no record of interview with him in the case files, only a couple of references made by Isobel's boyfriend, Tyrone. I'd be finding out more about the teacher from Sullivan. As one of the Feds working drugs at the time, I was hoping Sullivan would have the inside dirt on everyone. For the moment, though, Dunn was being defined as an 'evil viper' so I guessed there probably was something to those rumours of impropriety.

'He taught her, right?' interjected Maria curiously.

Eli nodded. 'He took advantage of her. Seduced her. She made love with him. She thought they were in love. I knew, I could see it. She didn't tell me very much about the viper, but I knew. I warned her. He was her teacher, for God's sake!'

As he calmed down I could see Maria's eyes narrow as if she were a sniper slowly taking aim at an intended target.

He continued, 'And she never knew where she stood with the police. One day they are charming and her best friends and taking her on a picnic, the next they are threatening her with ten years, or more, jail time for the importation of that drug. She didn't know it was a drug. She thought she was doing her teacher a favour. Bringing home a present from a friend. She wanted to impress him. She was naive, like all schoolgirls in the midst of a crush on a handsome wealthy older man ...'

He shut his eyes and rocked back on his heels, sucking in air.

'Stone was putting even more pressure on her. He'd drive past her house and stare at her. He'd follow her in his car. He'd call her up and tell her that if she said a word about him – to anyone – she wouldn't be celebrating her nineteenth birthday. He had others. Other men. They were police. I saw them, I saw them a number of times. They would always be driving around outside her house, maybe lounging on the bonnets of their cars parked nearby. They were besieging her.'

'How do you know they were cops?' asked Maria.

'You know,' he said, opening his eyes now and staring at us.

He was right. You do.

'Stone had visited her. He just walked straight into her house. One night Isobel woke up and he was sitting on the end of her bed. Warning her.'

Maria and I looked at each other. That information wasn't anywhere in the files. Of course not.

Maria changed the subject. 'This is a delicate question, sir ...'

'She didn't mention suicide,' he said, cutting Maria off.

'Of course. And we're not suggesting she did, but we have to thoroughly eliminate all possibilities. Did she say anything that might be construed as –'

'No.' Door closed: no suicide.

'What was she doing in the days leading up to her death? Was she seeing old friends? Was she cleaning up her house?' asked Maria.

A lot of people who take the suicide run do those sorts of things before they go – like most people who hang themselves, which is more of a guy thing, take off their shoes. I've never been to a suicide's house where it's a mess inside. Everything is clean and orderly. I don't get suicide, in fact I hate it, but you can't deny that some sort of calm seems to come over these people before they pull the plug and check out of the life they were blessed to have been given in the first place.

'You can look for yourself,' he answered.

That broke my reverie. 'What do you mean?' I asked.

'The house. Isobel's house. It's still there. It hasn't been touched since the day she died.'

I knew he owned the house but it had not occurred to me that, some twenty-five years later, it would still be there, as it was when she lived in it.

'I locked it up. Kept it intact. Hoping that one day you would arrive to unlock the truth.'

He reached into his pocket and took out a chain of keys. With his fingers gently shaking, he removed a silver key and handed it to me.

'I didn't touch a thing. You'll find everything as it was the night she died.'

—

WE CONSTRUCT WHAT we need in order to protect the memory of a loved one or because of fear. Some years ago I interviewed an eighteen-year-old kid over the murder and mutilation of his flatmate. The kid did it; he told me. He said he wanted to know

79

what it would be like to kill a friend and then, on top of that, like ordering a chocolate thickshake with your burger, what it would be like to chop up a body into a dozen pieces. But the kid was worried. 'Please don't tell my dad,' he implored me.

Old Eli was protecting Isobel's memory, and who could blame him. She was a princess, her life over so young, and there could be only one explanation. That of a bad guy. A killer. And if he happened to live in a tower of wealth with a moat of soldiers and footmen, all the better; that would explain why Isobel's death had not been avenged by the courts and the cops. Because they were in the powerful killer's thrall.

Hey, what the fuck: at the end of the day, old Eli might be on the money, I thought as we left his shop. I was trying to stay balanced and rational towards Dominic Stone, a man I'd never met, but my dislike for the guy was stacking up. I can't help it, when people are rich and arrogant I just want to hurt them. Like a few other personal traits, it's childish and I never let it intrude into my investigations.

Eli switched the door sign from closed to open and we stepped outside. When we'd first arrived, about an hour ago, it had been sunny and warm. Now a force-ten gale of ice and sleet was blasting the street. Melbourne is a city known for its idiosyncratic weather changes. In another hour's time we might experience a tropical front of mid-twenties heat and by night it could be snowing.

I'd been in town for less than a week and it still wasn't feeling like home. I didn't think it ever would again.

HAILE SELASSIE'S VOLKSWAGEN (i)

'I DID SOMETHING, TWENTY OR SO YEARS AGO, SOMETHING that might be exposed now, which could destroy my reputation.'

'The girl.'

There was a pause.

'Yes, then,' said the woman. 'Her. How do you stop this?'

'I can't. There's an investigation and it's been ordered from the very highest of authorities in the city.'

'How high? Who?'

'The Police Commissioner. The Attorney-General. The Premier.'

'Do you want to tell me what it is that you did? You never spoke of it and I never asked.'

'No.'

'You have to be able to stop it. You can't have your reputation ruined. I can't have it ruined. We can't let our family have their reputations ruined. There must be a way to stop it. You have to cover your tracks. Stay hidden. As we always have. You must protect me. Our children and our grandchildren.'

'There's an investigator. Actually there are two – they've been brought in from Queensland.'

'Then you eliminate *them*. Right?'

'One of them is a serving police officer.'

'So?'

'Isn't that a little drastic, if I'm supposed to stay in the shadows? Wouldn't it trigger even greater scrutiny?'

'It sends a message. Like that Hells Angel who told police he'd rape and kill their daughters and wives. Intimidation, as well as elimination.'

'I'll do what you say.'

'I'll hear the apology once all this has gone away. After twenty-five years, if this has come back, I am owed an apology. But first, do what has to be done.'

THE LOST CITY OF DUST

SOMETIMES A CRIME SCENE CAN YIELD VERY SPECIFIC EVIDENCE, such as hair or fibres that can be linked back to the killer. Sometimes a crime scene will reveal something about the killer's state of mind, if they've done something unique to the body. I'd been to a lot of crime scenes, many of them in homes, but I'd never stepped inside a house full of dust, a house that had been tightly locked up for over twenty years.

I'd read *Great Expectations* as a kid and I, like all readers, was fascinated by Miss Havisham's ghoulish dining room, a mausoleum frozen on the day she was jilted by her husband-to-be, complete with its table settings in place. I never expected to find myself walking into a similar environment as an investigator.

—

WE'D PULLED UP out the front. Osborne Street wasn't far from Eli's jewellery shop and it was the next street up from where Maria and I were staying. Though most of the houses along Osborne Street are almost mini-mansions in a Georgian style, facing a long, thin park that runs along a railway line, the top end of the street, where Isobel lived, is narrow and the houses are more like workers' cottages, jammed in together.

A well-kept hedge with a white cast-iron gate spanned the front; we stepped into a small, neat front garden. The house was detached, which was unusual, because most of these smaller houses had shared main walls. It was small, squat and narrow, made of weatherboard and painted white. The flowers in the garden were very English. Eli was obviously paying someone to keep the place looking tidy. So far I was reminded of the serene landscapes by the English painter John Constable.

It was a whole other world when we unlocked the door and stepped inside.

—

THE FIRST IMPRESSIONS of a crime scene, usually those of the responding uniformed officers, who are generally young and lacking in investigative techniques, can often taint and confuse what soon follows. When Buff and Al arrived at Isobel's house, they encountered a weeping, hysterical boyfriend – a confronting and awkward situation which hadn't prepared them for what they were about to discover next. An eighteen-year-old girl, naked, with a tie around her neck, attached to a brass hanger on the back of her bedroom door. One man, a Baptist, saw sin and found suicide. Another, Buff, saw sex and imagined a terrible accident. Murder didn't even cross their minds. In the boyfriend's wails, Buff heard the deep well of the young man's remorse and guilt. The double bed was unmade; the room, as they stepped into it, was defined by Isobel's sexuality. Snap – all of those thoughts had coalesced into first impressions, which were passed on to the next lot of cops and the ones after them and then the Coroner's people. Maybe a little snigger: that was a fuck she'll never forget. Of course there was little sympathy for the girl. She wanted to play it rough and weird, and, well, she sort of got what she deserved. Same deal with the grieving boyfriend. It wasn't until later, a few days later, that other theories began to emerge, but I wondered if they were ever taken seriously. The scenario based on the officers' first impressions was already too powerful.

So, as Maria and I stepped in, some twenty-five years after those first two cops, we took it slowly, starting in the front room, comprised of a living area with a kitchenette and bar, frozen in time, covered in dust, smelling of a deep mustiness. We simply stood and took it all in.

Eli had kept paying the electricity bills, but sunlight streamed through the windows, creating solid shafts as the dust from the floor swirled around the room, millions of tiny motes glittering in the sun's rays.

To the right of us was a corridor that led down to the bedrooms and the back door, through which I could see an outside courtyard. Nothing had changed in the past two decades. The TV was fat and wide, not an elegant flat screen, the sound system looked the same as mine back up in Noosa, the posters on the walls were of Madonna and Bruce Springsteen from his *Born in the USA* days, and the furniture was simple. On a bookshelf were some framed photographs of what I took to be Isobel in Bolivia. Aside from a Lonely Planet guide to Bolivia, there were only three books: *The Prophet* by Kahlil Gibran, *Siddhartha* by Hermann Hesse and *The Little Prince* by Antoine de Saint-Exupéry. All books on spiritual enlightenment. No *Catcher in the Rye*; I remembered a Detective Inspector laughingly telling me that most of the killers he'd arrested had a copy of *Catcher in the Rye* in their house.

I stepped up to the photos. Isobel with her arms around a good-looking young man her age. This was Tyrone, I presumed. Isobel in her school uniform with a bunch of other girls and a very cool and hip-looking teacher in the middle. All grins and confidence. This was Brian Dunn, I presumed. Isobel wasn't standing next to him in the photo, but the camera had caught her glancing in his direction. And then Isobel alone.

I was told as a rookie cop never to look into the eyes of the victim whose killer you are chasing, because you become emotionally attached and, the theory goes, potentially blind in your investigation because of that emotion. I've been looking into the eyes of my victims ever since. In this photo, taken when she was in her last year at school, her last year of life, she looked pensive.

Although her hair was barely shoulder length, it had been pulled back into a ponytail. She wasn't looking into the lens of the camera but off to one side, as if there was something out there that had captured her attention.

So we didn't lock eyes, Isobel and I, but I held my gaze and felt the connection and made the vow: I will find out the truth and if you were killed by another person, I will see he goes down and forever. He will feel pain.

—

As Maria and I became more accustomed to the dinginess – I hadn't turned on the lights yet – we also started to see the cobwebs. Thick, intertwined bundles ran along the ceiling and the edges of the walls, crisscrossing the spines of the books, connecting the back of the TV to the wall, the sound system, creating a curtain across the bar, like a grey shimmer between the kitchen and the lounge room.

The lively Prahran Market was only a couple of streets away, on the other side of the railway line, and in the deep silence of the house, its tomb-like atmosphere enveloping us, I could hear the shouts of the fruit-and-veg guys as they called out their deals, 'Kilo apples, half-price!' drifting across in the wind. When I was a rookie cop, freshly arrived in Melbourne having escaped mum's little farm in the Western District, on the road to Ararat, I'd go to the market on Saturday mornings, late, just before they closed, to buy the cheap trays of meat they were desperate to sell so they didn't have to throw them out.

The market had seen murder. I'd attended a stabbing there soon after joining Homicide, and up the road, a little further away, a father of two was shot in the head while pulling into a supermarket car park with his kids on a Saturday morning.

Tyrone had told the cops that after the party, which finished around two or three – he couldn't remember – he and Isobel had cleaned up. Maria followed me as I stepped into the kitchen, carefully wiping away the cobwebs from the entrance. The dishes were still piled up neatly next to the sink. He'd said that he and Isobel went into the bedroom after that, but all they did was lie down on the bed for a while. She fell asleep and he left, at about two-thirty or three-thirty, he couldn't remember. Undoubtedly the cops had the same thought back then that Maria uttered now.

'Why'd he leave? If they were lovers, why not stay the night?'

'He said he had to go back to his flat in Elwood to get ready for work. He had a shift at a local McDonald's.'

'Does that make sense?' she asked.

Possibly, yes, if that's where his uniform was.

There was no sign of a forced entry and Tyrone had told the cops that the front door was unlocked when he went back the next morning and found her. He said Isobel was hopeless at remembering to lock up.

Something I had noticed when we stepped into the house now got my attention again. I crossed the floor of the kitchen and looked down at the bar. There was, sitting amid the dust and also covered in cobwebs, an empty glass and an almost-full bottle of Jim Beam.

'She didn't clean this up,' I said.

'Somebody had a drink after she went into the bedroom?'

'Maybe the boyfriend, on his way out.'

'Maybe someone else on their way in?'

I leaned down and stared closely at the label on the bottle.

'Eli said the house had been kept locked and sealed since the last cop left at the end of the investigation,' said Maria, reading my mind.

'Yeah, but it's possible someone came in later and maybe had a drink. It looks old. No labelling about responsible drinking. No web address.'

'Can we get anything off that?' she asked, gesturing towards the glass.

Good question. Back when Isobel died, DNA was just starting to be used as a tool in solving crime. The first case of DNA being used in court was in Tasmania in 1989. Back then DNA had to be sent to the United States for testing and it took up to six weeks before the results came back.

'I guess if you can test the DNA of a five-centuries-old body found in a car park and prove beyond doubt that it's Richard the Third, you have a pretty reasonable chance of gleaning something from a glass that was used twenty-five years ago. We might get some trace DNA or maybe a fingerprint.'

'After this long?'

'Worth a shot.'

'But a killer wouldn't leave his prints.'

'No,' I said. 'Still, let's try to find out who it was who had the drink.'

I looked back across the bar into the lounge area. There had been sixteen people accounted for at the party. Among those sixteen, who Isosceles was trying to hunt down, were four drop-ins she didn't know, or maybe she did; these were the four cops who paid her a visit with their friend Ruby Jazz, who said they'd all left by one in the morning. I stared at the open front door, trying to imagine how Isobel felt, here at the bar or maybe over by the CD player or lounging on the couch or floor, among her friends, when four cops walked in. If she did know them, she would have been freaked, her stress levels ramping up to overdrive as she was faced with this direct, tough link to the threats she was getting daily. And even if she hadn't met them, had no idea who they were as they walked in, she would have still felt distressed: four testosterone-fuelled cops in their early twenties would have oozed threat and power, wherever they went.

In the official report, Racine said he had a few words with Isobel in her bedroom, that he was in there just a couple of minutes and then left with the others.

'What did you talk about?' was the question asked of him, noted in the police statement he made twenty-five years ago.

'I told her she had a nice house and I might have said I hoped it was okay for us to just turn up like that. We weren't invited, not by her, but by her friend who we'd met at the Underground nightclub.'

'Where do you think he was?' asked Maria as we reached the bedroom at the rear of the cottage. We stood at the doorway, looking in. 'Sitting on her bed? Do you think he followed her in or asked to have a private word? She must have been terrified.'

The bed, queen-size, was unmade, just as it had been when she lay in it after doing the dishes. The sheets and doona had pockets of green and grey mould and, like every other surface in the house, were layered in an accumulation of soft dust. The smell of dankness and mould was more intense in the bedroom. Maybe it was because a dead body had been left here, for some hours, before the police arrived. I didn't think so but, like every crime scene where a person's life has been cut short by an unnatural and unexpected incident, a *feeling* lingered there, and it wasn't good.

To the side of the bed was a small padded chair, dark blue with white stars dotted across it. On it were brightly coloured woven baskets. I guessed they were from Bolivia. Like the kitchen and lounge area, the bedroom was neat.

'If I was a cop wanting to intimidate her, I'd follow her in or maybe steer her in, from the kitchen, then I'd close the door and stand over her, with her sitting on the bed. I'd make sure she was in contact with the bed because of the sexual implications.'

'But if you didn't want to intimidate her?' Maria replied. 'If you genuinely wanted to apologise for turning up at a party uninvited, because a mutual friend said it was okay?'

'Then I'd say that in the kitchen, in a social environment.'

'What about the boyfriend? There wasn't anything in his statement that referred to Isobel being alone in the bedroom with a cop.'

'No, there wasn't. He wasn't asked that question. I suppose we'll find out pretty soon.'

We stepped inside.

We closed the door and stood back, away, to get a full view of where Isobel was found hanging.

The brass hook was gone, as the Coroner had taken it for evidence during his inquiry, but the three screw holes were clear to see.

Neither of us spoke for a moment. I wondered if Maria was thinking what I was thinking, which I then said aloud: 'Really, if you were going to have sex, that would have to be the most uncomfortable, awkward way to do it. For both of them. And if you wanted the experience of auto-erotic asphyxiation, why not do it while lying in bed, with your partner's hands around your neck?'

Maria was staring at the back of the door. 'People are strange. You taught me that.'

I shrugged. Yeah, people are strange, but as I looked around the room, I just didn't get the feeling that Isobel strung to the back of the door, fucking the boyfriend at three in the morning after doing the dishes and saying farewell to her guests, after being spoken to by Racine, fitted. Not that a girl fresh out of school couldn't be into kinky sex – we are, if nothing, complex and often contradictory characters reacting to myriad stimuli and events – but something was wrong with this picture.

It was too early to jump to conclusions, and only a twit would do that anyway, in an investigation as challenging as this, but as I tried to absorb Isobel's room, her house, her life, a darkness began to squeeze out the possibilities of suicide and sex accident, and a light, getting brighter and louder, said murder.

HUSH HUSH, SWEET ISOBEL

'CLOSE YOUR EYES AND LET ME MASSAGE YOU.'

She did what he asked and spread her arms out, across the surface of the bed, feeling her body sink into the white feather doona. She exhaled and tried to force calm. Everything was black, although pockets of light, shapes and edges, danced across the insides of her lids. His fingers pressed down on her forehead and he began to swirl them, gently. She felt his hands as they moved down the sides of her face to the back of her neck and softly lifted her head up, so he could knead her flesh. She exhaled, eyes closed.

He had picked her up on his Harley. 'Down at the corner of your street,' he'd said. 'Not out the front of your house; that dad of yours might not approve.'

And she'd laughed at that. 'I don't live there anymore. I have my own place,' she'd said, not without a considerable dose of pride, being the only one from her school year who had achieved that level of independence so quickly.

'You do? Where?'

'You know Osborne Street, in South Yarra? It runs between Toorak and Commercial Road. I'm up near Prahran Market.'

'Yeah, yeah, great part of town. I know it well. I used to date a girl in Osborne Street about ten years ago. Man, she was fucking wild.'

She laughed. It was still strange, still thrilling, to hear him talk to her like that. Like she was an adult now, no longer a schoolgirl. And he was no longer her teacher.

'Give me the address. Wait for me out the front.'

And she did. Waited for him by the hedge that ran on either side of the gate, pockets of white rose spun along its other side as a creeper. Waited for the sound of the growl, the *thump-thump* of his Harley.

—

'I'M SCARED,' SHE'D said to him on the phone.

'Don't be,' he'd replied. 'We'll look after you, you'll be safe. Let me come and get you, take you into the city, to Dominic's hotel. Wait till you see it. Five stars. Grand piano in the foyer. It's amazing. Let me take you there and we can just relax – we can have a drink and you can tell me everything. But Isobel, remember, I'll look after you. All of us, we'll look after you. Isobel, don't be scared.'

'Okay,' she'd said, even though she *was* scared. She was more than scared. Since being picked up carrying drugs at the airport three days ago, deep, hard quivers of anxiety had run constantly through her. She was unbelievably scared and who could she tell? Who could she confide in? Not her dad, not Tyrone, not her friends from school.

Brian – that's who she could confide in.

Brian. Who had asked her to bring in the cocaine. The 'gift', he'd called it. Brian. Who seemed genuinely shocked when she rang and told him what had happened. Brian, whose name she didn't give the police because she didn't know what to say or do, and even though she was terrified she thought that if she just said nothing and lied and pretended, then maybe it would go away. Brian, who rode up to her as she stood at the front of her house, waiting for him, who smiled and said, 'Hop on, you've got nothing to worry about, I'm here now,' and rode off with a burst of metal and fury as she clung to him until they finally arrived out the front of a twenty-storey five-star hotel in the middle of the city, in the heart of Chinatown.

He helped her off the back of the bike, then led her into the foyer, past the grand piano and towards the lifts. He pulled out a room key from his back pocket and spun it around his index finger as if it were a toy.

She froze but tried to hide her reaction.

'Don't worry, Isobel,' he said with a laugh, having seen her look of concern. 'Nothing improper, I promise. Dominic has given me a huge room up on the top floor. We're just going to go up there and take it easy.'

'Okay,' she said and stepped into the lift, thinking: He'll look after me.

—

'FEEL BETTER?' HE asked.

She opened her eyes and smiled. 'Yeah. You should do that professionally.'

He laughed.

She watched as he climbed off the edge of the bed, then walked across the room and into the large living area. He had opened the doors to the biggest hotel room she had ever seen. Two bedrooms and a massive lounge area with couches and a dining table. Glass doors that opened onto a balcony. They were on the top floor, just as Brian had promised. They had stood by the doors and looked at the view, across the city, down at the narrow streets and alleys of Chinatown, at the shops and restaurants and signs in Chinese neon, then across to Parliament House and the park next to it. From this height she could even see, in the far distance, South Yarra, where she lived in the house that her dad had bought for her.

Now she climbed off the bed, stretched and followed Brian into the main room. She *was* feeling better. She went to look out on the city again. It was raining outside now.

'Drink?' he asked.

'Yeah, thanks, that'd be great.'

'Beer okay?'

'Thanks.'

He joined her at the glass doors, handed her the drink.

'Cheers,' he said.

'Cheers,' she repeated.

'Dominic's going to come and join us.'

'Okay. He really owns this hotel?'

'Dominic is big money. When he comes, I want you to tell both of us what happened at the airport. Okay?'

'Okay, yeah, sure.'

'We'll fix it. Don't worry. You're not worried, are you?'

'A little. Yeah.'

'Dominic is very powerful. Trust me – it'll go away.'

She turned her gaze to a cathedral at the edge of the city, close to Parliament. She looked down on its steeple and thought that when it was built it would have been the tallest structure in the whole of Melbourne. Now she was standing on the top floor of a hotel owned by a guy called Dominic, who she'd met a few times, at his parties, but not properly, not to talk to. He was just around. The host of fun. Now she looked down on the cathedral, and Dominic would fix her problem.

'Did you know?' she asked. 'Sorry, I ... I have to ask.'

'Did I know ... ?' He seemed confused.

'The gift ... what was in it. When you called me and asked me to bring a gift back for you. Did you know there was going to be cocaine in it?'

He laughed, then walked across and held her, looked directly into her eyes and smiled.

'Would I do that to you? I mean, really? Isobel? Would I knowingly ask you to bring drugs back into the country? I might be a bad English teacher, but I'm not a bad guy.'

THE HIRING

'HELLO?'

'Do you remember this voice?'

'I remember everything.'

'I need your services again, assuming you haven't retired.'

'So, here's the thing: in the past twenty years the communications industry has kind of exploded. You might have noticed –'

'I'm calling from my granddaughter's phone.'

'Great. After we hang up you'll destroy it. Every call between us is on a new phone. At the end of each call that phone is destroyed and –'

'But –'

'That's twice.'

'Twice? Sorry? What do you mean?'

'You've now interrupted me twice. Don't do it again.'

'Oh. Sorry.'

'I'm going to give you an address.' It was on Errol Street in North Melbourne and he wrote it down. 'Go with a thousand dollars. The man who lives there will provide you a phone. Every time you need to call me you go to him first. Got it?'

'Yes. I'll go there now and call you back with the details.'

But he was talking into dead air. The other man had hung up. He stared at his granddaughter's phone. A Samsung Galaxy, brand-new. She'd spent all of last Saturday transferring her contact numbers into it. She'd downloaded the three most recent episodes of *Girls* onto it. She was sleeping now, which is how he had managed to take it away from her. She spent more time on her phone than she did anything else. With difficulty he removed the back flap, took out the battery and then smashed it with a hammer he found on a bench in his garage.

THE CHOW

'AFTER SHE DIED, THERE WAS A LOT AND I MEAN *A LOT* OF internal criticism that we had pressured the girl into killing herself, that our tactics were inept and inhumane – young girl, out of her depth, hassled by the Feds, can't take it and kills herself. The dad was bringing on some bad publicity, questions being asked by idiots in government, so the whole thing was shut down.'

Sullivan sat on the other side of the small wooden table, cradling a beer. He had been with the Feds for as long as I could remember. He was in his mid-fifties, a thin guy with blazing red hair and freckles. He would've been the kid who got bullied at school. We were wedged up against a wall, down near the back of a dark and very loud Chinese restaurant in the heart of the city. Little Bourke Street, hosting a narrow and extremely lively Chinatown, runs from Spring Street, up at the top of the city close to the stately Parliament House and Old Treasury Building, all the way down to its other end, near the train yards at Spencer Street. Chinatown, always full of people rushing this way and that, eating out in one of the dozens of restaurants, big and small, cheap and expensive, has been spread over the top few blocks of Little Bourke Street since the 1880s. Like pretty much every Chinatown, this one in Melbourne had seen a lot of blood over the years. Many murders. The Chow, which was our cop shorthand for the China Palace Inn, was a small diner, and like all busy inner-city Chinese diners it was loud and bustling, with impersonal but attentive service and excellent food.

The Chow was a cop institution, a great place to huddle and swap war stories or information. I'd eaten here so often I should have bought shares in the place.

'No arrests, then?' I asked.

'Nothing. Two years of a task force, which was operating well, and completely under the radar of your HQ – and then nothing.'

'It was just the Federal Police?'

'Yeah. We'd had a tip-off about a new player in town. He was wealthy, influential and, we'd been told, had a few police officers doing his grunt work.'

'Who gave you the tip-off?'

'Some deadbeat we busted bringing in smack from Bali.'

Our food arrived. The downside of eating at the Chow was that the food came quickly and leisurely conversations were often hurried along by staff eager to reseat your table. Sullivan had Singapore noodles and I had sweet-and-sour chicken, a dish that, try as I might, I can never recreate at home without the addition of a pre-made sauce.

I'd left Maria at her apartment. She was getting everything we knew so far up on the whiteboard, which was now at her place. Isosceles was joining her there, and the three of us would examine our leads and suspects later in the evening.

As soon as I had begun to write the names of four serving police officers on the whiteboard at HQ, I had realised we needed a more private location to be mapping out our thoughts. Maria had volunteered her place.

After the difficulty I'd had getting an office at HQ, I had, within a day, abandoned it. C'est la vie.

'Who was the target?' I asked.

'Dominic Stone. Why someone as wealthy as that would want to step in and get involved with drug importation was a mystery.'

'Unless he needed big cash fast.'

'Yeah, we wondered that.'

'Or if the original wealth was based on drugs.'

'Yeah, we wondered that too but he kept things pretty well hidden, lawyers and trust funds and corporate entities. He had layers upon layers of fucking walls around him.'

'How close did you get to him?'

'Isobel was the key. She'd met him, stayed at his house in Toorak, stayed at his beach house, been to his hotel. She would have seen him snort coke, maybe even seen him ordering some people around, but she wouldn't tell us.'

'How come she got sucked into his world? It seems unusual, a girl like that, fresh out of school, getting immersed in that glitzy life. People lead double lives, but on the surface there's nothing about her that suggests she was a party girl. Do you think she knew she was bringing in cocaine?'

'No, and she wasn't a party-girl type. Worked for the old man, had her sights set on university, was proud of her academic record. It was the sleaze-ball, the teacher.'

'Brian Dunn.' I thought back to the photo in Isobel's house. The teacher surrounded by schoolgirls, all smiles and joy.

'Yeah. They were almost like boyfriend and girlfriend. She was very protective of him. Real stars in the eyes, that sort of thing. Him, I wanted to nail more than anyone. I mean *really*, you ring up one of your students while she's overseas – she was an impressionable kid and he was the dude on a Harley – and get her to be a mule for you. He was close to Stone. Don't ask me how. He hung around Stone enjoying the champagne, fast cars and access to his five-star hotel.'

'Did her boyfriend, her actual boyfriend, the one who discovered the body, know about Dunn?'

'Had to.'

A jealous rage culminating in Isobel's death was something I needed to explore.

Another thought flashed across my mind: maybe Dunn and Isobel were lovers and maybe he'd turned up at her house later that night. The idea of two eighteen-year-old lovers, fresh from high school, engaging in kinky sex on a doorframe seemed a stretch, but a guy riding a Harley, a guy who was significantly older than Isobel, a guy who had convinced her to bring cocaine back into Australia … that was different. Dunn already seemed like something of a predator, happy to cross boundaries when it came to spending time with one of his female students … I could believe the auto-erotic asphyxiation if it was Dunn she was having sex with.

'Why didn't you put her into witness protection?'

Sullivan shoved another forkful of noodles into his mouth and ate while he spoke.

'Yeah, well, that wasn't my call. Hindsight is a beautiful fucking thing. Not that she would have agreed, most likely.'

'And the cops? Were they crooked? Were they working for Stone?'

Sullivan looked at me. 'We were circling them. Nothing proven. Nothing proven against anyone.'

'What's your gut feeling?' I asked.

'It's twenty years ago. More, in fact.'

'What *was* your gut feeling?'

'Who had the most to lose?'

'Stone.'

'Yeah. He killed her. I'm sure of it. If he didn't do it himself, he sure as hell sent the order to strap her up and make it look like a suicide.'

'Do you think any of those four cops could have been involved? Again, just a gut feeling – you were there at the time.'

'Nah. Too fucking stupid. No, not stupid, just moronic. They're all clever now, twenty years on and sitting behind desks in your HQ, but then they were boys with big dicks and no GPS to guide them. They were involved, I'm sure of that – you can read the look of fear and guilt, and I still remember seeing them at the Coroner's inquest. They had things to hide. Fuck, you should have seen them when I showed up, the fear of God in their eyes. Thought we had enough to bust them all. Sadly, by then, what we had was going into cardboard boxes and we were all being reassigned.'

There has always been fierce rivalry between federal police officers and state police officers: basically each organisation thinks the others are idiots. I wasn't sure if Sullivan's analysis of the four cops wasn't biased from that perspective.

'What *did* you have on the four cops?' I asked.

Sullivan swirled the last of his Singapore noodles on his fork – he was not a chopsticks guy; most cops who came to eat here weren't – and paused before looking up at me.

'The one they called Karloff ...'

'Boris Jones,' I said.

'He's out in the country somewhere. Runs a small rural station, watches over the kangaroos and drunken shearers. He opted out, chose the quiet, anonymous life. But the others, they're all very high up now, Darian.'

In other words Sullivan was going to be cautious, lest he ruffle the feathers of some high-ranking influential cops, even if they were state and he was federal. Everybody goes to the same police conferences held in swish resorts around the country and overseas each year; everybody has to appear to get along harmoniously.

'Nothing was ever proven, none of this got to court,' he said cautiously.

'No, because your eighteen-year-old witness died on you.'

'Yeah, thanks for that. I did my guilty time. It happened. It was a mistake.'

A mistake on his watch. I wasn't going to press the point, though. We all had innocent blood on our hands, because we were unable to be everywhere at once or see into the future.

'If I was bringing in drugs and needed cop protection, I'd go to the Drug Squad; that's where I'd be making my pay-offs,' he said. 'But Racine, Pappas, Jones and Monahan were uniformed constables. They didn't have influence.'

'But they *were* cops and they could move things around for him without drawing suspicion. A drug deal is always going to be safer if you have a cop doing it for you.'

He nodded.

'And why not have an out-of-uniform cop to bang a few heads together, to keep everyone in line. More influential than a Maori bouncer or a hired thug,' I added.

He nodded again. 'Racine bought himself a nice house in St Kilda. Pappas got himself a Porsche. Jones's wife stopped working and they paid off their kids' school fees in advance. Monahan took his girlfriend on a first-class trip around the world over Christmas that year. They weren't the smartest tools in the shed. Back then.'

'You guys were pressing her pretty heavily. Stone was pressing her heavily. Four cops turn up at her house. Did she show any signs of extreme anxiety, depression, anything that could link to a suicide?'

Sullivan leant back in his chair and downed the last of his beer. We'd both wolfed our food and the plates had gone. I was eyeing the banana fritters, one of those guilty pleasures that seem so right at the end of a Chinese meal.

'Yeah, you Homicide boys've got to ask that question, eliminate all the possibilities. But really, Darian? She strips naked, wraps a tie around her neck, attaches it to a metal hanger on the back of her bedroom door and says her last goodbye? I've seen some weird shit, probably not as much as you, but that doesn't make any sense to me at all. I've got daughters. From the age of ten or eleven all they want to do with their bodies is cover 'em up. They're embarrassed by 'em. That is not the psychology of a young woman wanting to kill herself.'

I nodded. Couldn't have articulated it better myself.

'I'm going to have the banana fritters,' he said. 'You?'

TENDRILS OF THE PAST

Isosceles had brought Maria a large bunch of pink lilies, a box of Lindt chocolate and two large whiteboards, which were now resting on a table and leaning up against the main wall of her apartment's lounge room.

Isosceles had been spending the past few days going through the case files and trying to locate all the players: Isobel's friends who were at the party; Dunn, the schoolteacher; Tyrone, the boyfriend; the insanely named Ruby Jazz, who supposedly took the four cops from the city nightclub to the South Yarra house; and, of course, Dominic Stone, who owned a house in Toorak, a house by the beach at Portsea, an apartment in Vanuatu and a holiday home somewhere in Europe.

—

Isobel's photo, one from her school yearbook, was pasted to the edge of one of the whiteboards. I walked over and stared at her. In this photo she had everything to live for. I remembered reading about her death when it happened. I was still in uniform. When I got to Homicide years later, I suggested to my boss that he reopen the case. It bothered me that her death had gone unsolved. I was told to shut up and focus on existing cases. There were a hundred active cases of homicide every year and that was why I was there. Anyway, said my boss at the time, echoing popular belief, it was suicide.

So I did. I forgot about her.

For the past few days I'd been ransacking this girl's life, considering her sexual behaviour, invading her privacy, as one does when trying to find a killer. She would become better known to me than she had been known to anyone else; me, the guy who was investigating her death more than twenty years later. She and I would become intimate. I'd see sides to her she didn't show her father, or her friends, or her boyfriend. I'd look into every angle, every thought, as I continued this journey into her world.

Maria had been in kindergarten when Isobel died. She'd mentioned this to me as we closed the front gate to Isobel's house and walked back across to my car. A kid in a playground somewhere up on the Sunshine Coast and a young woman down at the other end of the country, about to meet her last day of life; now, all that time later, linked, working together. I shrugged off that thought. I didn't know what it meant and the crossovers through the journey of life could have a lot of meaning to those who believed in fate or none at all to guys like me, who didn't believe in anything.

Isosceles broke my reverie. 'Brian Dunn is now deputy headmaster at St Josephine's. It's a girls' school in Toorak.'

I turned to see Maria staring at him in disbelief. 'A *girls'* school? Deputy headmaster?'

'He's a highly respected member of the Melbourne educational fraternity,' said Isosceles. He seemed to be unaware of the rising tempest that was Maria.

'Who fucked his eighteen-year-old student *and* got her to import cocaine,' she added.

'I doubt St Josephine's is aware of that part of his history,' he said, now clued in to her rage.

'They will be by the time I've finished with him,' she said.

I thought about pulling her up on that; we had a job to do and it wasn't getting revenge on a sleazy teacher for putting one of his students in peril by asking her to bring in some cocaine. I needed

Maria to stay focused on finding the truth behind Isobel's death, not on nailing Dunn, even though they could end up being one and the same. Still, an angry determination to obtain justice was a healthy drive for an investigator, and for the first time since Maria and I had worked together, she'd shown an edge, something I could relate to, different from her usual do-it-by-the-book approach. I liked it. I was feeling, also for the first time, that we were true partners on this one.

'By the way, Maria,' said Isosceles, 'I'd like to compliment you on your choice of clothes today.'

She smiled at him. Normally any woman would vomit at such rubbish, but she knew his idiosyncrasies and the lack of human interaction that caused him to utter such nonsense.

He turned to me. 'Shall I continue with the update on our suspects and persons of interest?'

'Stay with Dunn. Any record?'

'Clean.'

'Where does he live?'

'He purchased an apartment in Darling Street, South Yarra, many years ago. Lives alone. Never married.'

I nodded. 'Okay. Continue.'

'After Isobel's death her boyfriend Tyrone left Australia and backpacked through Asia and India for five years. He came back in 2001 and opened a small health-food store in Northcote, which went bust a year later. He drifted, doing odd jobs, and is now a swimming coach. He married in 2008, lives in Coburg and has two children.'

'Any record?' I asked.

'Yes.'

There was a pause, during which we all stared at each other. Sometimes talking to Isosceles is like talking to a robot.

'Do you want to enlighten us?'

'His wife took out a restraining order against him three years ago.'

'Why?'

'According to the court records he was drinking to excess and had become threatening and violent towards her and the children, both girls.'

'Are they still together?' asked Maria.

'Yes. She applied to have the restraining order removed after two weeks and they are still all living together.'

'Only the one restraining order?' I asked.

'Yes. Continue?'

I nodded.

'Nick Racine, Aristotle Pappas and Jacob Monahan are all based at St Kilda Road HQ, as you know. Boris Jones runs the police station at Nhill.'

'Nhill? What is Nhill?' asked Maria.

'A tiny country town close to the Little Desert, about four hours' drive from here,' I said.

'Unlike the other three police officers who were at Isobel's on the night,' Isosceles continued, as if Maria hadn't asked and I hadn't answered, 'Boris chose to leave Melbourne very quickly, putting in a transfer request three months after she died. He's been in Nhill all that time.'

'Didn't you say he was the most ambitious of them all?' Maria asked me.

'He was. I didn't know him, but I'd heard he was fond of bragging that one day he'd become Commissioner.'

'Is there anything on *any* of them since Isobel's death?' I asked.

'Nothing. All clean. Not even a drink-driving charge,' he said.

'Tell me about Ruby Jazz,' I said.

'After providing the police with her statement, which confirmed she'd run into the four cops at the Underground nightclub in the city and invited them to Isobel's house and party and then left with them at about twelve-thirty, Miss Ruby Jazz promptly disappeared. I can find no trace of her.'

'She was a schoolfriend of Isobel?' asked Maria.

'If she was she's not listed in the yearbook. Of course I posit that Ruby Jazz was not her real name.'

Isosceles had used that word *posit* on me before. I still had no clue what it meant but I got the gist.

'It's the name on her witness statement,' I said.

'I don't think we could accuse the police of investigating Isobel's death with great thoroughness, even after it became apparent that Isobel was in the grip of the Federal Police and that four serving officers of Victoria's finest had been at the party. The level of detail in the witness statements and corresponding files is, at best, scant,' said Isosceles.

'Because they all took one look at her in the crime-scene photo and thought she was a stupid girl who engaged in rough sex and deserved what she got,' said Maria, the anger levels rising another notch.

'Oh dear God, John Kerry is *such* a *fuckwit*!' announced Isosceles while looking at his smart phone. Maria and I stared at him. What that announcement had to do with the investigation – with anything, really – was beyond our collective wildest imagination.

He looked up at us. 'Oh. I do apologise. I get rolling tweets on the situation in Crimea and that idiot with the *Munsters* face and bouffant hairdo has just reduced the Russian invasion of Crimea to *Rocky IV*.'

That didn't really help us. We kept staring at him.

'*Rocky IV*, the film.'

'The one with Dolph Lundgren,' said Maria, still looking utterly bemused.

'Yes. That one. He just threatened Russia by saying they and the United States are not in a remake of *Rocky IV*.'

I knew this had something to do with Isosceles' obsession with the rather obscure Crimean War of the nineteenth century. I'd seen the news that Putin had gone in to annex that part of Ukraine, but I needed him back on track.

'Can you put the phone away, silence the tweets and stay focused?' I asked.

'Of course, Darian. My apologies.' He turned to Maria and almost bowed. 'My apologies to you as well, Maria.'

'Maybe Tyrone will remember a friend of Isobel who went by the name of Ruby Jazz,' said Maria, back on track.

'She's really important,' I said to Isosceles. 'Her testimony will go a long way to eliminating the cops. Or not.'

I had a thought and turned to Maria. 'Give Casey a call. See if he can remember a stripper or dancer or burlesque girl by the name of Ruby Jazz.'

She gave me a long look, as if to say *I'd rather not*, then nodded and moved off to the sliding door and stepped out onto the balcony.

'Holy fuck, it's cold out here!' she shouted as she took out her phone to speed-dial him.

Isosceles ran me through the guest list at the party. Three had died, two had moved overseas, and the rest, all Isobel's contemporaries, were still living in the Melbourne area. Their original witness statements were consistent. The party had started around seven, Isobel got drunk and might have smoked some dope (depending on who wanted to keep that part of the night a secret) and they all began to dribble home after two, leaving Isobel and Tyrone doing the dishes in the kitchen.

Both the Coroner and his assistant had died, which was immensely frustrating. I would have loved to find out what was going on in the Coroner's mind as he considered the evidence and accusations before him, coming up with an open finding, which essentially meant that he, officially, could not determine if Isobel's death was the result of self-harm, accident or foul play.

What Coroners *don't* put in their reports, especially when the death is controversial, is often the truth. It's not put in if it cannot be substantiated with the level of rigour required by a Prosecutor.

I heard Maria's raised voice echoing from the balcony, and then, after a moment of silence, she walked back in, looking like a blood-crazed Spartacus at the beginning of a war.

'Ruby Jazz was an under-age stripper and prostitute who specialised in performing in her school uniform and who hung in the circles of cops and certain nightclub owners. *I swear it was only the once, babe* were his final words just then.'

As delicately as I could, aiming to avoid enraging her even more, I asked, 'Does Casey happen to remember her real name, by any chance?'

'He thinks it was Holly something and he thinks she had an apartment on the Esplanade in St Kilda, which, he also thinks, was provided for her by an Italian gangster named Mario Brugnano. But he isn't sure about that, *Because I never visited her there, babe, I promise I didn't*. Thanks for bringing me into this investigation, Darian.'

Of course, it was my fault.

I'd never heard of an Italian gangster by the name of Mario Brugnano, but I turned to Isosceles and said, 'I think you've got enough to go on.'

He nodded, clearly not equipped to deal with the angry banshee in the room.

'Where's Stone?' I asked.

'Just over the hill, in his Toorak house.'

'Okay. Good.' I looked at the whiteboards. 'They're all under surveillance?' I asked.

'Of course. Phones, Google, email, every word and tap on the keyboard. Last I looked, our Mr Stone was reading his latest issue of *Gizmag* magazine.'

'He what?' asked Maria.

Isosceles leaned over to his laptop, fired it up out of sleep and hit the keyboard. Within seconds we were gazing at the face, full screen, of an elderly, wealthy-looking sun-tanned man. He was in turn gazing at his screen, his eyes scanning from left to right, taking in what was in front of him.

'I picked this up from friends at the NSA. I hacked into his life and set up a spy cam – using the inbuilt camera on the top of his laptop. I've done it to all of them. Stone spends hours reading *Gizmag*, which reports on all the latest technologies from around the world. They'd reported on the 3D printer at least a year before it hit the mainstream press.'

Maria and I leaned forward, our faces almost touching the screen as we stared at the man before us. Was he our killer?

THE STRANGER

MARIA WOKE AT THREE AND TRIED TO GO BACK TO SLEEP BUT couldn't. The sound of the wind tearing up Davis Avenue, twisting the old elm trees and their branches, kept her mind active and alert. She was hungry. She'd had no time to stock up on basic food, stuff like cereal, honey, bread and coffee. Normally she'd carefully choose these items at a big supermarket where she was able to get Free Trade and organic, but her need to eat and drink coffee of any sort was winning out. She climbed out of bed, threw on a pair of jeans and a T-shirt and some runners. There was a 7-Eleven around the corner. At this time of morning they might even have the local newspaper, which she could read while she ate. Grabbing her keys and a jacket, she left the apartment, walked down the stairs and within moments was standing outside on the footpath.

Above her the branches of the trees swayed, casting eerie, moving shadows from the dull yellow of the streetlights onto the street, which was empty and glistening from the light rain that had fallen overnight.

She hugged the jacket tightly around her and walked towards Toorak Road, which was lit up like a carnival. The trams would start to appear around five. She wasn't yet used to the sounds of their loud clattering as they rumbled along the middle of the Melbourne streets.

She passed one of the many narrow side alleys that dissected Davis. This whole area had a secondary maze-like world of tiny cobbled laneways. Darian had told her about a particularly nasty serial rapist who used these alleys to stalk and attack his victims in the mid-1980s. His capture had led to the formation of a Rape Squad to deal specifically with that crime; up until then women had to report to young morons at the front desk of the local stations. She thought about the morons who often manned the front desk of her station up on Noosa Hill. Freaky. *Are you sure you really didn't want it?* and *Maybe when you said no, you really meant yes.*

Darian had described the infamous Walsh Street killings on the other side of Toorak Road, just over the hill from where she was standing, where two young officers were ambushed and murdered in a payback a day after the killer's best friend had been gunned down by other cops in a shootout. Darian had also told her about a brutal decapitation in the Royal Botanic Gardens twelve years ago and a fifteen-year-old girl who'd been strangled by another, older girl, up around the corner from Eli's shop. Darian had pointed out pretty much every killing he knew of as they'd cruised the streets. He was like the tour guide from hell. After hearing about a woman whose face had been blown off by a jealous lover, which happened not far from the France-Soir restaurant, Maria had said to him, 'Enough, *enough.* Stop defining this city – this very beautiful city – by murder.' And he'd laughed and swung the car around and driven back down Toorak Road and parked just up the hill from the turn-off to Davis.

'Hop out,' he'd said.

And she did. 'What, a triple murder of five-year-olds?' she'd asked.

He'd laughed again. He didn't laugh often. In fact, she'd never seen him laugh back up on the Noosa River. Maybe he was at home here. She sure as hell wasn't.

He'd pointed to a real estate office housed in an old 1920s two-storey building on the corner of Toorak and another narrow street.

'That used to be the most famous restaurant in Melbourne. In fact, you could even say it was the most famous restaurant in the southern hemisphere. From maybe the nineteen-thirties to the sixties. I never went there, of course, but Copeland, our esteemed Commissioner, used to go when he was a kid. His father took him, every Friday night. Always ate the same meal: mashed potato and a boiled egg.'

'At the most famous restaurant in the southern hemisphere?'

'Yeah, well, that's why they get to be so famous. They cater, happily, to their clients' eccentricities.'

He'd reached out and taken her hand. She'd stared at him for a moment then gave in and let him lead her to the edge of the street. Traffic whizzed by.

'The restaurant was called Maxim's. One night, in 1959, Fred Astaire was dining at Maxim's. He was making that end-of-the-world movie, *On the Beach*, with Ava Gardner.'

'Who's Ava Gardner?'

'She was big. Like, a huge Hollywood star.'

'I know who Fred Astaire is,' she'd quickly said, slightly defensively.

'Anyway, Fred got a little pissed. As he was leaving, the staff opened the door for him and Miss Gardner and the two of them stepped out onto the footpath. Just there.'

'The car, limo, whatever they had in Melbourne in fifty-nine, was waiting, driver smiling, back doors open. And Fred Astaire looked down the street, down there.' He'd pointed to the vast long sweep of Toorak Road. 'It would have been about midnight and the street was empty. Fred Astaire stepped into the middle of the street, like this ...'

And to her horror, Darian had led her through the snarl of traffic and stopped, smack-bang in the middle of Toorak Road. Nobody had beeped their horns. People here jaywalked all the time – but they didn't just stop in the middle of the road on the tram tracks and stare down the street.

'... and he tap-danced all the way to the bottom of the hill.'

'Wow,' she'd said, the sounds of the traffic dissipating for the merest of moments as she saw the great man, in tails and top hat maybe, alone, tap-dancing down an empty boulevard, watched only by a fellow actor and a couple of amazed waiters, at a time when the world was, she imagined but couldn't be sure, a better, safer place.

—

SHE THOUGHT SHE heard footsteps behind her. She stopped, turned to look around.

There was nobody there, not that she could see. She looked up to Darian's apartment. His lights were off. Toorak Road was just ahead. Maybe it was all of those stories he'd been telling her, of murders in every street, but she was a little freaked and wished the sun would wash its light over her.

She kept walking. She thought she heard the sound of a man's voice, whispering. Again, from behind her.

She stopped and turned back. Nothing there. She stepped out into the middle of the street to get a better view of her surroundings.

She listened to the wind as it rattled through the branches of the trees, knocking them together above her, and she was sure she heard a man say, in a whisper carried down the street with the wind, *I just don't like killing cops.*

Had she imagined that?

Instead of hurrying to the brightness of Toorak Road, she began to walk back up along Davis, in the centre of the road, scanning both sides, the trees and the elegant gardens of the houses and apartment blocks.

Was someone out there?

Had she really heard a person say that?

By the time she had reached the end of Davis, she was just a block away from Isobel's house, where she and Darian had been that morning. The mausoleum. She hadn't seen anyone on the street, on the footpath, hiding behind a tree or in one of the gardens. Toorak Road was now way back in the distance. She kept walking. This time, however, using the moonlight to guide her, she turned off into one of the back alleys.

She walked along three narrow alleys, one after another. The cobblestones were large blocks of bluestone that the convicts had been forced to dig out of the earth across Victoria. They had shaped the stone into square blocks, then carried them to the city and laid them on the ground, thus forming the first series of roadways, back in the early 1800s. Darian had told her all about it. Coated in a mist of drizzling rain, they gleamed an inky cobalt as she stepped across them. Within minutes she was at the wooden fence of Isobel's backyard; she recognised it because she and Darian had examined the yard after they left the house. There hadn't been any signs of forced entry into her house, and it was assumed she'd left her back door open as well as her front door. One of the first cops attending the scene, from CIB, had mentioned in a report that he had a feeling, but no more, that somebody might have climbed over the fence from the other side. A throwaway line buried in the case file. A couple of broken shrubs in her garden might have indicated a person jumping into the backyard. Maybe. It seemed a stretch, but cops do have a weird sixth sense.

Curious, Maria scaled the fence easily, landing on the red-brick surface of the courtyard next to a towering white ghost gum.

There was a man standing in front of her. She couldn't make him out – he was dressed in black. The streetlights didn't reach this far and the moonlight was blistered by the canopy of the gum.

'What the fuck?' she heard him say as he ran towards her.

'What the fuck?' she heard herself say as he crashed into her. She fell, her head knocking against the bricks. She reached out to try to grab him, maybe pull him over with a swing to his legs.

He fell.

She tried to get up but her head was causing her serious pain and her shoulder felt like it had cracked.

She felt herself being lifted off the ground, she felt herself up in the air, she felt herself unable to control her body, her legs swinging in space and her arms flailing as the man held her. She tried to kick him and bite and spit at him.

He dropped her down, hard, onto the bricks and then he came down too, on top of her, all body and weight.

'Bitch,' she heard him say as she abruptly hit a place of black.

'I really don't want to kill a cop,' she heard him say as his knee began to squeeze down on her neck.

She heard a siren. It was far away. She saw a light. It was very close. She heard a lullaby. It was her mother at the end of her bed. She saw an explosion, a car ricocheting off the Bruce Highway and splintering into a hundred thousand bright spots of light, she saw a woman running through a field saving people who were on fire, she saw a woman firing a gun and a man, stumbling, falling, collapsing to the ground, and she saw a grave in the earth near an estuary where the body had been tossed and she saw the dead man smiling at her, she saw a dancer tapping his way down a boulevard and she saw a lover circling men on his motorbike and then running them over and again she saw this lover with his swagger and ponytail swinging and his body covered with tattoos and a smile that said, *Boy, do I ever love you, babe*, and she heard the sound of thunder, not close but distant, like the sound of a fighter jet that's passed overhead but continues to rumble through the sky for five minutes, even though it might be in another airspace by then and she felt the touch of her father, whom she never knew, and she re-read the letter she'd received at the age of eight, addressed to her school, saying, *I so love you*, and, *Please forgive me*, and she saw a darkness, collapsing and she heard Leonard Cohen singing about the crack of light and she remembered the time she stole Jackie's lipstick and painted her face and when she kissed Billy Waterson at his ninth birthday party at a Cooroy pub and that time when she sat atop a horse and screamed with fear and, despite the assurances of her parents, she had to climb down, and when she first held a gun and then she remembered, again, shooting a gun, seeing the explosion of crimson in his back and thinking, *Darian, you set me up*, and falling asleep at the wheel as the sun began to set and she thought about the surfboard she'd made her mum buy for her but she never rode and the blond idiot called Dave who flashed his dick at her end-of-year formal and said, *How about this?*, and how she laughed and ran and how, later, Dave and his friends called out to her, across the street in Maroochydore, *You frigid cunt*, and how she ran into the newsagency and sought refuge behind a copy of *New Idea* that had Kylie Minogue on its cover, and she thought about her lover with a seventeen-year-old girl who strutted around in a school uniform and lived in a flat owned by a gangster with an unusual name but not as unusual as Ruby Jazz, and how, when they first met, she had absolved him of the past and knew that he owned a strip joint and must have fucked hundreds of girls, even before she was born, yet how, now, as she was sinking into the black, it was such a betrayal and would she ever find a man who adored her and adored her forever and, really, was she that naive? She heard the sound of wind in the branches of elm trees and the feel of the moon, she heard the sound of the night and the loss of her mother. She imagined herself with Darian, beside him, the feel of his chest and the press of his body into hers, the scent of his breath and the look in his eyes as he came within her. She saw an old woman and it was her. She heard the creak of bones and they were hers. She heard the sound of kids and they were running towards her. She felt the swell of a river and the undulation of the sea and saw that she was floating off the coast of Fiji. She saw a kid in a playground surrounded by boys and heard their cries. She heard the footsteps of soldiers across the frozen tundra of Siberia and saw an old man named Eli who was a child staring through a razor wall as the echoes of their approach materialised into men on horseback appearing on the horizon after two days of riding, the land so still and flat that sound carried for hundreds of miles, and she heard those beats as she felt the breath within her ebb away and she knew that this man, in black, was extinguishing her, as someone did Isobel, more than twenty years ago.

Then she heard the sound of a gunshot.

THE MAN WITH THE GOLDEN ARM

She had called Tyrone and said she was staying the night with her dad and not to bother coming over, as they'd planned. She'd catch up with him later on tomorrow. She'd call when she got back home.

He was fine with that. He didn't suspect anything. He never did.

Dominic had walked into the penthouse with a 'There she is,' and shaken her hand like they were old friends. He wore a white suit and pink shirt, which Brian had told her had come from Savile Row, and he had a smooth face, tanned and soft, full of teeth. His long nose somehow made her think of Persia but she didn't know why. He had a tie pin clipped halfway down a red tie with blue spots and he smelt of aftershave and he was always smiling and his shoes, which Brian had told her also came from some exclusive shop in London, were polished so much that they reminded her of her mum's patent-leather high heels, her favourite shoes. He spoke softly and quietly and he exuded confidence. Often she'd seen him with the buttons of his shirt undone, to reveal his hairy chest. A thick gold chain hung around his neck and on his wrist was a gold Rolex, studded with diamonds, which Brian had told her was worth over two hundred thousand dollars.

Brian watched as Dominic guided her to one of the couches and sat in a chair opposite her. A low, long glass table with the latest copies of Paris *Vogue* was between them. She noticed that Brian's demeanour changed when Dominic was there. He was … she had trouble figuring out exactly what it was, but she could see that Brian wanted to impress. How she felt around him, that's how he seemed to be when he was around Stone. Which unnerved her.

He won't try to scare you, Isobel, he'll try to make you his best friend. That's what the Federal Police officers had told her about Dominic. *It will all be an act. But you tell him what you want. Or hey, maybe he won't try to make contact with you at all.*

Who is he? I've never heard of Dominic Stone.

He's the guy who asked your boyfriend –

He's not my boyfriend. He's my teacher.

Okay, he asked your teacher *to call you and get you to bring some of that cocaine back into Australia. Dominic made a deal with a new supplier and he wanted to check its quality.*

She'd lied to the police. She'd met Dominic Stone a number of times. Brian, who was still Mr Dunn back then, had taken her to the Underground nightclub one night and they'd had vodka martinis and danced and she'd been introduced to a whirlwind of people, among them, Brian shouted into her ear as the music was so loud she couldn't hear a thing, 'One of the richest men in the city and the best fun!' at which Stone, all tan and smiles, had grinned and kissed her hand like in an old-fashioned movie, which she had thought was both cool and a bit slimy.

This was about the time she was finalising her application to spend a term of her final year in Bolivia, about a year after she started going out with Tyrone, soon after Mr Dunn had kept her back at the end of English and asked if she'd like to hang out on the weekend. She'd told none of this to Tyrone. Or her dad. This other life was secret. Nobody knew. Just Brian and his friends.

'I'm here to help,' said Dominic as he sat back in his chair and rested his legs on the table, putting his feet on the cover of *Vogue*. 'Tell me what happened, then I'll tell you how we'll fix it.'

'After I got my bags off the carousel, these two men walked up to me.'

Isobel Vine?

'They knew my name. It was like they were waiting for me.'

Can you come with us, Isobel? We need to have a look inside your luggage.

'They took me into this room. They went through all my stuff and they found the parcel I was bringing back for Brian.'

'Then what happened?' asked Dominic, smiling, calm, relaxed.

'I tried to pretend I didn't know how it got there, that I hadn't packed it.'

'But they didn't buy that?'

'No. They said I was in big trouble.'

This is jail time, Isobel. How old are you? Eighteen? Just about to finish school and you're caught importing cocaine? Your life is fucking ruined, Isobel, and you haven't even begun it.

'But then they made you an offer, huh?'

I've got a kid your age, Isobel. I have. And she gets up to stupid stuff. Hell, I used to do stupid things when I was your age too. I understand. The Federal Police are not in the business of locking away teenagers for a ten-year jail stint if it can be avoided. So, Isobel, let's avoid it. What do you say?

'What did you say?' asked Dominic.

'I asked them what they meant. I was freaking out. I was crying and I couldn't think straight.'

You want a coke, Isobel? Coca-Cola, that is. Ha. Something to relax you. You need to calm down.

'What did you say?' asked Dominic again. He was smiling, still looking relaxed, but she wasn't sure how deep that went beyond the exterior.

'I said yes.'

'Uh huh. Okay. Good girl. That's exactly what I would've said too. I mean, what was the alternative? Say no and they'll throw the book at you. Cops are like ex-lovers: they're prone to bursts of irrational anger. So, what exactly do they want you to do? What are the terms of this offer – which is now a deal – they made to you? I get what *their* part of the deal is – they won't press charges – but what's your part, Isobel? What do they get from you in return?'

She looked at Brian, then back at Dominic.

'They want me to tell them everything I know about Brian.'

'And?'

'And … you.'

'Me.'

'Yes.'

'They mentioned my name?'

'Yeah.'

'Hey, Brian, we're famous! The Feds are after us! So, Isobel, what have you told them?'

'Nothing.'

'Nothing?'

'I'm meeting with them on Monday.'

'Who? Did they give you their names? Maybe their business cards?'

'Um, yeah, one was called Sullivan and the other was Bellini.'

'Okay. Great. Good recall. Can you stand up for me, Isobel?'

That's a weird request, she thought, as she did what he asked. Suddenly she regretted her choice of clothing: tight pink miniskirt with white singlet and black leather jacket.

Dominic got up out of his chair and walked around to her.

'Hey, don't be offended. By the suspicion. Or the touching.'

He reached out and grabbed her, pulled her to him and held her pressed to his body while his hands glided down her back, across her skirt, over her bum and around to her front. Then, gently pushing her away from him, just ever so slightly, he ran his hands up over her stomach and her breasts and then through her hair.

'I'm looking for a wire,' he said. 'I don't, for a second, imagine I'll find one. But you've got to be sure about these sorts of things.'

While he did this she tried to stay still, but her eyes sought Brian. He was looking away.

'Fantastic!' said Dominic as he finished. He stepped back and clapped his hands together like a kid about to meet Santa. 'All right, let's all go down to Portsea and have ourselves a party! Brian, call down to room service, get 'em to put a crate of Krug in the boot of my car.'

ASSASSIN

I HAVE SHOT – ALTHOUGH EXECUTED MIGHT BE THE BETTER word – a number of men in my time, and they all deserved an early death, not because of a determination on my part to exact revenge or justice, but to ensure that their ability to destroy other people's lives was terminated. I have no qualms about what I've done and I don't believe in a God or a hell, so I sleep in peace. I am not tormented by these actions as are most other men and women. Police officers are trained to shoot with maximum effect, at the head or the heart, if a violent offender is in the throes of attack and that officer's life, or the life of another, is at risk. People often decry this training and suggest that the police officer should have, really, gone for a leg, even an arm, perhaps a foot. It's bullshit. If someone's coming at you with intent to hurt and they ignore the warnings, they go down. All the way. It's what you're taught, it's what you learn, it's the only option. It's also one of the biggest nightmares that cops have: being confronted by an immediate and very dangerous risk, pointing your gun at someone and them ignoring your warnings, counting down the milliseconds before you know you've got to pull the trigger and kill them. Just because they won't fucking listen and drop to the ground.

There are very, very few cops who last in the job after one of these incidents. No cop joins the Force to kill a person. Not even me. I just got to that point after years of watching bad guys stroll out of jail and reoffend, watching clueless judges and parole boards lap up the stories of remorse from heartless psychopaths who've learned how to be charming and act like a Leonardo or a Brad while in their cells or maybe even earlier, at school, as they alternated between torturing their neighbour's pets and assaulting kids in the playground.

As soon as I saw the heavy-set man dressed in black straddling Maria and trying to choke her, his knee digging in hard against her windpipe while he grabbed her by the hair in what looked like a prelude to her head being smashed back onto the concrete, I took aim with my Beretta and pulled the trigger.

He went down immediately.

I'd been sitting in the cold dark of my balcony when I noticed her on the footpath, walking in the direction of Toorak Road. I saw her hesitate and look back. Then I saw her step out onto the street. Clearly she'd heard something or someone. I hadn't, but the wind was playing a light orchestra through the leaves of the elm trees directly in front of the balcony. I watched as she walked back up Davis and then it seemed like she was following someone. It seemed unlikely that either of us would be the target for an attack, but the streets of South Yarra at four in the morning, particularly the cobbled alleyways, have a well-deserved reputation for danger. I grabbed my Beretta and left the apartment. Less than a minute later I was on the street some eighty metres behind her as she walked towards Isobel's house. Was she being lured there?

—

GENERALLY SPEAKING, WHEN you shoot a guy in the head at four in the morning in the backyard of a house in the middle of inner-city suburban Melbourne, the neighbours are going to wake with a start, people are going to call triple zero and the sounds of angry sirens are going to close in on you within minutes.

I ignored, for the moment, the dead guy and went straight to Maria.

'You're okay,' I said.

She was in shock, gasping and reaching for her bruised neck.

'What the fuck just happened?' she said when she could put words together.

'Don't move. Just take in deep breaths and try to exhale slowly,' I said.

Ignoring my advice she propped herself up on her elbows and looked across to where her attacker lay.

'He just came at me. What was he doing here? Who is he?'

I crossed over to him. I could hear sirens in the distance. At least three sets of police sirens.

I rolled him over and searched for a wallet. There was none. His pockets were empty. No mobile phone either.

Maria started to laugh. Uncontrollably, like she'd just seen George Carlin or Billy Connolly perform a gag. Gales of laughter, resonating with the profound shock at almost having been killed, swept through her. I'd seen this reaction before. Funnily enough, it's not that unusual … although it sure as hell is the first time you witness it.

—

WHEN THE FIRST set of uniformed cops arrived, pistols drawn, stepping into the backyard stealthily lest they be gunned down, they must have wondered what was going on. A dead guy lying facedown on the concrete, a woman laughing like a raving lunatic, and me, sitting cross-legged, hands open and flat, resting on my knees. My Beretta was three metres away, on the ground, too far for me to lunge at.

'I am a police officer,' I said. 'So too is this woman.' I gestured towards the dead guy. 'This person was trying to kill her and I shot him. It might be a good idea to call the Officer in Charge of Homicide. His name is Zach Reeve.' I recited Reeve's mobile phone number.

They were young. Clueless. They'd probably never seen a dead body before. They certainly wouldn't have seen this kind of dramatic tableau.

More cops arrived. Constables. First responders. They didn't exert muscle or attitude, which was gratifying. Within ten minutes Maria had stopped giggling and we were both staring at six young men and women, some of Melbourne's finest.

—

'Is THAT YOU, Darian?' I heard from the front yard of the house.

Dawn's grey wash was approaching, and with it the temperature had plummeted. An hour had passed. Reeve and a crew from Homicide had arrived, the Coroner's people had arrived, forensics had arrived, two ambulance crews had arrived (with blankets) and the crime-scene investigators had arrived. Maria had told the ambos to fuck off when they said she had to go to hospital and we had both consumed two cups of steaming black coffee and given our first statements. Everyone was giving us the sympathy and respect you give when fellow officers are put in the line of fire – *there but for the grace of God* stuff – when I heard the familiar voice.

Commissioners don't attend crime scenes.

Copeland lumbered into the backyard and everybody froze. *What is the Commissioner doing here?* Walking briskly behind him was a woman in her late twenties, dressed in a black suit, her thick, dark hair tied in a swinging ponytail. I knew her. She was vivacious, with big eyes and a bigger smile, although not today. This was Michelle Alessandro. She was Head of Media Liaison.

Reeve strode up to the boss.

'Sir. We don't yet know the identity of the assailant. But he was attacking Senior Constable Chastain when Darian pacified him.'

Pacified?

Copeland brushed past him and walked straight up to Maria.

'Miss Chastain, are you all right?'

'Yes, sir, thank you.'

'Copeland. None of this *sir* bullshit.'

'Yes, Copeland.'

He turned to me. 'What's the meaning of this? Can you tell me, Darian?'

'The dead guy was following Maria. He's not carrying any form of ID, which suggests he was hired by someone who wants to put the frighteners on us. We need to facial recognition him and trace him back to the contract. It might lead us closer to the person responsible for Isobel Vine's death.'

Reeve bristled. I was telling him how to do his job. I didn't care. The dead guy could have been hired by someone sitting in an office one floor above Reeve, who might now want to exert some friendly influence on the current Head of Homicide.

'Darian, you're saying there is a person responsible for her death?' asked Copeland, seemingly taken aback. 'It wasn't suicide?'

'Boss, have a look around you. We're standing in her backyard. Twenty-five years after the Coroner couldn't make a decision. There's a dead guy who tried to out Maria. We've seen some weird shit, you and I, boss, but we've never seen an effort to cover up a suicide. We haven't ruled anything out, of course, but I've got to tell you, after tonight, it's looking the least likely cause of her death.'

He stared at me for a long moment. I got the feeling it wasn't the answer he wanted to hear.

'They think they can stop us?' After all, he was the Police Commissioner, one of the most powerful men in the state.

'They think they can spook us. Destabilise us.'

He turned back to Maria.

'I take personal responsibility for this. You are here in Melbourne at my invitation.'

She nodded. She wasn't used to Commissioners being respectful, let alone caring.

He turned to Reeve. 'Ignore the protocol. These officers need to continue their duties.'

The protocol was that when a police officer discharges their firearm they are immediately put into a kind of twilight zone and Internal Affairs jump in to investigate. They are suspended from their duties to await the outcome. This is a longstanding formal process that applies in each of the states. At the same time the police officer is forced to attend counselling so that they can be advised on how to deal with the stress.

And then, as if he'd made a faux pas, Copeland reached out to Maria, took her hand in his. 'That is, of course, if you wish to continue. Forgive me.'

'We're finding the truth behind Isobel's death,' said Maria with conviction.

He smiled. 'If you ever want to abandon Queensland and come work down here, you have my total support.' And then he turned to me.

'He was shot with …?'

'I have a firearm,' I said cautiously. I'd shot the guy with my Beretta, which had been given to me by Casey a couple of years earlier. The gun was unlicensed and I'd been carrying it – now firing it – illegally.

None of this would be a surprise to Copeland. He had a Colt .45, which he kept locked in a safe at his home. He well knew my love for the Beretta and my predilection for having an unregistered one within easy reach. Police officers have to check their weapons out at the beginning of a shift and then in at the end of it. They don't go home with you and you don't buy pistols in secret, on the black market, from gangsters. Or if you do, you don't get caught.

I'd just got caught.

Maria was staring at me, goggle-eyed. This was her worst nightmare: Casey's nefarious activities would come to haunt her as an officer of the law. She'd always known it was going to happen one day, but I was guessing she hadn't expected that day to come so quickly. We never do.

'Who has the gun?' Copeland asked, looking around at the assembled crime team. One of the Homicide boys stepped forward, carrying the Beretta in a sealed plastic evidence bag. Copeland reached out for it, then turned back to me.

'I'll give it back to you when you return to Queensland. I presume it was purchased in Queensland?'

I could feel Maria squirm. Copeland, never missing a beat, saw her discomfort.

I nodded.

'It'll be in safekeeping.' He turned to Michelle, who had, until this moment, kept back in the shadows of the sprawling magnolia tree in the yard, waiting for instruction.

'An unidentified person was fatally shot in South Yarra this morning at approximately three-fifty. There are no suspicious circumstances. Local police and officers from the Coroner's Office attended the scene. Please direct any inquiries to Michelle Alessandro at Media Liaison.'

She didn't need to write it down. She was word perfect with a radar memory.

She nodded, turned to me. No vivacious smile. Just a look. Which, still, even in these circumstances, couldn't hide a past.

Which Maria read correctly.

THE KID

HAROLD HOLT WAS AN UNUSUAL PRIME MINISTER. HE WORE Panama hats; he had a house in Toorak by the Yarra River where he would sit, when not in Canberra, in an office covered with leopard-print wallpaper; he handed out matchbooks with his photo on the cover and his signature on the back; and he liked having his snap taken in diving gear at the beach in Portsea surrounded by young women in bikinis. He died in late 1967, while swimming in the notorious Portsea rip where two aggressive tidal swells converge and create a dangerous undertow that can drag even the most experienced swimmer out to sea within seconds, caught among the waves and helpless to fight back. That's presumably what happened to Harold Holt, after he was last seen wading into the rip-tide during an early weekend swim, waving at friends with a smile. To commemorate his death, Melbourne named an indoor swimming pool after him in what is possibly the most bizarre and inappropriate memorial to a nation's leader in the world. The Harold Holt Memorial Swim Centre is on High Street in Glen Iris; you turn left off Chapel in South Yarra and drive for about twenty minutes in a straight line and end up at the place, situated in yet another English-themed park with towering oak and elm trees. Tyrone, Isobel's boyfriend of twenty-five years ago, was a swimming coach there.

We crossed Orrong Road, where, in my thirties, I'd attended a murder–suicide in which a husband, fed up with life, had shot his two sons and wife then turned the gun to his temple. We crossed Kooyong Road, where, eight years ago, I'd found the body of a Vietnamese girl who'd been raped, tortured and then had her throat cut by an angry lover. We passed Mercer Road, where, in 2004, a teenage girl by the name of Janelle had been abducted, her dismembered body later found in the bushlands of Eltham. Off Mercer Road was Myamyn Street, where a well-to-do elderly gent lost his temper one night in 2001 and bludgeoned his next-door neighbour to death over a dispute regarding the fence between their properties.

We pulled up out the front of the Prime Minister's memorial.

'Is this for real?' asked Maria.

'Good promotion for water safety,' I said as we climbed out and walked towards the entrance.

—

IT WAS AFTER nine. We had evaded the gathering press, who had scented a story regarding a gunshot in the outwardly calm and genteel streets of South Yarra as dawn broke. While Michelle was giving them the four-line explanation of the event, well away from the crime scene, Copeland, Maria and I exited quietly into waiting cars. The attendance of the Police Commissioner at such a shooting would have drawn a startled curiosity. Copeland had completely overturned protocol in allowing us to continue with our investigation. We had given our statements and the next step for the cops was to ID the dead guy. That usually doesn't take very long, but I had a feeling in my gut that this wasn't going to be the usual process. Only professionals carry no trace of ID on them. I'd asked Maria if she wanted to take the rest of the day off. She said no. I'd asked her if she'd like to see someone about the violent attack and near-death experience. She said no. I told her I didn't mind, wouldn't think any less of her if she'd said yes to either of those suggestions, because they seemed like good ideas to me. She said no, she wanted to go back to the apartment, have a shower, get dressed and then be taken out for a monster breakfast before we went to the interview.

—

I HATE WATER, except, of course, the stuff that comes out of taps. I hate the water in the ocean and I especially hate the water in indoor swimming pools, with its deep wash of chlorine and vague scent of kids' piss. The chemical smell overwhelmed us as we walked inside.

The swimming pool was, at this time, largely empty of people but for a couple of elderly diehards, the sort of old men and women I see powering through the waves at Noosa Beach every morning in an admirable and regular burst of keeping up the energy as their long day wanes.

There was a kid. He might have been eight, maybe nine. It was a school day, so I don't know what he was doing standing at the farthest end of the pool in a pair of dark blue Speedos, arms wrapped around his skinny chest, shivering, soaking wet and listening to his coach berate him in words I couldn't hear but with an attitude that was unmistakable.

'That's him?' asked Maria, staring at the coach.

I nodded. Tyrone was now in his mid-forties. Maria and I had seen the photos, framed and hung in Isobel's house, of a cocky young sportsman, his future an ocean of opportunity. All he had to do was choose and the winds would unfurl before him. He had wanted to be a champion skier. His dream was to compete at the winter Olympics and his fallback was to coach in Austria. None of that happened. After Isobel's death, he floated, and by the time he came to the surface with anything that might resemble a plan he was thirty years old. Now it was fifteen years later and he was a slightly overweight, slightly balding angry guy taking out his everyday frustrations at his lost hopes on a kid who hadn't swum the pool fast enough.

We walked the length of the pool towards them. Tyrone watched us approach as he continued to tell the kid how to do better, as opposed to being a loser who was wasting everyone's time. Maria and I in almost-matching black suits made it pretty obvious that we hadn't turned up for a swim. He barked at the kid – 'Go!' – and pumped a stopwatch as the boy dived into the water and began to power up the lane, arms swishing over his shoulders with grace and skill.

'Hello, Tyrone, my name is Darian Richards and this is Senior Constable Maria Chastain. We'd like to ask you some questions about the events surrounding Isobel Vine's death twenty-five years ago.'

He turned away from us and stared at the kid, who was about a third of the way down the pool. I noticed that his posture had sagged, as if a breeze had rippled through him, removing his energy. 'Yeah, okay,' he said.

I let Maria take the lead. She was gentle and caring and her questions were uttered with a tone of compassion. Tyrone said that many of the events from that night were now hazy, but he clearly recalled leaving Isobel at about three in the morning. 'I had to get back to my flat to get my uniform for work, then get to work on time. The boss was a prick, a nineteen-year-old kid who thought that McDonald's was going to make him a millionaire.'

'Do you remember what happened after everyone left?' Maria asked. The kid had completed his lap and was now sitting on the edge of the pool, waiting for further instruction, watching as the coach spoke to strangers on a nearby bench. The kid's legs were dangling in the pool and every now and then he'd kick up his toes, flicking water away from him.

'Yeah, I dunno. We went into her bedroom. I remember thinking it'd be good to call in sick and spend the rest of the night with her, but I needed the money.'

'And can you describe to us, as best you can, what happened in the bedroom?'

'Why are we doing this?' he asked, looking at Maria, then at me. 'I mean, what's the point?'

'I think we'd all like some closure,' said Maria in a soothing voice.

He bought that and continued. 'We just lay on the bed. Yeah, that's right. I remember thinking, I better not fall asleep or I'll miss the shift.'

'Did you have sex?'

He didn't reply. He was staring at the now-empty lanes of the swimming pool. When asked this question twenty-five years ago, Tyrone had said no, he and Isobel had just lain together, and after she went to sleep, he quietly left the house through the front door.

'Tyrone?'

He turned back to Maria. 'You look like her,' he said. 'A bit. She had short hair, though, just shoulder length. She looked like Clara Bow. You know who Clara Bow is?'

'No, I don't,' said Maria. I did, but I didn't think it was appropriate to butt in with a history lesson on 1920s film stars.

'Look, we need to be really thorough, Tyrone. Perhaps you might say that, all those years ago, the investigation was a bit rushed, but now ...' She let it hang for him to take up the pause.

'Yeah, we had sex.'

'Okay. Thanks for being honest. I'm going to have to ask you this: *how* did you and Isobel have sex, and *where*, exactly, did you and Isobel have sex?'

'It wasn't on the back of the door,' he said with a trace of anger. 'It was in bed. It was always in bed.'

'Was Isobel conservative in bed? Or was she maybe a bit experimental? Sorry, I have to ask these questions.'

'She would never want to be choked. I mean, we were kids, we had no clue about that sort of stuff.'

'That's not what I asked, Tyrone. Was she the type of girl who liked to do things – in sex – a little differently?'

'No. She was kind of modest and we were very boring. Sometimes I had to turn out the light before she took off her clothes and got into bed.'

'Okay. Were you wearing a condom?' The Coroner's report had said there was no sign of semen in her body, nothing that he could try to test for DNA.

He nodded. 'She was terrified of getting pregnant.'

'And then, after you guys had sex …'

'I left. Kissed her on the forehead and left.'

'She was asleep?'

'Almost.'

His time frame panned out.

'Can we go back to the party? Do you remember when the four men arrived?'

'The cops?'

'You knew they were police officers?'

'Fuck, yeah. Those arseholes were hassling the shit out of Isobel. I couldn't believe it when they walked in.'

'What do you mean, they were hassling her?'

'Ringing her, hanging around. All the time. Ever since she'd been caught with the cocaine. They were working for Dominic Stone.'

'Did you ever meet Stone?' I asked.

'No, but everyone knew who he was and that they were on his payroll. It was obvious.'

'And they arrived with Isobel's friend, a girl named Ruby,' said Maria.

'They arrived alone. I don't know any Ruby. They just walked in like they owned the place. It was pretty tense.'

'Tense in what way?'

'Well, we all knew about the situation. Isobel had told all of us; that's why we had the party, to try to cheer her up. Then the very guys who've been spooking her turn up.'

'What happened after they arrived?'

'They were drunk. I asked them to leave. They ignored me and spread out through the house. One of them goes into the kitchen and pours himself a drink, another goes to the couch and tries to chat up Di –'

'Di Strong?' I asked. She was listed as one of the partygoers, a schoolfriend of Isobel.

'Yeah, and one of them just goes up to Isobel and takes her by the arm and walks her towards her bedroom. I tried to stop him. I went up to him and said, "Mate, can you fuck off," and he pushed me away, kept walking Isobel down the hall, and I watched as he took her into the bedroom and closed the door behind him.'

'Can you describe this man?'

'It was that guy Racine. I saw him at the inquest.'

By now the kid had realised the coach was in another world, so he'd jumped back into the pool and was slowly doing laps on his own.

'What happened next?'

'I don't know. They were in there for a few minutes, then he came out and left. The others left with him.'

I could sense the feelings of powerlessness in him, even now, years later, at having been unable to protect his girlfriend from a bully who'd invaded her house, her bedroom, her mind. I wondered what I would have done, at his age, if faced with the same circumstances. I would have been paralysed. Like the kid now floating on his back in the pool, we seek answers and guidance until one day self-confidence, and with it, assuredness, moves us forward.

'I went into the bedroom. Isobel was, like, shaky but was trying to laugh it off. I asked her what he'd said but she wouldn't tell me. We went back to the party and she tried to make light of it, popped open a bottle of vodka and said we should all get pissed.'

Maria took him through the events of the next morning and his recollection vibed with his statement at the time. She asked him about Isobel's state of mind, probing around the possibility of suicide, and he was resolute in his answer that she was, despite being hassled and caught between hard cops and bad guys, determined to see beyond the immediate world that had encircled her. 'She was looking into the future, she wasn't facing the abyss,' was how he put it.

'One more thing,' said Maria as she was about to wrap up with him. 'After everyone left, you and Isobel cleaned up?'

'Did we? I suppose we did. Isobel was like that. A cleaning nut … yeah, that's right. I'd forgotten that. She insisted we do the dishes. I just wanted to go to bed before I had to leave.'

'Do you remember doing all the dishes?'

He frowned. 'We would have. As I said, she was a cleaning nut.'

'But there was a glass. On the bar between the kitchen and the living area. Next to it was an open bottle of Jim Beam. Maybe you had a drink on the way out, after you left her in the bedroom.'

'Nah. Jim Beam? Nup, not me. I might have had a glass of water, but if I did I would have washed it up and put it with the rest of the dishes. I was a beer guy anyway. Never drank spirits; they made me sick.'

'Okay. Thanks, Tyrone,' said Maria.

He was about to get up, thinking the question time was over, when I asked: 'Did you know that Isobel was seeing Brian Dunn, her schoolteacher?'

'Yes,' he said tightly.

'Were they in a sexual relationship?'

'I don't know.'

'Come on, she was your girlfriend. You must have had some idea if she was cheating on you.'

'We didn't talk about it.'

'You didn't discuss with your girlfriend what she was doing hanging out with her English teacher, the same guy who was responsible for her getting caught with the cocaine?'

'No.' He was lying.

'Was she infatuated with him?' asked Maria.

'I don't know,' he said.

'But it must have made you angry; your girl hanging out with an older guy,' I added.

'I didn't kill her,' Tyrone said.

Maria glanced at me. It's never a good look when a person denies committing a crime they haven't been accused of. It's like when Richard Nixon went on TV during the Watergate scandal and said, unprompted, 'I am not a crook' – which later turned out to be exactly what he was.

———

As we were leaving I noticed that the kid was now in the middle of the pool, treading water. He was staring at me, his gaze following me as I walked. I turned and gave him a wink. I used to like that when I was a kid.

He didn't wink back.

EVERYTHING THAT RISES MUST CONVERGE

BORIS COULDN'T GET OUT OF MELBOURNE FAST ENOUGH. The city was on fire. He was a burning man. Said to his wife, *Janey, baby, we gotta go, we gotta go as far as we can,* and she said, *Where?* with a rising fear and he replied, *Out to the edge of the desert where they won't come after me.* Packed up their stuff, their two little girls and the dog. The transfer had come through. He'd got what he'd asked for: a one-horse town in the middle of nowhere. *Nil?* Janey had asked. *Is that a place? How can a town be called Nil? It's Nhill,* he'd said, *spelled with an H and a double L.*

They'd driven for hours in the baking heat with the girls in the back, asking, *Why did we leave Melbourne, Dad?* and her thinking, *How bad was it, for us to be running like this? And what did he mean when he said, 'They won't come after me?' Who was he talking about?* She'd stared at the landscape as it flattened out, as they drew closer to the border with South Australia, as the trees began to vanish and a red, endless plain of dirt began to take hold, as the distance between the last car and the next that they passed grew from ten minutes to half an hour and as the girls grew fidgety then finally fell asleep, as her husband kept his gaze firmly on the road ahead, never once speaking.

That was so long ago. The girls had gone now. Fled the town as soon as they were able. Janey had stuck with Boris, through thick and thin, whatever that meant. There was more thick than thin or maybe it was the other way around; all she knew was it had not been the life she expected. It had not been the life he had promised her.

Why had they run? And from whom were they running? She never asked him. But she'd made a guess. From the cops, is what she thought. That's why we're living on the edge of a desert four hours' drive away from Melbourne.

It was all so far in the past. Everything had been fine. Boris had settled into the new job at the local police station, and she had eventually found a position at the local state school. The small farming community of two-and-a-half thousand people was close-knit and friendly. They were welcoming. Most young families skedaddled out of Nhill, and few arrived. They were old-fashioned people with care in their hearts and a warmth in their smiles. At first she'd detested it, but then, as the months lapsed into years and the years into a decade and then another, she realised that the quaint town of Nhill was exactly where she was meant to be.

Everything had been fine. Until this morning.

—

I HADN'T INTENDED to interview any of the four cops until much later. I'd planned to gather as much information as possible from Isobel's friends and develop a thorough understanding of her – to be her, in fact – before moving on to the forces of antagonism that were encircling the girl. The assault on Maria had changed that. Whoever ordered that she be attacked – the cops, according to Isosceles, had yet to identify the assailant – was a person of means and desire, a person with a lot to fear and a lot to lose. People like that don't shrug their shoulders when the first attempt goes awry and say, 'Oh well, we gave it a shot.' Already cornered, they become more dangerous. If the assailant had been hired by a cop, I needed to match that move and up it.

And cops, especially cops in high places, think they can get away with those sorts of actions. The sad truth is, they can. And do.

We were on the road to Nhill. We were in the Studebaker, top down; for a change the day was sunny, with a slight cold breeze. For most of my time in Melbourne so far I'd chosen to be anonymous, riding around in a police-issue white Holden Commodore, yet another of the all-purpose globally made instruments of mediocrity, designed to offend no-one and offer minimum human skill and intervention to the art and fun of driving for the drivers. Today in the Studebaker I cranked the gears and felt the engine. The car was left-hand drive. We cruised along the Western Highway, having worked our way out of the stop-start traffic on the fringes of the city's outer suburbs. On either side ran a stretch of undulating dull green farming land, with pockets of gum trees and the occasional mountain range, grey–blue, off in the distance. Running along the paddocks, on both sides of the highway, was an endless old low stone wall, built in the early nineteenth century, when convicts were forced to scour the landscape picking up any big rock, mostly bluestone, and carry it back to the wall-in-progress. I guess it was a hard-labour punishment. It always reminded me of something you'd expect to see in Scotland or Wales.

We would arrive in Nhill by nightfall. I had called Boris – aka Karloff – and introduced myself, explaining that he was to make himself available at nine the following morning. He'd sounded freaked, which was exactly the response I had hoped for. I was working on the theory that he was a guy whose instinct was to flee and deny. I wanted to spook him and then I wanted him to get on the phone to the boys back in the city, demanding to know what was going on and why, after twenty-five years of silence, suddenly the case was back in the top ten.

Isosceles was standing by, all ears, waiting for that phone call to come through. So far, however, there was only the silence of a scared man, uncertain, I imagined, of what to do.

Following the interview with Tyrone, we'd driven to see Isobel's friend Di.

Di had clearly fallen on hard times. She offered us vodka but we settled for water. We sat in her lounge room while she smoked Stuyvos and listened as she told us that Isobel had indeed been infatuated with her schoolteacher, *that cunt, scuse the language but that's what he was.* Isobel had confided everything in her friend. She and Dunn had had sex. A heap of times. Isobel had told her friend that Dunn was 'awesome'. She had thought – *even though I told her she was being a naive fuckwit* – that when all the hassle was over, they'd get together, maybe even live together.

'Did Tyrone know?' asked Maria.

'Sure. Yeah. He wasn't too happy about it.'

'In what way?' I asked. 'How did he express that unhappiness?'

'He was all over the shop. One day he's crying, next day he's threatening to bash her head in if she keeps it up. But he'd never do that. Tyro was, well, he was a kid. Him and Isobel, it was his first love. He didn't know how to handle all that stuff.' She laughed and added, 'Not that you ever do.' Di, we had noticed, lived alone with two dogs.

'But did you ever see him being physical with her? Did he ever push her or touch her while he was in this threatening mood?'

'Nah, Tyro would hit a wall. Smash a bottle. He wouldn't hit *her*. You guys are barking up the wrong tree if you think it's Tyro who killed her.'

'Why is that?' asked Maria.

'He loved her. You don't kill what you love.'

Well, many of us do.

Di's recollection of the night of Isobel's party was identical to that given by Tyrone: four tough guys barging in, throwing their weight and power around, one of them trying to chat Di up, one of them taking Isobel into her bedroom. Four cops. After they'd left, after the party had revved up again, at Isobel's insistence, determined not to let those guys intimidate her, she and Di had an argument. This was at about two in the morning, Di thought. She and Isobel were alone out in the backyard.

'She said Brian would fix her problems with the cops. I said: "Isobel, he's one of them. He is not your friend." That went down like a balloon full of shit. She was blind to the guy. That's infatuation, for you. She said she was going to call him. Get him to come over.'

'That night?' asked Maria, suddenly alert, just as I was.

'Yeah, she was going to tell Tyro she was too tired for him to stay over, and after he left, she was going to call Brian and get him to come and stay. He'd been staying at her place quite a bit.'

'Excuse me,' I said and got up from the couch. Moving to the kitchen, I called Isosceles.

'Is there *any* way we can access Isobel's phone records?'

We had already been over this. Twenty-five years ago Telecom, as it was then called, did not log incomings and outgoings. There was no such thing as caller ID.

'They that had fought so well, came through the jaws of Death, back from the mouth of Hell,' he replied and hung up.

I didn't need a translation into conversational English; this was the geek quoting Alfred, Lord Tennyson's famous poem about the ill-fated charge of the Light Brigade during the Crimean War. It was his shorthand, albeit florid and obscure, for: 'Yes, leave it with me. I will do what you ask despite the tremendous difficulty.'

Meanwhile I could hear a somewhat angry Maria ask, 'Did you tell this to the police? At the time?'

Di didn't answer.

'Or to the Coroner?'

I walked back in as Di said, 'Look, it was hairy back then, okay? After Isobel died it was really freaky, you know what I mean? I mean, we'd just left school and all this shit was happening. Cops and fucking drug dealers. So, no. I didn't tell anyone. I was scared. Okay?'

Maria and I stared at her. She was crying.

Yeah, I thought, it's okay.

—

'WHY HAVE WE stopped here? I am starving and there's not a place to eat that I can see, in any direction. All I can see, Darian, are sheep and paddocks and a mountain with a stupid name. Why would anyone call a mountain Disappointment? Disappointed by what?' asked Maria.

I'd pulled over on the side of the road. I was staring at Disappointment and the little wooden farmhouse that nestled in its shadow.

'Is there something wrong with the car? Ararat's, like, only another half an hour away, isn't it? There's a restaurant there called Sicilians. I googled it. I've already looked at the menu,' she said, holding up her iPhone like she might use it as a weapon against me. 'I love it when they post the menu online. I'm going to order the shish tawook.'

Hungry people are relentless people.

'It was Major Mitchell,' I said.

'What the fuck? What are you talking about?'

'He was an explorer. Searching for the great inland sea.'

'Can we not have a history lesson by the side of the road? Can we do it, like, maybe, in the restaurant? Over food and a beer?'

'When the English arrived in Australia –'

'Oh fuck,' she said and slumped in her seat.

'... they assumed – why, I don't know – that there had to be a massive sea, or at least a lake, in the centre of the country. They couldn't, I suppose, conceive that such a huge land mass would be arid from coast to coast. So, they set off to discover it.'

'And they never did because it wasn't fucking there. Yeah, I know. I went to that history class. *I am starving!*'

'So, off hiked Major Mitchell. He'd got this far and, in the tradition of most of the explorers at that time – English twits, really – he imagined he'd come across the great inland sea after a day or so's walk out of Melbourne.'

'Maybe we could do this while driving?'

I turned and looked at her. 'Okay.'

'Thank God.'

With a final glance at the little house under the mountain, I put the car back into gear and drove for about five minutes up the highway and pulled over again.

'What!' Maria yelped, then turned and saw another mountain. A sign on the other side of the road said, *Mount Misery*.

'Okay. I get it. They're connected. He's disappointed and now he's miserable.'

'He was. Having climbed the first, expecting to observe the sea from its top, he named that mountain Disappointment.'

'And then he got all fired up about this one and, getting to the top and not seeing the big fucking ocean, he named it Misery. Imaginative guy. Can we go?'

I drove on.

She saw the next road sign looming up ahead. 'Don't stop, Darian.'

I pulled over by Mount Despair.

'Right. Okay. Now he's despairing. What's next? Mount Suicide?'

'No.' I pointed up ahead. In the distance, on the horizon, was another mountain. None of these mountains were very high. 'Mount Ararat.'

'Finally. Let's get going. Let's get to Ararat.'

'*Like the ark we rested*, he wrote when he reached that one.'

'Jesus, he thought he was Noah?'

'Twits and arrogance. That's the world around us.'

She narrowed her eyes, sat up in her seat and looked at me. 'How do you know all this stuff? This is way too obscure for a history lesson. Were you stationed out here? I didn't know you did a stint out in the bush.' She looked around her, at the rolling paddocks, the hills, the gum trees, the convict wall made of blue rock, the sheep and cows. 'God, and I complain about Noosa.'

'Wait till you see Nhill,' I said and planted my foot, kicking up stone and dust as I pulled back onto the highway and hammered it in the direction of her shish tawook, away from that little wooden house beneath the mountain named Disappointment, where, many years ago, I had fled as a young man, abandoning my mother just as my dad had some desperate years earlier.

—

'WHAT IS IT?' asked Janey. 'Do you want to talk about it?'

They were sitting in the kitchen. She'd made him roast chicken and corn fritters smothered in gravy. Every night they sat in the kitchen and ate dinner together, drank a few beers and then watched some TV before going to bed. It was routine, warm and reassuring.

'It'll be fine. It's nothing,' he said unconvincingly.

'Has it got to do with why we left Melbourne? Is it about that girl?'

That girl.

She couldn't, wouldn't, articulate that girl's name.

Janey had read everything about *that girl*, when she was news, in the papers, when her death was somehow connected to Boris in a way that he had never explained; they were husband and wife, but this one subject had remained inaccessible, out of bounds. He'd chosen to never talk about it and she'd chosen not to ask. She wished it wasn't so. She wished they had a perfect life, but all couples have secrets, don't they, and nothing's perfect. But that little out-of-bounds territory, like a floating island that sat on the other side of the horizon, bobbing up every now and then like a mirage, never let go of her. She knew Boris, all of him, but for that little floating island on the other side of the horizon. And now, she thought, as she cleared away the plates, it's here. On this side of the horizon. I can't see it and I don't know what it is or what it means but it is here.

Someone was coming for him, that she knew. He had cleared his schedule for the morning. She'd overheard him on the phone. 'Yeah, yeah, cancel that, I'll do that next week,' she'd heard.

Someone was coming for him. They'd fled to the edge of the desert, she and Boris and the girls, and now she thought: I don't think we fled far enough.

THE BREATH OF GOD IS STILL

WE ROLLED INTO NHILL AT ABOUT ELEVEN IN THE EVENING. We had eaten at Sicilians in Ararat and Maria had the shish tawook. We left town as night was falling and she used her iPhone to find us somewhere to stay in Nhill. Surprisingly, for a town of two-and-a-half-thousand people on the fringes of the Little Desert, which is not a tourist destination, it had almost no vacancies. The rodeo was in town. She had finally managed to locate us a room in a place called the Zero Inn.

'Zero at Nhill,' she said after she hung up. 'What *is* this place we're going to?' she asked, staring out the side window. Beyond Ararat was Horsham, a large country town, and beyond that were smaller towns and a lot of flat nothing on either side of the road. Beyond Horsham most drivers were in for the long haul over the semi-desert, over the border into South Australia. Out here, at night, it's dead and still. There aren't many cars even though the highway connects two capital cities. Once, years ago, I'd driven over the border and was in the middle of nowhere in the middle of the night. I'd been listening to the radio but then, like something out of *The Twilight Zone*, all the stations crackled away into deep space and were gone. I drove on in silence, unnerved by the emptiness around me. I didn't have a CD player in the car. I was twiddling the knobs on the dial and finally I picked up a hazy connection. It was a radio station from somewhere in Tasmania,

149

thousands of kilometres away, across the Bass Strait. They were playing gospel but even that, after a few minutes, drizzled into the vast nothingness.

I pulled into the Zero Inn. There was a porch light on; they were waiting, a friendly couple who ran the place. They gave us the room key and pointed in the direction of the car park.

It was freezing, like desert-at-night freezing. Still and icy.

'Oh,' said Maria as we stepped into the room.

Oh indeed. I had heard her say, when she rang and booked ahead, that we needed a twin room, meaning in most people's language a room with twin beds, as in not one but two.

There was one bed. Queen-size. And there wasn't much else to the room. A bed, a TV, a kettle next to the TV, and floral wallpaper.

She shrugged and dumped her overnight bag on one of the chairs.

'I'll sleep on the floor,' I said.

'Don't be ridiculous,' she replied, 'it's not as if anything is going to happen.'

And nothing did happen. She went into the bathroom and closed the door. I heard the shower running for what seemed like six hours and then tried to keep my eyes averted as she came out, climbed into the bed and pulled the doona up around her. I too went into the bathroom and had a shower. A brief shower. I was amazed there was any hot water left. I hadn't packed pyjamas – because I do not own any and did not expect this situation to occur – and wondered what I would wear. I settled on a fresh pair of boxers and a T-shirt. I climbed into the bed, we said our goodnights and I turned off the light.

Maria and I had shared a motel room once before, on the Gold Coast, and I tried not to think about that time, when I had woken at about four in the morning and stared at her while she slept.

When I woke at four in the morning in our Zero Inn room, I'd been dreaming about chasing a killer down a long, dark tunnel that stank of dry ginger ale and was littered with the broken bodies of his victims. I hadn't had that dream for some while but it was familiar. Not so familiar, especially associated with that dream of The Train Rider, was the press of a woman's body as she lay across me. During the night Maria had, somehow, managed to nudge into my side with one of her legs crossed over my hips and her breasts pushing into my chest and her head exceedingly close to mine, so much so that I could feel the breath from her nose as she slept quietly. I eased out of bed quickly.

It was still dark outside. I needed coffee – I always need coffee at four in the morning – but all that was on offer in the motel room was a sachet of instant. I pulled on my jeans, boots and my thick coat and stepped outside in search of an all-night roadhouse, thinking that perhaps the reasoning behind my desire to have Maria join me on this investigation was a little more complicated than I'd told myself.

—

I WAS ON to my third coffee when she joined me, slid into the opposite booth at my table and scanned the menu.

'What time did you get up?' she asked.

'About an hour ago.'

'Have you eaten?'

'Avoid the eggs.'

A waitress came over and Maria ordered a T-bone with chips, bacon, English sausages, baked beans and hold the eggs, with a pot of green tea because she was health-conscious.

'For an old guy, he's kind of hot,' said Maria.

'Who are you talking about?' I asked, perplexed.

'Copland. Cool nickname too. Do you think he meant it about me getting a job here if I wanted?'

'Of course he did. He's a man of his word. Always has been.'

'It's weird seeing you like somebody.'

'I like people.'

'You don't. You hate most people. You told me so yourself.'

I didn't bother arguing. 'Yeah, okay, you win. I do. But I like him; I always have.'

'How come? He would have to be the sole living example of a police officer, myself excluded I'd like to hope, whom you don't hold in total, utter, complete contempt.'

I laughed. It was true. I respected her, I respected Copeland, and pretty much everyone else was a drone to be avoided; I think this reflects more on me than on these other people. I'm sure most humans are perfectly nice and charming and clean the house regularly. I'm sure it is me who has the problem. I don't think about this very often, and when I do, I don't care.

'He saved me. If it wasn't for Copeland Walsh I would most likely have been dismissed from the Force, with red flags popping up against my name whenever anyone searched for me on a database.'

'Did you get caught executing a bad guy?'

'No, Maria. I never get caught. It was over an investigation I was running, just over twenty-five years ago, maybe the year before Isobel's death, maybe a bit earlier. I was a Senior Constable with CIB in Prahran. Young, still learning. Mostly watching and soaking up the work of the experienced guys around me.'

'*Running* an investigation?'

'That was the point. I'd attended the death of a young woman. She was found by her flatmates in her room, in bed; it seemed, on the surface, as if she'd died from natural causes. No signs of violence, nothing. About a year later, I attended another death. Another young woman, also found in her bed, also with a complete lack of violence or anything that looked suspicious.'

'No such thing as a coincidence.'

'Exactly, but as far as the police were concerned, it was a coincidence. Young people die of natural causes. But I didn't like the feel of it. On both occasions the girls were alone at night, they were young, they were pretty, they were naked. Smothering a person with a pillow is an excellent way to kill someone without leaving a trace behind. I started to ask around and soon discovered that there was a link. Neighbours had seen a police car outside the buildings where they lived, parked there for no apparent reason, in the days leading up to the deaths.'

'You thought it was a cop?'

'I thought it was a cop. Cops kill. Not often, but murder ain't a discriminating behaviour.'

'Was it?'

'No. As it turned out. I ran my own secret investigation, which pretty soon was not a secret.'

'That would have made you popular.'

'King of the kids, top of the pops; I was everyone's favourite guy, on the verge of being not only kicked out but brought before an internal inquiry with the likelihood of being charged ...'

'For what?'

'They were scouring the Crimes Act; they would have found something. That was just a formality. The main game was crucifying me. It didn't matter how. Just as long as it happened.'

'And Copeland stopped them.'

'More than that. He was Division Commander. He took me aside – in fact, he took me to the Chow in the city – and told me about the threat to my career, but he also explained how my line of thought was flawed. He'd been doing his own checking into the two deaths and was starting to link them to a serial rapist. There was evidence that put this guy in the vicinity of the girls' places. He gave it to me, handed me what he'd done, then told me to take the very cops I'd offended by looking into their whereabouts, and arrest the guy. I made those cops into local heroes. There was quite a bit of media coverage about it. They called the killer The Whisperer on account of him smothering the victims. Lesson learned, all was forgiven and I was transferred across into Homicide. After that Copeland became my mentor. Taught me the politics as well as a bunch of other stuff. Best cop I've ever known.'

'I could never live in this state. Too bloody cold,' said Maria as her food arrived, a mountain of meat with a blanket of baked beans. Me, I'd had a muffin.

—

'Who's this?'

'It's Boris Jones –'

'Whoa. Hey. Boris. Don't call me on this number, okay. People are listening.'

'Racine –'

But by then Racine had hung up.

Isosceles had emailed us the voice recording he had taped at 12.34 this morning. Boris had ignored the warning and had tried Racine's number another four times.

'He *is* freaked,' said Maria.

I smiled. Just how we wanted him.

'What's with the Karloff nickname?' she asked as we threw our bags into the back of the Studebaker ten minutes later. It was just past nine o'clock. We were going to be a little late. That was Maria's idea, to sweat him a bit more.

The cop I'd worked with three years earlier had become a different person. Although she would never admit it, she was, I thought, becoming more and more like me.

'Boris Karloff was a famous movie star, back in the nineteen-thirties. He did the original monster in *Frankenstein*, and all those B-grade Edgar Allan Poe movies in the sixties.'

'Edgar Allan Poe … is he that gloomy guy who wrote about ghosts?'

'Yep, that's him. One of my favourites is "Spirits of the Dead". It's a poem. I wonder if our Boris has ever read it.'

'There he is,' she said, pointing. 'Why don't you ask him?'

I looked up ahead. Boris was standing out the front of the police station, waiting for us like an attentive schoolboy. It was only six minutes past nine but I had the feeling he'd been out there, waiting, for at least half an hour.

I parked the car directly in front of him. He stared at us, not moving. He had a sort of statue thing going on. We climbed out of the car slowly, doing our best *Law & Order* impersonation, that old *this is serious* cop look.

'Hello, Senior Constable, my name is Darian Richards, and this is Senior Constable Chastain.'

He nodded, tightly. 'Yes,' he said.

'Let's go inside. We've got a few things to talk about.'

I led the way.

TELL ME

'Born to Run' was thundering through the Bentley.

'Do you like Bruce Springsteen?' yelled Dominic over the music.

'Yeah, I do,' said Isobel.

'I know him. He's a friend of mine.'

'He is?' she asked, impressed.

'Yeah, he stayed at my hotel when he was touring a couple of years back. Next time he comes, if you want a ticket – fuck, if you want to *meet* him – just ask.'

She laughed.

She believed him.

They were driving at high speed down the Nepean Highway in his convertible. Brian was on his Harley, close behind, and another car was following him. As they'd left the hotel walking to Dominic's car parked by the front entrance, doors open, waiting for them, Isobel had noticed a car full of four guys, young, tough, sexy-looking guys, waiting. They're the cops, she'd thought. Bodyguards for Dominic, something like that. She'd met them, sort of but not really, although one of them kept on giving her a look that said, *Any time, babe, I'm here ready and waiting.*

'I've met everyone,' Dominic was shouting. 'Give me a name. Someone famous, *real* famous.'

'Madonna.'

'Yeah, she's a friend.'

'She is?'

156

'Yeah. She's stayed at the hotel. Wanted a thousand white roses in her room. Can you believe that? So, what do I do? I call the Netherlands. That's where the roses come from, snap-dried, frozen, that's where they come from, and I say I need a thousand, no fuck that, I need *ten thousand* white roses *tomorrow*. Get them in the fucking plane now.'

'And what happened?'

'They arrived. Madonna, she walks into the room, the same room we were just in; how about that, Isobel? You just walked out of the room Madonna stayed in, and she was, well … she was *very* appreciative. She called for me and told me that no-one had ever done that sort of thing for her before. Confidential … okay?'

'Okay.'

'We fucked.'

'What!'

'Madonna and me. Hey, you give a girl ten thousand roses, what do you expect? Gimme another. Another name.'

'MC Hammer.'

'Yeah, he stayed at the hotel too. Crazy guy. He rings me up at four in the morning and says, "Dominic, I gotta see the sunrise over the ocean." And I say, "No worries, brother," and I pick him up and take him down to Portsea, where you're going to see the sunrise in the morning tomorrow, and he sits there, looking out over the ocean, waiting, until finally the sun appears and he turns to me and he says, "Thank you."'

He cranked up the volume.

She laughed. There was, she had to admit, a voice somewhere deep inside that was saying, *Watch out*, but how can you deny the attraction of owning a hotel, of owning a Bentley and driving down to a house at Portsea with a crate of French champagne in the back? She felt safe. Dominic sang and she sang with him.

—

THE HEADLIGHTS OF the Bentley swept across the facade of an old two-storey sandstone house that clung to the edge of a cliff overlooking Port Phillip Bay, the lights of Melbourne spotting like fireflies in the far distance and the deep rumble of the wild waters of Bass Strait behind her as she stepped out of the car. As she breathed in she felt the chill in the air. The lights of the Harley, along with its familiar grumble, washed over her. It was followed moments later by the other car, the car with the bodyguards, the four guys who finished the convoy.

Wind swept through her hair. She stood, while around her came the gentle cacophony of party preparations, Brian grabbing the crate of champers, Dominic lighting a cigar and saying, 'Isobel, wait till you see the inside of this fucking joint,' and, 'Hey, boys,' to the four men as, in slow motion it seemed to her, they climbed out of the car, four doors opening at once, four sets of feet hitting the ground and four smiling faces, in the moonlight, in the wash and brine of the beach night. 'Hey, boys, go to the pub, get a mega-load of spirits and I want some Bénédictine and I want some Drambuie and get some birds, sexy birds, no fucking dogs – Isobel, babe, you don't mind, do you? You're not, like, off to a fucking nunnery, are you? We're gonna have some fun tonight; you don't mind if the boys bring some birds and we all sit in the spa? You don't have to partake, my darling. Brian will look after you, won't ya?'

And like in a movie where everything had been in slow motion, now it was freeze-frame on her with everyone watching.

'No,' she laughed with a little too much force. She was cool. 'I'm cool.'

And, as if someone unseen had pulled a lever, everything changed and the world around sped up. She felt as though she had been drugged. But it wasn't a drug. It was the swirl of Dominic's wild life, a hedonistic Gatsby-swirl of the sudden, the unexpected, always laced with fun and laughter, sex and music.

Champagne – hey, this is Krug, have more.

Where is that fucking Bénédictine? Pour it onto her. Now, on her tits!

Hey, Isobel. Dance with me, baby.

Hey, gorgeous, who are you? Where'd you spring from? What's your name? Joni? Just like Joni Mitchell. I know her. I fucked her once.

Just a little snort, Isobel, nothing more.

Look at the rack on this girl! Will you look at that!

Emma? Everyone this is Emma and this is her friend ... what's your name, darling?

Racine, get that fucking spa on.

Who can sing a Beatles song backwards? Anyone here who can do that, I give them ten grand.

What's your name, darling?

Fuck, I gotta lie down. Wake me in ten ... no, five! Ha! The sun rises at six – who the fuck asked that question? Who cares what time the sun comes up? Where the fuck is Boris?

Boris! Come 'ere, do the Frankenstein impersonation. Oh my fucking God, this guy is hilarious. Ruby Jazz? That's a name? Fuck me, I love it; show me your tits, Rube.

I own the biggest hotel in the entire fucking city of Melbourne and Bruce Springsteen is my friend!

Go talk to her.

No, now. No. Now.

It's easy, mate – you go talk to her and you make sure she ain't talking to no cops.

Ruby, don't you go away, baby!

You come back and report. You tell her, she talks to the cops, I shove this bottle of Krug up her cunt and then I kill her. I slice her fucking throat, but I fuck her first. Rube, show me those tits! You tell her, my grandfather was a Serb who killed more than a hundred men. One little pussy cunt bitch is not, is not, going to ruin my empire. Got that? Good.

You tell her.

You come back.

You report.

Dunn stepped back, shocked. Dominic was, most of the time, a fun guy, always laughing, nothing ever a problem. But then he could change like the wind. One moment all charm, the next a ravaging monster. This cold fury appeared rarely but when it did you wouldn't forget it in a hurry.

—

'Hey.'

'Hey.'

'So … ah, how you feeling?' he asked.

'I'm okay.'

'Better?'

'Yeah,' she said.

'Dominic's cool.'

Isobel nodded. They were in the lounge room, a wide room with a view over a black bay of water and far away, the lights of Melbourne. Over there, in the lights of Melbourne, were her dad and Tyrone and her years at school.

'I remember the first time I saw you.'

'You do?' she asked.

'I thought: there is my siren.'

She smiled, soft, hazy. She was drunk, she was floating, but everything was still happening in fast-forward even though she was gripping the edge of the chair to keep it slow, to keep it real.

'You know what I mean?'

'Yeah.' Hazy, floating. *Am I going to fall?*

He stepped towards her. Close. In fast motion she saw them in bed, naked and having sex. In slow motion she saw his hand as it closed upon hers.

'What do I mean?' he asked lazily.

In slow motion they were kissing. In fast motion she was running to him.

'Sirens are like mermaids: they sing, they call to men,' she said.

'Why?'

He touched her. His body was against her and she pushed into it.

'They want to seduce them,' she said.

'And they do.'

'They do,' she said through a thickness that she tried to fight away.

'Come with me,' he said. And she did.

He led her into a bedroom. He kept the light off. The bedroom smelled of cinnamon. She could hear the sounds of the party from afar and beyond those came the smash of the waves from the base of the cliff below the house, and she thought about Tyrone and her dad and her mum who had died years before and she thought about that phone call he'd made while she was in Bolivia – *You're my special girl, right? You can do me this favour, right?* – and she let him remove her clothes for the first time, though she had imagined this moment between them many times, and then he lowered her onto the bed and she let him enter her as she said, *I love you*, to which he said, *I love you too*, and she believed him, she did, she really did, and she held him tightly, she gripped him, knowing that, really, everything was going to be okay, as Dominic had said, as Brian had said, and she thought, *I must let go of Tyrone, it's so unfair, and when Brian moves in with me I'm going to cook him the best food every night and I'm going to look after him, not like the girls from his past, I will be different and he will adore me.*

Then it was later, much later, maybe it was two in the morning, and the sounds of the party were pounding from outside.

I need to sleep. Hold me.

'Hey.'

'Hey.'

'This whole thing about the cops ...'

Don't.

161

'It's, like, really important that you *do not* talk to them.'

Don't.

Hold me.

'Tell me, okay,' he said.

'Okay what?'

Don't.

'Tell me you won't say anything to them.'

Don't.

'I won't … Promise.'

'Promise?'

'Promise.'

Don't. Please. Just hold me. Encircle me and let the waves take us away. Drunk, stoned and fucked up, she said: 'You know the sirens?'

Her eyes were closed and she was drifting to sleep. His body was against hers.

'Yeah,' he said.

'They were dangerous.' She laughed and rolled into him, gripped him and held him. 'They lured sailors to their death.'

She was almost asleep.

'But that's not you, is it, Isobel?'

'No.'

She woke with a start. She'd been asleep for maybe ten seconds.

'I lure them elsewhere,' she said and collapsed back into the dark world of slumber.

—

HE CLIMBED OUT of the bed. He removed the doona that covered her. He turned on a bedside light. He stared at her. Naked. He reached out and stroked her back. She was out to it. He rolled her over, face up. He remembered the first time he had seen her walk into his classroom, remembered thinking, I so want to fuck this girl. He stroked his cock. Like a lion examining its prey, he stared at her, erect, poised over her. He rubbed against her. She moaned, but it was a moan from far away. She was unconscious, but he knew she could feel him. She would feel him. He placed the tip of his dick against her and pushed. In. Push. 'I love you,' he said, just in case. He began to thrust.

'How does that feel?' he asked.

She was unconscious. She wasn't going to answer him. He knew that.

'Tell me.'

He pushed into her.

'Tell me it's good.'

She didn't answer.

'Tell me.'

He layered her with kisses and said, again, 'I love you,' as the rush, the hit, the life within him rocketed out with a flood of loss, as if he were being depleted but at the same time energised – and then he collapsed on her, on the beads of sweat between her breasts and her belly, and again he said, 'I love you.'

Knowing full well that it was the orgasm speaking. Knowing it was, really, I love coming inside you. And no more.

'Tell me.'

FRANKENSTEIN

CRIME IS RELATIVE: THE BIG ISSUE FOR THE NHILL POLICE over the past few years had been the search for the person or persons who had severed in half a pet Pomeranian and then dumped both bits into the owner's front yard.

The station was quiet as Boris led us through to his office, at the rear, with a view over the backyard. The other two uniformed officers stared at us with expressions that ranged between bemusement and contempt. Contempt towards me, the ex-Homicide guy hassling their boss, and bemusement towards Maria. Most men want Maria as soon as they see her, want to possess her, make her their own. Beauty is a blessing, but it can also be a curse when you're surrounded by Neanderthal halfwits.

Boris closed the door behind us as we walked inside.

'Where would you like me to sit?' he asked.

He was cowed, even before we'd begun.

'At your desk, Senior Constable,' said Maria with a lethal smile.

He did as instructed. Boris was in his late forties. The blue uniform doesn't really suit cops at that age; it says *loser*, or maybe, a little more generously, *lack of ambition*. The uniform hung on Boris like the gloom of failure. He was tanned from, I guessed, living by the Little Desert, which is an area of flat land about a thousand kilometres square, covered in scrubby broombush off to the left of the town. Sullivan from the Feds had described Boris, back then, as fit, aggressive, muscular and a slightly older rookie with a chip on his shoulder and a few things to prove, but also a guy who would always be a follower. The man sitting at his desk in front of us now had run to fat and his eyes – which might once have been sharp and on the lookout for any perceived slight – were watery and his lids drooped. The buttons on his shirt strained against his gut. They looked as if they were about to pop. He had an issue looking you in the eye. He looked like a guy who had a problem greeting the mornings. He waited for us to lead the interview, like a guy who knew he was doomed to his fate.

'Boris,' I asked, 'have you been in contact with Detectives Racine, Pappas or Monahan in the past twenty-four hours?'

'No,' he answered.

Brilliant: let's start with a dumb lie. At least Maria and I knew now how this would play out. I sat back as Maria took the lead.

'Tell us about Isobel,' said Maria.

'Like what?' he answered. As a general rule, cops are hopeless when they're the ones being interviewed. He wasn't prevaricating, not yet, he was just unused to being questioned, and particularly by a policewoman in her late twenties.

Maria didn't respond. She just stared at him. I did too. Silence can be a great weapon when interviewing a sweaty guy. Boris looked from her to me and back to her again. Maria, to my delight, had even taken the awkwardness a step further: she was now smiling at him as if agreeing with something deeply profound that he might have uttered.

'I only met her the once.' He tried a shrug. 'She seemed harmless.'

Maria bristled. *Harmless?* What sort of description was that of a dead eighteen-year-old girl?

He corrected himself. 'I mean, she seemed quiet. I don't know. I can't remember. It was a long time ago.'

'Tell us about the time you met her,' said Maria.

'Well, I didn't really *meet* her. I just went along to that party at her house and she was there.'

'Why'd you go to the party?'

'We were invited.'

'By whom?'

'I don't know. It was years ago. There was this girl. We were at a club in the city, and this girl, I think she was Racine's friend, well, she said she was going to a party and would we like to come along.'

'What was her name? This girl at the club?'

'Ruby Jazz.'

'Who was with you at the club? When you say *we*, who are you referring to?'

Every now and then Boris would glance in my direction as if wondering whether I was going to jump in and ask a question. I'd followed Maria's lead and was giving him smiley-faced Darian.

'There was Racine and Pappas and Monahan.'

'You four would hang out a lot together?'

Another glance in my direction. *Who the fuck is this girl to be asking me questions like this?* Or maybe I misread it. I didn't think so.

'I don't know,' he shrugged.

'Yes, you do. You guys were a team. You all graduated from the Academy at the same time, you were known to frequent clubs together, spent weekends together.'

'So, if you know the answer to the question, why bother asking in the first place?' he said in a momentary flash of anger.

'We want to hear it from *you*, Senior Constable. I was just prodding you to help us find the truth. So, what happened exactly? What *exactly* did Ruby say to you? Take us through the details.'

'I can't remember. I think Racine came up to me and said Ruby had invited us.'

'What did she look like, this Ruby?'

'Pretty. Young-ish, I suppose.'

'Okay. How'd you get to the party?'

'Huh?'

'How'd you get to the party?'

'What do you mean?'

'What I mean is how did you physically get from the nightclub in the city to Isobel's house in Osborne Street in South Yarra?'

'I dunno, it was over twenty years ago, for fuck's sake.'

I leaned in a little towards him and spoke softly.

'Hey, Boris?'

He snapped his gaze away from Maria to me.

'You're aware that Senior Constable Chastain and I have been tasked by the Commissioner on this one.'

He nodded.

'And he's been tasked by the government.'

He stared at me. No nod this time.

'And the Commissioner wants this to be not only thorough but also expedited. As such, we've been granted some rather draconian powers of arrest for what we might conceive as anything less than total cooperation. Contempt-of-court sort of stuff.'

What I'd just said was bullshit but how was he to know? When you're in the grip of fear you'll believe anything.

Maria didn't miss a beat. 'How'd you get to the party?'

'In a car,' he answered, starting to get surly.

'Try to be more specific, please, Senior Constable. What car and who drove?'

'Pappas drove. Pappas always drove.'

Maria leaned back and stared hard at him.

'Senior Constable, we've got a problem,' she said in a disarmingly reasonable tone. 'Because Pappas drove a Porsche.'

Boris was staring at her, waiting.

'A 964 Turbo model, to be exact. There is what you could *call* a back seat in that model, in any Porsche, really, but Porsche never really designed the back seat for *people* and the 964 would not be able to fit four well-built young men *and* a girl by the name of Ruby Jazz. Even if you all tried to squeeze in, even if Ruby said, "Hey, I'll sit on your laps, guys" – it just isn't going to work.'

Maybe because Boris had referred to Isobel as *harmless*, Maria didn't stop: 'Square peg, round hole. Know what I mean?'

Maria watched him for a moment before speaking again.

'I'm going to suggest to you, Senior Constable, a proposition that you can confirm or deny: that this girl Ruby Jazz did not go to the party with you,' said Maria.

There was a long moment as Boris weighed up his options. He and the other cops had been reciting this story about going to the party because they'd been spontaneously invited by Ruby – as opposed to a more sinister version of events, in which they went to strongarm Isobel – for more than twenty years. It was rote. It was easy and safe. Until now. It had been a life raft. Until now. Now the story was starting to unravel. Neither Maria nor I believed it and I figured it would just be a matter of time before we'd pulled it right apart, revealing the truth. We'd get to that point through Ruby, when we found her, or through a weak link like the sweaty cop sitting before us.

After a moment I could see Boris had made up his mind. His eyes had narrowed as his story clicked into shape.

'Ruby was in the back seat. She was stretched out over Racine and Monahan.'

—

MARY SHELLEY WROTE *Frankenstein* when she was a teenager, about the same age as Isobel when she died, which is a remarkable achievement, considering it came about through a bit of fun when the poet Lord Byron suggested one drunken night that she and a gathering of other literary figures come up with a ghost story to entertain themselves. She clearly nailed it, going on to write one of the most influential books in the English language. Some people get confused and think Frankenstein is the monster, but he's in fact the doctor who creates him. I'd heard that as a party joke Boris would do cheesy impersonations of Boris Karloff's monster from the old movie from the thirties; these impersonations made him a popular guy around the police stations in the late eighties, although I doubt he bothered with one on the night he went to Isobel's house.

Really, it's all about choice. The decisions we make. Frankenstein chose to create a living creature – the monster – and then, to his horror, discovered that his creation had a mind of its own. But that came later. Upon looking at the creature Frankenstein ran, horrified at what he'd done. Did he think about what he was creating? What the repercussions might be?

The creature was left confused and upset. Without any moral guidance, without anything, he did what any creature will do – try to survive – within a world of people who took one look at him and freaked. Eventually he tracked down the doctor and told him that he'd been shunned by everyone. Please, he implored, create a woman for me. You made me, make me a companion. Frankenstein agreed, but then, later, spooked by his own work, he destroyed his female creation, thus sending his creature – the monster – into fury. Why would you kill my companion? Why, if you created me, would you kill the only thing that would make me happy? Content. At peace. At one. Why?

Did Frankenstein think about what he was creating the second time? The female? What the repercussions might be? What are, indeed, the repercussions of anything that we choose to do? Do we consider them? Do we act randomly, with a snarl of spontaneity and fuck the consequences?

The story doesn't end well. The creature – the monster – ends up killing Frankenstein's wife, Elizabeth – not the first person he has killed. The narrator of this story is entombed in ice, at the North Pole, and the book ends with the creature on an icefloe, drifting towards the horizon, towards certain death, as night begins to fall over the frozen white world, bereft at what he has done.

Maria glanced at me. Time to shift gear.

'Were you aware that the Federal Police had instigated an investigation into Dominic Stone and alleged drug importation,

and that you were also being investigated as part of that inquiry?'
I asked.

He shifted uncomfortably. 'I don't know anything about that.'

'When, to the best of your recollection, did you first meet Dominic Stone?'

'I never met the man.'

'Boris, I'm going to do you a favour. I'm going to pretend I didn't hear that answer and I'll ask the question again. But before I do …'

I reached down to my briefcase, opened it and pulled out a dossier, which I placed on the desk.

'I want you to know that the Feds were very thorough in that investigation, which was abruptly halted soon after Isobel's death.'

I indicated the dossier.

'That's their file.'

THE ILLUSTRATED MAN

CASEY RODE LIKE A GALE.

He'd torn off his sarong, dragged on a pair of Levi's, found some socks, from somewhere, snapped shut the boots over his feet, rifled through his clean washing on the floor by the end of their bed and found his *I Like Ike* T-shirt, prized even though he was dubious about Dwight Eisenhower's presidency, and snatched up his black leather jacket, surreptitiously given to him by a cat from the Hells Angels back in 02, all member logos removed. He grabbed his wallet as he strode through the house, and then his mobile phone and another three mobiles and one of his seven Glocks, which he tucked into the back of his jeans, and the sawn-off shotgun he kept hidden under the sofa on the outside balcony. As he walked outside the sprawling, rambling old wooden Queenslander he and Maria had shared for almost five years, as a couple, as deep lovers, as a team, he knew he was in danger – not from anyone who might think to harass him with a little smash-bang, but at the core of his life: Maria, and his relationship with her. He climbed onto his Harley, ignited the growl of the engine and, without a backwards glance at his home, which he hadn't bothered to lock, burned dirt and gravel at an alarming speed.

Drivers gave way.

At the first red set of traffic lights, he told himself to calm. Don't run the red. Don't run the law. You're carrying two serious weapons. Meditate. You can run all the fucking lights from here to Melbourne, Case old fella, and what? You'll end up there twenty minutes ahead of the groover who took it easy. With this in mind he inserted his newly purchased baby headphones and plugged Frank Zappa's *Hot Rats* into his ears, his head, his mind, his body and his heart, loud and without pause, on a loop as he rode all the way from Tewantin on the Sunshine Coast to Davis Avenue, South Yarra.

—

AND WHY DID she fall in love with me? he wondered.

And, like every human with a heartbeat, he then asked: *Does she love me? Am I worthy of her? And worse: Is it just a trick?*

How can the most sensuous, beautiful woman in the history of womankind love a guy like me? Me, the guy with the too-long hair and the seventies look, the guy with tatts that cover my body as fear covers a body, as swagger and bullshit cover fear, as fear covers unease, as swagger and bullshit cover unease and everything within, all that stuff that makes you scared when you're a kid, makes you wanna go out and bang a few heads and pretend you are who you are not. Tatts cover that and I am covered in tatts, have been since I was fifteen, when I said to him: You cover my back, from arse to neck, or I break your head, and he did, he covered me in a sprawling tatt of an eagle, swooping.

For a year he knew they'd been drifting.

Some days apart, some days close. He needed to grab her, keep hold of her.

She hadn't told him very much, only that there'd been some sort of attack but she was okay, and don't worry, babe, be back in a few weeks.

It was more than that, more than wanting to find the fucker who'd ordered the attack on her and stomp on him until his head bled with ooze and then trash the fucker into another eternity far from here. It was also about Ruby.

Casey couldn't lie. It was an affliction. When Maria had asked, *How do you know her?* he couldn't pretend. Ruby with the school uniform and the body set to create a world war. *Jesus save me,* he thought as he told her the truth. Whereupon she had hung up and stopped returning his calls. Whereupon he thought he better get down there, no this or that, and reignite the flame.

The past is the past, he thought as he wove through the traffic, on his way out of the Sunshine Coast and onto the Bruce Highway, heading south, heading some thousand or so kilometres away to his girl. But the past is now, he told himself. It's here, with me. Ruby, the sixteen-year-old kid I fucked twenty-something years ago, is with me now, between me and Maria. Now. And I gotta connect the past with the now and make it right. Or else I lose the woman of my life.

Casey's first tatt had been needled into him a long time ago. 'Make it hurt,' he'd said. And it did.

He hated helmets but he wore one anyway. He hated staying within the speed limit but he observed it as he plundered down the highway, stopping only for petrol.

He'd put the word out – his word was strong and carried far: my girl got monstered the other night, in Davis Avenue, South Yarra, some fucker tried to kill my girl, he tried to crush her windpipe, and I am on the way down, *now,* and we have to find 'em both: the prick who did it and the prick who set it up. And they're both dead, bullet in the noggin, for each of 'em.

He'd been retired for almost ten years but the loyalties stretched back, like tendrils. Tell everyone, he'd said.

And they had. While he rode listening to *Hot Rats* his phone rang incessantly. He'd put it on silent. He would check it when he stopped for fuel.

Melbourne was his land. There was no-one, not even now, a decade later, who could tramp the land of Melbourne without Casey knowing, if he wanted to. He wanted to. He wanted to kill.

He wanted to reaffirm his love. He wanted to say: Babe, look at what I've done. For you. Blood on my hands. For you.

Would he lose her?

He'd lost so much. Start with mum, cut to dad. Gone. Cut to Jane. Gone. Cut to Dolores. Gone. Cut to a whirlwind of girls. All gone. Cut to everyone. Gone.

But for Maria.

Maria: he would reclaim her.

THE FOG OF WAR

'I HATE COMING HERE,' SAID STOLLY. 'THERE ARE BODIES under the car park over there, almost ten thousand. Dead people. Did you know that? And here, under where we're walking now, another ten thousand. Dead. Bodies. Bones, you know that? Bones. We are walking across a cemetery, bulldozed a hundred and fifty years ago. To make way for this fucking joint, so that the immigrant population of this great city could sell cheapo imitation rugs, Elvis T-shirts and deep-fried doughnuts.'

'Shut up, keep walking,' said Racine.

'Why are we here? Why couldn't we meet at a Chinese in the city or down at the beach? We could be walking along the beach with fish 'n' chips. Fucking great. Love that. But here we are in this dingy shithole.'

'I don't like it either,' said Monahan. 'The stallholders recognise me.'

'Shut up. We are three detectives walking through the market at lunchtime. No big deal. Looking to choose between the kebabs and the sushi. Stop being paranoid and acting suspicious, both of you,' said Racine, who was clearly beginning to lose his cool.

—

QUEEN VIC MARKETS. *One hour*, Racine had written, in pen, on paper, last-century style, and then hand-delivered the note to both

175

men, Monahan in his office a few doors down from Racine's and Stolly, down one floor, in Homicide.

The Queen Victoria Market was on the other side of the city. St Kilda Road HQ was on the southern fringe of Melbourne's inner city, and the old, rambling market, spread across seventeen hectares, the largest such market in the southern hemisphere, was on the north-western fringe. The market was largely under cover, a sea of long corridors between stalls that sold mostly useless junk and cheap imitations. Food stalls abounded. Tourists and locals crammed the aisles, many with a bemused look on their faces saying, *Is this really one of the city's premier tourist attractions?* as they shuffled from one loud shop owner to the next.

The smell of kebabs and deep-fried doughnuts, the shouts of Greek and Vietnamese and Lebanese and Italian punctured the air without pause. Trams rumbled past and thick traffic snarled Peel Street on one side and the wide Victoria Street on the other.

A raucous din in every which way.

'Richards uses that geeky gimp with the stupid triangle name. We've got to assume he's listening in to everything we say, every thought and grunt we make. So, come here,' he said to the other two.

They were in an aisle that hosted a florist, tubs of fresh carnations, roses and tulips laid out on the ground, next to a nut shop. On the other side was a stall that sold gardening equipment that sat between a towel shop and a place that specialised in crystals and offered, on Tuesdays and Thursdays, half-price for first-timers, a reading with Mr Electro, genuine clairvoyant, direct from the Adelaide Hills.

'Boris talked,' said Racine.

'You were meant to handle him,' said Monahan, annoyed.

'Yeah. Well. That didn't work. I told him what he had to say and he went off course.'

'Off course? What the fuck does that mean? What did he say to them?'

'He told them about us and Stone.'

Monahan's eyes flared in anger. 'He *told* them?'

'Everything,' said Racine.

'Whoa. Boris, brother, am I going to kill you,' said Stolly.

'Why did he do that?' asked Monahan.

'Richards has the file.'

'From the Feds?' asked Stolly.

'Yeah,' said Racine.

Stolly rounded on Monahan. 'You were meant to have that destroyed.'

'It *was*.'

'Then how the fuck does Richards have a copy of it?'

But Monahan wasn't listening to words – only to the tremors inside him. 'This is bad,' he said. 'We've got to take him out.'

'None of this would've happened if it wasn't for you,' said Stolly to Racine.

'What's that supposed to mean?'

'You and your big ambition, wanting to become Police Commissioner.'

'I didn't ask for this investigation. Copeland sprung it on me.'

'Yeah, but you asked to become Commissioner, didn't you?'

'Of course I did, and you heard it here first: I'm going to be.'

'You reckon? With your past?' Stolly scoffed.

Monahan was just staring at them. He had an unnerving tendency to stare and not say anything, as though silently scheming, but this silence belied a spontaneous and explosive temper, often triggered by the most trivial things.

'What's that meant to mean?' asked Racine, eyeing off Stolly.

'You were a bagman for a drug dealer, for fuck's sake. We all were. It's not usually one of the selection criteria for the Police Commissioner's job.'

'You always were a space cadet. Do your research, Stolly. Corruption may not be a requirement for the job, but it sure isn't a hindrance,' Racine said. 'And I'll tell you one other thing, mate:

better I'm in the chair than some prick who'll take one look at *your* history and decide to hold a few inquiries.'

He turned back to Monahan. 'Anyway, Richards is investigating the death of that girl ...'

That girl.

None of *them* could bring themselves to say her name, not even twenty-five years later.

'So, she's his focus, not us moving stuff around for Stone,' said Racine.

Monahan was staring into the nut shop, his mind snapping through a series of obstacles and how to solve them; he was like a triathlete, preparing for the course, imagining it before he commenced. 'We've got to take him out,' he repeated. 'It shouldn't be that hard; I'll get onto it today.'

'What do you mean *take him out*? Who are you talking about?' asked Stolly.

'He's talking about Boris,' said Racine. 'Boris has to be destroyed, we've got to discredit him, set him up. We need to go through his file, see what we can find on him.'

Monahan started talking, started weaving a story.

'I've heard the bikies have a cop friend up in Nhill, some fella they like to use to help import their meth from over the border. They've got a cookhouse up there, on the outskirts of Nhill, and this cop knows all about it. He's been on it for a few years now. He's had a lucky run: two grand a week. Thought he could keep getting away with it, all the way out there, but no, the Drug Squad heard about the operation in March this year. So, under the orders and direction of its head, Detective Inspector Jacob Monahan, a sting operation was set up to nail the crims and their police protector, Senior Constable Boris Jones. *Prior to the raid, sir, I received information that Senior Constable Jones had been alerted to the fact that we knew about his criminal activity, that he had been taking bribes for many years and also that a warrant for his arrest was about to be drawn up. It was at this time, sir,*

*that, coincidentally, retired Detective Inspector Darian Richards
and his partner Senior Constable Maria Chastain, working on
an internal inquiry for the Commissioner, interviewed Constable
Boris Jones and he used this interview to try to denigrate the
reputation of not only myself, the Head of the Drug Squad,
but also two other high-ranking and respected police officers.
Additionally, sir, I have also been informed that Senior Constable
Boris Jones has, over the years, downloaded some three thousand
images of child porn, some disturbingly violent; this information
was passed on to me by my informant, the previously mentioned
member of the bikie gang. I forwarded this information on to the
relevant task force, sir, and I understand a hard drive has been
located.'*

Racine and Stolly had been staring at him for the duration, like
kids listening to a Roald Dahl story.

'Man, you are a genius,' said Stolly eventually, laughing.

Racine just nodded. 'Okay. Good. Let me know what you need
to make it work.'

'Nothing. It's easy. I've done this shit before,' Monahan said
and then turned to leave, satisfied that his career as the Head of the
Drug Squad – fuck Racine and his bid for the Commissioner's job;
he couldn't care less about that – was inviolable.

'Hang on,' called Stolly. Monahan stopped, turned back to him.
'What about Chastain? And Richards?'

Monahan turned to Racine. 'Who put the hit on Chastain?'

'It wasn't a hit. She was just supposed to be roughed up –
raped, her face sliced a bit. I told him not to do it. Did he listen?
Nah. Idiot.'

'And the point of that being?' asked Monahan.

Racine shrugged. 'Just to spook them. Get her out of the
game. Destabilise Richards. Let him know that even with the
Commissioner on their side, he's treading in dangerous waters.'

'Don't fuck with Richards,' said Stolly. 'You either kill him or
stay out of his way.'

'Sure,' shrugged Racine again. 'Whatever. He's going for the girl again. Same deal. He thinks she's Richards' weak point. This time, I said to him, "You do that sort of shit, you better get someone who knows what they're doing."'

'Maybe you could volunteer yourself, mate,' replied Monahan.

Racine laughed. 'Those days are gone.'

'Shame. Fun days they were,' said Monahan.

1984

WE WERE ABOUT TEN MINUTES OUT OF HORSHAM, ONE OF the largest towns in the area, and about an hour south-east from Nhill, when I heard the siren and saw the lights. A cop car chasing us down. It had to be us because there were no other cars up ahead, and anyway, you know, in the pit of your gut, when it's you in their sights.

'Were you speeding?' Maria asked.

'I never speed,' I lied. But in this case, I hadn't been.

'Maybe it's Boris, wanting to recant his story,' she said airily.

Boris had told us everything that we already knew, or had surmised, about his and the others' involvement with Dominic Stone's drug syndicate. That's not to say it was not of use, it was: it was confirmation. It brought Racine a step closer to Isobel's body on the back of her door at three in the morning.

And it was the crack in the wall; all it takes is one to break the cabal of silence and others tend to follow as self-interest kicks in.

Perhaps stubbornly or perhaps truthfully, Boris had insisted that he and the other three men did go to Isobel's party at the behest of Ruby Jazz, whom Isosceles was still in the process of hunting down. And, again either stubbornly or truthfully, Boris had insisted that all five of them, four solid and tall men plus one under-age stripper, did pile into Pappas' car, the Porsche, tightly squeezed in with Ruby draped over the laps of Racine and Monahan. He had embellished the memory, real or imagined, with a disapproving description of Racine's hands moulding and squeezing various parts of her body as they drove at speed from the Yarra River end of Spencer Street, over the bridge, along City Road until it turned into Alexandra Avenue, a gracious tree-lined boulevard that ran alongside the twists of the Yarra and a popular spot for a bit of late-night speeding because there are so few traffic lights. 'Pappas hit the ton,' said Boris, 'and we all laughed because we were cops and no-one could arrest us, even if they tried, because we were lords of the empire living in the kingdom of the strong.'

—

As the police cruiser drew closer – they must have been doing at least a hundred and forty – I slowed and pulled over into the dirt and gravel on the side of the highway. I opened the door and started to climb out when I heard *Stay in your vehicle* boom out through one of their George Orwell loudspeakers cops love to use as a party trick.

Another party trick these cops love to pull is to make you sit in your car for what seems like an interminable period of time while they do Important Business in theirs, like checking you out on the computer, via the licence plate, against who knows what sorts of databases they have – perhaps they'll check your Facebook page or download your iTunes library too – before they finally deign to step out onto the road and do the *This is a very serious matter* walk towards you.

Unfortunately our cops were young and male, which, for me, puts them into the bin of Dumb and Disdainful. I call them the DD. Fresh out of the Academy, eager to make a mark and as many arrests as possible, surging full of testosterone that isn't helped by the pistol and taser on the belt around the hips, and awash with the belief that they're all powerful. Just like four drunken off-duty cops riding in a Porsche some twenty-five years ago, on their way to a party where a girl dies and no-one, at the time, hammers them for accountability.

One of the cops walked to my side, the other to Maria in the passenger seat. My guy was Luke Douglas and Maria had the pleasure of Rod Cooper's company. Cooper took one look at her, grinned and leaned on the side of the car, close to her.

'This is a left-hand drive vehicle,' noted Douglas with amazing powers of observation. I didn't bother replying.

'Do you have the appropriate paperwork to prove that you can drive this vehicle?'

'Yes,' I said.

'What year was this car made?' he asked.

'Nineteen-sixty-four.' A car with left-hand drive has to be more than thirty years old before you can drive it in Australia.

'We would like you to come back to Horsham with us so we can verify that this car is roadworthy and has with it the appropriate certificates.'

'No, I'm not going to do that,' I replied.

Maria might have been remembering an incident a couple of years ago in which she and I had been driving along a motorway up near Noosa and I'd taken out two cops in vaguely similar circumstances. She was giving me a look of concern, lest I turn on a repeat performance.

'Excuse me?' said Douglas. Cooper also turned my way with a look of shock and a flex of muscles.

'I said, no, we are not driving back to Horsham. We just drove through it and have no intention of returning.'

Douglas muscled up and gave me his serious voice. 'I just told you to drive back to Horsham. If you do not obey me, I will arrest you for the obstruction of justice, handcuff the both of you and drive you there myself and then shove you in the lockup.'

I began to open the door.

'Stay in the car!' barked Douglas as Cooper took a step back, clearly anticipating some action.

I got out of the car.

'Get back in the car!' Douglas commanded.

I put my hands up, as if surrendering. 'Calm down,' I said. He put his hand on the pistol by his side. Jesus H, did they screen cowboy movies for them at the Academy these days?

'Who told you to pull over the red Studebaker, Constable Douglas?' I asked.

He gawped at me, then looked to his colleague, then at Maria and then back at me.

'Get back in the car, sir,' he replied.

'I don't have to get back in the car. I don't have to follow that direction from you – in fact, I don't have to do anything but give you my name and address, but you've already got that; no doubt you were given that information when the officer from St Kilda Road – eighth floor or ninth, Constable? – rang and instructed you to harass and intimidate the driver and passenger in the red Studebaker that would be passing through your town around midday, on their way down to Melbourne from Nhill. What they failed to mention, I suspect, is that the driver and passenger are working for the Police Commissioner and are on official police business, or maybe they told you that this was just a bullshit cover story, so you shouldn't believe it. In any event, here we are. You've pulled over two serving officers of the Victoria Police, and *you* are, in fact, in the process of obstructing justice, as Officer Chastain and I are on duty. So, you've two choices, boys. You can either withdraw back into your vehicle and let us continue on our way, or Officer Chastain and I will forcibly disarm you, perhaps even break a few bones in the process, and then charge you with as many crimes as we can muster.'

This was the basic Fred Flintstone approach to these sorts of cops: fire back with greater intimidation. Yabba Dabba Doo. Not so dumb after all, Douglas took his hand off the gun and stepped back, calling out to Cooper, 'Let's get out of here.'

We watched them retreat through our rear-view mirrors.

'What will they do to Boris?' Maria asked, a little shaken. She wasn't referring to traffic cops on the highway.

'Do you care?' I asked.

She shrugged. 'No.'

—

BORIS HAD ALSO stuck to the line about arriving at the party and then leaving shortly afterwards. He seemed to be telling the truth, but then he told us that when they arrived Racine had recognised Isobel from some of the parties that Stone had held, in his house at Toorak and at his big house in Portsea.

'So it was coincidence? Not buying that one, Boris,' I'd said.

'It's true,' he insisted. I let it pass.

He told us that Racine had taken Isobel into her bedroom and had a talk to her.

'About what?' Maria had asked.

'About not talking.'

'To?'

'The Feds. She'd got caught bringing in some cocaine for Stone. They were hassling her to tell them everything.'

'How'd you hear about that?' I asked.

'Monahan told me.'

'How long, at that time, had you been working for Stone?' asked Maria.

'We weren't *working* for him, okay? It was nothing. I never even saw any drugs. All we did was, like, drive him around or maybe his wife, deliver some stuff for him, talk to some of his colleagues.'

'And threaten anyone who might be a threat,' Maria added.

He didn't answer her.

'Let's agree to disagree on the definition of *working*, Boris, and continue on: how long were you working for him?' I said.

'Nineteen-eighty-four was when we started.'

'The year you graduated from the Academy.'

'Yeah.'

'How'd it come about? This relationship with Dominic Stone,' asked Maria. Boris stared at her as if she had no right to ask such a question. *You were hardly even fucking born then, so what would you know?* is what the look implied.

'Racine,' he eventually said.

Maria stared back at him until he looked away.

'He said they met in Toorak. Racine had gone to see *2001* at the Trak, the old cinema with the big screen, midnight screening. He was stoned and there was this guy sitting next to him, also stoned, and next to *him* was this chick Racine thought was hot. Apparently Stone leaned back and said to his girl, "He wants to fuck you, darling," and Racine, he's never been shy, laughed and said, "Hell, yeah." So, this girl gave him a blow job as the two astronauts disabled Hal – the computer, yeah? – while Stone had one eye on the screen and the other on the two of them.'

Later that night, around three in the morning according to Boris, Stone had approached Racine out on Toorak Road and said, *You're a cop, aren't you? I need some cops.*

'For? Why did Stone need some cops?' I asked.

'Like I said before, we drove for him and –'

'No, Boris, that's not why you want cops. If you need someone to drive you around, you get a driver. Cops provide specific services.'

His face went through a series of contortions, as if he was having trouble articulating the answer. 'We'd sort of lean on people.'

'Threaten them.'

'Yeah. If they were out of line.'

'How would you lean on them? What exactly does *lean* mean?' asked Maria.

He stared at us for what seemed like a long time, then shrugged and said, 'If they didn't do what we *asked*, then we'd rough 'em up a bit.'

'Tell us when you first met Isobel.'

'She used to hang around. She was Dunn's girl. He'd bring her to parties, take her down to Portsea and, when Stone's wife was overseas, to the house in Toorak. There were a lot of girls at the parties.'

'This was before she left for Bolivia?'

'I didn't have anything to do with her. None of us did. She was clearly under-age, I mean, she was still at school, for Christ's sake. Maybe Stolly tried to chat her up – he was like that – but she was really just another pretty face at the pool.'

'And then that changed.'

'Yeah. Then she became the most important person on everybody's mind. Specially Stone's.'

'Tell us about the first time you heard that Isobel had been picked up by the Feds.'

'I was at soccer practice with my oldest girl. It was a Saturday. No mobile phones back then. Well, there were, but they were huge and expensive. Racine turns up, in the middle of soccer practice, and I'm thinking, *Oh shit, what now?* And he tells me we've got a problem, like a huge problem.'

'What did he say? Can you remember? As best as you can remember.'

'Nah, I can't. But it would have been something like, *Isobel's been arrested at the airport, carrying in some dope for Dom –* that's what we called him – *and the Feds are pressuring her to talk. And if she does, we're in trouble.*'

'So, this was immediately after her arrest?' asked Maria.

'Yeah, I think she was still in their custody. Dunn was waiting for her in the arrivals lounge. He called Stone when she didn't come out. Stone must've called Racine ... so, yeah, it was all happening.'

'This was seven weeks before Isobel died,' I said.

He shrugged as if the time frame wasn't important.

'So, that would be seven weeks of you, Pappas, Monahan and Racine all leaning on her,' I said.

He got the message and started to fidget.

'Seven weeks. And during those seven weeks she hadn't yielded, otherwise there would have been no point in Racine taking her into the bedroom on the night she died to pressure her, yet again.'

He didn't answer.

'Seven weeks is a long time to have that sort of thing hanging over you. Any day Isobel might have caved and fessed up to the Feds. Must have been a tense seven weeks, Boris?'

'I didn't kill her. I swear.'

'Take us through exactly what happened after you left the party.'

'We drove to see Stone.'

'Where?'

'The Toorak house.'

'With Ruby? All five of you packed into the Porsche again?' asked Maria.

'No. We dumped her on Toorak Road, told her to find her own way home.'

'What happened with Stone? What was said?' I asked.

'I dunno. He was angry. He wanted the problem fixed.'

'How? Did he say?'

'No. He didn't say.'

'How long were you there? At Stone's house?'

'Not long. Maybe half an hour.'

'And then what happened?'

'I called a cab, went home.'

'And the others?'

He shifted in his seat. 'Dunno. Suppose they went home too.'

MAN ON THE RUN

Isosceles was staring back into a prehistoric world, in which the digital footprint was a thing of the future. He felt like an anthropologist. This was a strange world, one he didn't understand. He'd grown up with apps and computers and texting and the internet. He knew, of course, that these things were recent innovations, but to live in, or even contemplate, a world without them was like having to light a fire to cook food, instead of ordering it in, online.

Darian had tasked Isosceles with numerous jobs. He wanted old phone records, which were proving elusive; current addresses of the rest of Isobel's friends who were at the party; the true identity and whereabouts of Ruby Jazz; the current location of the neighbours who had lived next door to Isobel and also those who had lived in the same Elwood apartment block as Tyrone; and finally the report from Darian's private forensics guys who were examining the empty glass from Isobel's house.

Darian had rung yet again about Isobel's phone records. Had she indeed called Brian Dunn hours before she was killed? If she had, and if Dunn had gone to her, then that clearly made him a chief suspect.

But nothing was more important, for Isosceles, than discovering the identity of the man who had attacked Maria. He swooned for Maria, lusted for her in an adolescent way, knowing that his great fantasy would only ever be that – a fantasy – but it was one in which he luxuriated. He saw himself as her saviour, much as he sometimes imagined he was Batman sweeping across the Melbourne skyline at night. Thus he was infuriated by the attack on her. Since then he'd had her under twenty-four-hour surveillance provided by a drone, owned by the Americans but commandeered by him; a drone that followed her every move. Added to the drone were CCTV cameras recently and secretly installed in and around the apartment block where she was staying. Careful not to cross a moral boundary, he made certain that there were no eyes in her bedroom or bathroom.

The police had yet to identify the assailant, which he put down to a cover-up or, more likely, ineptitude, so he decided to take matters into his own hands. He had hacked into the Coroner's system and slid a bug inside their video monitoring of the man's autopsy. Within moments of the body being laid out on the table, ready for the Coroner's buzz-saw, Isosceles had frozen the image of the man's face and run it through his facial-recognition software. Within another few moments he had a name and criminal history.

—

WHEN YOU RUN a murder investigation, you plan it and structure it according to the evidence and the suspects and the degree of urgency, deciding whether, and how soon, another killing might take place. You try to keep an open mind and not jump to conclusions. You determine to whom you want to speak first and when and how. We had already gathered a swathe of information pointing to Dominic Stone, but he wasn't the only suspect capable of killing Isobel. If indeed she had been killed. There were other people with other motives floating around. I was not ready to interview Stone. Before I got to him I wanted to talk to the other cops and to Brian Dunn, the schoolteacher who also seemed to have been working for the wealthy guy. I figured that Maria and I were some days away from knocking on the door to Stone's Toorak mansion, ready and armed. We needed to be across all the material, as much as we could be, before we heard his version of the story.

But sometimes investigations get away from you and take on their own life.

Isosceles rang us as we hit the outer suburbs of Melbourne. The sky was deep metal grey. Another storm was about to lash the city. I put him on speakerphone.

'The name of Maria's assailant is Gabriel Vasquez. He is Bolivian by birth but, some twenty years ago, migrated to, and became a citizen of, Vanuatu, island home to numerous Australian tax dodgers and shelf companies shielding drug syndicates, many of which I've had the pleasure of investigating over the years. This circuitous journey of citizenship would be, I posit, the reason our colleagues in the Victorian constabulary have had so much trouble uncovering Señor Vasquez's true identity.'

There was the word posit again.

'Vanuatu is, Maria, a most interesting case study in the phenomenon of colonial history.'

Maybe it was nerves, maybe it was showing off, maybe it was brain wiring, but away he went and it was pointless trying to stop him.

'In that it was, from 1906 to 1980, ruled by both the French and the English in what they called a condominium. Every morning on the island a French flag would be raised at exactly the same time as the Union Jack, and if one was raised or lowered ahead of the other, an international row would occur. Every government edict, indeed every stamp, was printed in both English and French. Of course both nationalities loathed each other, and the locals could only look on them all with extreme befuddlement. Curious, don't you think?'

'Can we go back to the Bolivian?' I said.

'Indeed, *mon ami*. Ha, that's French for "my friend". *Ma chérie?* That's French for "my darling".'

'The Bolivian!' I shouted.

'Indeed. He appears to have travelled to Australia many times, over the past thirty-two years. I've accessed his phone records through Telecom Vanuatu Limited, and most curiously, three days before the attack on Maria and a day after arriving in Melbourne, he took a phone call from a seventeen-year-old girl by the name of Sara Southy.'

'Who's she?' I asked.

'Sara lives in Toorak. She has her mother's maiden name as a surname. Her grandfather is Dominic Stone, who has, I might add, just checked in to Melbourne airport for a flight to Zagreb in Croatia, first stop Singapore, next stop Dubai.'

—

WE'D JUST DRIVEN through Bacchus Marsh, an apple-growing town with the famous Avenue of Honour, a stretch of road lined on either side with almost three hundred Canadian elms. They'd been planted back in 1918. The branches formed a magnificent canopy creating a forest tunnel through which we had passed. I wanted to show Maria. Off to the right, about ten kilometres away, was a remote little spot where I'd executed a crooked cop some years ago, an old bruiser who had caused the suicide of a young policewoman because of his bullying. I can't remember the date exactly but it would have been about six or seven years after Isobel had died. I didn't mention this to Maria.

I gunned the engine, turned back onto the main highway and drove too fast until I turned left at the Melton Highway, in the direction of Melbourne airport.

—

IN THE MOVIES it goes like this: Maria and I would burst into the airport and, unimpeded, run to the first-class lounge and grab a startled Stone, handcuff him and read him his rights, then drag him back to our car, which we would have left out the front, tended to and guarded by a compliant security guard. And perhaps if the movie was B-grade, en route to HQ old Dominic might burst into tears and confess his role in the killing of poor Isobel, a terrible crime for which he's been harbouring shocking guilt for twenty-five years and please will we all absolve him, just a little?

None of that happened.

First up, as we drove along the highway, at least thirty minutes away from the airport, was the issue of how to get ourselves in. The main airports around Australia come under the jurisdiction of the Federal Police, not the state cops. In a world of inter-agency tension and rivalry, we couldn't just drive in on official business. We needed permission. Of course, most of the time that's done after the event, during the event, or as a very simple matter of formality before the event. In this case, though, we had a problem. My colleague from the Chow, Sullivan, who'd given me the case files on the drug investigation from twenty-five years ago, a copy he had stored away privately, knowing the original file would probably be destroyed, had gone on leave. Fishing somewhere near Anglesea. His replacement said yeah, they'd get on to it, but just wait a bit, because they were in the middle of dealing with yet another possible terrorist crisis. I couldn't imagine securing the assistance of the Head of Homicide, the Head of the Drug Squad or Assistant Commissioner Racine, none of whom really needed to see Dominic Stone, blast from the past, walk into an interview room at HQ, and Copeland was in surgery having an endoscopy. We could deal with it when we got to the airport, but I didn't want to waste time explaining myself; better to have them alerted to our arrival as we were travelling.

At the same time, I had to deal with the small problem of how we were going to prevent a citizen, a first-class passenger, no less, from boarding a flight to Singapore, which didn't have an extradition treaty with Australia, then on to Dubai, which also lacked an extradition treaty, and finally to Croatia, which – guess what? – didn't have an extradition treaty either; he'd chosen his flight path well. If we asked him to come in for questioning, he'd refuse. So, Maria and I had no alternative but to arrest him, then and there, in the Emirates lounge.

There was precious little to arrest him on – the call from his granddaughter's phone would not, in the land of judges and courts, be enough – but, under the Victorian *Crimes Act 1958*, which I had memorised at the age of twenty-one, section 458, subclause 1, paragraph c, amended in 1986, we could, and we would, place him under arrest for avoiding apprehension. It was still a long bow, but it would keep him from Zagreb for a little while.

If we made it in time. The clock was ticking, traffic was dense and the wheels of bureaucracy were turning slowly with the Feds, meaning we were being blocked, meaning we were going to be blocked when we arrived. Telling them that we intended to arrest a wealthy and powerful businessman in the middle of the first-class lounge wasn't going to help smooth the way through the blockage either.

Additionally, we had to deal with the boring issue of airport security, now a major hassle if a car is left unattended or parked anywhere near the entrance to departures for longer than two minutes. Isosceles was onto that, although I had more pressing business for him.

'Can you stall the plane's departure?' I asked.

'I've never had to do that before,' he answered.

'But can you?'

'I can do anything,' he said without thinking.

HAILE SELASSIE'S VOLKSWAGEN (ii)

THERE WAS A TIME WHEN HE USED TO LEAVE HIS MOBILE phone on up until the very last second, usually well after boarding, after the doors to the plane had been closed and he'd consumed his first glass of champagne. He was the guy the flight attendant would tell with a smile, now is the time to turn off your mobile device, thank you, sir. Not anymore.

He loved the sanctuary of the lounge and then the flight. No-one to bother him, nobody able to contact him, no problems to solve, which, for that time in limbo, in the lounge and in the air, made it possible to pretend there were no problems at all.

After many years, as he would settle into his first-class seat and say, yes, I'd love a glass of champagne, thank you, he would think, I'd prefer to be alone, now. And then he'd switch off his phone. That desire to be alone – in that calm, problem-free space – began to elongate backwards, to the moment where he passed through the gate and began to walk towards the inviting open door of the plane, then to the moment when, back in the lounge, his flight would be called, as he stood up and collected his carry-on, then back to a random moment about fifteen minutes before he'd have to leave the lounge to board his flight, and then, finally, as he was passing through security, before he even arrived at the lounge and ordered a glass of champagne and yes, thank you, some smoked salmon would be very kind.

He wasn't prone to self-pity but there were moments he'd slip back into those times, back into the eighties, which had almost led to his ruin. When the world was loud and brash and it was great to be alive, when the high rollers bulldozed into every facet of business with wads of cash and fat smiles, with lit cigars and girls on both cheeks, when there was no fear, in sex or investments, before the crash of the eighties when banks went bust and bankrupt and the girls became classified as under-age. When he, along with all others, lorded over a world of personal debt because – guess what? – debt makes you richer. When he was plunging cash into property and racehorses even though he didn't like horseraces and into surfie fashion design houses and then the brilliant idea of building a twenty-five storey, five-star hotel right in the middle of town, across the road from those stuffy Georgian terraces where old Geelong Grammarians sat and snorted snuff and inhaled sherry. When, rashly in hindsight, he made a decision after downing far too many drinks and being blinded by the light of yet another nubile girl thrust into his lap by another carpetbagger with yet another scheme for fast-cash-no-hassle and, hey, Dom, there's also the frisson of danger but danger is no problem for a powerful man like you, am I wrong?

It was the mid-eighties and banks had gone bust and dreams had evaporated, not just for Dominic Stone but for many business investors, guys who crawled through the stock market in search of greater wealth and status despite already having both. But the hotel was built, a testament to Dominic's can-do prowess and his fuck-you-Melbourne-old-boy-network determination: a dark black tower of glass and steel rising from a forgotten corner of Russell Street, once a slum for the Chinese in the previous century, now his kingdom of steel, Stone's five-star hotel, an edifice to his immortality, he liked to muse. The kids were all at private schools and he had an assemblage of cars and two houses and a wife he adored who enjoyed shopping in Hong Kong, and who was he to deny her or their kids; but then, hello, hello, debt really wasn't all that it had been cracked up to be. Debt was, he came to realise as the afterparty of the eighties slugged him and others across the head during the middle of the decade, something that had to be paid back and not really the first floor in the elevator to wealth. He was a rich man with a lot of glittering ornaments and not a penny in the bank. He needed cash and he needed it fast. Guys like him, who were already rich and stable in the late seventies and early eighties, had joined a conga line of dazzle, gambling a secure world for the excitement of another – and they now found themselves in deep shit.

So, after too many drinks and a little champagne-pouring onto the tits of the nubile, in the depths of a city nightclub, he listened as the other man spoke of the great ease of bringing cocaine into the city. Coke, no harm, no drama, no dirty scummy stuff like needles and smack; coke, it's the Moët of the new world, my man. No different from bringing in a shipment of cement. Easy, and the bucks are big.

Was there fear? No. Dominic might have overextended himself, but the banks loved him and his parties and the girls and the grog, and, as he stood on the top floor of his hotel and looked across the flatlands of the city around him, he felt like an emperor. And emperors have no fear. So, it was without concern, of being caught, of breaching a moral code – truth be told, he had none – that he leaned back on the banquette in the disco and with one arm around the nubile put the other arm around his friend and said, 'Yeah, far out, man, let's bring in a ton of coke. When do we start and who do we bribe?'

—

'I START WITH nothing, Dominic, just a cardboard suitcase, and do you know what? Two words; that's all I knew. Your mother, the same. Both of us, two words: *hello* and *thank you*. With nothing we start. But I got a job and I work my way up. You know what I was? Before your mother and I came to this country?'

Yes, Pop, I've heard this story many times. You were a cutter.

'I was a cutter. I cut fabric. I make dresses. I make them back in Lviv, then, after your mother and I escape from the Germans and then the Russians, both as evil as each other, after your mother and I arrive here in Melbourne, I make dresses. From nothing we start, and look at us now.'

And he would make his son look; Sunday mornings after church, every week without fail, Julius Stojmenovic would drive Dominic, his only son, through the working-class suburbs of Richmond and Collingwood, down narrow streets, and show him the small factories that he owned, where his clothes were manufactured, and more, for Julius had expanded beyond making cheap women's dresses. He had, from the early sixties, begun to buy houses. Cheap working-man's cottages, cramped together in narrow bluestone streets in the run-down inner-city suburbs that encircled the CBD. Into these brick cottages he installed tenants. Sunday mornings after church became rent day, when Julius would drive down the myriad back alleys and narrow streets with his son in the front seat and, having passed the profitable factories, pointing them out to Dominic as if for the first time, he would then drive to each of his houses, sit in the car, out the front, and wait while his son went inside to collect the rent.

There were times when the tenants couldn't pay their rent. His tenants were all poor. Julius had warned his son of this. 'When they see a boy coming to collect their money, if they are behind or do not have enough that week, they will think they can cajole him, lie to him, make a fool of him, with biscuits and sad talk. Guard yourself against this. Never come back to the car without the rent.'

Julius would make Dominic lock the passenger-side door as he closed it, before he walked to the front door of each house. He would only be allowed back inside the car, his father leaning over to open it from inside, if he had been successful. It was a test, of strength. Of will.

For many years Dominic hated Sundays. First church, prayers to a God he didn't understand or care about, then another drive around the ever-expanding factories and shops that his father owned, then, finally, the rent collection. By the time he was fifteen, there were more than thirty-five houses, thirty-five tenants and, more often than not, thirty-five excuses to a young man of whom no-one was frightened. Up to thirty-five disappointments for his father, staring at him through the locked passenger-side window of his car. These were hard days for the people who rented off Julius, so why, Dominic kept asking himself, did his father install poor people into his houses in the first place? People who clearly struggled to put food on the table week after week, people who really should have been in a government housing commission flat.

Ten years of collecting rents as a child, then as a young teenager, then as a young man, for it was soon after his fifteenth birthday that Dominic felt confident enough, strong enough and finally determined enough never to see that look of disappointment on his father's face again, the look that said *My son is a failure*; he decided to exert some muscle. And he did. He was strong. Men and women, even children, had scoffed at him for years. Not anymore. Now, he would prevail. At the first house, in which an elderly man by the name of Mr Summers lived, chronically behind in his rent but always with enough for whisky and bets on the races, Dominic held the old man down and broke his index finger. Mr Summers revealed a Nescafé coffee jar full of crumpled ten-dollar notes. Dominic took them all. At the second house, in which a young woman by the name of Connie was also full of excuses week after week, Dominic also prevailed. He punched her in the stomach, began to choke her and threatened to cut her throat, whereupon Connie paid up in full including all the arrears. At the fifth house Dominic held a knife to the cheek of an eight-year-old girl and felt regret when her parents hysterically paid their overdue rent, as the thrill of his power was becoming addictive.

By the time he was sixteen his father didn't bother to lock the passenger-side door anymore. His son had triumphed.

Julius had a heart attack while sitting behind the wheel of his car, parked out the front of a dusty little shack in a Fitzroy back alley on a Sunday afternoon. Dominic was inside having sex with the forty-year-old woman who rented the house. Sexual favours for rent reduction had become part of Dominic's game by the time he was sixteen. When he stepped outside he saw his father slumped over the steering wheel. He climbed into the passenger seat and stared at the old man. All he could think about was his inheritance and that now, finally, he could wake up on Sunday mornings without tremors of fear for what the rest of the day held.

—

HE WISHED HE'D fucked Isobel; that was his one regret. She had caused him such immense grief, twenty-five years ago, and now, too, that somehow, if he had fucked her – she had been a gorgeous-looking girl and he had so craved her little body – his situation might not seem so unfair. To have been torn asunder by a girl whose body he had not enjoyed seemed unreasonable. Had he fucked her like Dunn had fucked her, then he could reconcile, at least partly, the trouble she had caused him. Then he would have got something out of her. And frankly, he mused, a fuck would have been a tiny price for her to pay.

People were leaving the lounge. Was it time for him to board? He looked around and noticed that his flight had been delayed. No matter. He was more than happy sitting in the cocoon of the first-class lounge. Why not have another glass of champagne? Soon he'd be back in Croatia, where he had bought a small house in the town of Rogoznica, overlooking the Adriatic Sea. He would stay there until this whole event, this new, unexpected and entirely unwelcome investigation into that girl's death, was over and, as it had been for the past twenty-five years, forgotten. Let sleeping bitches lie, he thought as he poured himself a glass and enjoyed listening to the bubbles pop on the surface.

He noticed a man and a woman walking into the lounge. She looked vaguely familiar. Very beautiful; had they fucked? he wondered. How was it that he seemed to recognise her? She was looking around the lounge, as if searching for someone. So too the man she was with. Then, as he sipped his champagne and sat back, staring at the woman, trying to place her in his orbit of pretty women, he noticed that she was now staring directly at him. For an instant he thought to wave and smile at her.

But then he realised that there was something about her demeanour as she walked towards him, the man in tow, which wasn't friendly.

And then he remembered where he had seen her and who she was.

FUCK-YOU MONEY

'I HAVE A PLANE TO CATCH,' HE SAID AS WE APPROACHED HIM, getting up from his chair and reaching for his carry-on luggage. We hadn't even introduced ourselves but he clearly knew what was going down.

He was moving quickly for a guy in his seventies. I put my hand on his shoulder and pushed him back down into his chair. I sat on one side, Maria on the other.

'My name is Darian Richards and this is Maria Chastain,' I said.

He nodded quickly.

'You know why we're here?' I asked.

He nodded again.

'Good,' I said comfortingly. 'Maria and I have some questions we need you to answer, so I am afraid you're not going to catch your plane. We're going to leave the lounge now and then exit the airport. Okay?'

'No,' he said firmly. 'I have a plane to catch. I'm flying to Croatia. I have to go. It's urgent.'

I put my hand on his arm, to calm him. And to intimidate him.

'We need to ask you about Isobel.'

He nodded again.

'And ... we need to figure out why a phone call was made to a hit man, if I can call him that, in Vanuatu, a couple of days ago, who then tried to kill my good friend Maria, here. A phone call made from your granddaughter's mobile.'

He froze. Stone was sun-tanned in a fake way, especially for a guy living in cloud-covered Melbourne. He was short, about five foot two, but he had that *Fuck you I'm rich* feel to him. Tall in the walk. A swaggering type of guy, all full of bombast, which was, with a tiny breeze, gone and replaced by a childish helplessness. He had that desperate-to-please thing going on. He looked ridiculous in a silver double-breasted silk suit with a white T-shirt underneath. He smelled of aftershave. His teeth were perfect and his nails were clipped.

'I have a plane to catch. You can't do this.'

'Yeah, I can. I can and will arrest you. You can accompany us, or we can haul you out of here, if you like. It's your call.'

He stared at me, his mouth moving without speaking, like a fish, which made me very briefly think back to my failures on the lake before Copeland came into my life with the lure of the gig.

And briefly, momentarily, to my dad, when he threw me out of that boat.

'I need to call my lawyer,' he said.

'Of course. Due process. We love that. All for it. But, and you might have heard this before, if you hide behind a lawyer, then it looks bad. For you. And frankly, Mr Stone, it's looking bad already, so think about how you want to play this.'

I leaned in. 'We really hate it when a person tries to harm a police officer.'

He turned to Maria, who had been staring at him, then looked back to me. 'I am not answering any of your questions. I am calling my lawyer. I insist that you refrain from this deprivation of my liberty and allow me to catch my flight.'

I pulled out the handcuffs and slapped them around his wrists, just below the diamond-studded gold Rolex on one arm and a trendy gold-and-platinum Celtic bracelet on the other. Then we hauled his sorry arse up from the chair and escorted him out of the lounge with a suggestion to the startled Emirates staff at the desk that they might want to retrieve Mr Stone's luggage from the plane.

There'd been no hassle with the Federal cops once we'd arrived at the airport; as usual Isosceles had come through for us by contacting one of his colleagues there. We'd been escorted through security, showing our Special Constable badges and our weapons, then through immigration and then on to the Emirates lounge.

On our way back out Stone whined a little, head down low to avoid the stares and the snapshots from kids and teenagers on their smart phones, his silver silk jacket draped over the cuffs.

Once we reached the car we allowed him to call his lawyer, who expressed outrage and advised that if I continued with this gross violation of the human rights of this important man, then I would be charged and imprisoned for crimes against humanity. Or words to that effect; I wasn't listening. I told her I'd call when we had arrived at an interrogation room with her client and hung up, noting that Stone had fourteen missed calls in the past hour. Someone trying to warn him of our approach.

Before I put the car into gear I turned to look at Stone. Sharp blue eyes, sun-tanned cheeks, flaming white teeth perfectly crafted in neat rows. Thinning dark hair, swept back and a little too long on the neck. What was going on behind his sullen, angry face? He stared back at me, then at Maria.

'I will not be answering your questions and you will, both of you, regret this outrageous behaviour, and, I might add, I *will* be taking action.'

I put the car into gear and drove off.

Murder takes you everywhere, into all sorts of homes and to people from all walks of life. I'd seen guys like Stone before. Wealthy guys who owned mansions in the plural and maybe choppered to work to literally stay above the hoi polloi. An accumulation of great wealth allowed them to believe they were untouchable. They have so much money they can afford to say to anyone, *fuck you. I don't care, you can't touch me, I'm too wealthy, I can pay off anyone or anything to solve this problem, so get out of the way and fuck you.*

The truth is, their fuck-you money can and does, in almost every situation, buy them out of a problem. Stone was angry not so much at the danger we posed to him but rather at the inconvenience of his freedom being curtailed. As I glanced back at him in the rear-view mirror I knew he was thinking he could buy his way out of it, like maybe he bought his way out of the threat Isobel represented twenty-five years ago, paying four cops big money to be his men.

——

'Excuse me, Inspector ...'

'Hello, Maria. Call me Zach. How are you?'

She stood in the doorway to his office. The crews of Homicide were busy on phones and computers behind her. She could feel Stolly's gaze boring into her; he'd smiled in a sleazy way as she'd walked into the offices.

'I'm fine. Thanks. I was wondering if we could use one of your interrogation rooms. Do you have a free one?'

'Yeah, no problem. I think they're all free unless one of the crews has taken someone in without telling me. Better bloody not have,' he said with a laugh as he rose from his chair to escort her towards the row of small, narrow, box-like rooms that are nothing like what you see in American TV shows.

'Yep, all good,' he said moments later. 'Who are you bringing in?'

'Dominic Stone,' she replied.

He smiled. Some cops love it when the temperature ramps up and life gets interesting and controversial.

'It's all yours,' he said and walked off.

Moments later Maria watched the look on Stolly's face as Darian escorted Stone through the Homicide office and into their interrogation room. All of Stolly's previous swagger and *I'm your man, baby* crumbled, as she and Darian had known it would.

—

STONE HAD NOT been questioned after Isobel's death. Of course it was only after her father, Eli, had jumped up and down and made accusations of murder that Stone was associated with the case. Still, he wasn't even called to the coronial inquest after these accusations were made and, more importantly, reported in the press. That was his fuck-you money talking.

'Where were you on the night of December the twenty-first, nineteen-ninety?' I asked.

'That's a ridiculous question. I have no idea, and in any event, I am not going to answer any of your questions. Where is my lawyer?'

'I'll help you with the time frame: that was the night Isobel Vine died in her house in Osborne Street, South Yarra. At approximately one-thirty in the morning you were visited by four serving officers of the Victoria Police. Do you remember that?'

'I will not be answering any questions.'

'Constable Boris Jones has told us that he and three other police officers drove to your house. Who were the other three officers?'

'I will not be answering any of your questions.'

'Constable Boris Jones has also told us that the subject of discussion that night, indeed the purpose of the visit, was Isobel Vine and the likelihood that she would be passing on certain information to the Federal Police. Do you recall that conversation?'

'This is ridiculous. I will not answer any of your absurd questions.'

'Give me your passport.'

'What?'

'Your passport. Give it to me.'

'I certainly will not.'

I clamped my hands down on his wrists, held them tight. 'It's in his jacket pocket,' I said to Maria.

'What are you doing? This is outrageous!'

Maria stepped forward, reached into his jacket pocket and removed it.

'There's a shredder next to Reeve's office, just around the corner,' I said.

She looked horrified for a moment, then shrugged and walked out of the room.

'You can't do that. That's illegal. You can't destroy my passport!'

'We just have.' I leaned in, letting go of his wrists. I could feel a building anger inside me. Cool it, I told myself. Just because he's rich and thinks he can buy his way out of this and just because you think he is the reason why Isobel died, cool it. Emotions blind you when it comes to murder, when you're sitting in front of the guy you think is the killer.

'This is the end of the road,' I said. 'You've got away with whatever involvement you had in Isobel's death *until now*. I have enough on you to put you away for drug importation. I can and will, if you like, finish the job that the Feds started twenty-five years ago. I also have enough to get an obstruction-of-justice conviction against you, and I haven't even begun on your relationship with Gabriel Vasquez and the attempted murder of Senior Constable Chastain. All the cop protection you had has now vanished. All the court protection you had has now vanished.'

He looked around him, a bit like a scared ferret, then back at me as I continued:

'You get involved with trying to harm a cop and you lose every friend you ever had, even the bad cops who might have something to lose, because, Dominic, we cops are clan-like. Tribal. Even the dodgy cops. Even the worst of the worst; cops might kill gangsters and crims, maybe even civilians, but they don't kill other cops and they hate it when someone tries to. You are ruined. You can figure it out now and start cooperating or you can figure it out next week and start cooperating then. Or you can be a martyr and clam up, keep telling us you won't be answering any questions, hope I'm wrong and that the money will keep you safe. Give it a shot, see how that'll work for you, but believe me: it's over. You're done.'

He stared at me, then at Maria, who returned sans passport, then back at me, hard and cold.

'I will not be answering any of your questions.'

NO WAY OUT

'You know what I hate? I'm going to tell you what I hate: I hate it when people like you think you can avoid telling me the truth, when you think you can get away with silence and prevarication. You think this is a fucking game?'

'No,' said Isobel.

'No,' echoed Sullivan. 'Good, because it's not a fucking game and you cannot just sit there and pretend I'm going to go away. Because I'm not. You tell me what I want to know and we can make a deal, or you go to jail, and, Isobel, you're a cute little girl, got a real nice virginal sweetness to you, darling, and that's *just* what the butch bitches in jail like. You think it's just the guys who get it bad in jail? Believe me, it's worse in the women's jail. I'm going to walk out of here now, for five minutes, then I'm coming back, and in that five minutes you are going to do two things: you are going to reassess your attitude towards me and then you are going to contemplate how it would feel to have a broom handle shoved up your sweet little fanny while another is being shoved up your sweet little a-hole with a couple of butch dykes drooling all over your sweet little titties inside your prison cell, day and night for ten years.'

She heard, between the tears and horror, the sound of the interview room door slam shut and she thought back to this morning, when she'd woken with a start to find two men sitting at the end of her bed.

'Hello, Isobel,' Stone had said.

The other guy – his name was Nick something – was one of Stone's cops. She'd sunk deeper into the bed, pulling the doona up tighter around her neck. How did they get into her house? Why didn't she lock the doors, like Tyrone had told her?

'We were just passing by and thought we'd drop in and say hi. You spoke to Brian?'

She nodded.

'Brian told you how important it is that you keep silent?'

She nodded.

'Brian told you we'd look after you?'

She nodded.

'This is Nick. Have you met him yet?'

'Yeah. I think so.'

'Hey, Isobel.'

'Hi, Nick.'

'Nick's a cop. So, what that means is – you're protected. Safe. He'll look after you. Make sure all the threats that the Feds are going to throw at you are ignored. The value of having a cop like Nick on your side ... I can't emphasise it enough; it's just wonderful. As much as it's a terrible nightmare if a cop is not on your side. If that happens, if a cop from the Victoria Police, or *four* of them, were not on your side, then life wouldn't be worth living. That right, Nick?'

'That's right, Dom.'

'Give me an example, Nick.'

'Walk down the street, get arrested for jaywalking. Drive your car, get arrested for running a red. Sit at home watching the telly, get arrested for disturbing the peace. Travel home at night, in a dangerous suburb like this ... we had a bit of an issue with a serial rapist a couple of years ago in this suburb, remember that, Dom?'

'Yep, sure do. Bad business. Lots of poor innocent girls. Lives ruined.'

'Yeah. Walk home at night, get attacked, call for the cops but maybe they don't come in time. Same goes for just sitting here at home. Break-in. Armed robbery goes wrong and a shotgun goes off. It's an endless list. Really, the possibilities are limited only by your imagination.'

'I won't be telling the Feds anything. I promise.'

'Good girl.'

—

TICK-TOCK. SULLIVAN WOULD be back any moment. She closed her eyes and fought off an urge to throw up. She thought back to the movie *Quadrophenia*, which Brian had taken her to see at the Astor cinema at the St Kilda end of Chapel Street one night. The Astor was a 1930s movie house with two floors of seats that showed old movies on double bills every night. *Quadrophenia* was about the gang warfare between the mods and rockers in England during the 1960s. The music was by the Who, and Sting, from the Police, one of her favourite bands, played one of the mods. At the very end of the film the lead character rode his motorbike over the edge of a massive white cliff, killing himself. He had sailed through the air like a hero, smashing into the ocean below.

She wanted a bike and she wanted a cliff and she wished she were there, at the edge of the cliff, so she too could sail into the ocean below before the five minutes evaporated and Sullivan came back in.

THE FALL GUY

PEOPLE WERE STARING AT STOLLY. COPS, ON HIS FLOOR. WORD was getting out.

It was like he'd been transported back twenty-five years to when his reputation was on the line, when cops in corridors were taking sidelong glances at him and whispering about whether he was corrupt. He'd weathered that storm, but now it was back. And worse: now he had more to lose. Then, he'd been a kid, in his early twenties. Easy to jump and get another job. Now, in his mid-forties, he was a high-flying Homicide detective with a big fall looming and not much chance of finding a new career. He could, he imagined grimly, become a private detective, but what the fuck? Chasing down randy guys cheating on their wives? Was that the future? Was that what all this was coming to?

And that was the best-case scenario. Worst was that he would find himself up on charges relating to their work for Stone, with a possible jail term.

'He'll talk.'

'He won't,' replied Monahan.

As soon as he'd seen Stone being led into the interrogation room, to be questioned by Richards and Chastain, Stolly had gone upstairs, to Monahan's office.

'I wanna steak sandwich,' he'd said and Monahan, without responding, had risen from his desk and walked out with him, across the office floor to the lift, down to the foyer and outside, across St Kilda Road and into a cheapo snack bar on the other side. School was out and the joint was crowded with boys in their Melbourne Grammar uniforms, grabbing a burger or hot chips before their tram ride home.

'He will. Richards will spook him, tell him it's the end of the road and he can either cooperate with them and maybe avoid some jail time or he can go down. Stone's a coward. Remember? Back when we told him we weren't going to work for him anymore? How he barked loud until we threatened him? How he folded like a pussy? He'll do what it takes to preserve his life.'

'He won't talk. Too much to lose.'

Stolly stared at him and wondered exactly what Monahan meant by that.

'What did happen that night?' he asked. 'After I left?'

'What do you mean?' asked Monahan.

'I left you and Racine with Stone, at his house, at about two-thirty. What did you guys talk about? What did you plan? What happened?'

Monahan paused. They had never spoken about the events of that night, after the party, after they'd driven to Stone's. The events of that night were kept in silence. Better that way, better for all of them.

'Stone rang Dunn.'

'The teacher?'

'Yeah. Told him to go see the girl, told him to fix it. Gave him the old line about being able to buy silence or make silence, and that we'd tried to buy her silence and that hadn't worked so now it was time to make her silent ... and that Dunn had to do it.'

'What? He told Dunn to kill her? Are you fucking kidding me? We're implicated in a murder?' Stolly whispered urgently.

'You think she killed herself?' Monahan asked incredulously.

'Yes. I did. Maybe. Or that the boyfriend killed her accidentally.'

'Don't be so fucking naive, Stolly. Jesus, you of all people.'

Suddenly the worst-case scenario was looking catastrophic.

'This is Racine's fault,' Stolly said. 'If it wasn't for his ego, none of this would be happening.'

213

'Yeah.'

'He was meant to ensure Stone left the country.'

'Did a great job on that.'

'And Boris. Did he even talk to Boris? Warn him? Or is he too fucking busy having his photo taken with politicians and putting out press releases on how the crime rate's gone down since he became Assistant Commissioner?'

A waitress came over with two large plates. 'Two steak sandwiches?'

'Thanks, darlin',' said Stolly, for once not following her with his hungry stare as she walked away from their table.

'Fuck,' said Monahan, angry.

'What?'

'Every time we come here and I order a *rare* steak sandwich, it comes out more overcooked than a hide of buffalo that's been roasted in a crematorium. I'm fucking over it.'

He stood up and shouted to the waitress: 'Hey! I ordered rare! I want a *rare* steak sandwich, not a grizzled piece of leather!'

'Mate, shut up,' said Stolly as the schoolkids all looked at Monahan as if he were a nutter and then, realising he was most likely a cop from across the street, looked away quickly. The waitress hurried over to scoop up his plate with a litany of apologies and then bustled back to the kitchen and the startled cook, who looked to be all of eighteen.

'Jesus, calm down.'

'I *am* calm. I just want a steak sandwich that won't break my fucking teeth. Is that too much to ask? Tell me that's too much to ask and I'll go over there and apologise to the cook. I'll tell him: My friend Stolly thinks I'm being a prick because I overreacted to the fact that you never cook a meal according to the order.'

'No, mate. Not too much to ask. It's all good.'

'I'm going to France in October,' Monahan said, seemingly out of the blue, leaving Stolly bemused by the sudden change of subject.

'Good for you, Jake. Nice place, France. You know the language?'

'Yeah, a few words. Enough to get by.'

'Super. October? That's their autumn, isn't it?'

'Yeah. Lorna's coming with me, and the girls.'

'Awesome, mate.'

'We're going to the Loire Valley.'

'I went there once, with a bird I picked up in London. Soho, London. She was a stripper on the run from this loony fucking Belgian gangster. Anyway, we hightailed it out of London and flew to Paris and hired a car and then drove to this amazing chateau in the Loire Valley. Great week. What'cha going for?'

'Conference. Organised by the Europol Drugs Unit; we're looking to see if the recent decriminalisation of weed in those US states has had any impact on crime rates. We're actually ... here comes my steak!'

The waitress placed the plate before him with a nervous smile. 'Sorry about before, sir. Let me know if there's a problem with this one, but cook says it's rare, just how you like it.'

'Thanks, honey,' Monahan said and began to munch. 'Perfect.' He shouted across to the cook: 'Awesome!'

The cook nodded and smiled and the waitress breathed a sigh of relief.

'Decriminalisation. Specially of weed. It's the only way to go. My job is to sell it to the government; I figure that falling crime rates is the way to do it. We've booked the tickets. The girls are really excited. They're doing some special assignments for school based on the trip, and Lorna, well, she hasn't been on a holiday with me since that trip to Hawaii eight years ago.' He swallowed and looked straight at Stolly. 'My point in all this, Stoll, is that I think you and I need to take some decisive action in the current circumstances to ensure that events do not overwhelm us. I think you might be right.'

'About what?'

'Stone. He will talk. Eventually. They all do.' Monahan finished the last of his steak sandwich. 'I've got to be more pessimistic about people. Sometimes I forget that people are fucked. He needs to go for a swim.'

'A swim.' Stolly repeated the word quietly, his attention now fully with the man sitting across from him. He looked – and felt – shocked. This was getting more and more out of control.

'Nice bracing winter swim down at Portsea. I'll organise it,' said Monahan. He looked at Stolly again. 'You got a problem with that?'

'Nah. No problem.'

'Good. Don't go pussy on me.'

WINGS OF DESIRE

Despite all the bluster and outrage she could summon, Stone's lawyer did not facilitate a happy outcome for her client. A very dour-looking Stone was led into the court, to the shock of the Magistrate, who no doubt knew him socially. The Police Prosecutor, a nifty little Irish bulldog in the court environment, went in for the kill.

In my experience, judges get a little antsy if they are informed by Counsel that there is a potential for the accused person standing before them, be they innocent or guilty of the charges, to do an overseas runner. It makes them look bad if they've let a guilty party abscond, especially if said guilty party then turns up in the tabloids sitting by a jacuzzi with a bevy of sexpots on a tropical island, having evaded justice.

So, after the Police Prosecutor explained that Mr Stone was required to stay in Australia for the purposes of helping police with their inquiries and that Mr Stone had refused, hence his unfortunate but necessary arrest at Melbourne airport, the Magistrate reluctantly, it seemed to me, ordered that good old Dom surrender his passport and cooperate with police inquiries.

Naturally this led to an eruption from Dom's lawyer, who went all human rights on me and the police, specifically one Senior Constable Chastain, as she and Detective Inspector Darian Richards had not only stolen her client's passport, but they had illegally destroyed it.

Naturally I lied to the Magistrate and said it was a spurious and outrageous allegation, for which there was no basis in fact.

One thing I can say about judges is, they are mostly dumb fuckwits, and they all buy it when a cop lies to them.

Dominic was out on bail, charged with resisting arrest, adrift and alone in Melbourne, far from the sanctuary he'd been craving.

He was all mine.

—

No MENTION HAD been made in the courtroom of the call from Stone's granddaughter's phone to the Bolivian hit man who was lying in the Coroner's slab-room. That had to be kept off the court record because we had obtained both the guy's identity and the phone records of Stone's granddaughter through secretive and very illegal means. Best to keep that sort of stuff away from the Magistrate.

I grabbed Stone's lawyer on the steps of the court, a modern glass and brown rendered concrete box in William Street, not far from where Dom and the boys used to party at the Underground nightclub, down near the bottom of the city.

'Is your client ready to talk to me?' I asked.

'I'll be in touch,' was all she said as she took Dominic by the arm and shepherded him away from the gathering media, who'd just been tipped off to the arrest of a well-known Melbourne identity, owner of a five-star hotel, for ...

... something. But what? They had no clue, although the whisper was quickly becoming a loud confirmation that he had attempted to flee the country.

Why? they wondered. Could it be that Dominic Stone – wealthy patriarch of a Toorak family, owner of racehorses, man about town, friend of rock stars and fashion models alike, bon vivant – was somehow involved in crime?

Could it be, wondered the older members of the press, that this had something to do with those unfounded rumours from twenty-five years ago when Dominic Stone briefly made the headlines after it was suggested he'd been involved in the tragic death of a young girl – though whether it had been suicide or a kinky sex game gone wrong, no one knew.

Surely not, not after all this time.

I grabbed the lawyer before she had a chance to walk three steps, alarming her, freaking Stone and catching the attention of the journos.

'Tell your client that if he has commissioned another whack job on my partner, Senior Constable Chastain, he is to abort now. Or else he's a dead man.'

'Are you threatening my client?' barked the lawyer.

'Yes,' I said, staring hard at Stone, 'and I expect thorough and complete cooperation by no later than nine tomorrow morning. The clock's ticking, Stone. You'll be on the news tonight and there are a few angry, powerful police officers who might want you silenced before the sun rises. I'd be staying in the penthouse at your swish hotel. With a crew of bodyguards.'

My phone buzzed with an incoming text message.

It read: *found ruby.*

GOING PUSSY

Night falls swiftly in Melbourne winter. Darkness comes early, soon after 5pm.

Streetlights snapped on, beaming orange tungsten into pools along the wide boulevard of St Kilda Road, its lanes clogged with cars and trams and office workers hurrying home, raincoats and jackets drawn tightly around them. A light rain whistled across the sky, dousing people and leaving the street glistening, the headlights mirroring up from the bluestone surface.

Stolly pulled his car out from the car park below HQ and turned into the grind of traffic. It was Thursday, which meant it was Caffé e Cucina night: drinks, the best calamari in the city and some pasta in a narrow, bustling genuine slice of Italy on Chapel Street in South Yarra, just up from the corner of Toorak. Thursday was his night with Florina, an Italian woman he'd started dating eight months earlier. Unlike Stolly, who'd been single all his life, Florina had recently divorced and had not been searching for another relationship, especially with a Homicide cop, whose work hours were probably the least reliable in the entire spectrum of emergency responders. She was a real estate agent and had a good, independent single life; so did Stolly, or so he'd thought, until he met her and until they had begun a frivolous, easy-to-get-out-of ritual of Thursday night dinners at the Italian down the road from her place.

He had been imagining a time when he would propose to her. He had been waiting for them to ease into familiarity, a culture between them, built over time, over the Thursdays at the cafe and sometimes on weekends.

Tonight, as he was driving towards the restaurant, that was all starting to crumble and he was wondering if indeed he should cancel. But it was frail, their relationship. He was on his toes, his best behaviour, on guard when around her.

He'd been terrified that she would discover the truth of his past. Now he was even more terrified that she would discover the truth of his complicity in the events unfolding at a freakishly rapid pace. The past was easy: you can lie and paper over the past and hope that no-one steps forward to shred the lie. But the now; for fuck's sake, Dominic Stone was on the evening news, and how much longer would it be before Stolly's name was dragged through the dirt?

And what about Monahan? Holy shit: killing Stone? Making it look like a swimming accident? This was spiralling into dangerous chaos. Stolly felt himself going down, sinking into a morass, and it was worse than the old days, when he'd been born into a morass and dragged himself out of it, like an angry kid who pulls himself out of a swamp.

What he had told Florina, the woman he hoped to marry, was this:

I was born into a hard family in Richmond. My father hit me and my mother was never around. I wasn't too good when it came to school attendance. As soon as I could get off the streets, babe, I did. Became a cop. Found a real family. Worked my way up from the bottom, as my dad, God rest his soul into damnation, always said you should.

And she believed him and held his hand, tightly, in the cafe and then, later, led him home to her house, where he stayed the night.

What he had not told Florina, the first woman he had ever met who he thought about beyond a fuck, was this:

I grew up in the hard yards of Richmond, driving stolen Monaros to school without a licence, punching schoolteachers and students if they got in the way, especially on the football field.

221

I played in the reserves team for the Richmond Football Club and drank with my buddies in the pubs along Swan Street, in the few remaining drinking outposts of the white man in what had become, in the late seventies, Little Vietnam after the massive influx of boat people.

I wasn't averse to kicking a few slopes on a Friday night and didn't mind a bit of touch-and-fuck with the slope chicks either. They couldn't speak English and were all scared of cops, because of where they'd come from – they'd never report a crime to the authorities anyway. Great days, Florina.

After I bashed a slope prick nearly to death in one of the laneways near the Foster's Brewery I decided to become a cop. When I got home to my mum and dad's house, a brick worker's cottage in a narrow back street, and went to bed after showering, I took time out to think about life. It seemed to me that I was destined to a life of violence. Footy on the weekends, bashing and fucking during the week. I wasn't a dumb kid and I knew that if I continued this way I'd end up in jail, like a lot of my friends. I wasn't going to become an A-grade footballer, I knew that.

The next morning I walked down to the old station, which looked like a fort, stepped inside and asked the cop on the front desk how I could join up.

Then, nearly thirty years later, I met you.

And now it all seems like it's going to dust. And I've got to fix that.

I've got to talk to Darian Richards and tell him everything. For me. For you. For us, darlin'.

—

THIS HE WOULD have to do quietly, because he had no doubt that Monahan would kill him too.

THE FIX

'Is that you, Nick?'

'It's me, boss. Can I come in?'

The lights of the city at night were spread out in every direction, like a sparkling carpet, nine storeys below Copeland's office. The morning's newspapers, delivered every day, were neatly piled on his desk, as were dozens of files. On the walls hung framed photos giving testament to a long and successful career as a police officer.

'You wanted to see me?' asked Racine as he sat by the Commissioner's desk.

'Are we any closer to finding out who ordered the attack on Senior Constable Chastain?' asked Copeland.

'The assailant is a Vanuatu national who was born in Bolivia. He had some links with the Brunswick mob, back in the nineties.'

'As?'

'As a standover guy. He's been off the radar for at least a decade.'

'Who brought him back?'

'We're not sure, boss, but it's possible the attack was linked to Chastain's partner. A man by the name of Casey Lack.'

'How so?'

'He owned a string of nightclubs and brothels around the city, Fitzroy and Collingwood from the late eighties up until about seven or eight years ago, when he moved, or fled, I heard, to Queensland. He managed the old strip joint that went up in flames about ten years ago; killed all the strippers.'

'Organised by a group of jealous wives? I remember that. Who could forget? He managed that place?'

'Yeah, so we're thinking that with her arriving down here on a high-profile investigation, the attack could have been linked to some payback for the boyfriend's time before he went up north.'

'What a curious choice of partner for that policewoman.'

'She's got a bit of a reputation herself, boss.'

'She has?'

'Her officer in command, Adam Cross – remember him? He used to work down in Frankston. Anyway, he rang and told us not to trust her, that she ...' He paused. 'You don't want to hear this stuff, boss.'

'Keep going, Nick.'

'He told us that she spreads her legs for both criminals and powerful cops. Said she was doing some Homicide guys in Brisbane to try to get ahead, up the ranks, that she's been doing Darian ever since he arrived up there; that she's an ambitious psychopath.'

'Her officer in command said that?'

'Exact words.'

'And what do *you* think, Nick?'

'I think Adam Cross is a lazy, envious, sexist oaf.'

Copeland leaned back and smiled. His thoughts exactly. He noticed that Racine was looking at a framed photo of Jan on his desk.

'You were married, weren't you, Nick?'

'Yes,' Racine said.

'But you got divorced?'

'Yeah. Quite a few years ago now.'

Copeland looked at the photo of Jan. 'She was a wonderful woman, my Jan. The bedrock of my moral code, my greatest supporter. I miss her very much.' He paused for a moment, then said, 'We had a bit of a high-profile arrest this afternoon.'

'Yeah. We did,' said Racine, thinking, *This is why he wanted to see me. Has he spoken to Darian? Does he know that Boris has talked? What does he know?*

Copeland rose from his desk and walked around to take a seat next to him.

'What are your thoughts on that, Nick?'

'From what I've heard, Dominic Stone was at the airport and refused to be questioned by Darian. He was about to board a flight, I believe. Darian felt he had no alternative but to arrest him.'

'But what are *your* thoughts on the matter, Nick?'

'I think …' He proceeded carefully. What he really thought was that the sooner Stone was dead, the better. 'I think Stone was foolish to try to run. If that's what he was doing.'

'Fleeing the country?'

'Yeah. That's what it looks like.'

'Why would he flee? I mean, I understand a person running from the law, trying to evade capture. Hell, you and I have had many a car chase with criminals trying to outrun the sirens and lights. But I would have thought, in this instance, that Darian's investigation into that girl's death was very low-key. Not the sort of thing that a retired businessman looking after his grandkids would hear about.'

Racine shrugged. Best not to give a verbal answer to that one.

'Could he have been tipped off?'

'I couldn't say, boss.'

'Nick, let me ask you a question: where do you think this will all lead?'

He was leaning close to Racine, adopting a kindly pose, like a caring dad.

'I suspect it will lead to a complete and final clearing of my name in relation to the girl's death. An exoneration if you will, boss.'

'Yes, Nick, I know you had nothing to do with that girl's death, but what if there's collateral residue? This was always going to be a possibility, and Dominic Stone's foolish behaviour today makes it all the more possible for that to occur.'

He leaned in ever closer.

'Nick, we're in this situation because you very aggressively lobbied the government, not to mention the union and the men, for the job of Commissioner – and good on you for that, good on you, really – and the Minister then in turn forced me to run an investigation into the past to ensure that your nomination and subsequent announcement would not be sullied: this investigation into Isobel Vine's death. None of us really paid any mind to those rumours about you and the other three police officers working for Dominic Stone. I hear those sorts of rumours, and worse, far worse, about so many police officers, every day; why, look, we've just been discussing such scurrilous rumours about Senior Constable Chastain. But, Nick, I'm wondering if we might find ourselves in a bit of a bind here, now that Dominic Stone has been arrested and maybe he was somehow involved in that poor girl's death. I'm wondering, just between us, if you might want to reconsider your desires. If you might want to rethink your ambition to become Commissioner. If you might want to withdraw your interest, let the government know you've had time to realise the job isn't really for you. No shame, of course. If you were to take that stance, old son, then I'd call off Darian and his investigation, shut it down, as there'd be no need for it to continue, the original reason – your bid – no longer being the instigating factor.'

'Would he shut it down?'

'Darian will do what I say.'

This was not what Racine had expected from the meeting. He had to think fast. The old man was cunning and always about ten steps ahead of you. Nick had learned how to play him – just – but he needed to be pinpoint accurate in his response.

'I didn't harm the girl. And it's the girl's death that Darian is looking into. Or has the brief changed, boss? To include, as you put it, collateral residue? Because, as you say, everyone in the police department has had to put up with scurrilous and unfounded rumours, especially if they get to the position of Assistant Commissioner.'

'The brief hasn't changed, Nick. Darian's job is to determine who, if anyone other than the girl herself, was responsible for Isobel Vine's death. I'm just taking the opportunity to take stock, as it were, of where we are and where we might end up.'

'As I said, as I've always said, I did *not* harm that girl. Her death cannot be a hindrance to my getting the job of Commissioner. Provided, of course, I can still count on the support of you and the police union and the government.'

'Of course you can, Nick. We all want you to take the position. You'll make a fine Commissioner.'

'Then maybe, boss, I could make a suggestion?'

'Fire away.'

'Perhaps Darian needs to stay focused on the actual death. Instead of running off, chasing imagined drug lords.'

'I'll be sure to pass that on, Nick.'

HAILE SELASSIE'S VOLKSWAGEN (iii)

THE HOUSE WAS EMPTY OF FAMILY WHEN HE ARRIVED HOME. Catastrophe was occurring in tiny increments.

First came the phone call from Racine telling him that an investigation into Isobel's death had been ordered by the Commissioner, under instruction from the Attorney-General himself. After all these years. It was so unfair.

And why? Because Racine wanted to be the new Commissioner. Ego and vanity; Dominic had never liked him. Racine even spoke as if he welcomed the investigation. Talk about arrogance and hubris. Said he had nothing to hide and they had nothing to fear; talk about getting it wrong on that one. Now they had everything to fear.

Then came the news that the investigation was being handled by this top gun ex-Homicide investigator, a guy with a solve rate above that of anyone in the country.

Next was his own foolish – yes, he admitted it to himself, it was stupid, but who could blame him? – action in hiring Vasquez from the old days and using his granddaughter's phone to make the call.

Then his granddaughter's discovery that he'd taken her phone and that it, with all its data, had gone. *Lost?* she'd asked. *How?* she'd asked, becoming increasingly angry, then suspicious.

Then Vasquez's bungled attempt on the policewoman. Why was he surrounded by incompetents?

Could it get any worse? Sure it could: Boris the quiet cop went and blabbed.

And yet another late-night visit: go, leave now, was the message. They're getting close and you're best off out of the country. Sure, drop everything and run like a fugitive. What do I tell my wife? My children? What do I say about a sudden long-term visit to the holiday house in Croatia? Missing my youngest daughter's engagement party in a month's time and my wife's string of winter cocktail parties.

His family was furious. No sympathy, nothing. Cared only for themselves. And now that he'd been caught at the airport, handcuffed and arrested, his passport shredded, dragged like a common criminal into court, having to listen to all those allegations about him, his wife and daughters having to endure the phone calls and knocks on the door by the scavenging press, they'd gone. House empty. His wife and family gone. Not even a note.

Here he was, Dominic Stone, alone like a wandering outcast, in an empty home.

Not a phone call of support.

He'd been abandoned.

As he wandered through the empty house, turning on every light in every room in order to give himself the solace of illumination as opposed to the darkness of fear, he remembered the story of Haile Selassie, the last Emperor of Ethiopia, a story he'd read with fascination many years ago. Dominic loved to read about emperors. Haile Selassie's lineage went back to King Solomon and the Queen of Sheba. He was also a victim of incremental catastrophe. Huddled in his vast palace in Addis Ababa, a whirlwind of change and doom ate away at him. Each day another of his ministers would vanish, leaving their master, until there were none left, and then, slowly, day after day, everyone else left, the cooks and the servants and the gardeners, until finally the Emperor was alone, having been totally abandoned, leaving only the Marxist rebels who clamoured at the gates. Until finally the leader of the Marxist rebels had arrived at the palace and said to the Emperor: *It's time*.

He led the great man, who carried within him the blood of the Queen of Sheba and King Solomon, out of the palace to a vehicle that would take him away, out of the city and away from any residual power to which he might have been clutching.

Waiting for him at the base of the steps to the palace was a Volkswagen.

The ultimate humiliation.

'No, please, not that,' said the Emperor, more concerned with appearances than with the fact that he had lost an empire. The Marxist leader shoved him in anyway and they drove him away. A few weeks later he was executed and his body thrown into a ditch.

That was how Dominic Stone felt: a man with nobody, deserted by everybody. Increments of catastrophe.

All because of that stupid girl. Like Haile Selassie, Dominic knew that it was more than desertion. He was squeezed. If he talked to the cop he'd go to jail, he was sure of that. If he didn't talk to the cop, they'd kill him anyway. Those four men, whom he had once ruled, were ruthless and they had a lot to lose. Cops, top cops, going to jail? They'd be dead. So, they would kill him first. His death would bring them silence.

He snapped out of his reverie as he heard the growl of a Harley motorbike on the street outside. The sound reminded him of the times Brian Dunn would pull up and park his bike between the Mercs and BMWs of his neighbours. One of them had complained and Stone had told Dunn to park it in the driveway. The street was a typical quiet tree-lined avenue with old-wealth mansions and Melbourne-club establishment types living their enviable lives behind hedges and metal gates. He'd bought into it soon after his father had died, after he'd inherited all the money and before he'd embarked on the acquisition of a splashier investment portfolio than his father could have ever imagined. He'd held cocktail parties on the lawn in daylight and dinner parties at night, inviting the best from the street and as many influential and important people from the city that he could rub up against. It had worked. Ten years of this and he'd reached the level of society he had craved.

He heard footsteps on the gravel driveway. Instinctively Stone took a step backwards and wished he hadn't turned on all the house lights, advertising his presence.

And then he heard the doorbell ring.

HARD RAIN'S GONNA FALL

CASEY HADN'T TOLD ANY OF US THAT HE WAS COMING DOWN and although Maria seemed less than enthusiastic about his arrival, I couldn't blame him for wanting to reassert himself into her life, even if she was busy in another city on an investigation. He rumbled in at about eleven that night, his Harley's engine audible over the din of cars and trams in the Toorak Road traffic.

'Hey, babe,' he said as he rang the buzzer downstairs, 'your man is here.'

She, Isosceles and I had been whiteboarding the latest information, going over where we were and the plan of attack for the next twenty-four hours. Thanks to Isosceles, we now knew that Ruby, who had reverted back to her original name of Holly, lived in Albert Park, a very high-end suburb by the beach, not far from St Kilda, full of parks and old churches, mopeds and outdoor cafes. Ruby was long dead, apparently. Maria had called her before I returned to the apartment after leaving the Magistrate's court. Holly had answered and said that, yes, she'd happily talk about those years and that specific time, but only between the hours of ten in the morning, when her husband, a city banker, had left for work and after she'd dropped the kids at their private school, and three in the afternoon, when the mum duties resumed. Ruby could only be brought out and discussed in the absence of the family, who knew nothing of her wild and illegal past.

I'd received a text message from Stone's lawyer, who advised me that her client was prepared to talk, at his Toorak home, at nine the following morning. She wanted immunity and protection for her client. I said immunity was out of the question if there was murder involved and I wasn't particularly interested in pressing twenty-five-year-old drug charges, so it all depended on her client's involvement in Isobel's death; as to protection, that was different. Stone was a man in the firing line. Cops had much to lose and he'd be losing it for them.

At the time I didn't know that her client was already dead.

Maria was going to interview Holly about Ruby while I spoke to Dominic at his Toorak house – or that was the plan – then we would pay a visit to Brian Dunn at his exclusive girls' school. Aside from Racine, Pappas and Monahan, Dunn was the last of the most important people for us to interview; the last on our list of possible killers.

Isosceles was getting nowhere with the phone records from twenty-five years ago, just as he was finding it hard to locate any witnesses from the night, including Isobel's then-neighbours and Tyrone's then-neighbours. My forensics guys were still working on the glass and, more promisingly, the paper label on the bottle that had been left behind on the kitchen bench at Isobel's house. They were trying to lift prints and get trace DNA, the latter of which can hold, we'd learned, for twenty to twenty-five years. Forensic science, which Homicide detectives so rely on now and take entirely for granted, is a wonderful thing.

We were eating the last of our takeaway pizzas, baked around the corner at Pinocchio's, an institution dating back to 1971, still made by the same guy for more than forty years, when we heard the sound of the buzzer. Then we heard the sound of a swagger-man, who'd ridden twenty-one hours down the highway to reaffirm the love of his girl.

'Oh shit,' Maria muttered under her breath. 'That's the last thing I need.'

Actually I thought Casey's arrival could be helpful. He'd certainly ensure that she was safe from another night attack and he was always reliable for help and muscle, not to mention street info, if we needed it. If anyone knew the back streets of Melbourne, it was Casey.

—

'YOU SHOULDN'T HAVE come,' said Maria after Darian and Isosceles had left.

'Yeah, I knew you'd say that, which is why I didn't tell you in advance. But, babe, it ain't natural when lovers are not together. I won't get in your way and I can help move shit around if you need help moving shit around, and the other thing is that if anyone comes at you again they have me to deal with.'

'What are you going to do here while I'm at work?' she asked. Which might have been, she realised, a question she could have asked him back home, because he did precious little aside from sitting in his armchair, made out of a seat taken from a 1954 Chevy and grafted onto a solid wooden rocking chair, on their wide verandah, staring out across the valley to the azure waters of the Coral Sea. He owned and ran Casey's Antique and Second-hand Emporium, a place of mystery and treasure, a dumping ground for an increasing amount of junk spread over their acreage that her lover pretended was both valuable and of use.

Before he had a chance to answer, she answered for him. 'Don't you go hanging around strip joints and nightclubs like you did in the old days.'

'Scout's honour, babe,' he said raising two fingers to his forehead in what purported to be a symbol of honesty.

'No illegal gambling in the Greek cafes on the other side of town either.'

'How'd you know about them?'

'You told me, Case. You told me everything about sin-city Melbourne and your sinful life before you met me.'

Everything, that is, except for fucking an under-age stripper named Ruby not long after I was born. A woman I have to meet tomorrow. Which is going to be even weirder now that you are here.

'And no trawling the clubs, strongarming guys for unpaid loans.'

'No strongarming, babe. Promise. I'm just here for you.'

She smiled – yes, he was here for her and that made her feel good – and then she held out her hand, which he took, and led him into the bedroom, turning off the lights.

Outside the wind picked up and a light rain began to fall, sending people leaving the clubs and restaurants scurrying along the footpaths of Toorak Road.

DEAD MAN

OF COURSE I KNEW THAT STONE'S LIFE WAS IN DANGER FROM the moment we hauled his sorry arse out of the Emirates first-class lounge and paraded him in front of the police department, the courts and then the media. As I drove up over the hill, out of South Yarra and down into Toorak the next morning, I imagined Eli watching the TV news the night before, seeing his nemesis brought before the court, wondering if finally Isobel's death was about to be avenged. I imagined the four cops also watching, and I wondered if they had wives or girlfriends, kids maybe, who were vaguely aware of the glimmers of this past, which was, at a rapid speed of knots, catching up with them. Boris we had already seen, but how had Racine, Pappas and Monahan reacted to the news? According to Isosceles, there was dead silence over the airwaves; not a beep from them in the digital telecommunication world. Maybe they'd resorted to pigeons to stay in touch; staying in touch, I knew, was something they would be doing, increasingly.

As I drove through the Toorak village, as it was called, with its cheesy mock Tudor buildings looking like something out of Grimms' fairytales, I received a phone call from Unknown.

'Hello,' I said.

'Darian?'

'This is Darian Richards; who's calling?'

'Stolly.'

He sounded drunk, drained and beaten. I was happy about that. I waited.

'I need to talk.'

'Okay. Good. That's *real* good, Stolly.' Affirmation. Stolly was a jerk and he wanted to off-load something that was going to make me dislike him even more, but it was a game, and my part at that moment was to play the supportive nice guy. 'I'm really pleased to hear that. Where are you, man?'

'At home.'

'Okay. Great. Where's home? Can you give me an address?'

'Yeah. I'm in Duke Street, Windsor, off Chapel.'

'Yeah, I know it, Stolly.' A Vietnamese kid had gone nuts and knifed his entire family in Duke Street, back in the late nineties. Including three kids. The killer, the kid, was upset over some traffic fines that his uncle had refused to pay. A few years later a young woman high on meth had severed the head of an elderly pensioner on his way home from a nearby pub. And a few years after that the Sudanese gangs had decided they had a problem with a house full of uni students and torched them all alive while shooting their AK-47s, wherever the fuck they got them from, into the walls to prohibit any attempt at escape.

'I know Duke Street well. Stolly?'

'Yeah?'

'Are you on duty today?'

'Yeah.'

'Call in sick, hey? I'll be there in a few hours' time, round midday. Stay put and wait for me. Okay?'

'Yeah. Don't go to work.'

'Best not, Stolly. Know what I mean?'

'Yeah. I do. Darian?'

'Yeah?'

'It's fucked.'

'I know,' I said.

'Yeah. That's the thing. I know you do.'

'See you at midday. Stay at home, and, Stolly?'

'Yeah?'

'After this call, turn off your phone and remove the battery, okay?'

'Gotcha.'

'Stay cool.'

'Am.'

—

Stone's house was a two-storey brick mansion, probably built in the nineteenth century, gracious and, unlike many of the other houses in the street, not at all ostentatious. A high brick wall ran along the street, covered in ivy and a circular driveway carved its way under a portico. Sparrows buzzed around the jasmine and magnolia.

I knocked on the door, an ornate number that must have been transported from the rainforests of Indonesia. No answer. I rang the bell, which rang out with a computerised version of Queen's 'Bohemian Rhapsody'.

Nothing.

And then I heard the sound of a car's engine, humming softly. Like a monotonous drone. Coming from the garage.

That's where I found him, attached to a hose, which was attached to the exhaust pipe.

He looked composed. No sign of struggle. No sign of murder. Peace in death.

I called it in and drove very quickly to Duke Street, Windsor. By the time I arrived, Stolly had gone.

RUBY

'How did you find me?' asked Holly.

She'd invited Maria into the house and led her down the airy wooden corridor past three fluffy and sunny bedrooms and into the large open-plan kitchen, dining and living area, large pop-art paintings on the wall in a splash of the sixties. She had made a pot of herbal tea, then opened the sliding glass doors and invited Maria to sit in the sun in the outside courtyard. The back fence was covered in the spray of a tiny white rose creeper. The same as at Isobel's house.

'From a connection in the old days,' said Maria.

She could see Holly narrow her eyes and try to rattle back through the years to make the connection. Holly was in her early forties and looked a stately version of the wild Ruby. Hair that had been pink and blonde twenty-five years ago was platinum now, swept up and tied back to highlight flaming blue eyes and high cheekbones. The rebellion of the mid-eighties had been replaced by a cool poise in the second decade of the new century; she reminded Maria of Grace Kelly, or Beyoncé when she was being a wife and mother as opposed to a music goddess.

Maria, still distracted, as she had been from the moment she laid eyes on this beauty when she opened the front door, stuck to the script. 'You were Isobel Vine's friend?'

'Yes. We went to the same school, but we weren't friends until final year. I thought she was too stuck-up and prim and all Laura Ashley and she thought I was wild and dangerous.'

Holly laughed and pulled out a cigarette, which she lit.

'I was,' she said as she inhaled.

'You called yourself Ruby?'

'Ruby Jazz. Brian gave me that name.'

'Brian?'

'Brian Dunn.'

'Tell me about Dunn.'

Holly leaned back and stared at the sky. Fat clouds were forming across an otherwise-perfect canopy of empty blue. 'At the time he was amazing. He'd put you on the back of his Harley, take you into nightclubs, snort coke with you, drink with you, fuck you. Everything a wild teenage girl expects from her teacher.'

She returned her gaze to Maria. 'Now that I'm a mother I look back on him – and me; what an idiot I was – and think: how did he get away with that stuff? Where were the parents and where were the other teachers? Dunn's a sleazy paedophile who likes to impress then fuck schoolgirls. Have you interviewed him yet?'

'When did you and Isobel become friends?'

'Brian and I were having sex in my final year. I was sixteen – that was the year Ruby was born. I got into coke, a bit of smack, I got into everything. I started stripping and … some other things. As I said, Isobel was freaked by me but then she and Brian got close. This would have been before she went to Bolivia. She started hanging out with him. I think he helped her with the application. In fact, I think it was because of him she was accepted into the exchange program. Anyway, she was suddenly on the scene. Miss Goldilocks in her Laura Ashley was starting to go wild in the spotlight.'

Holly leaned forward and looked at Maria closely.

'It was great back then, but these were dangerous guys that we were hanging around. Crims and crooked cops. We didn't really know it at the time. We loved it, Isobel and me, we were just having fun. But we knew deep down, even though we never said anything, that these guys were heavy. So we, like, hung out together. For support. By the time she went to Bolivia, we were

240

close, and when she came back and things got really heavy we became closer. Sort of.'

'Sort of?'

'She needed someone to talk to who understood the world. But her dad? Forget it. Her boyfriend? Forget it. Most of her other friends: they thought coke was a brown fizzy drink.'

She lit another cigarette. Maria waited.

'So, I could sympathise because I got it. At the same time, these creeps were putting the pressure on me to make sure she didn't talk to the Feds, so it was, like ... I was torn.'

'Which creeps?'

'Stone. Creep number one. Dunn. Creep number two. There were sleazy Italian guys from Lygon Street. All creeps. Then there were the cops that Stone liked to have around. He'd show them off –'

She stopped as if suddenly gripped by a frightening thought.

'Am I going to have to testify? This is just a chat, right? I don't have to go to court and be a witness? Because I won't.'

'Just questions,' replied Maria soothingly and not exactly truthfully. 'Were Isobel and Dunn in a sexual relationship?'

'Yes. She replaced me, which pissed me off at first, but not for long because then I found my man.'

'Mario Brugnano.'

'Best sugar daddy a girl could wish for. He once flew me to Los Angeles just for a shopping weekend. My parents thought I'd gone to Torquay on a school outing.'

'How long were Isobel and Dunn in this relationship?'

'A few months before she left for Bolivia, and then when she got back, that was when they got really close. Like she thought he'd save her and they'd live happily ever after.'

'Was Dunn ever violent?'

'No. The opposite. He was weak. In mind, in spirit, in bed. He made up for it all by riding his Harley.'

'Did Isobel's boyfriend know about Dunn? I mean, the relationship between Dunn and Isobel?'

'Yes.'

'Did you know Tyrone?'

'Yes.'

'Did he ever talk to you about Isobel and Dunn?'

'Yes.'

Maria could feel her heart beating a little tighter. Three terse one-word answers made her feel like she was on a trail and about to reach its end point.

'What did he say?'

Holly stared at Maria. Since the first *yes*, she hadn't moved and had kept her gaze on the policewoman, as if she knew where this was going to lead. 'He said that if he couldn't have Isobel, then no-one would. I asked him what that meant and he said he would kill her unless she stopped seeing Dunn.'

'He was eighteen; did you believe him?'

'I was stoned at the time but I never forgot it. I've forgotten a lot of stuff from the Ruby days but not that.'

'When did he say that?'

'On the night of the party.'

'You went to the party.'

'The cops forced me.'

'How?'

'I was at one of the clubs in the city and Racine came up to me. He said they had to go to Isobel's and talk to her. He said she wasn't listening. He told me I had to go with them.'

'Why?'

'I don't know. Maybe to get them through the door. Maybe they wanted me to talk to her as well. So, we went, all piled into the back of someone's Porsche, and when we got there Racine grabbed Isobel and took her into her bedroom. Later, after we left, he said that he'd given her the last warning. He said that if she talked she would be dead.'

'Did they say anything else?'

'No. They pulled over in Toorak Road and just threw me out of the car, onto the footpath. Pricks. Too late for a tram and there were no taxis. I had to walk home.'

'Did you hear from them again?'

'About two or three weeks later, after Isobel was found dead, Racine called me and told me I had to make a statement.'

'What about?'

'Saying that I took them to the party. That I invited them to my friend's place. That it was my idea, not theirs. That it was innocent and had nothing to do with Isobel and the Feds and Dominic Stone. Up until then I thought it was Tyrone.'

'What do you mean?'

'When I heard that Isobel had died, I thought Tyrone must have done it.'

'What about the possibility of suicide?'

Holly shrugged. 'Maybe. But Isobel was pretty strong. Who knows? A few of my friends had killed themselves and it was a huge shock. But the way Racine was at me to cover for him and the others … it freaked me out. I made the statement. I went to Prahran police station, told the police that it was all my idea, said everything Racine had told me to say and then jumped on a plane and backpacked around Europe for two years.'

'Did the police ever ask you about Tyrone?'

'No.'

'You didn't think to come forward and tell them what he told you that night?'

'No.'

Maria let it pass. This was a fact-finding mission, not a journey into a person's moral and ethical responsibilities.

'Did Tyrone talk to you after Isobel's death?'

'Yes. He rang a few days later. He was distraught.'

'What did he say?'

'He didn't say anything. He just cried.'

2.45AM
12 DECEMBER 1990

'I LOVE YOU. SAY YOU LOVE ME TOO.'

'I do. It's just ...'

'What? It's just Dunn. Isn't it? It's always about him.'

'I'm really tired. Can we talk about this another time?'

The party was over, the guests gone and the dishes cleaned. Isobel and Tyrone were lying on the bed, fully clothed, exhausted, drunk and stoned.

'Do you love him?'

'I don't know.'

Which he took as a yes. 'I'm going to report him.'

'Don't. Tyrone, don't.'

'I don't get it. I mean, he's the one who got you into this nightmare. You think he's going to get you out of it?'

'I don't want to talk about it. I want to go to sleep.'

He leaned up on his elbow, stared down at her. Her eyes were closed. She wanted to sleep. She felt his fingers fumbling at the buttons on her shirt.

He was caught betwixt love and hate. How could that be? How could he both love her and hate her? Maybe there was no such thing; maybe the emotions of love and of hate didn't really exist. Maybe it was just the intensity of feeling for a person. Maybe love was an illusion. Maybe hate was too. Otherwise how could he feel these contrasting feelings?

'No,' she said but he didn't stop. He opened her shirt and lay on top of her, kissing her.

'Tyrone,' she said, which he chose to interpret as an invitation.

I just want to go to sleep, she thought, as her lover and boyfriend from the past – she really did care for him, she had loved him, she sort of still did love him, but not like that, like in the old days, not anymore – reached into the back pocket of his pants, which were now around his ankles, for a condom, which he slipped on.

'You've got to go home and I've got to sleep,' she said as he pressed inside her. She let him, she held him, she didn't say stop; she felt sorry for him, she knew how upset he was about Brian. It was better this way. No yelling and screaming and, hopefully, no carrying out of threats against Brian.

Afterwards he rolled off the bed and left without speaking. As she pulled her pyjamas on, she heard him flush the condom down the toilet and then she thought she heard him cry. She rolled over and hugged the doona up around her, tight.

She heard the front door close softly and maybe she heard the sound of the front gate. As she was drifting off, she tried to close out the horrible parts of the night: Racine here in this bedroom, her fight with Tyrone. She wondered if she should call Brian again and ask him to come over, but after what had just happened with Tyrone she thought it was gross and disrespectful. To Brian. Tomorrow, when she woke up, then she'd call him.

Then she heard what sounded like somebody jumping over the fence in the backyard, landing on the bushes, falling onto the brick pavement.

SEA OF GIRLS

WAS IT SUICIDE? I WONDERED FOR ABOUT TEN SECONDS AS I drove to pick up Maria on our way to interview Dunn. I was in a hurry. Because if it wasn't suicide, there would be no reason not to kill the other guy who knew too much about four crooked cops.

If it was the cops who had killed Stone.

The attending cops and, eventually, the Coroner would rule it a suicide. Stone had just been humiliated publicly; the narrative would be of a man wanting to end it all instead of fighting to clear his name. Naturally the suicide implied guilt. But of what? Nothing specific had been mentioned in the brief court proceeding the previous day; allegations of drug importation might be hinted at but nothing could be proven. When the accused dies, you drop the charges. Stone had evaded justice.

If it was murder, I could be pretty sure that it wasn't Stolly who did it. He must have thought Stone was about to talk to me, but now that Stone was dead he wouldn't give me the time of day, not now that he felt he was back in a safe world. All we had now was Boris's statement – and they'd do a job on him, discredit him, set him up as corrupt, destroy him.

And Dunn.

If Racine and the other three were involved in Isobel's death I needed to prove a clean line of motivation, and Dunn was our best shot. On the other hand, Dunn was looking all right as the killer himself; he had as much to lose as Stone and the cops.

—

MARIA KNEW.

In her heart. Straightaway. As soon as Darian told her about Stone.

Casey had killed him.

Any man touches my girl, he is dead – that's what he would have thought as soon as he heard about the attack on her. Ride down to Melbourne to exact revenge and then stay close and protect her. That's how her man's mind operated. His network of informants in Melbourne was as strong and potent as Isosceles' skill at extracting information from the cloud.

Casey, killer.

She'd always feared that his criminal life would intersect with her life as a cop and now here it was. Murder.

She stared out the window at the passing serenity of the oaks and elms on either side of the street.

—

ST JOSEPHINE'S SCHOOL IS one of the more exclusive all-girls schools in Melbourne, nestled down a hill at the bottom of a tree-lined avenue in Toorak, surrounded by mansions with lawns, willows, magnolias and oaks, rose gardens and hedges; cars whisper as they drive along these streets. Sounds are absorbed by the layers of garden and protective fences, and inside, by layers of rooms: entrance halls and drawing rooms and dining rooms and sunrooms. Stone lived up around the corner, a few streets away. It's an expensive world in the avenues that flow from Toorak Road down to the river.

We drove past a mansion done in a gaudy *Gone with the Wind* architectural style that was popular with the new rich as they moved into the suburb back in the eighties and nineties, a two-storey monster where, in 2008, I'd attended a home invasion gone wrong that had ended in murder. Two adults and three kids had been killed by a methed-up freak with a machete and angry voices in his head. I didn't bother telling Maria, not because she'd overdosed on my dark trips down memory lane as we drove around Melbourne but because she had another murder, close to home, on her mind. After spending ten seconds wondering if Stone had killed himself, considering his arrogance and vanity, and wondering then if our crooked cops were responsible, I had reached, by about the eleventh second, the conclusion that Casey was the guy. I could see that Maria had also figured that out.

Where this was going to take us, I wasn't sure.

———

I HAD EXPECTED to have to search for Dunn, braving countless gatekeepers and secretaries on our unscheduled visit to one of the most exclusive girls schools in the city, but there he was, surrounded by a sea of teenage girls, in an open quadrangle, holding court like a prince. We angled our way towards him.

The guy was sharp. He saw us coming, squinted a little and I could feel the wheels turning in his mind as he continued his chatter with about ten girls, all aged around fifteen or sixteen.

As we grew closer he peeled his way out of the circle of girls and walked towards us. He was about fifty but he held it well with a full head of wavy blond hair and a genuine suntan, a taut chest, shoulders alert and head straight, long strides and a big smile. I hated the guy on sight. Way too handsome. But I would have hated him anyway, regardless of his good looks.

'Hello. Can I help you?' he asked.

'Brian Dunn?' asked Maria.

'Are you Mr and Mrs Preece? Have you come to talk about Michaela?'

'No, that wouldn't be us,' I said with a smile to equal his. 'We're police officers, and we've come to talk about your role in the death of Isobel Vine.'

He didn't miss a beat. 'Sure. But now is not an appropriate time. Okay?'

He turned and began to walk off, clearly thinking he could get away with it.

'Hey!' called out Maria, who since last week had been ready to eviscerate him.

He stopped walking.

'I had nothing to do with Isobel's death,' he said, turning back.

'Mr Dunn!' We all turned to see a girl running towards him from one of the old brick buildings.

'Vicki ...'

'Mr Dunn, you told me you were going to show me that scene at lunchtime. You know, that scene from *Citizen Kane*, that old movie you said was awesome.'

'Oh yeah, sorry, Vick, let's go.'

And, to our amazement, he began to walk off with her. To show her a scene from Orson Welles' *Citizen Kane* during lunchbreak, because that's what cool teachers like him do.

Maria turned to me with an *Is this guy for real?* look on her face.

Maybe he imagined that in this city of girls he was inoculated with fairy dust. I reached out to him and held him back.

'Vicki,' I said, 'you're not going to be watching a movie with Mr Dunn today. Catch it another time.'

There was a momentary stand-off as Dunn defiantly stared at me and Vicki looked completely confused, before Maria grabbed him by the other arm.

'We're doing this now,' she said.

'Mr Dunn?' asked the girl, worried.

'You can't do this,' he hissed at us. 'I am at work. This is outrageous.'

'Brian?' called another voice.

What now? I thought. The leader of the harem?

Maria and I turned to see a middle-aged woman approaching us. Behind her was a posse of girls, apparently incensed that their

Mr Dunn was being manhandled in the school grounds by two strangers.

'Who are you?' the woman demanded.

'We're police officers,' I said.

'You don't look like police officers,' she said, reminding me of all the horrid headmasters and headmistresses I'd encountered as a kid. 'What are you doing with Mr Dunn?'

'We're going to ask him a few questions,' said Maria.

'Gloria, I don't know what this is about,' said Dunn. 'It's ridiculous.'

The gang of girls were surrounding the woman called Gloria, and for a moment I thought that if this were a black-and-white B-grade movie, Maria and I might be attacked and chained up in a dungeon for insulting the good virtue of sweet Mr Dunn.

'I think you should leave,' Gloria said to us.

Maria stepped forward, pulling out her badge. 'I'm a police officer. He's a police officer too, and we're arresting this man.'

The girls all gasped.

'For what?' screeched Dunn.

'Sex with a minor, for a start. There will be numerous charges.'

Gloria took a step back, as if suddenly aware that the world of her school had just changed forever, and not in a way that would reflect well on it or her. Dunn slumped a little and the posse looked horrified, although I swear to God some of the girls gave him a *I knew you were a sleazy perv* look.

THE SILENCE

'WHOA, WHERE ARE YOU TAKING ME?' ASKED A PANICKED DUNN from the back seat as I turned off Toorak Road into Osborne Street.

We didn't answer him as I drove up the street and pulled up outside Isobel's house.

'Remember this house?' asked Maria.

He didn't answer.

'When was the last time you were here?' I asked.

He was staring at the front gate and the little house beyond. I climbed out of the car, opened the back door and said, 'Get out.'

He was like a man walking towards a firing squad but he did as he was told. We led him inside.

A sharp beam of sunlight razored through the side windows of the lounge room. A million particles of dust were illuminated, buzzing about the room like stars in the cosmos. The house was still and otherwise dark, full of the smell of faraway mould. Cobwebs hung from the corners of the walls and from the ceiling.

'Sit down,' I said to Dunn, who still hadn't said a word.

He sat on the lounge, clasped his hands and stared at me, then at Maria, then back at me. We were standing above him.

'Why have you brought me here?' he asked.

'Let's start with some basic facts, Brian,' I said. 'Some basic truths that we can all agree on.'

'Like?' he asked.

'Fact one: you were Isobel Vine's teacher?'

'Yes.'

'Fact two: you helped arrange her trip to Bolivia under an official schools program.'

'Correct.'

'Fact three: while she was in Bolivia, you made contact with her a number of times.'

He hesitated for a moment and then agreed. 'Yes.'

'Fact four: during one of those times you asked her to bring a small amount of cocaine back into the country.'

'Okay. I get it now,' he said, in what appeared to be a sudden rush of relief and confidence. 'That whole arresting-me-for-under-age-sex thing at my workplace was just a ploy to threaten me. And I didn't sleep with her anyway. Not until she was over eighteen. I didn't. You guys are the Drug Squad, aren't you? You sure look like Drug Squad. And you want me to rat on Dominic Stone. That's why we're here and not in some police station where I'm being formally charged. Hey, that under-age thing? That's an allegation, okay. We've got to fix that with the school. You want me to talk about Stone and his drugs? Fine, on the condition there's something in writing that rescinds the under-age-sex allegation. Okay?'

'Fact four: you spoke to Isobel while she was in Bolivia and you asked her to bring back some cocaine. Correct?'

'Maybe I need a lawyer,' he said, confidence and relief gone.

'Forget it. That's not happening. You asked Isobel to bring back some cocaine, right?'

'Who the fuck are you guys? Are you even cops? Show me your badges.'

'Yes, we are cops and we're investigating Isobel's death,' said Maria.

'You're a bit late. The Coroner already did that over twenty years ago. Read his report.'

Maria kneeled down and stared at him, eye to eye. 'We *will* charge you with under-age sex, and we have proof of that, maybe not with Isobel, but with another girl, if you don't stop being a smart-arse and start cooperating.'

'Okay. Got it. Loud and clear. I'm cooperating. Isobel's death.'

He then pulled out his mobile phone and began texting.

'What are you doing?' asked Maria.

'Oh, sorry. Won't be a sec. Just texting Gloria at the school to tell her that the under-age thing was a mistake and not to worry.'

I hated this guy. Maria reached out and swiped the phone from his hands. 'Stay with the moment,' she said lethally.

'Sure,' he said, leaning back into the couch. Turning to me he said, 'I was passing on a message. To Isobel, about the coke. I was the facilitator of the communication.'

'To bring it into the country.'

'Correct.'

'Fact five: you were, at the time of Isobel's death, a friend of Dominic Stone.'

'I was.'

'And it was Stone who asked you to, as you just put it, facilitate the importation of the coke.'

'Yeah. It was some new dealer he had made contact with. He wanted Isobel to bring back a small amount, to test its quality.'

'Okay. We're almost done with the fact checks, then we're going to ask you some questions and you're going to tell us everything you know.'

'It'd be really good if I could just text Gloria at the school.'

'No,' said Maria.

He gave her a look I interpreted as saying, *You're hot and I'd love to see you naked but you're scary and I can tell you hate me, so I'm going to pretend you don't exist.*

'Fact six: you and Isobel were having sexual relations at the time of her death.'

'Look, you'd remember,' he said, pointing at me, 'at the time, back then, it wasn't a big deal. As far as I was concerned, Isobel was an adult, and you know, I think she was eighteen – she *was* eighteen – when we started going out anyway. It was a consensual relationship. We were very close. She looked up to me.'

If he was expecting any trace of sympathy or understanding from us, he didn't get it.

'She called you her boyfriend.'

'Yeah, maybe, I dunno. She just called me Brian. I dunno what she called me to her friends.'

'Where were you on the night of her death?'

'At my apartment. I live in Beverley Hills, down near the river.'

Anyone in Melbourne who tells you they live in the Beverley Hills apartment blocks – two rambling towers of Art Deco flats, huge, ancient and expensive, overlooking a small park and a tree-lined section of the Yarra River – is showing off, because the address has had an uber-cool cachet with the hip and beautiful since the seventies.

'Was anyone with you? Who can confirm that you were there?'

'No. I was alone. I think I was doing some marking. I can't remember.'

'Did Isobel call you that night?'

'No.'

He fidgeted. It's all in the body language.

'We've got your phone records,' I lied.

'Yeah, okay, so she called me. After some guys had crashed her party.'

'What guys? Who were they?' I'd taken a gamble with the lie about the phone records and the question about calling Isobel. It wasn't great policing. We knew that Isobel had said she would call him, after Tyrone, the boyfriend, had left, but we had no idea if she had. Like lawyers, police don't like asking questions they don't know the answer to but, like lawyers and everyone else on the planet, sometimes you just have to leap off the cliff like a crazy blind guy, hold your breath and hope for the best and not a blowback.

'I don't know. She didn't say.'

'What did they want, these guys? Why did they crash her party?'

'I don't know. She didn't say.'

'Then why did she call you about it? About them?'

'I don't know.'

'Brian,' I said, 'I've had a lot of experience with people who think that by staying silent they're doing themselves a favour, that by not talking, especially about others, they are protecting themselves. It's the theory that silence buys loyalty, that staying silent means you're safe. In fact it's the exact opposite. People like me, and I've been a cop for decades, understand this. People like you, who listen to hollow threats from scared guys and who watch too much TV and come to think that the world of fiction might be real, don't understand it. But it's simple. You're a teacher. It's a bit like two plus two equals four. Silence is dangerous. Silence will get you killed. Because, you see, the people who want you to remain silent, the people you're protecting by not answering our questions, know that, eventually, you'll talk. Everyone talks. They know that. I know that. Maria knows that, and you know it too. So, the longer you maintain the silence, the greater the threat you are to them and the faster they'll make the decision to ensure your silence forever. For them it's insurance. Good business. Therefore, paradoxically, the second you begin to speak and break the silence, you're safe. No point in taking out a guy to ensure his silence if he's already talked. Sure, there's the issue of payback and revenge; I'm sure that's going through your mind, but let me assure you, Brian: these guys who you think deserve your silence, they can't make a move against you the second you speak. It's too public. They're on the radar, being watched; every move they make, people like me and Maria are watching. And really, the other thing: only Italian mobsters and bikies do the revenge thing. Revenge is only an issue when you've got generations of crime, in the past and into the future. Speak to us, Brian. And then you'll be safe. Stay silent, you're a dead man.'

He stared at me, goggle-eyed, as if I'd thrust him into an online game of *The Godfather* and he was the shooting target.

'I don't know if you caught the news on TV last night, but Dominic Stone was arrested yesterday. By us. We didn't get to talk to him, but we had it lined up for this morning. Nine o'clock at his house in Toorak. He was murdered last night before we got to speak with him.'

I could see Maria glancing at me, realising I had reached the same conclusion about Stone as she had.

'See? That's what silence will do to you,' I told Dunn.

He exhaled very slowly, took in a deep breath and began to nod, as if trying to reassure himself. Then, after a few moments, he smiled as if we were secret buddies. He reminded me of a tennis coach you might see in Los Angeles or on an episode of *The Love Boat.*

'Got it.' He looked up to Maria and nodded seriously. 'Got it,' he said to her as well.

'Fact seven: the guys who Isobel called you about were cops.'

'Yeah.'

'And their names?'

'Pappas, Monahan, some creep called Boris, can't remember his surname, and Racine. Nick Racine.'

'Let's go back to that conversation, on that night. What did she say?'

'Yeah, they'd barged into her place. That was their thing. Being all high and mighty and throwing their weight around, especially Racine. Dom … Stone was hassling the fuck out of them to silence Izzy. It was dreadful. I mean, I felt so terrible for her. I was the one who Stone had forced to call her. It was my fault she was in this horrible, horrible bind. I did what I could. Really.' He was staring at Maria like she was about to hand out some absolution. 'I told her to call me anytime, if they were scaring her. I told Stone too. I said, "Just stop, will you? Isobel won't talk. She won't spill to the Feds."'

He turned to me.

'That thing you just said to me, about the danger of silence? So true, man. As you were talking to me, just then, I was thinking back to Izzy. But what could she have done? Talk to the Feds?

Then what? I mean, Stone was just a fucked-up wealthy Toorak guy who decided it'd be fun to import cocaine. He wasn't the mob, he wasn't born into that world; for him it was like buying art. This week I'm into modern African paintings. Next week I'm into rare Argentinian wine, week after that it's a nightclub I'll buy or maybe I'll become a movie investor or how about we all go wild and become drug runners? He was a prick. I'm glad he's dead. He had her killed. I'm sure of that.'

He rolled back in the couch and closed his eyes.

'Look,' he said after a moment, 'there's something I've got to tell you.'

We waited.

'I'm feeling good about this,' he said. 'It's cleansing.'

'Uh huh,' said Maria. He didn't notice the attitude. We both let him ramble.

'After Isobel called me – I don't know what time it was, but it was late – I got another call.'

He sucked in some breath, like he was doing yoga, all lotus-and-exhale-with-focus intent. The cleansing thing.

'From Stone. This one, it was late. I was in bed. I was asleep. Dom … Stone called and he told me that the guys, the four cops, had gone to see her, which of course I knew because Iz had already called me about them, and he told me I had to go see her.'

'Why?' I asked.

'To tell her not to talk.'

'But they'd already done that.'

'Yeeeaaahhh … but he, like, wanted it to be reiterated.'

Fidgeting again. He was telling us the truth and also lying. I could pursue that now or let him complete the story and go back at him.

'Did you go? See her?' asked Maria, solving the issue of which way to press the questions with him. Usually I hate it when a colleague intrudes on my line of thinking in an interrogation and especially when I'm mulling over a direction to pursue. But in this case I didn't. Maria and I were very much in tune on this one, for the first time, and I was happy to let her step in and take the lead when normally I'd be angry. The reason Stone had asked Dunn to go see Isobel, so late, and after the cops had already seen her, wasn't to reiterate what they'd just said, and I knew. He had a more sinister reason ...

Let him speak.

'Yeah. I did.' He spoke slowly, anxiety now creeping into his voice. 'I drove over to see her. I got to her house at about three, maybe later. Maybe four. It was still dark.'

'And?' asked Maria.

'I came in. I had a set of keys. I walked in through the front door. There.' He indicated the door behind him. Twenty-five years ago he had stepped into the room we were now in.

'And I called out –'

—

'HEY! BABE? HELLO!' he called as he stepped inside. The house stank of beer and wine and smoke, from ciggies and weed. As he closed the door behind him, gently, he noticed that Izzy, as he had begun to call her, had cleaned up. All the dishes done. Everything packed away, stacked by the sink. But for a bottle of bourbon and an empty glass.

'Iz? Izzy?'

Nothing. Everything was still. Outside there was a hard and cold wind buffeting the sides of the wooden house and the tin roof. Rain had begun to fall.

—

'I WALKED DOWN the hallway.'

He walked down the hallway.

'I called out her name again.'

'Iz! Izzy! Babe, you here?'

He reached the door to her bedroom.

'It was closed, and that was a bit odd because she never closed her door. Isobel was a little claustrophobic.'

He turned the knob and started to open the door.

'But it wouldn't open properly.'

So, he pushed.

'So, I pushed.'

And as the door gave way to his force and as he began to enter the room, seeing that it was empty, he realised the door was too heavy, that something was dragging it.

'Like there was a weight hanging on it. I just pulled it back shut as I stepped into the room – and there she was.'

Isobel was hanging on the back of the door. Her hair, her bob, was slung over her face, her head had fallen forward onto her neck and her entire body was slumped, her arms hanging, dangling. Around her neck and then looped up through the solid metal hook on the back of the door was a man's tie. A long red welt was beginning to form on her skin where the tie cut into her.

—

THIS WAS A girl whose body he had dreamed of, as a teacher, as she walked into his classroom, a girl he had lusted over and seduced, a girl whose body he had finally conquered, had smothered and licked, whose very core he had penetrated and, as he came within her, had again and again conquered and with each vanquish she became a girl he had fallen in love with, deeper and deeper, for vanquishing was what he wanted, needed, had. This body, dangling like a puppet, was his body.

He wept; he told us he wept.

'Was there any sign of a break-in?' I asked.

'Not really. I can't remember. I just left, after I saw her.'

'What time was this?' asked Maria, businesslike.

'I don't know. Before dawn.'

'That's the bottle of bourbon,' I said, indicating the empty bottle that sat on the bar between the kitchen and lounge room.

It actually wasn't. Both the bottle and the glass that Maria had found when we first walked into Isobel's house had been carefully secured and sent for DNA and fingerprint testing. We had replaced them with a recently purchased bottle and a glass from Isobel's cupboard, to preserve the crime scene as it looked back then. The fingerprinting and DNA testing were proving challenging: the DNA trace, from a person's lips as they drank, was extremely hard to find.

'Has this place been locked up since that night? Whoa. That is freaky. That'd be her old man, right?'

'You didn't drink from it? You didn't open it? It was there when you arrived?'

'Yeah. I remember being a little worried, when I walked in, when I saw it.'

'Why?'

'Bourbon was what her boyfriend drank. I thought he might have been in here … which was why I was so careful walking down to her room.'

'How do you know he drank bourbon?' asked Maria.

'Isobel told me.'

'And why was it that Stone had asked you to go to see her?' she asked.

'He just did.'

'Yeah, but why?'

'He was freaking out.'

'Which is why he sent four cops to heavy her. But after that, after they'd come here to heavy her, he called *you*. He asked you to come over and see her. At, what, four in the morning? Why? What was it that you could do that the cops couldn't?'

He shifted his weight from one side to the other and his hands went into a whirlwind of preparatory explanation without words and he smiled and looked savaged, all at once. I knew the answer and so too did Maria.

'You were told to kill her,' said Maria calmly.

'She was dead when I got here,' he said by way of defence.

'I think that might be bullshit, Brian,' she said, still calm. When you get closer to the truth, you slow down and concentrate. 'I think you got here, at three-thirty or four, and you killed her, strung her up on the door, like a girl who had to be vanquished, and smothered her. Maybe you fucked her as well. Maybe you told her she was your Venus, your lover, your muse, or maybe you just stuffed a pillow into her face and strung her up on the door and watched her die, then had a quick shot of bourbon and let yourself out into the night. Is that right, Brian?'

'No. I did not kill her. I loved her.' He stared at Maria. 'I know you think I'm a sleaze, going out with a girl her age, but it was special, what we had between us.'

Maria didn't respond.

'I'm telling you the truth. Give me a lie-detector test. I don't care. I had nothing to do with her death.'

'Let's go down to her bedroom,' I said.

CLEAR HISTORY

Nick's fiftieth birthday had come and gone without a whisper, a card, a phone call, without any form of notice – and that was just how he wanted it. His ex-wife, wherever she was, dead or alive, he didn't know and he didn't care, would be going into tailspins of anxiety and depression about turning another year older. Like so many, she saw a birthday as a time of failure, a time of regret. Others saw it as a time of celebration. Nick saw it as a time to ignore. His ex-wife's name was Amanda and they had lasted three years, more than twenty years ago. She had trouble with his devotion to the job and he chose to discard her like roadkill on the highway. The only reason he married her was because he was in lust with her. That firebrand passion lasted a few months after the wedding, then, like everything now with Nick, it was replaced by the job. He loved the job. He didn't love her. He loved arriving at work in uniform. He dreaded arriving home, but one night, close to the time he was about to turn thirty and soon after she just had, he walked through the door and told her it was over. Pack your stuff and I'll drive you to your parents. I'll give you the car and all that we have in the bank but I keep the house. He loved the house far more than he loved her.

But that was Nick. A guy who could adore an inanimate object more than he could a person. His dad had been an addict and his mum had been worse. They had both abrogated any attempt at parenting well before he was born and didn't bother to even consider that a kid needed some form of looking after, let alone that idea called love, which had, Nick knew but still could not forgive them for, eluded them.

After disposing of a frozen and stunned Amanda and never seeing her again, Nick had returned to his Edwardian red-brick house in Chaucer Street, St Kilda, a wide street just one block away from the beach and across the road from a park through which he could see the rides at Luna Park, an ancient funfair built sometime in the late nineteenth century with a roller-coaster that ran along a rickety white wooden structure that rose above the walls and from which the screeching patrons could see the flat waters of the bay. Soon afterwards he bought a bird and put it in a cage. It wasn't a talking bird. It never spoke and Nick never spoke to it. He would stare at it and wonder how long it would take to crush its heart. Over the years, still living in the same house, as the screams of kids on the roller-coaster carried across the park with the wind, Nick replaced many birds. He never gave them a name, never spoke to them, only fed and stared at them. He wondered if they were afraid of him.

Most people were, and he liked that. Fear bred loyalty as much as kindness, compassion and consideration. The latter traits did not come easily to Nick but he understood their value. As the man about to inherit the mantle of top police officer to almost six million people, he had worked hard to stay fit, alert, in tune with the many people around him, to listen and respond to their concerns not only with the appropriate emotion but with an action plan.

Nick, who had raged through a childhood of neglect and anger, who realised early that there was nothing and that everything was fucked, who bit and tore at anyone close to him, who partied with coke and weed and booze and smokes and sex and speed, had, like Jekyll, adopted the cloak of respectability and goodness, letting his Hyde recede into the mists of darkness as the dawn approached, as the cop returned. At about the age of thirty, maybe when he tossed Amanda out onto the scrap heap of uselessness, he had decided with a firm steel-trap determination to cleanse himself, erase the past, get fit, get healthy, get focused, get ambitious, to forget and put behind him the whiners and the partygoers, the cokeheads and crackers, the pops and spags, the whores and hangers-on, the low-lifes and the Toorak-riders of glitz and boredom, of mansions, girls and Portsea parties, the aimless, the no-hopers, the vacuous, the snazzies and fuck bombs, the boys at the track and the girls in the shadows, the smiles of danger and the thump-thump of disco on the dance floor at two in the morning, the neon of nothing, seen through a fucked-up haze from the back seat of somebody else's car in the streets of South Yarra or the sex-end of the city, down by the river.

Click. Delete. Clear history. I'm a new man now.

The text came in at 3.13am. He was awake. He was waiting for confirmation of death and he got it, only in a way he hadn't anticipated: *stone already dead looks like suicide*

Nick stared at the phone's screen, then removed the back, the battery and then broke the phone into two and walked across the park, where, in the distance, he could see the Kublai Khan minarets of Luna Park illuminated by strings of fairy lights, buffeted by the winds off Port Phillip Bay, less than a hundred metres away. Hookers trawled the park even at three-thirty in the morning in the depths of winter, their tight short skirts ridiculous as they swung at him with offers of blow jobs, leering out from behind the trees.

He killed himself? wondered Nick. Really? The world's greatest egotist? He decided to snuff it out?

It seemed unlikely, but frankly Nick was just mightily relieved that Stone was a dead man. Dead men don't speak. They hold the silence; another life – click, delete, clear history – was gone.

He threw the cheapo phone into a bin. He could hear the sounds of the water rolling onto the sand, down at the bay. It was enclosed, safe, not like the wilds of the dark surf at Portsea where, twenty-five years ago, the other Nick – click, delete, clear history – had spun out like a whirling dervish on the acidic bursts of sex and drugs. That Nick was gone. This Nick was ascetic. This Nick took cold showers every morning. This Nick stared at caged birds without speaking. This Nick never succumbed to emotion. Or feelings. Feelings were dangerous, even though, as the Man Who Would Be King, the man to serve six million men, women and children, feelings were necessary. They needed to be appropriated.

This Nick didn't go to the movies very much, but he had seen Alain Delon in *Le Samouraï*, a 1967 movie about a hit man who didn't speak, who had no emotion, who lived underground in Paris with a caged bird. That was Nick. That was his appropriation. A fictional hit man in a sixties movie in which nihilism and existentialism – I am and there is nothing else – fused with killing people.

As he walked back towards his house, the large red-brick home built more than a hundred years ago, with a garden of rose and daphne, a woman appeared from behind one of the massive trees.

'Hey,' she said.

She was in her twenties or thirties; it was hard to tell. Still, she was lithe and her breasts were large and firm beneath a thick woollen top, her legs were thin and fully revealed, long sexy stalks covered in black silk sheen, and her hair was alarmingly blonde and her teeth were wide and her lips were red and she looked as though she could do with a sleep or a bath and she was pretty, or so it seemed to Nick, who only had sex with hookers but never with hookers from the street or a park, only the escorts from a website at no less than $500 an hour.

'I'm lonely,' she said.

Normally Nick would have kept walking, but this morning, with the great and wonderful relief that Stone was dead, he was feeling buoyant. The last time he'd had a fuck was ten weeks ago when he smashed down a Vietnamese hooker who might have been eighteen in a South Melbourne brothel. Fucked her every which way and choked her as well. Tight. The bitch started freaking out but it was all good. He let go of her throat before she went blue, while she could still understand his words.

Say a fucking word, bitch, and you are dead.

And of course she didn't. She was pliant and stayed quiet and she pretended to have the orgasm of the century and she told the man crouched above her, like a praying mantis with his dick inside her, that he was her master, her hero, her saviour, the man she had been begging for. And, to her great relief, as she slid from underneath him, he believed her.

'I'm lonely,' said the woman under the tree.

Yeah, thought Nick, in a weird sudden rush, me too.

Maybe it was the intensity of the past few days, Darian and Maria edging their way closer and closer to him, to the truth of the past, as the future – the crown – began to shimmer like a precarious rainbow's end. Was he losing control? He wasn't sure. At times, like now, he felt as though he needed to steady himself. He kept seeing himself falling. There was a hole beneath him. It had always been there, but he always stepped over it, easily. Not so now. Now he was having to keep looking down as he walked, lest he fall, deep into the earth. He looked at the girl, the hooker from under the tree, and once again he felt uncertain, as if he might tumble. She reached out for him and steadied him. 'You okay?' she asked. He didn't answer.

'You live just over there, don't you? I saw you come out. I'll take you home.'

And he let her, something he would, normally, never do. But the days of normal had gone. They had fallen into a hole in the ground.

—

'STOLL, I HEARD YOU called in sick this morning.'

'Yeah, Nick, felt like shit.'

'That's no good.'

'Feeling better now.'

'That's not like you, is it, Stoll?'

'What do you mean, Nick?'

'You. Being sick. I checked, old buddy: you've been sick, or, better put, you've called in sick, once in thirty years, which is a pretty impressive record. So, when I heard you called in sick this morning I was rather shocked. Taken aback, you might say.'

They were walking – Nick, Stolly and Monahan – along the St Kilda foreshore, where the bay enticed gentle waves, where seagulls hovered like vermin, where people huddled in their coats as they were buffeted by the cold wind.

It was safe. No-one could hear them.

'Yeah, as I said, just a glitch. Better now.'

'A glitch? Mate, a *glitch*?'

'Yeah, Nick. Yeah. So, who killed Stone, or did he do it to himself?'

'Stoll?'

'Yeah, Nick?'

'I'm a little worried.'

They stopped walking. Monahan stared out across the bay, at the low point where the grey sky meshed with the grey water, a point where there was a line of vague connection. He appeared disengaged. Stolly said nothing but flexed his biceps, as he always did when about to be attacked.

'I think you might be a weak link here, mate. What do you think about that?' asked Nick.

—

NICK WAS USUALLY laser-focused. But he couldn't help but return his mind to the woman from behind the tree, in the park, before dawn, the hooker who said she was lonely. He'd taken her back to his house. He had, in fact, taken her hand, warm and soft, and she led him across the icy grass to his home, in through the front door and into his bedroom. He was fully aware that he was about to become the next Commissioner of Police, fully aware that any misstep or scandal would ruin him before he was anointed.

He was soft with her and he asked her name.

Bree, she'd said.

'I'm Nick.'

'Hi, Nick.'

How had Stone died, he'd wondered as he'd crawled across Bree, as he thought about the past, the future. And what of his colleagues? Pappas and Monahan? Could he trust them?

—

'NICK, THERE IS no way. Mate, there is no way. I am solid. Believe me.'

Racine didn't need to look at Monahan, who'd been the one to suggest they couldn't trust Stolly, to get a sense of where he stood on that response ...

Stoll's lying.

'Come 'ere,' said Racine, arms outstretched to Stolly, smile on his face. We're all in this together, the famous five, the secret seven, pals, come 'ere.

—

BREE FOLDED INTO darkness. She reached out and took his hand. He didn't speak.

'Come here,' she said in the night.

Why am I lonely? he asked himself, as he came to her, as he let her enfold him, as he allowed himself to be taken into her body, as he allowed himself to breathe out slowly in the night. Somewhere not so far away waves rolled onto the beach, kids screamed on the rides of Luna Park, and couples sat and danced in the cafes and clubs of St Kilda, along Acland Street and beyond, where, somewhere, an addict lay in a grave and another had burned, where words of love from these chimeras had been lost, in the wind maybe, in the wind that rattled through the trees of the park across the road from his house, the house in which he had sat with a woman whom he had loved, briefly, as a wife, whom he had then thrown out in anger, the house in which he had adopted a life of hard steel, in which every morning he woke to remind himself: I am to become the most powerful man in the state, in which he had, this morning, woken to find the girl called Bree sprawled naked in his bed and he had stared at her and thought: what have I done and do I throw her out now or do I cook her breakfast?

And what did he do? The man who would be king? He bent to her and stroked strands of her hair from her forehead and he remembered her warmth and he said: 'Hey.'

She roused.

And he said: 'I've got to go to work.'

And she said: 'What time is it?'

He said: 'It's six.'

And he wavered, this samurai, he wavered, unsure of what to do and how to act.

'Should I go?' she asked.

No. Stay. She wants money, she's a hooker, but ...

Stay.

He stared at her. Hard.

'Well, hey, look ...' he said hopelessly, for the rarest of moments adrift.

Bree needed a place to stay. She unfurled herself, all breasts and thighs, out of the doona, and reached up to him. Slow. Careful. Don't push it, she thought.

'I can be here for you. When you get home. But don't let a dumb girl like me get in the way.'

All breasts and thighs, out of the doona, hair tousled, all emotion and loss, as he said: 'Great.'

'Great.'

'I'll be home at six-ish.'

'Really? Awesome.'

As he disentangled himself from her, as he left, he thought: How stupid am I? I leave my house to a hooker? Because of some lost lust?

He turned around, went back into the bedroom. Bree was back under the doona, looking for another few hours of nothing.

'You know who I am?' he asked.

'No,' she said.

'I am a bad guy. Do not fuck with me.'

She held the look and got the message. Then he leaned down and kissed her cheek. 'You tell no-one about me. You tell no-one anything. You're in a cocoon. Okay?'

A shiver of fear, not for the first time, from him, quivers through her.

'Yeah, sure, of course. See you tonight.'

—

'I WANT YOU to go away, Stoll. Maybe everything is cool and maybe I'm being paranoid, but I want you out of town. Get on the next plane. Go far away. Go to Bali, Bangkok, go to Zanzibar, just go, and after all this is over, after I'm Commissioner, then you can come back. Indulge me.'

'Nick, I can't. I'm on two homicides; Reeve will never let me go. We're understaffed already.'

Racine turned to Monahan, who was still staring at the waters of the bay, like a kid bearing down on an insect he was about to dissect.

'Jake?'

Monahan turned around. 'Family tragedy, Stoll. Compassionate leave. Your dad dies. Brain tumour. Just like poor old Doc Neeson. Unsure how long I'll be away. Me poor old mum is on the edge. Got to look after her, got to do the right thing, got to put home and family ahead of the job. Sorry, Zach, but you understand, don't you, you having some troubles with your dad in the nursing home and your mum who's just been diagnosed with Alzheimer's?'

It could have been a bullet, thought Stolly as he looked from bad guy to bad guy and thought: how did I get here? And ...

... how bad am I?

THE SPIDERS FROM MARS

'TELL US WHAT YOU SAW,' I SAID TO DUNN.

We were in the bedroom, the door closed, staring at where Isobel had hung. Dunn was looking pale and his hands were trembling.

'She was leaning forward. Her feet were touching the floor. Her head was down. Her arms were kind of, you know, dangling ... Do we have to do this? It's creeping me out. Can we go back into the lounge room?'

'Keep going,' said Maria.

'Okay,' he said resigned. 'She was, well ... naked. The tie was around her neck, looped back over the metal hook on the door.'

'Tell us about the tie,' I said.

The tie, a rather vital piece of evidence, had not made it through the test of time; in other words, it had vanished from the evidence box. Due to first impressions of suicide or kinky sex, not murder, the gathering of evidence and photographing of the crime scene had been sketchy.

Dunn had his hands behind his back, like he was Prince Charles, and was staring at the white carpet, which was dense with dust and gave off an odour that reminded me of dead refrigerators.

'It was blue,' he said without looking up.

'Can you be more specific?' I asked.

'It was dark blue,' he said to the floor, 'and there were no patterns and it was polyester.' He looked up and turned to Maria. 'I hate polyester,' he said.

She didn't answer.

Maria and I exchanged a look. Police regulation ties were dark blue and polyester. Still, it seemed odd that if it was a cop who killed Isobel, he would have used a police tie. Only a twerp like Dunn would have noticed the difference but I was glad he had.

I left the room and made a call.

'Buff?' I asked into my phone.

'Make it quick,' he replied. 'I'm about to go round-to-round with the government over holiday pay.'

'Can you describe the tie that was around her neck?'

I heard an intake of air being sucked into his chest.

'You know it was over twenty years ago, Darian.'

'Not an issue for a man with an elephantine memory.'

'Blue.'

'Was the tie familiar?'

'In what way?' he asked, prevaricating.

'Was it a cop tie, Buff?'

'I am late for this meeting, Darian. I have to go. Good luck with the search.'

———

TYRONE FLOATED. HE lay still, allowing the water to undulate beneath him. And he thought of Isobel, the girl he had crashed into love with so many years ago. His name meant power. That's why his parents had given him the ridiculous name, after Tyrone Power, a movie star he'd never even seen. But once upon a time, back in the years of Isobel, he'd liked it. Not now.

Monahan had soccer practice with his daughters.

Nick went home to his hooker. Bree had stayed in bed for the morning, then decided to stay a bit longer in bed, until the midafternoon, then decided she might make the man – who would be king – some noodles. Thai style. But then she remembered the last time she made that and it tasted awful. Like everything else in her life, she'd fucked it up. A simple fucking noodle dish.

Tyrone dreamed about the girl he had once loved and thought about the woman he was now married to and, unfairly, compared them. Isobel, of course, came out ahead.

Dunn stood in the bedroom of the girl he had seduced and stared at the door upon which she was found hanged.

Maria thought about her lover, the killer.

Next to Monahan was another dad, shouting like a fuckwit at the coach. 'Give it up,' said Monahan to the guy. 'Let him do his job.' The other guy ignored him and kept shouting.

Tyrone remembered that he'd been going to ask Isobel to marry him even though, at the age of nineteen, he didn't understand marriage. Now, in his early forties, he did and thought it was a doomed concept. Even though he had great kids, he hated his wife. The water beneath him, in the Harold Holt memorial pool, was cold and he pissed into it.

'Hi,' said Bree, as this man with whom she had connected, to take his money and anything else, despite his danger, walked into the house through which she had paraded all day.

'Hi,' said Nick, back to her.

Casey was cooking his lover a dish of spaghetti with olives and zucchini. He splashed some red vino into the pot and hummed 'Too Much of Nothing' by Bob Dylan.

I was thinking about Rose, the woman I had loved, had left behind, in Byron Bay, by a lighthouse that swung its beam through the night sky as I drove away wondering if I would ever see her again. It had cast its brief spotlight into the void of gloom, of night, of terror, its hope, her beauty and wonder. Would I ever be with her again?

I thought about The Train Rider, the monster I had let get away. Would I ever find him? Could I ever kill him?

I thought about the many I had killed. Bad guys, one and all. Executions. And a God said thus it is to you. I thought about a father in Thailand, in a smashed-up room with hookers eager for his cash, and about a mother I hadn't seen for too many years.

I thought about Isobel and the blue tie and Brian Dunn, the creep, and how we could nail the prick for being a prick – but was he the killer? And I thought about Racine, the slender man, smooth and cool, all Italian suits and aftershave.

Tyrone climbed out of the pool and wiped himself down with a towel. He had to get home, to the kids, his wife, he had to play it real.

Nick stared at Bree. She was wearing the clothes from last night but they had been, he thought, washed and ironed. Fresh. New. She'd showered. The bird was in its cage. It stared at them.

'Hi,' she said. 'I made you dinner.'

During the day, between meetings, Nick had remembered his insane foolishness at having invited a hooker to stay in his house. I am the next Police Commissioner, he reminded himself. But after each of those acrimonious moments fled through him, he settled back into the memory of her flesh and her warmth and he reminded himself that he had power over her; he could do what he wanted.

'That's great,' he said. 'What is it?'

'Spaghetti a la Bree.'

'Come here,' he said.

And she did. She did as she was told, as she had since she was a child.

He unfurled his arms and held her and thought: This is good.

And she thought: This is good.

And Tyrone thought: Why have the cops come after me? Do they think I did it? And he thought back to when he saw Isobel, his Isobel, dangling on the back of the door.

'Hey, so … Maria? Can we, like, leave this room now?' asked Dunn. 'I have told you everything I can.'

'What else did you see?' she asked.

Stolly caught a flight. But before: 'Florina? Hey, it's Stoll.'

'Hi. You sound a little stressed.'

'Nah … Hey, look, I've got to go away for a bit. The job. We've got a homicide that's taking me to Auckland. I'll be away for a bit.'

Florina didn't believe him. 'Okay,' she said.

Tyrone left the pool, angry, wanting to bash his wife.

Monahan turned to the sprouter on the soccer field and said: 'Shut up,' and the guy, the father of a girl named Naomi, looked into the eyes of this man and decided to keep quiet.

Casey was no fool; he knew he was in trouble. But would he apologise for killing Stone? No. No way on God's great earth.

Spiders crawled across Tyrone's body. He couldn't see them but he felt them, spiders of doubt, of anger, of remorse, spiders from another world, from Mars.

'What else did you see?' asked Maria again.

'Oh,' Dunn said, as if a memory had suddenly returned and both Maria and I looked at one another, wondering if this was going to be something, or just another of his annoying banalities. 'She was wearing a ring.'

'Was that unusual?' asked Maria.

'Yeah. She never wore one before. I assumed her dad must've given it to her or that Tyrone, her drippy boyfriend, gave it to her. Whatever. It gave me the shits, to be honest.'

There was no reference to a ring in any of the reports. Either it had been removed or, more likely, ignored, taken for granted.

'What sort of ring was it?' I asked.

'I don't know. Gold, I think. It looked antique.'

'And you'd never seen it before?'

'First time. As I said, it gave me the shits. If she was going to get a ring, it should have been from me.'

The charmer himself.

'What finger was it on?'

'The wedding ring finger.'

CRASH BURN

THE RING BOTHERED ME.

We called Eli, and no, he hadn't made his daughter a ring and she didn't wear one, and nor could he explain how she had one on her.

'Why do you ask me about a ring?' he asked. I hadn't answered.

We called a belligerent Tyrone, and no, he hadn't given Isobel a ring either and, as he curtly reminded us, he was, at the time, a kid working on a dead man's wage at McDonald's.

'I couldn't afford a ring,' he'd said and hung up on us.

It wasn't that there'd been no prior mention of a ring that concerned me. This had been a scrappy investigation with few details noted or questions asked until it was too late, until after Isobel's body had been cremated, when the Coroner started to wonder if the suicide or accidental-death scenario might be replaced by something rather more sinister.

Might it have been the killer who put the ring on Isobel's finger? That is what Maria and I silently pondered, what bothered the both of us, as we drove around the corner from Osborne and down the narrower and densely tree-lined Davis.

We'd left Dunn on the footpath back in Osborne, complaining about the mistreatment he'd received at our hands, asking for a lift to his apartment at Beverley Hills and gazing sleazily yet again at Maria, who looked ready to clobber him to death.

'The ring,' said Maria.

'Yeah, the ring,' I answered.

'Would Racine do that? Stone? Any of the other cops. Put a ring on her finger? If they killed her?'

'People do weird shit,' I said helpfully.

By now I had pulled up outside our apartments. Maria stared up at the balcony to hers, no doubt thinking about Casey and the weird shit he'd pulled in the past twenty-four hours. Stone's death was a monumental blow to us, a crucial voice now forever denied us. Casey's reckless vengeance, no doubt an act of valour and honour in his eyes, left us with a huge loss. Stone would have talked, nonstop. If Isobel had been murdered it was, we assumed, on his orders. If it was an accidental death, it might have been Dunn or Tyrone. We had all but ruled out suicide.

But this new fact, the fact that she was wearing a ring, meant there was now an unexpected and even more challenging dynamic to be considered:

That Isobel's killer was none of the men we'd been looking at.

PART II

KILLER

'Like one that on a lonesome road
Doth walk in fear and dread,
And having once turned round walks on,
And turns no more his head;
Because he knows, a frightful fiend
Doth close behind him tread.'

SAMUEL TAYLOR COLERIDGE – *THE RIME OF THE ANCIENT MARINER*

THE RECKONING

I KNEW THAT THERE WAS A PERSON INSIDE MY APARTMENT AS I walked towards the door. Someone had broken in, picked the lock, was waiting for me. Whenever I'm on an investigation, I always leave a tiny sliver of a restaurant's business card, in this case from France-Soir, wedged in the crease of the door as I close it every morning. It's an old habit of paranoia. I do not do this back home in Noosa, but, unlike everyone else in the Friendly World of Sun and Smiles, I do lock my door; as Maria and I had just noted, people can do some weird shit.

Given that Stone had, before he expired, put out a hit on Maria and might have, before he expired, put out another one, on her or me, I pulled out the Glock that Casey had kindly loaned me last night, away from Maria's gaze and knowledge, assuring me it was all cool, brother, because he'd get a new handpiece the next morning, another Glock, from one of the Lebanese boys in Lygon Street.

You can't open a thick wooden door to a modern apartment quietly, so I didn't bother trying. As I pushed through the door, I held my finger on the trigger, ready to fire, and made sure I didn't present as an open target.

'Darian, it's only me.' I heard a familiar voice.

I stepped inside and found Nick Racine sitting at my dining table next to the open kitchen. Smooth as always, dressed in a ten-ton suit, hair slicked back, aquiline features and a look of self-assurance, or congratulation, I could never quite figure it, on his face.

'I thought you were a Beretta man,' he said.

'Tough times,' I said, shoving the gun back into the belt around my jeans.

'I was searching for something to drink but then I remembered you're an alcoholic. I was going to make myself a coffee but thought, fuck it, wait till I get home, have a few snorts then. How's the investigation? When are you and the girl going to schedule an interview? You know I've got a very, very busy schedule. Of course I'll push aside whatever to work with you and the girl, to accommodate your needs, but a little warning would be most appreciated. Thursday's looking good.'

'How about now?' I asked.

'No girl?'

'No girl.'

He unfurled his arm and made a point of looking at his watch. A Rolex.

'Can't. I have an appointment. But, anyway, I want to do it with the girl. I like the girl. Actually, it's about the girl that I came over here.'

I said nothing, waited.

'I've heard, from the streets, where I have excellent sources, that the girl's boyfriend, Casey Lack, ex-nightclub owner and minor-level gangster, has rolled into town. Rode all the way down from the Sunshine Coast is what my sources tell me. Armed to the hilt.' He indicated my belt, where the Glock was resting.

'My sources tell me that Mr Lack, friend of yours I believe, Darian, was on a bit of a mission. Of revenge. Dominic Stone was the most egotistical man I ever met. Didn't like the guy at all. He gave a good party, though, and the girls were endless. Didn't I invite you once? I'm sure I did. I'm sure, way back in the late eighties, I told you to come along to his place at Portsea. You, being a solitary guy who only fucked hookers, a bit like me, really, you would have loved Dom's parties. Back in your vodka days too. Man, why didn't you come along, Darian? Too late now, old mate. Now we're men of respectability.' He chuckled.

'Anyway, back to the conundrum: Casey Lack, lover of the girl across the street, in her nice little apartment that we in the Service are paying for, like yours, my old friend. I think Mr Lack, all tatts and attitude, might have been the one who killed Dominic Stone because, despite the opinions of the morons who attended the scene, Stone was not a man to off himself. Fucking pussy, if nothing else. Didn't have it in him. Have you fucked her?'

I didn't say anything, just let him talk.

'I hope so. She is beyond hot. Best tits I've seen in years. And you, being the sage old wise man, you must get her juices flowing. But it's gotta be tough when Casey the Lack is a buddy. Another conundrum. Me, I would abort old Case and fuck the living daylights out of Maria Chastain. When you do, because I know you will, let me know. Okay? Send me a text. I wanna know how she felt. Inside. The warm pussy stuff.'

I truly wanted to reach over and throttle the prick, but when you're dealing with monsters, you get down to their level and play in the garden.

'You'll be the first to know, Nick.'

'It's a bit like Isobel,' he added. 'I didn't fuck her and I certainly didn't kill her, and the sooner we have that established, old mate, the better, but I wanted to. Fuck her, that is. Ha. Have you seen the photos? Not of her dead. No, of her leading up to the death. Mate,' he said leaning across the table at me, 'have you seen the photos that Dunn took of her in bikinis, down at Stone's Portsea house, by the pool? Victoria's Secret meets Porn Hub. I would have loved to fuck her. Hey, so this is me being honest; a killer doesn't talk like this, does he? But, old mate, back to the issue of Mr Lack. What do we do? Because if I were to initiate an investigation, which I'm inclined to do, Mr Lack might find himself charged with murder. The big numero uno. Swing swing. His fingerprints will be there. No-one can do a kill like the kill on Stone and not leave a trace, especially a biker moron covered in tatts. And then, gee, that Maria with the tits and ambition, what happens to her? Do you care? I would. I'd be keen to protect her. Maybe not you. But you know what?'

He leaned in towards me again. I still wanted to throttle him, and maybe I would, after we'd got to the end of the investigation. I'd killed a number of cops before, bad cops, and it seemed to me that Racine was opting for nomination.

'I think you will. I think you're in love with her and I think you'll do anything to protect her. Casey going down for murder would destroy her and I think, correct me if I'm wrong, you'll do anything to stop that. She's a beautiful girl – really and truly, I mean it, call me or email or text me after you guys have fucked; I want to know about her nipples and the tightness of her cunt –'

It was at this point I reached for my belt, pulled out my Glock and smashed it onto his forehead.

He went down like a sack of spuds.

I would have thrown him off the balcony onto the street below, but I was three storeys up and it would have killed him, so I dragged him down the concrete steps and out onto Davis Avenue, where I flung him onto the footpath.

Yeah, I kicked him in the head as well.

I looked up and across the street, to Maria's apartment. The lights were burning and I wondered how she was doing.

ORPHAN

CASEY SAW IT IN HER EYES, HER MANNER, HER MOVES, AS SHE walked through the door. He saw pent-up anger and stress and so he decided to go for the jugular.

'I killed him. Okay? I rode direct to his house and I killed him.' He couldn't help but add, 'I did it for you, babe.'

'I fucking hate you,' she screamed and smashed at him, all fists and spit. 'You killed our main, most important witness. I fucking hate you.'

Case had never been great at relationships. This was an assault he was expecting but, like the generals in World War One, he had no clue how to navigate it, despite having worried about this moment all day.

'Babe,' he said, hopelessly.

'Don't fucking *babe* me.'

'I did it for you.'

'No, you moron, you did it for *you*.'

He was lost. Where do I go from here? he wondered. All that I do I do for you, and you are the only thing in this mother-fucking trembling world of detritus that I care for. I know you're a cop and I know I've crossed the line and compromised you. But I love you.

None of this he could articulate.

He stared at her like an orphan.

'Get the fuck out of here,' said Maria.

His mum, when he was eight, had told him to *Get the fuck out of here*, and he had, with tears squashing through his face, wondering where the fuck out of here he would go and why, why did Mum tell me to fuck off? And his dad, smashed with dope and smack, had told him, the day after, to *Come 'ere, kid, and meet your Uncle Bruce*, and Casey had recoiled, knowing that Uncle Bruce wasn't an uncle and had nothing good to do or say. Run.

He ran. Mother-fucker, did he run.

'Get out! Get out, get out, get *out*. Now. I fucking hate you,' screamed Maria.

And he did.

He left.

But before he went he smiled at her and said, despite the sound and fury, 'I love you.'

'Make it hurt,' he'd said to the tattooist. And it did.

—

I HEARD THE grumble of a Harley and I knew that it belonged to Case and that Maria had gone thermonuclear on him. I guess if I were her, I would have too. I texted him and said: *There's a bed here my brother*, and he texted back and said, *am in the wind but u call me if u need me 2 do anything and keep my girl safe.*

—

MARIA FELL FROM a cloud. She hadn't meant to. She'd been gripping to its edges, her nails biting hard into the folds.

Where she was falling she didn't know. Was it a friendly place or a place of warfare? She rolled around in her bed and mourned the loss of a great love and wondered if she should text or call him back to her, now that anger had subsided and a sense of *I get where he's coming from* crept in. She thought about adoration and devotion. Casey was an old-school, dumb warrior knight who adored her – *And baby, you will adore me back.*

He'd said it with a smile. And she had.

There was a problem: she had no-one to talk to. Deb, her oldest friend, wouldn't understand; Jackie, her next oldest friend, would tell her to meditate and take in some sun on the beach; and Billie, her third closest friend, was still outraged that Maria was taking in the trash in the form of a biker in tatts. She could march across to Darian's and try to extract some of his wisdom, but the last time she had broached her relationship with Casey with him he'd done a Road Runner backwards exit; he was possibly the most emotionally retarded person she'd ever met, despite his brilliance as a detective.

Men are fucked, she came to conclude and rolled over and tried, yet again, and without success, to absolve herself of blame and go to sleep.

Sleep never came.

FREEFALLING

My phone buzzed at 3.57am. I answered, rolling out of bed and reaching for the remote to change the room temperature from Reykjavik to Kalahari.

'Hey,' I said. 'Anything?'

'Yeah,' replied Buff. 'I finally remembered. She *was* wearing a ring. You were right.'

'Do you remember what sort?'

'Not really. But I think it went through my mind that it was expensive. I think, don't quote me on this, it was gold, really old, with two diamonds, small, and a sapphire in the middle. In fact, as I'm talking now, I think I remember it looked like my grandma's. Why is this important?'

Because whoever put it on her finger was possibly the killer.

'Thanks, Buff. Speak to you soon.'

'Real soon,' he said.

—

There are, of course, many types of killers, but when you remove the identities and characters of killings, you're left with but a few profiles. The person who kills for financial gain. The person who kills in blind anger, spontaneous or pent-up. The person who kills because they have been ordered to, as a job. The person who kills for revenge.

It's usually about love or money.

Then there's the person who kills for fun or perhaps to satisfy their twisted inner needs.

And when a killer leaves their victim, they will flee in horror at what they've done or retreat calmly, satisfied at what they've done, or in panic, scared by the ramifications of what they've done, and sometimes in remorse, shamed at what they have done.

But the killer who has killed for fun, to satisfy a black inner need, will extricate himself, or herself, with regret that the game is now over. It might be like pulling back from a glorious kiss on the lips with your lover, a kiss of such sensuality and glow, of such erotic entanglement, that you just want it to last forever but you know it cannot. And as that kiss is broken, as it comes to its end, you reach out, usually, to touch the person, maybe a hand on theirs, or across their cheek or down their arm, like a coda or an affirmation of that brilliant moment which has just passed. This is when the killer will remove something from the body that he knows he now must depart. A trophy, a lock of hair or a piece of jewellery or some clothing. Or, alternatively, the killer may leave something of his on the body that he must now depart. Something for her to remember him by. Something to symbolise their shared kiss, when he took away her life, as she looked into his eyes knowing they would be the last thing she would ever see. This is dangerous, though, because precious gifts left on the body, whatever they might be, are obvious clues to the people who will now discover it. Who will now pore over it, in search of your identity. Whatever you leave behind needs to be anonymous, a secret between you and the person you've just killed.

They have honoured you, this person. They have given their life to you. They have sated your desperate need. They have forsaken their body to you. They have allowed you to shatter them.

So, reward them. Honour them in return. Show them your gratitude.

Put a ring on their finger.

THE DEEP

Somebody is in my house, thought Isobel as she pushed away the wave of sleep and sat up in her bed.

'Ty?' she called.

No answer.

Why do I think someone is in my house? she wondered. What did I hear? Or is it just a feeling, like when I was a little girl, scared of the dark, of cats, of waves at the beach, but found solace in the arms of my dad?

'Brian?' she called.

No answer and no sounds, of feet on the carpeted floor, of creaks in the floorboards or from doors opening. Just wind and a steady drizzle outside, spattering her bedroom window.

'Hello?' she called out.

There was nothing in response, just a big, empty, dark silence. Which she was rapidly filling with fear.

Had she heard the sound of someone coming over the back fence, falling onto the bricks? Or was that a dream? She'd been asleep, hadn't she? Since Tyrone had left. When was that? It felt like hours ago, but it couldn't have been any longer than ten or twenty minutes. She reached out for her watch on her bedside table.

And then she heard, coming from the other side of her partly open door, from down the corridor:

'Hello, Isobel,' in a whisper.

A man's voice. She froze and fought a sudden urge to vomit. She didn't speak, didn't move. Her gaze was on the door.

'Are you ready for me?' said the man, again in a whisper on the other side of the door.

She started to cry.

'Everybody's gone, so it's just us now.'

The door began to open inwards. He was coming into her room. Who was he? The voice was vaguely familiar, but she couldn't locate it, and in her desperate panic, all she could think about was her dad and how he would grab her out of the surf and laugh and raise her high above the water in his arms, always there when the water crashed down.

'I've got a present for you,' he said as the door opened, and through the dark and gloom, she saw a man, dressed entirely in black, step into her room.

And she knew that this time there was no dad to raise her out of the surf. She knew that she was dead.

THE LEDGER

BECAUSE THE INVESTIGATION HAD BEEN INSTIGATED IN AN effort to exonerate Racine, everything had been framed around his connection to her and the inevitable consideration of whether a lover was involved. There had been no contemplation of Isobel being killed by someone she didn't know. The nature of her death was not only unusual, it hadn't been repeated, before or after, which left me puzzled, because I was now considering an unknown person who treated her death as artistry. And death artists are great at repeating themselves. But as far as we knew – and another like hers would have stood out – Isobel's death seemed to be a one-off.

'Does this mean everyone we've been working on is eliminated?' asked Isosceles.

The three of us had gathered in my apartment early the next morning. There was no mention of my evening visitor nor of Casey's departure.

'No,' I replied. 'Everyone is still in play. We're just opening a new line to consider, to go hard at.'

'Dare I say it,' he said, 'but this cold case has just gone glacial.'

'That's not very fucking helpful,' snapped Maria.

Isosceles looked as though he was about to cry.

'I'm sorry,' she quickly said. 'I had a bad night.'

'Anything I can do to help?' he asked.

'No. But thanks.'

Peace restored.

'We need to look at all the other aspects of her life. There was an intersection between something she was doing and the killer. He knew her. At the very least he'd seen her and followed her. The type of guy we're now looking at studied her moves, knew her routine, maybe kept watch on her. And that's what we've got to do now: stalk her, track her every move for the seven weeks leading up to her death.'

The magnitude of this task, discovering the minutiae of a person's life in a pre-online world, was not lost on Isosceles. 'What do I do?' he asked.

'Keep searching for the whereabouts of her neighbours. Any eyewitness testimony, even twenty-five years later, to the events of the night, will be helpful.'

He brightened up.

—

ELI LOOKED SUSPICIOUS.

'Why are you asking me these questions?' he said. For many years he had harboured a deep hatred for the man he thought was responsible for Isobel's death. As far as he was concerned, we had entered his life, days earlier, to confirm that, not to question it.

'Why ask me how she got to work? Did she walk or did she drive? What sort of question is that?'

'We have to examine every facet of her life,' Maria said smoothly.

'Is it because Stone is dead? He gassed himself. I saw it on the news. I was happy, but now I think you will never prove it was him. So, instead you come here asking me questions about the route Isobel took to get to my shop when she worked here.'

'You might want to take Stone's death as a *sort* of resolution,' I said. 'We are just tidying up things.'

He didn't know what I meant and I wasn't going to elaborate.

'And the police officers who worked for him?' he asked.

'We are looking closely at them. But we need your assistance. You have to tell us everything you remember about Isobel, in the months before she died, but not about the pressure she was getting from the Federal Police or from Stone's men – we know about that, we've done a lot of work on that – but on the mundane details of what she did and where she went, what her routines were or if there might have been anything out of the ordinary. Who she visited, who she talked to here in the shop, where she went for lunch, if it was the same place. I know it's a long time ago and I know we are asking you to recall very ordinary facts, things most of us forget in a few weeks or months, but we need you to try to recall as much as you can.'

'I have forgotten nothing,' he replied simply.

Indeed he had kept her alive by memorialising her, in every way, from the most trivial to the most significant. Just as he had preserved the house in which she had briefly lived, so too had he kept her bedroom at his home, where she had grown up. We scoured her schoolbooks and the diary she wrote while in Bolivia but found no mention of Dunn, of his request to bring in the small amount of cocaine.

Her presence also resounded in Eli's jewellery shop. Being an old-fashioned guy who still belonged to the world of the previous century, he hadn't bothered to computerise his business. Isosceles would have loved him even more. He recorded all the sales in an old-style ledger. I hadn't seen one in years, but in his back office, a tight, dingy little space made warm by a bar radiator, a wall was stacked with rows and rows of these old books. Proudly he took one down and opened it, showing us Isobel's handwriting, where she recorded the sale of a piece of jewellery and to whom.

'How far do these go back?' I asked.

'To the first day I opened this shop.'

'Where's December, nineteen-ninety – the month she died?' asked Maria. 'Actually ...' she said, correcting herself, 'can you give us the ledgers for all of that year?'

Justice can be ugly.

I wished he'd thrown those ledger books away and clung only to the visions in his mind. Maria and I saw the name at the same time. It was like it popped out at us. Like a joke, a taunt, an evil game. A name we both instantly recognised. And, next to the name, in the second column, was the purchase.

A ring.

WHO ARE YOU?

'IS THAT YOU, DARIAN?'

I'd caught the lift up to the ninth floor. I was back in the kingdom of the strong and mighty.

Copeland was standing by the window, looking out at the view of the bay in the distance. It was an unnaturally sunny, warm day. I'd left Maria back at her apartment.

'It's me, boss,' I said as I closed the door. He turned to face me.

'I saw Nick this morning. He was saying some terrible things about you. Alleged you struck him with your pistol. He does have a nasty bruise, too.'

'You didn't tell me you'd met Isobel.'

'No, I didn't.'

No hesitation, no blink, no sign of surprise.

'How come?'

'I didn't think it relevant.'

Uh huh.

'Why don't you tell me about it now?'

He turned around to face me. A blank look. We might have been about to discuss how to cook up the perfect ratatouille.

'Are you investigating me?'

'Covering all the bases. Just like you taught me.'

'Good boy.' He hadn't moved, hadn't blinked, hadn't changed his expression.

Well, after you dice the zucchini and capsicum and salt the eggplant …

'You went to her father's jewellery shop.'

He nodded. Good boy, Darian, keep going. I know you'll get there in the end, like you always do, as I trained you, mentored you. You are the best. Only you, Darian, only you can solve it. And you always do, don't you?

'You wanted to buy a ring for Jan. I remember you telling me, on the day of her funeral, that you two had some troubles in your marriage in the late eighties. You thought a piece of jewellery might help; a ring would be an ideal gift.'

He nodded again.

Then you cook them both on a high heat before you add in the chopped tomatoes.

'And behind the counter was a beautiful young girl.'

'Isobel,' he said. His gaze hadn't left mine. Staring right at me. Keep going, old son, and let's see where this takes us, I dare you.

'Tell me about the problems between you and Jan.'

'Of no relevance,' he replied.

Don't forget to add the basil – fresh, a whole bunch. And we've put the garlic in, haven't we? Cook it slow. Give it at least six hours.

'Okay. That part of the story, how you met Isobel, is pretty clear. Help me with the rest.'

'There is no rest. That's it. I met her and she was beautiful, I admit it. But that's the end of the journey, Darian. Which is why I felt this was of no relevance, why I didn't bother mentioning it to you.'

Make sure you have some parmesan, Reggiano if possible, and cracked black pepper. Delizioso!

'Okay,' I said.

For a moment we just stared at one another and didn't say a word. Life's full of choices, and which one are you going to take now, old son?

THE MONSTER'S CHOICE

'THIS IS INSANE. IT DOESN'T MAKE ANY SENSE. WHY WOULD he hire you to investigate a death if he's the killer?' Maria had said as we left Eli's store.

'And,' she continued, 'just because he didn't tell you he met her, it doesn't add up to guilt.'

I didn't answer. I was listening, though. She was correct. But why would he neglect to mention it? My head was doing a spin – I was having trouble staying focused.

'Maybe he forgot,' she went on. 'Maybe he didn't even know that the girl who served him in the shop was the same girl who was later killed.'

Through the haze it sounded to me as though she wasn't buying what she was saying.

Copeland had bought the ring two weeks before Isobel was found dead. Stay focused.

Of course he knew she was one and the same. Her death became big news. Her photo was in the papers. And Copeland was not a man to miss anything, nor was he a man to forget people.

But just because he'd purchased a ring from Isobel and she was found dead with a ring on her finger that none of the men in her life had bought, it didn't necessarily mean he was the killer.

Yet …

An omission of vital information is a lie.

And …

There is no such thing as a coincidence in a murder investigation.

As I drove away from my brief meeting with Copeland, away from HQ, back towards Davis Avenue, as I tried to drill focus and rational thought back into my brain, Maria's essential question of *why* began to take form with answers.

At the time of Isobel's death, Copeland's marriage was in some trouble. Jan was ill. The cancer would take her two years later. It's all very well to think you'll be a good and strong husband and care for your wife through sickness and in health, but when the sickness comes – and does not go – the pressure can become crippling. And, without being too crude, your sex life evaporates. Twenty-five years ago Copeland was a tough, virile guy in his late forties and while he was too polite to discuss things like sex, he must have, after some time, yearned for the press of a woman's flesh.

Then, maybe, a young and innocent-looking girl crossed his path and maybe her smile dazzled him and maybe – it happens – he became obsessed with her. Maybe he began to follow her. Maybe he began to fantasise about her. Sexually. Maybe that led to a break-in at her house, on that night, after Tyrone had left at about two-thirty in the morning, before Dunn turned up a couple of hours later, before Tyrone turned up again even later, instead of going to work, and found Isobel, triggering the events that led to me here, now, in a whirlwind of what the fuck is going on?

How could I prove any of this? And, I reminded myself, all of this was pure speculation.

—

AT THE TIME of Isobel's death, Copeland had also been a senior and highly respected police officer. He was, he would have assumed correctly, beyond suspicion.

By the time he came to visit me in my little cabin by the lake, just a couple of weeks earlier, he had long been the most powerful man in the state. Police Commissioners can tangle up governments and bring down Premiers. Every voter wants their street to be safe, their home to be safe, their kids to be safe. They understand there are bad cops, corrupt cops; that goes with the turf. It is something that has to be condemned but to which a blind eye can be turned, because when the lights come down and the streets turn dark and the kids are in bed, you want to know that the good guys will protect you. Without the good guys, what have you got? If you don't know, roll back to 1923, when the good guys went on strike and trams were overturned in the streets and stores were looted and people were shot; chaos in the heart of the city.

As Commissioner, Copeland was a man above suspicion.

But if the investigation into Isobel's death, ordered by the government, an order he would not've been able to have reasonably resisted – *Why and to what purpose, Commissioner?* – had to be sanctioned, then who to run it? Who among the levels and desks of HQ?

Why not Cold Case? Why not Internal Investigations?

Because there was somebody else, a gifted son, a former detective who had not only held you as you wept at your wife's funeral in a car park out the back of the church, but a man who owed his career to you.

But wait, Darian, I could hear him say, *there's more.*

There is more.

Like the Beretta he had taken from me in the backyard of Isobel's house and put into safekeeping. The boss knew of my excursions into summary justice. The executions of bad cops and crims who would have kept on killing unless someone put a bullet through their skulls and threw their corpses into a deserted gully or mine shaft. There were many such killings, and while we had never talked of this, we had an unspoken understanding that I would never be investigated or charged with the disappearance of these bad guys.

'You'll look after me,' the boss had said the next morning, after we'd had breakfast in the cabin. The fog had begun to clear and from far away I heard the sound of a four-wheel drive groaning up a mountain, its diesel engine chug-chugging as he went to leave, an old man taking care not to slip as he walked down the icy steps onto the white, frozen lawn towards his car. I had told him I'd do the job.

For him.

Because he was more a dad to me than my dad had ever been, that's for sure.

And, like he had wept for the loss of his wife, his Jan, I had poured out my vitriolic, vodka-infused story at his house one night, about the dad who'd left a message, scribbled by hand, pinned to my pillow as he crept out of our home in the middle of the night, a note that said *I love you, kid*, and then, maybe a year or two later, sent a copy of Pink Floyd's *Dark Side of the Moon* – the LP – through the mail with a note of love and regret.

—

WHO AM I?

This morning I was righteous and strong. I clobbered Racine like an old-fashioned hero in an Erskine Childers novel, asserting the honour of my colleague. I had, for close to thirty years, been a cop dedicated mostly to good. I had been groomed and taught, I had been led, honoured, case after case, justice found, my victims' desire for justice sated. I had looked into my victims' eyes, become the first person to stare into them after the killer had fled, after he had stared into their eyes, leaving an imprint, an imprint for me to find, tease out, that he thought was invisible, just as he thought he could flee, could get away with it – *ha, look at me, I'm invincible*. This moment often reminded me of an old-fashioned negative, developed in the darkroom after the photograph is taken. All of the detail is there in the black-and-white image on the strip of film, but it is only when black becomes white, when negative becomes positive, that the picture becomes clear and real.

Yeah, that was me. The good guy. The hero. Only you, Darian, only you. And sound the trumpets now, old son, for he shall march forth; I have, your mentor, groomed you to become the absolute best homicide investigator. That solve rate? Ninety-eight per cent?

Wow.

All those interstate calls, from politicians begging for you to come across, over the state lines, and solve an embarrassing murder?

Wow.

Who are you, Darian?

Easy: you are the man I made you.

So, where now, old son, do we go from here?

THIS IS THE END

THE MAN STEPPED INTO HER ROOM.

'Who are you?' asked Isobel.

'I'm death,' he replied, as he turned on the bedroom light.

He smiled at her and she froze. Her death. A man in his forties, a man who had smiled at her in the shop as he bought a ring for his wife and said, 'What's your name?'

'Isobel. This is my dad's shop,' she'd said.

'I drive past this shop every day and I would have never realised that inside were not only the most beautiful rings but the most beautiful girl.'

Yuck, she'd thought, but smiled at him, because her dad had taught her to be polite and accommodating to every customer.

'You work here all the time, Isobel?'

'No, part-time. I'm hoping to go to Melbourne Uni next year.'

'Congratulations.'

'Thanks. Is there anything else I can get you, Mr Walsh?'

'My wife – I bought this ring for her – looked just like you, when I proposed.'

Yuck, she'd thought again as she smiled and pretended to be impressed.

'What's that look, Isobel?' he'd asked.

'What?'

'You gave me a look of disquiet. Is that what it was? Did you think I was being perhaps inappropriate?'

'No, of course not. Not at all.'

'I'VE BEEN FOLLOWING you, my beautiful girl,' he said as he took a step towards her bed. 'I've been watching you. You are very, very beautiful and I want to consume you.'

Isobel was no longer frozen. Now she was freaking out. I'm going to die. Mr Walsh is going to kill me. Now. Here. Ty … Brian …

Dad.

He was now above her, at the edge of her bed. There was nowhere for her to go; she was up against the wall. She was crying and she was pleading.

'Please. Please. Please. Don't. Please. I'll do anything. Please.'

Which, it seemed to her, in a flash-then-gone moment of clarity, was like a salve to him.

'Pull back your doona, my beautiful,' he said.

And she did.

Please.

'Take off your pyjamas.'

And she did.

Please.

'Rub your clitoris, my beautiful.'

And she did.

He sat on the bed and watched her.

A man dressed in black and … Fuck! He told me he was a policeman, she remembered.

'Stop,' he said, after a few moments, still staring at her.

And she did.

'I have a present for you.' He reached into his back pocket and pulled out his wallet. He fumbled inside, while keeping his gaze on her.

'Here.'

He held out the ring that she had sold him.

'Put it on.'

And she did.

'I bought it for you.'

No, you told me you were buying it for your wife who was sick and dying of cancer. It was meant to give her strength. Make her happy. You told me that she needed to be reminded of the glory of life and I remember, for a moment, how I liked that phrase.

The glory of life.

You told me that buying it from a beautiful, gorgeous young girl like me – yuck – made it all the better and yet again I smiled at you, like my dad told me to.

'It suits you, doesn't it?'

'Yes.'

'Remember what you said before I bought it?'

'No.'

'You said: "Diamonds are a girl's best friend." That's not very original, my beautiful, but a young girl like you, who's to understand these things?'

Maybe he won't kill me. Maybe, if I touch him, fuck him, he will go away, this man who calls himself death.

'Do it again,' he said.

'What?'

'Touch yourself. I want my ring inside you.'

She did as she was told.

And he watched.

'Have you ever been choked? During sex?' he asked

Choked? During sex? Was there such a thing? There couldn't be; what did that mean? Suddenly she realised her bowel was full. A ridiculous thought flashed through her mind: she wanted to ask him if she could go to the toilet, to avoid a terrible accident in her bed; she was losing control of her body. This was fear, she knew.

'No. Clearly not. Let me show you. Stop with the touching, my gorgeous.'

And she did.

He stood up.

'Get up,' he said.

And she did.

He reached into his back pocket and pulled out a tie, dark blue and wide.

'Go over there,' he said, pointing to the door.

—

SHE HAD DONE everything he'd asked. Backed against the door and allowed him to wrap the tie around her neck and allowed him to pull it tight. She was hanging, the tips of her feet trying to stay firm on the floor as she watched him step away, his eyes never leaving her, as he began to undo his shirt, which he then let drop to the floor. He smiled at her as if this strip was amusing. He undid his belt, then the buttons on his pants and pulled them off. He removed a pair of boxer shorts. He was naked in front of her. He inhaled and flexed his arms, like a bodybuilder. She watched, in horror, as his penis became erect, as he stroked it, never once taking his eyes off her.

He reached down to his pants and removed a condom packet, tore at it, placed the empty wrapper back in his pants pocket and, with one hand now reaching out to stroke her cheek, his other rolled the rubber onto his erection.

He stepped up to her, rubbed his penis between her legs and, without warning, thrust inside her, his knees bent at first, as he then pushed his way up into her.

He moaned and she smelt his breath.

Then he reached up to the tie, above her, and began to pull on it.

He fucked her, as she was pinned to the door, as he pulled tighter on the tie and as he smiled when he came inside her and said, finally, just a moment before she fell into darkness:

'Good.'

As if she had appeased him.

And she had.

—

As SHE FELL into that darkness, a word, a yearning, a moment, a life, a series of dreams, chaos and rest and joy and despair came to her. Words.

Dad.

Surf.

I love you. You held me up as the waves beat me.

I love you so much, Dad.

And then she was gone.

OUTLAW

I HATE TRAFFIC LIGHTS. OR, TO BE MORE SPECIFIC, I HATE being forced to sit and wait at a set of red traffic lights when all I want to do is move. I was at the corner of Punt and Toorak, staring down the boulevard, past France-Soir on my left, amidst a cacophony of cars and trams and pedestrians, the clink and clatter of screech on the busy roads, cars jammed up against one another and people scurrying in all directions. As the signals changed to red again, after I had crawled another three metres towards the intersection, I noticed a tribe of young girls in school uniform gathered by the traffic lights closest to me. They were doing what all tribes of schoolyard teenagers do: lounging in groups, texting and messaging, scrolling through Facebook postings, pressing 'like' without thinking and gathering close for whispered conversations. The light turned green for them and en masse they ran and walked past me. It was a too-easy connection, but I needed a too-easy connection: Isobel had been one of these girls, and every teenage kid deserves the right to be free and cool, certainly alive, away from the hassle of a sleazy teacher and an arrogant, vain millionaire; every teenage kid deserves the freedom to go to sleep at night without a man stepping into their room and snuffing out their life, their dreams.

Copeland might have been relying on my self-preservation instincts as his ultimate means of staying safe, but he had forgotten my susceptibility to the victims and my unconscious yielding to their pleas and cries. I hadn't succumbed yet to a nightmare of a wraith-like Isobel floating above and around me, imploring me to find the man who killed her – I hadn't had those nightmares for some time – but I didn't need her to come back and remind me of the job that needed to be done. Just like the schoolgirls crossing the street, the awareness that Isobel once lived in the still-empty house up and around the corner from where we were staying kept me, and Maria and Isosceles, determined to see her put to rest.

It's not easy bringing down the top cop in the state. He has a lot of resources and a lot of laws that can be enforced to thwart the closing in of enemies. Copeland was, of course, relying on his place above suspicion, but emperors can be toppled; it was just a question of how to do it. But I wasn't exactly sure three lone rangers could match the might of the police force.

And that's what we were: three lone rangers. I couldn't turn to any of the detectives in Homicide, not even the ones I trusted. They were in a castle and we were on the outside; Copeland would see to that. He would be seeing to it now.

I drove down to the apartment and parked out the front. As I stepped out of my car, an anonymous blue late-model Ford cruised slowly by. I'd spotted it while ruminating at the traffic lights on the corner of Toorak and Punt and then watched, in my rear-view mirror, as it followed me into Davis. It didn't pull over but it was clearly a message.

A somewhat anxious Maria and Isosceles were waiting for me.

'What did he say?' asked Maria.

'He said that his meeting Isobel was of no relevance to our investigation.'

'Of no *relevance*?' she repeated.

Isosceles started to rock backwards and forwards. 'This is bad,' he said.

'Darian, we're fucked. What do we do?' asked Maria.

I was looking at our whiteboard, our list of suspects. Dunn, Tyrone, the four cops, especially Racine – the leads we had been following. Now there was a new lead, a number-one suspect who had trumped all the others. We had yet to add Copeland Walsh's photo to the board.

'As a start, we connect the ring that he purchased to the ring on her finger,' I said. 'Even if the lab comes back with a print on the bourbon bottle that matches his, it's not enough. We need to follow the ring.'

—

THE LAB CAME back with a print from the label on the bourbon bottle. It was a match to the then Division Commander, Copeland Walsh.

It wasn't enough.

SEND LAWYERS, GUNS AND MONEY

'THAT DOESN'T HELP US. HE'S A COP; THERE WOULD HAVE been dozens of cop prints at the crime scene,' I told Maria and Isosceles after the results came back.

As a matter of procedure, every cop is fingerprinted so as to avoid confusion. When the lab goes through all the prints, they crosscheck the cops who entered a crime scene, logged in and out, and then, as a matter of routine, eliminate them. The assumption, correct 99.9 per cent of the time, is that a cop is not responsible for the crime.

'If the print had been Dunn's or Tyrone's, that would be a different matter, as both of them denied touching the bottle and drinking from it.'

'But he was a Division Commander in a suburb miles away. There would be no reason for him to be at the crime scene and I bet he wasn't logged in. This is proof, Darian,' said Maria.

'Yes, it confirms in our minds that he's the killer, but it's not enough. You're right: he won't be logged in, because there was no reason for him to attend the crime scene, but so what? He'll say he went anyway and, as we all know, the case file is littered with sloppy police work. How many times have I walked into a crime scene and the constable meant to be logging you in is nowhere to be seen? It's not enough. Not yet.'

'But it is outrageous!' thundered Isosceles. 'It is a taunt, a blatant act of sheer arrogance,' he said.

And he was correct. Soon we would recreate the night of Isobel's death, from the perspective of a killer who had stalked her and murdered her for sexual pleasure. We would trace back to the moment of intersection between Isobel and Copeland, in the shop, when he purchased the ring before she died. In the meantime, however, we had an insight into what Isosceles had called the mind of sheer arrogance. We could only assume that Copeland had hung Isobel up and then had sex with her while he choked her, knowing that he was going to kill her, and then, afterwards, casually strolled into the kitchen and poured himself a glass of bourbon, no doubt savouring the taste and feeling rather pleased with himself. It was a deliberate act and there was nothing rushed about it; here was a killer who, after murdering someone, was taking his time, leaving his prints on the bottle and the glass as well, no doubt fully aware that if those prints were ever found, nothing would be done. He was bulletproof.

'We have to connect him to Isobel, and specifically, until any new avenues are opened, the ring that was on her finger,' I said.

'How?' asked Maria.

Good question. Where was the ring? After her body had been removed from the house in Osborne Street, it was taken into the care of the Coroner, who then, after his inquest, released it back to Eli. It had been sent directly to a funeral director on his behalf. Eli promptly arranged for his daughter to be cremated. Any items of jewellery that are on the body in a Coroner's care are also, at this time, released back to the next of kin. Eli had told us that there was no ring. There was no jewellery. Just his daughter. Her body, already decaying.

Somewhere during that journey, from Osborne Street to the Coroner then back to the funeral director, the ring on her finger had disappeared.

Or had it?

But before I could follow that line of thought, before we could create a road map to follow this new and urgent line of investigation, it was time to move.

—

A SANCTIONED INVESTIGATION is one in which doors open and people cooperate. A private investigation is another matter entirely. The cloak of power that the badge provides is extremely useful; people feel, and are, compelled to talk to you. Abandoning it, going rogue, not operating as official officers of the law, is fraught. This course of action frequently pits you against the cops and they don't like it when others intrude on their turf.

Copeland had told me to wrap it up, finish the job. Make it suicide, make it an accident, take down the boyfriend if you want, but do it, Darian, and do it quickly. Exonerate Racine and let's all move on. By Friday, close of business, no later, old son. I'm tired and it's time for me to let a younger man take the chair, and maybe I will go on a cruise after all. Always wanted to visit the South Pacific islands.

I guess he expected I'd obey.

I didn't.

We shed our badges, Maria and I, then left the apartments, left the company car parked out on the street, packed our bags and clambered into the Studebaker. We drove to a safe house, a two-storey Victorian home with an abandoned look, set back from the street, Grey Street in St Kilda, not far from South Yarra but out of range and out of sight, a place I had used, when I ran Homicide, to hide witnesses who were in the firing line. It was owned by the same Algerian gent who had gifted me the Studebaker after I rescued his son many years ago. Loyalties run deep with guys like him, and with one phone call we had the keys. Although I'd declined the offer, we also had two young and highly buffed Algerian boys sitting in a parked car out the front playing bodyguard with shoot-to-kill smiles on their faces as they watched us park the Studebaker in an alley running alongside the house and then walk up the path to the front door, closing the gate behind us. Isosceles had gone straight back to his bat cave, assuring us that it was, like the real cave in *Batman*, off the radar, unknown to any cop in the country, known only to pizza delivery boys and the occasional real-life woman he might have had sex with once a year.

Unlike Isobel's tomb, the house was clean, warm and well furnished. We could have been in Algiers: thick rugs and old French-colonial-in-the-Ottoman-style furniture, a massive fireplace and oil paintings of long-forgotten sheiks on the walls.

'Wow,' said Maria as we walked inside, then, as she sat in one of the lounges, 'What do we do next? Can we eat? I'm starving and I saw there was an Indian place just down the road.'

—

WE HAD UNTIL Friday. Three days. Then, if I hadn't ordained it suicide or accident, maybe Tyrone's fault, if we were still investigating, they would come after us. Or maybe they'd come after us sooner. Maybe they were after us now. I was inviting wrath and bringing Maria into the game.

'Maybe you want to think about calling Casey?' I said to her as she rummaged through the fridge in the extraordinarily large kitchen, which looked onto a small walled garden thick with pomegranate trees and rose bushes.

'He's gone home,' she replied in a dull, wan tone.

'No. He hasn't. He's around the corner, in Elwood, hanging out in a friend's hotel.'

She turned and looked at me with a *how come you know so much about my man?* look.

—

314

'BABE?'

'Babe! It's you. I'm here.'

'Darian told me you're in Elwood.'

'Yeah, I couldn't leave. I couldn't leave you. Hey, look, I'm real sorry, honey, I just did ...'

His voice drifted off. Apologies weren't his thing. He only ever made them to one person, and it was to her.

'Are you all right?' he asked.

'Yeah.' But he knew that meant no.

'I can come over ...' He let the rest hang. Don't push it, Case.

'Yeah.'

Long silence.

Don't push it, Case, but this doesn't sound good. While he waited he grabbed one of his other three mobiles and began to text.

may need help

Then he added, for clarification:

muscle

'The investigation's taken a twist and it's ... bad.'

get everyone

'How come?'

'We've had to move into a safe house in St Kilda. There's a cool-looking Indian restaurant around the corner ...'

we're going to st kilda

'You there with Darian?'

'Yeah.'

'Bad how?'

There was a long moment. Casey waited, his finger hovering above the touch screen of his other phone.

'Our lead suspect is the Commissioner.'

thermo AKs the lot

'Gimme your address,' he said gently. 'I'll come over. I'll look after you, babe.'

'Okay.' And she gave him the street number. Then, moments after hanging up, she walked outside and across to the car where the Algerians sat.

'My man is coming,' she told them. 'He'll be on a Harley. He has long hair and he looks dangerous. But he's cool.'

And they said: 'No worries, sister.'

They offered her a bit of the falafel they were eating, which she happily took.

—

QUEENSLAND HAD RECENTLY enacted a law that banned bikies from congregating in groups of more than three, a little like the old redneck days when the government had banned groups of more than three people, no matter who they were, being together in public, lest they foment revolution. Victoria doesn't have a similar bikie law.

I heard the full-throttle grumble of Harleys around noon, around the time I was rolling back into the years when I knew Copeland as a Detective Inspector, in the late eighties, trying to recall the man I knew, trying to cast light on the man I didn't know; were there any trails I could pick up on?

Fourteen Harleys, led by Casey, rode into the laneway by the house.

Thirteen bad guys with maybe eight square metres of tattoo, led by Casey, walked into the house, each of them with a pistol tucked into his belt and a sawn-off shotgun, or, in the case of a couple of the fellas, an even more highly illegal semiautomatic rifle, holstered over their shoulder, under their jacket. Miraculously they hadn't caught the attention of the cops.

'We rode the laneways,' said Casey by way of explanation.

I was in *The Good, The Bad and The Ugly*.

'We're here,' Casey added, somewhat unnecessarily.

SEARCH

NO-ONE KNEW HIS LOCATION. HE WAS SAFE. IN THE CAVE.

Like Batman.

He bolted the doors and stared out through the wraparound windows of his apartment on the top floor of one of the city's tallest buildings. All of Melbourne spread out before him, from the urban tangle that surrounded him to the flat stretch of suburbs beyond, and then, far in the distance, mountains, hazy blue and grey. He fired up the pulse, his massive mainframe connected to a wall of screens on his desk, connected to the cloud and, secretly, into thousands of other computers and online storage facilities and databanks, even the NSA, though they didn't know it, and typed in two words: *Copeland Walsh*.

And then he hit the return button.

Search.

—

THE BIKERS, ALL of whom had imaginative names like Anvil or Thud, concluded that there was no immediate danger to us, no storming of the castle, so they ordered pizza – twenty-six large – and massed upon the floor of the lounge room, around the flat screen, and watched *Legally Blonde*.

Go figure.

I left them to it. I went out the back, into the garden, and lay on the grass, staring up at the blue sky and wondering if indeed

I was in the Maghreb. The enclosed walls covered with jasmine and the ground peppered with pomegranate evinced a fragrance that I caught in wafts. I was in Richard Burton's *The Book of the Thousand Nights and a Night*, I was the Sheik of Araby and there were rolling sandhills, more than a million, I swear, stretching to a dusky West African sunset. I was floating.

A voice said: 'Darian.'

I ignored it. It was Maria's voice and it seemed like she had something important to say but, for the moment, I was, for the first time since discovering that Copeland was Isobel's killer, allowing myself a little private retreat. I'd retired to the Noosa River for a life of hammock-swinging and little else, and I was deeply cursing my weakness in having accepted the offer to clear up a twenty-five-year-old death in my old home town.

'Darian,' Maria called again.

—

THE FIRST TIME I took a hit of vodka at five in the morning – like, the hit of an entire bottle – was after I'd attended a crime scene in Mornington, down south on the bay, where I had stood over a four-year-old boy named Tim whose body had been cut into eight. All eight pieces of Tim had been assembled like Lego blocks on the dining table of his house. I had seen worse and I'd seen a lot of murder and a lot of mutilation and I tried, I tried, I really did try, but Tim was a body too far. He had green eyes and soft brown hair and dimples on his chin. I leaned over this grotesque statue, a nightmare effigy, and stared into his eyes and said *I will get the person who did this to you and if they don't go down for the rest of their life in a cell, I will kill them and personally throw them into a pit of bile,* and then, that night, having assured myself that yeah, I'm good, all good, I'm fine, no problems, no torment, I went home to my house in Collingwood, but on the way I stopped at one of the few 24-hour liquor stores where occasionally I'd buy some wine or maybe a bottle of Campari and I pointed at a large bottle of vodka behind the counter. I took it home and downed it in twenty minutes. Here's to you, Tim. Here's to you, Darian.

I don't do that sort of thing anymore, and as I lay on the grass I wasn't feeling vulnerable in having to reach out for a bottle. But I was feeling vulnerable in having my world recently give way.

'Darian?' Maria called again, this time a little more loudly.

Leave me alone, I wanted to say back to her, give me ten more minutes of reflection, ten more minutes to try to get my head around this betrayal. But I didn't.

'Yeah?'

She kneeled down next to me, on the grass.

'The ring. If what Dunn says is true and Copeland did put it on her finger as he killed her, then …'

'Yep, let's do it.' I sat up. I'd been putting it off, lost in marvel at how a man I thought I knew was a totally different person.

Maria had arrived at exactly the same point I'd got to.

—

'Buff?'

'Hey, Darian, I hear you've pretty much wrapped it up.'

He was on speakerphone, Maria and I on the other end of the line. While the boys were in the lounge room guffawing at Reese Witherspoon and providing X-rated commentary on all the blondes they knew, Maria and I were hunkered down in an office upstairs.

'I hear Racine's been exonerated and you're going to say it was a suicide,' Buff said.

I didn't respond to that. Instead I asked a question.

'The boyfriend, Tyrone: you told me that he was in the lounge room of the house while you and Al went into the bedroom?' I said.

'Yep.'

'You also told me you felt sorry for him.'

319

'I did, yeah. At the time. As I said, I didn't think he had anything to do with it. At the time.'

'After you came out of the bedroom, how long was it before CIB, or in fact any other cops, arrived?'

'About ten, maybe fifteen minutes.'

'You were alone in the house with Tyrone during that time.'

'Yes.' He was beginning to sound wary.

'I remember you as being a very compassionate man, Buff. I'm sure you still are,' I said.

He didn't answer.

'So I'm wondering if by chance you might have allowed him, Tyrone, back into her bedroom. Given that you felt sorry for him. As a sort of farewell. Even though it might have seemed a little gruesome. If he was innocent, as you thought he was, then maybe it seemed, at the time, like an act of compassion.'

He didn't answer.

'Caring for the bereaved, they teach us not to worry about that, they tell us that the feelings of the families of the victim are irrelevant. But the good cops, the cops who care, take all those lessons on board and then, when the time comes, a time of extreme anguish, make their own decisions. I certainly did. On many occasions.'

He didn't answer. I waited. After a moment he said, 'Yeah, he wanted to say goodbye to her. He told me he wanted to hold her hand one last time. Al didn't care; she was going straight to hell anyway, as far as he was concerned. He was in there for a couple of minutes. Alone. I remember hearing the sirens approaching and shouted to him to get out.'

What Al and Buff had done was, of course, a serious breach of protocol, but it was the sort of thing that cops do. We aren't averse to breaking a few rules when we believe it's the right thing to do.

From the corner of my eye I could see that Isosceles had arrived at the house. He had come into the room where Maria and I were hunkered over my mobile phone. He was agitated. We signed off from Buff.

'Here,' Isosceles began excitedly, 'is a most curious and, I suggest, combustible situation: while keeping a GPS track on all our suspects, I have just noted that Tyrone, ex-boyfriend of Isobel, has just arrived at the abode of Brian Dunn, also known as ex-boyfriend of Isobel.'

PAYBACK

THE LAST TIME HE HAD SAT OUTSIDE BRIAN DUNN'S apartment, in the oh-so-very-fucking-swanky Beverley Hills block overlooking the river, was twenty-five years ago. Days after Isobel's return from Bolivia. Doubt had turned into suspicion when, after she seemed more distant with him and had postponed a couple of dates together, he'd overheard her on the phone, whispering, giggling, saying Brian this and Brian that. Could it be that she was seeing that slimy teacher?

He had staked out the apartment block, sat and waited. Felt like a fool, felt like a dummy from a z-grade detective movie, all the while thinking, am I paranoid?

But no, he wasn't.

There they were, strolling out of the building, hand in hand, laughing as they walked to his Harley, as they climbed onto it, as they roared off, his girlfriend's arms clasped tightly around Dunn's waist.

A wave of revulsion swept through him. He almost vomited. He decided then and there that he would kill Brian Dunn. For the shame and the betrayal, for taking his girl, for messing up her life ...

He was beyond angry. He'd never had feelings like this.

Sitting now out the front of Dunn's apartment, twenty-five years later, Tyrone remembered that anger. Isobel had been used by the guy. The guy had asked her to bring drugs back into the country and, naive beautiful girl that she was, she did it, without realising what she was doing. Dunn had put her in the firing line, put her on the precipice of destruction, and still, yet still, she was laughing and throwing her arms around him.

Had they fucked? he wondered back then.

Of course they had.

He had blocked his eyes shut as he tried to force away the visions of his girl, spread out on a bed, naked, with that older man, also naked, on top of her. The more he tried to push those images away, the more they came right back at him: Isobel naked on top of Dunn, Isobel sucking his dick, Isobel kissing him on the lips while he came inside her. The more he tried to block those images, the faster they came. Isobel kissing him on the lips while he came inside her quickly morphed into Dunn ejaculating into her mouth as she looked up into his eyes, all full of love and adoration at the same time – a series of images, all horrid, getting worse, without limit or control. As the rage and jealousy tore through him like a tsunami, they blew away all reason, all control. There was no logic. There were only his uncontrollable emotions, hurtling through his brain, creating visions of his girl wrapped around the body of another man.

Dunn's snaring of Isobel had dwindled him. He had felt like the character in *The Incredible Shrinking Man*. Twenty-five years ago, after he had confirmed that they were together, after he vowed to kill Dunn, he had driven away, tail between his legs. For another six and a half weeks, he endured knowing that Isobel was in love with another man, a bad man. He felt impotent. Not sexually, but in the core of his being. Isobel had been his everything and now that had been displaced. By another man. A man who had used her. It was so unfair.

And then …

Isobel dead. Isobel naked. Isobel hanging on the back of her door, in her house. Isobel having had sex. With Dunn. It had to be. When Tyrone saw her, on the back of the door, naked, dead, his world evaporated. He had lost his love.

He didn't know it, at the time, but he had also just lost his life. Nothing was ever the same afterwards, just a series of losses, disappointments, bitterness, all matched with an increasing roar of anger and cynicism.

After he'd called triple-O, after the first uniformed cops had arrived, as he stood trembling in the lounge room, now with a new image of Isobel in his head, one that had become imprinted on his mind, like a freeze-frame in a movie, he kept thinking: Dunn did this.

Dunn came here after I left, he fucked her and then he killed her. It wasn't deliberate, it was an accident, during some weird-shit sex, but he killed her.

It's Dunn.

And what did he do, back then, after the body was removed from the house, as the coronial inquest was launched, as he sat in the court and watched the proceedings?

Nothing. Yet again cowardice kicked in.

—

ALL OF THESE feelings, from over two decades ago, had come back in a violent rush after the cops visited him at the pool, asking him questions about Isobel's death. Suddenly her death felt as though it were yesterday, and so too did the power of these feelings, long buried.

So now, he determined, he would do what he was too cowardly to do back then. He wouldn't *kill* Dunn. That was stupid. But he would hurt him.

It was payback time.

Tyrone climbed out of his car. Tucked into his belt was his weapon. What would he do? He didn't know. But he would hurt him bad.

TURN OF THE SCREW

Rescuing Brian Dunn from being stabbed by a screwdriver-wielding Tyrone was probably not high on Maria's list of priorities. Certainly not on mine. We drove quickly, knowing that a confrontation between these two players would not end happily for either of them. Preventative policing is always a good thing, but if it wasn't for a belief that Maria and I shared about Tyrone and the ring, we most likely would have got Isosceles to make an anonymous call to the nearest station and report the likelihood of some criminal violence at the Beverley Hills apartment block.

We pulled up out the front, illegally parked and ran towards Dunn's open front door. The two towers of the apartments are impressive. Built in a 1930s Art Deco style, they are unique in the city. They have an unmistakable Los Angeles feel to them.

Dunn's apartment was on the ground floor, which was convenient. As we approached we heard shouting and the sounds of a scuffle from inside.

Dunn was on the floor, doing a crab-walking thing with his hands and feet, shouting and trying to get away from Tyrone, who seemed to have frozen with uncertainty, a screwdriver raised above his head as if he was going to plunge it into the other man. I walked up to him and simply took it out of his hand. He looked dazed and offered absolutely no resistance.

'I want him charged!' screamed Dunn as he clambered to his feet. 'I want him charged with attempted murder! Break and enter! This is outrageous and it will not go unpunished!'

Maria walked up to him and pushed him backwards. 'What the …?' he spluttered as he lost his balance and fell back into a couch.

'I would suggest you shut the fuck up. How does that sound?' she said.

He stared at her and gulped. It seemed to be sounding just fine.

We escorted the world's worst assassin out of the building and plonked him in the back of the Studebaker.

'I want to go home,' were his first words, as I sat in the driver's seat and turned around to face him.

'We need to talk to you first,' answered Maria.

'I'm sorry. I didn't mean to do that. I dunno, I just wanted to hurt him. He killed her, didn't he? I knew they were lovers, but I did nothing about it. I could have stopped her from seeing him. I was going to report him and I should have. She'd still be alive. It's my fault that she's dead.'

'It's not your fault. You're feeling guilt that's entirely unwarranted,' I said. He didn't respond. I don't think he even heard me. I needed him to focus.

'Tyrone. The night she died,' I said.

'Yeah?'

'When you left, do you remember seeing anyone out on the street? Parked cars, that sort of thing?'

It was a long time ago, but it was also a night seared into his memory like no other. He would have replayed the events of the night and following morning over a thousand times.

'No. Nothing,' he said.

'Okay. The morning that you discovered her.'

'Yeah?'

'Remember the first two cops who arrived? They were in uniform.'

'Yeah.' He was talking like a zombie, like he was on autopilot.

'They let you back into the room. To be with Isobel. Like a last farewell sort of thing.'

'He told me he'd get into trouble if anyone found out. But he was kind to me.' Still talking as if he was on autopilot. No hint of emotion at all.

'There was a ring on her finger. Did you take it?'

—

THE RING INFURIATED him. It was a symbol of another man's claim to her. Dunn's. Dunn must have bought her the ring. When? Maybe he had given it to Isobel ages ago. Before she went to Bolivia perhaps. Maybe it was like a secret between them. Maybe she would bring it out and put it on her finger when she was with him. Then remove it, hide it, when she was with Tyrone. Whatever, as he stood in the lounge room, as he tried to hold back the waves of revulsion and grief, as he tried to make sense of his girlfriend now dead and in that terrible, terrible way, hanging on the back of her bedroom door, all he could think about was the ring on her finger. A ring he had not given her. As grief and confusion gave way, in brief snippets of clarity, to anger, Tyrone found some focus.

He had to remove that ring. His girlfriend, she was his. They had made pledges. Dunn had ruined all that they had, all that they'd talked about. The future together. Dunn had poisoned her and smashed their dreams.

Dunn had killed her. Tyrone didn't know how it'd happened, but he knew that Dunn was responsible. He had killed Isobel.

And now Dunn's ring was on her finger.

Tyrone had to get rid of it. It represented a cancer that had permeated and now destroyed their lives.

He turned to one of the cops. 'Can I go in and just say goodbye to her? For the last time? Please?'

—

'WHAT DID YOU do with it?' I asked.

'I took it off her finger,' he replied.

'Yeah, and then what did you do with it?'

'Do you still have it?' asked Maria.

He looked up at us from the back seat then out through the side window, back towards Dunn's apartment, as if trying to remember where he was.

'Why would I keep it?' he asked. 'It was poison.'

—

HE HAD TRIED to crush it. But it wouldn't yield; the gold was too strong. The ring was stronger than his brute force, all that he could muster.

So he threw it.

'It hit the wall. I can't remember where. I just threw it. I wasn't even looking at where it went.'

—

MARIA AND I STEPPED into Isobel's bedroom, for the third time and this time with the explicit intention of finding, hopefully, a precious ring bought twenty-five years ago by a killer, then removed and flung away by a jealous and confused Tyrone. The bedroom was carpeted. Thus far, as we had walked around the house, we had been careful where we stepped, lest we kick up walls of dust. Now we had to sift through it.

We were wearing overalls and face masks. More than just being a meticulous job, it was going to be a dirty one too. After Tyrone stumbled out of the car and promised he'd drive straight home and not try any revenge-inspired attacks on Dunn again, we had driven towards Isobel's house, discussing whether we should pick up a vacuum cleaner along the way. It seemed, at first, like a good alternative to crawling around the bedroom floor on our hands and knees. But then we remembered how thick and deep the dust on the carpet was; a vacuum cleaner bag would fill within twenty seconds, having barely made any progress over the surface.

'Welcome to the glamour of a murder investigation,' I said.

'Better than being in a cruiser watching roadworks,' Maria replied.

We moved slowly, digging our hands through two decades of thick, solid dust, reaching down towards the surface of the carpet then edging our fingers in all directions, like I'd imagine a suddenly blind person walking through a dark space, arms outstretched, hoping not to stumble and fall.

Time was not on our side.

—

WHO WAS THIS man, this man from another time, a successful and highly respected cop in his mid-forties? Certainly not the man I thought I knew. Who was Copeland Walsh back at the time of Isobel's death?

After he had bought the ring, he must have then stalked her, maybe on the same day, waiting for her to emerge from work, following her home as she walked the twenty minutes down Chapel Street, turning left at Commercial Road, walking past Prahran Market and then down Osborne. It wouldn't have taken long to determine where she lived. Maybe he did the dumb thing and found her address on the cop database – Isosceles was checking – but it was extremely unlikely he'd leave such an obvious footprint. Then, once he knew where she slept, it was a matter of getting to know her routine. Did she live alone? He would have discovered that she did, very quickly. Just a few mornings and nights checking out her house and he would have realised that, yes, she did live alone, although there was a bit of foot traffic coming and going. Tyrone the boyfriend and Dunn the older boyfriend.

He would have established a pattern. Isobel's life. He would have got to know all the details, the minutiae of this young woman's life, just as I had, walking now in his tracks.

All of this would have been time-consuming. As a Division Commander he would have had a full day at the office, every day. Some of that could have been carved out for his shadowing of her, but most of it had to have been outside of work hours. These were her private times and when he was free from the constraints of the job. I needed to go back and look into those times.

Isosceles was searching. There was one person, hopefully still alive, who I thought might shed some light on those private hours of our elusive killer.

—

WOULD THE RING still even be there? Tyrone had not been the last person to exit the bedroom. After him were tribes of cops and the Coroner's people but not, luckily, anyone remotely connected to forensics. The lackadaisical nature of the investigation was, for the first time, a significant advantage for us.

We hoped.

Isobel had lived in the house for a very short period of time; her dad had bought it for her, as a (rather generous, I thought) graduation present, for having completed school and, in particular, for being chosen to go to Bolivia. So it was surprising just how much we found on the floor: an endless number of bobby pins and cheap bangles and bracelets littered across the surface of the carpet.

After what seemed like a two-week visit to an internment camp, Maria shouted, 'I've got something!'

She was in a curiously spider-like position, half-twisted around one of the bedposts by the wall, her overalls, like mine, coated with a thick film of brown dirt.

I crossed to her and watched as she explained that she was carefully wrapping her fingers around a circular metal object, which she then lifted up through the thick layers of dust.

It too was coated in dust.

She blew at it and a hundred thousand tiny particles spun into the air around us. It was a gold ring, antique in style, with a setting of a sapphire between a small diamond on either side.

—

ELI RECOGNISED THE ring straightaway. Like all of the rings he had either made or reconstructed, it bore a tiny little stamp, an imprint on the inside of the gold band.

'What is this?' he asked. 'You call me, ask me about a ring, now you show me this ring. What does it mean?

We didn't answer him.

The ring was confirmation, but we needed more. Our killer could easily claim that the ring had been stolen or that maybe he had taken it back to the shop for sizing and forgot to pick it up afterwards, that Isobel might have taken it for herself. Conclusive evidence, or a mountain of circumstantial evidence, was what we needed.

As we left Eli's shop and drove away my phone buzzed.

I put it on speaker as I answered the call. The phone was brand-new. Casey had organised two phones, for Maria and me, a few hours ago.

'Is that you, Darian?' asked Copeland.

'It's me.'

'I'm here with Nick and we're both wondering how you're going, if we might get a result from you tonight perhaps.'

The speed with which he had found my new number was not lost on Maria, who was looking decidedly worried.

'I'll have it to you by Friday.'

'There've been some developments. Nothing to be concerned about, but developments that have made the need for your final report rather urgent. I'm sure you're just at the stage of correcting the spelling mistakes and the grammar, but don't worry about that. All we need is the conclusion. As we discussed.'

'Just tying up a few loose ends here,' I said. 'We don't want any misunderstandings, do we?'

'That's my boy. By the way, were you unhappy with the lodgings in Davis Avenue?'

'Not at all. We just thought we'd work from a larger space.'

'Super. Great idea. I'm very fond of Grey Street – you're just a short walk from Nick's house. He's saying that you could drop over and hand him that report later tonight.'

'If we're done.'

'Indeed. Nice chatting, Darian. Send my best to the lovely Miss Chastain.'

And with that he signed off.

I put the car into gear and kept driving. This was a dangerous game; I could feel Maria's fear as I silently contemplated how great respect, maybe even love, can turn so quickly into the opposite. In my case all I had were feelings of anger and hatred.

Betrayal, which wasn't really the best motivator in an investigation, had been replaced.

TILL DEATH DO US PART

WITH ONE FINAL THRUST HE CAME INSIDE HER.

By then she was dead. She had tried to fight him off as he pulled hard on the tie around her neck, but she was not strong enough. He just pulled harder, choked her tight and kept on doing what he'd been fantasising over for two weeks.

He opened his eyes and stared into hers. Her dead eyes. For a moment he was ignited again but then an overwhelming feeling of shame and disgust rippled through him. He carefully eased his penis out from inside her. Making sure that nothing from the condom leaked onto the floor, he removed it and then wrapped it up in a tissue that he had brought along especially. He placed the tissue with its deeply incriminating evidence in his pocket as he pulled his pants back on and then hurriedly dressed.

I need that drink, he said to himself. He had brought the bourbon along because he knew he'd need a long hard bolt afterwards. Everything had been planned. It was waiting for him on the other side of her bedroom door.

He felt the warm burn from the hit of alcohol, as he stood in the kitchen, staring at the neat array of dishes, washed and stacked up. Really? Who does that after a party? His baby girl, hanging on the back of her bedroom door, was certainly a little homemaker. He felt good. Shame and disgust had gone. The bourbon had seen to that. This was good, he said to himself. I could do this again.

But I won't. I cannot. Isobel, my beautiful dimpled girl, Isobel, you were like a blazing star across my orbit and now you are gone and I shall, as I must, retreat back to my humdrum life with that cancerous woman … who I really do love.

Oh my Jan, I am so sorry, my darling, but your husband has needs. Desires. And while we cannot talk about these things, I am sure you understand.

I needed you, Isobel, and thank you, my darling. My little sweet girl. You made an older man so happy.

—

DID SHE KNOW? I wondered as Maria and I walked through the open gates towards the front door of the house ahead of us, perched on a small hill overlooking a blistering ocean below. Did Jan know, before she died, what her husband had become? Did she discern a change in the man after his kill? As her body was collapsing and she was facing death, could she have known that Copeland had returned to her, one night in 1990, having extinguished the breath of a young woman, having stripped her naked and hung her on the back of her bedroom door?

We were travelling unexposed. No mobile phones with their GPS trackers, no connection to the outside world. We had driven down to Queenscliff, a gracious seaside town to the west of Melbourne. I'd turned left out of the city and we hadn't got lost.

Port Phillip Bay, upon which Melbourne had grown around the fringes, hugging its edges and spiralling out in all directions, is shaped like a duck's head. Think Donald and you've got it.

The entrance to the bay, where the ocean is calmed as two fingers of land coming in to the east and the west or, in Darian-speak, the right and the left, channel the swells, where Harold Holt was lost in the rip, is home to two towns. Queenscliff on one side, Portsea on the other. Maybe Isobel had stood on the cliff at Portsea above Dominic Stone's house and stared across to the city beyond. Maybe she had glanced in another direction and looked towards the town only a kilometre away, across the water, where, almost three decades later, investigators would seek the proof to nail the man who was, at that time, scheming to kill her.

—

'I REMEMBER YOU. You're Copeland's friend,' said the woman in an accusing tone.

'He was my boss. We were close, but that was a long time ago.'

'We are investigating the death of a young woman twenty-five years ago,' said Maria. 'If you're worried about misplaced loyalties, don't be; the only loyalty Darian and I have is to the dead girl.'

We were standing at the front door to the house. Patricia was three years younger than her sister Jan. I had asked Isosceles to find her for us. I knew the sisters were close and I was hoping they had confided in one another. It was a long shot and, on the drive, Maria had panicked, albeit briefly, saying that we were idiots to be driving all the way down to Queenscliff to waste time talking to the sister of the bad guy's dead wife of over twenty years. *I mean come on, Darian. We should be chasing some fucking evidence!*

She was correct, but we were fresh out of evidentiary leads and, even though we might get a grand total of nada from the sister, it was a conversation we had to have.

Okay, okay, I get it, I had told her. It's all about dotting the i's and crossing the fucking t's.

And on we drove.

Patricia was in her late sixties, although she told us she was fifty-four. Maybe she'd reached sixty and started counting backwards with the passing of each year. She was tall, dressed in a woollen suit, had steely blonde hair and looked like a golfing version of Emma Thompson on the moors. There was no-one in her life but for three cats, who slinked around her ankles as she stood in the entrance to her house and calmly appraised us.

'What possible relevance could I have to an investigation of a murder that happened over two decades ago?' she asked.

'We'd like to ask you some questions about Copeland,' I said.

There. I'd said it. I'd mentioned his name in response to her question about a murder. I knew Patricia and Copeland had fallen out over Jan's burial so, even though it was decades ago and for most people such disputes are resolved over time, I was hoping that if the sisters were close and talked, then we might get an insight into Jan's thinking at around the time her husband killed Isobel.

Her eyes narrowed and she stared at me, then at Maria. Then she stood back and held the door open for us to walk inside.

'My sister worked for the police. Did you know that?'

'I didn't. No,' I replied.

We were in a sunroom, glass walls with a view out onto the ocean beyond the cliffs. I felt like I was in Wales. The sun was out and it was hot. Soon, given the vagaries of the local weather, there would most likely be a southern gale whipped up by Antarctic winds. We were sitting on a large floral-covered couch. We had tea. I'm not used to an English atmosphere, all that stiff upper lip and formality going on. Interestingly, I couldn't think of having attended a homicide down here in Queenscliff, ever.

'At the Police Forensic Science Lab, in the city. She went to Monash Uni. Graduated with a masters of science in biochemistry.' Patricia looked proud and, thinking back to how it must have been for a woman in those days, in those fields, of science and forensic cop stuff, I could understand why. The Police Forensic Lab was established in 1965. In the years before DNA it was all about blood typing, fingerprints, fibres and hairs; 'Every contact leaves a trace,' is what Dr Edmond Locard, who created the first forensic lab in the world, in Lyon, famously said.

'She met Copeland Walsh on a case. She thought he was handsome and dashing. I thought he was too. In fact, for many years, I was jealous.' She flicked her hair and drank some tea. 'They got married and Jan left her job. She told me that he wanted her to stay at home. "Why?" I asked. She didn't answer. But she did it. Gave up her career. That was a long time ago. She was still in her mid-twenties. They both were.'

'Can you remember back to the early nineteen-nineties for us?' I asked.

'Jan was very sick then.'

'Did she talk to you, at that time, about him? Was there, for instance, anything she might have said about a change in him?'

'That's a very vague question, Mr Richards. Applied to a time that is quite distant. Perhaps you might be better off asking me something more specific.'

'Okay. Sure,' I replied. One usually doesn't ask specific questions. It's called leading the witness. 'Did Jan express any concerns to you that her husband might have crossed some kind of moral line? Into, perhaps, criminal territory?'

It was still a vague question, but neither I, nor Maria, was about to ask her point-blank if Jan had confided that her husband had raped and killed a young woman.

'She found a used condom. In the pocket of his pants. Which he had stuffed into the laundry basket. That was the answer, by the way.'

Both Maria and I were flummoxed by this comment. Seeing our look, she explained:

'He wanted her to stay at home so she could do his laundry, make their bed, cook his breakfast and then have a meal waiting for him when he got home. She wouldn't answer my question because she was embarrassed. Anyway, she found a condom. Used. Can you believe that? At first she thought it evidence of marital betrayal. But then she thought: why would he keep it? It was wrapped up in tissue. If a man cheats on you, he'll do everything in his power to keep it a secret. No-one wants to be caught. So why not, like every other cheating man on the planet, flush the evidence down the toilet? Why wrap it up in tissue and place it in your pocket? Well, there could only be one answer, she told me. It had to represent more than just a simple infidelity.'

'When was this? Do you remember?' asked Maria.

'No. Not with any accuracy. But it was after she discovered she had the cancer and very soon after the first mobile phones went on the market.'

'Did she ever happen to mention the name Isobel Vine?' I asked.

'No. Who's she?'

'She was the young lady who died. Back at around this time.'

'It's her death you're investigating?'

I nodded.

'How old was this woman?'

'She was young. She had just finished school,' replied Maria.

Patricia closed her eyes and sat back in her chair, as if she was trying to remember something. 'That's strange,' she said, with her eyes still closed. Then, after a moment, she sat forward.

'Jan went to a young woman's funeral. I remember she came around to see me the same day. This was years ago. I asked where she'd been. She was all dressed up. And she said she'd been to a funeral. Oh, who died? I asked. A young girl, she said, who had just finished school. Did you know her? I asked. No, she said. And then she started crying. It was quite odd. And we never spoke of it again.'

'What did she do with the condom?' I asked.

'DNA had just been discovered. Jan had read a lot about it and knew it would be the most important tool in crime-solving. She was upset that by the time it would be regularly used in the courts to prove guilt she'd be dead. The cancer was very aggressive. So she froze it.'

'Sorry?' Both Maria and I were confused. 'She froze …'

'The condom. She left it in its tissue, placed it in a Tupperware container, one of the really small ones, and put it in a freezer.' She paused for a moment, then: 'I've lived here in this house since I was eighteen.'

She was leaping from one thought to another with no apparent connection between them. Maria glanced at me and I gave her a *let's just roll with it* look.

'My husband and I bought it. He died very young. Sweet man. He built tractors. I vowed I would never leave this house, and why would I? Sitting up here on this promontory with wonderful views of the ocean. I told Jan. I said to her: I will die in that house, and she said, yes, I know you will. Which is why she gave it to me. She needed a place where it could be stored safely, for a long time, just in case, as she said to me. Just in case, one day, if it's needed. You can't do very much with it now, she said. I won't do anything with it now, she said to me. But in the future, maybe in five or ten years, then it might unlock something. Which might *need* to be unlocked. Do you think she was talking about that young woman? The one who'd just finished school?'

She stood up. Maria and I were reeling from the shock that, within maybe twelve hours of Isobel's murder twenty-five years ago, Jan had put aside crucial, utterly damning evidence which would, if anyone bothered to investigate, convict her husband.

'I'll go get it for you. It's at the very back of my freezer.' And with that Patricia walked out of the sunroom. True to form, a southerly squall was kicking in, and through the windows we could see that clouds of cobalt blue were beginning to scud across the horizon in the far distance.

Every murder, every rape, every act of wanton violence, is a snatch in time, but those incidents don't come out of nowhere; there's always a time line where the person who commits the crime sets out on his or her journey and, for whatever reasons, intersects with their victim and then, following that crossroads of violence and mayhem, tendrils are left behind. Guilt, shame, remorse, anger, feelings of retribution or hopelessness. Evidence, too, the traces of the contact. These tendrils, both physical and psychological, never, it seems to me, vanish. Here we were, twenty-five years later, and evidence from the day after the murder was about to bring this all to an end.

That is, of course, unless Copeland decided to fight back.

SPIRITS OF THE DEAD

I'VE NEVER BEEN THE MARRYING TYPE. I FIND MY SOLACE IN the arms of the game I play with hookers – you pretend you love me and I pretend you love me – and a river that flows through the mangrove lands of Noosa. It's kind of pathetic but I don't care anymore. I was proposed to once and I said no, even though I wanted to say the opposite. I was scared. Of what I didn't quite know, but I'd seen the marriage of my parents and it was a horror ride in the Ghost Train. I get marriage, I do; I see it and I admire the people who endure it. They have kids, they have a house, they have, as Anthony Burgess wrote, a culture. And that's cool, because at my age, in my mid-forties, I have a culture of one and it's boring talking to yourself after a few days. I had hoped to make it work with Rose, but the longer we remained separated the more I felt it was over between us. Totally over. That's what she had said to me: 'Come back when it's totally over.' She was talking about my addiction, the living for murder. It would never be totally over and we both, in our hearts, knew it.

I used to admire Copeland and his marriage to Jan. It was one of those old-school stories: they met at a very young age and swore eternal love to each other, or so I imagined, and then stayed in that one street, one house, one bed. Until she died.

Now I knew better.

Her grave, in one of Melbourne's older cemeteries, became a monument to his wife but also to Copeland's principles and beliefs. Like the old-fashioned guy that he was, he'd even purchased the plot of earth next to hers so that when his time came he would be laid to rest, body to body, earth to earth, next to her.

I walked along a path, past ornate nineteenth-century gravestones, angels with wings and sonnets of eternal love.

He had betrayed her. Sex and murder. She paid him back with another betrayal. Justice.

It was just past six in the morning and a hard dawn was starting to break, the sky grey with plumes of black. No wind. Being an ancient cemetery, this one had rows of hundred-year-old trees and above me I could hear the whistle of sparrows as they fluttered around the low branches, empty of leaves this time of year.

The sound of my feet cut short, crisp echoes, breaking the silence as I walked along a broken concrete path, tufts of grass sprouting where the edges had come apart.

Up ahead I could see him. I paused and watched. Every Thursday morning at six he would travel to her grave, on his way to HQ, and spend half an hour with her. This was a ritual of which few knew. His driver would be waiting at a set of gates on the other side of the cemetery.

He must have heard me approach, but he didn't look up or acknowledge me. I stood close by and watched.

What do you say to her? I wondered. What *do* you say to the dead?

'You were careless,' I said.

He didn't answer. Maybe he prayed when he came to her grave. Maybe he pretended to speak to her, like you see in the movies. Or maybe he was asking her, or himself, for atonement.

'Or maybe a better way of putting it is that you were just too arrogant. At the crime scene with the ring and the glass of bourbon, but especially when you went home, leaving the used condom in the pocket of your pants. I guess that when you went to retrieve it, to throw it away, and found that it was missing, you thought: Oh, Jan must have discovered it. Not to worry, she won't say anything. She's my obedient wife. That was the arrogance which has nailed you.'

341

He still didn't answer. He was standing at the head of her grave, his hands clasped together, behind his back.

'I can connect you to the ring, but we both know it's not enough. I can connect you to the bourbon bottle, but we also know that's of little use. What's going to finally convict you is the condom.'

He almost turned to look at me. Almost. He managed to resist the temptation, which would, in his mind, be seen as weakness.

'Jan kept it. On the inside your DNA. On the outside, Isobel's DNA. That, boss, is the clincher.'

He turned his back on me and began to walk away.

'I'll have the results by tomorrow morning.'

He hadn't stopped walking, but I thought I could see him falter, for the merest of moments. And then he turned a corner, into another pathway lined with silver birch, and disappeared from view.

For a few minutes I stood there, not moving, thinking about frailty. I heard footsteps behind me. An elderly Greek woman, swathed in black, was shuffling along the path, head bowed as if praying, walking towards, I guessed, her husband's grave.

What would Copeland do?

There were a few options. He could fold and bite the dust. He could flee. He could fight back. We were ready for any of the above, but he had schooled me, so I was ready for the most likely alternative.

As I approached the gates, passing a row of sculptured marble angels, their wings and arms reaching out to embrace the dead and maybe the living, I saw, from out on the street, the familiar red and blue circles of police lights. Lots of police lights. As I stepped through the gates I counted five cruisers and twelve uniforms, all with their guns levelled at me.

Also joining the crowd were two crews from Homicide and Zach Reeve, the Officer in Charge, leading them.

This was alternative number three: fight back.

Zach called out, 'Darian Richards, you are under arrest for murder. If you have a weapon, remove it slowly and place it on the ground. Then place yourself on the ground, facedown, hands behind your back.'

'Who'd I kill, Zach?' I said.

He looked uneasy. He'd been tasked to do a job by an old man who might or might not be on the way out and the order would have been rife with non-specifics. The uniformed cops didn't care. They were blindly doing what they were told and nothing they did when following orders would be used against them. But Zach, Officer in Charge of Homicide, in one of the most responsible and scrutinised positions in the Service, would be held to account for his every move and decision. And clearly he was bothered.

'We'll get to that later,' he replied.

'Victim? Chain of evidence? The basic stuff that even eight-year-olds understand from watching *CSI*. This is ground zero, Zach; I shouldn't have to tell you that the arrest needs to be perfect, needs to fall into place like logic 101 so that when the team from the Public Prosecutor's Office come to take over nobody is embarrassed. Maybe there's something I can help you with.'

He stared at me for a few seconds, then said: 'If you have a weapon, remove it slowly and place it on the ground. Then place yourself on the ground, facedown, hands behind your back.'

THE WAITING GAME

I WAS DRIVEN TO HQ, TAKEN DIRECTLY UP FROM THE underground car park to the eighth floor and put in an interview room. They had chosen not to handcuff me.

Nobody spoke. There was, of course, nothing to say. They were awaiting orders and every passing second went by with an even louder thump that said: not protocol, this is not good, we are in the middle of a power play.

I hadn't been sitting there for longer than five minutes when the door opened and Racine, wearing a bandage on his temple, came in.

'What is going on?' he asked.

'Your boss didn't like the way my investigation went.'

'What does that mean?'

'It means he's the killer.'

He stared at me as if I'd told him we'd just discovered alien life on the third floor.

'Isobel's killer?' he asked in disbelief.

'Yeah.'

'That's bullshit. You're insane.'

'I've got the proof, Nick. DNA proof.'

Such statements are not made in jest by a former Officer in Charge of Homicide. He looked a little shaken and backed out of the room quickly.

—

WITHOUT EVIDENCE YOUR case is as dead as your victim. You can try to make it up, try to build a circumstantial case based on suggestion and motive, and sometimes you can get that through.

Confessions are gold. Cops love a confession and the courts swoon over them, played loudly and in Dolby quad sound for all to hear. Without a confession you have to rely on the next best thing – evidence – and the more you have, the stronger you are.

Whoever was moving the train to have me arraigned before a Magistrate on a murder count was busy somewhere, sweating to find evidence they could use against me or manufacture some that would stand up in court; not, in the second decade of the twenty-first century, as easy as it once was.

And as much as one side relies on evidence to nail their point, the other side relies on its destruction.

And whatever side you're on, there was only one approach, as I'd been taught by the man who mentored me: go at it hard and take no prisoners.

———

THERE WERE NO sirens, only lights flashing from behind the grilles of the cars. Four police cruisers driving at massive speed, weaving through the early-morning traffic, braking hard outside the safe house in Grey Street.

Eight armed cops jumped out. Behind them another two cruisers and three motorcycle cops pulled in.

The Algerian boys vainly tried to halt the approach of the cops as they walked towards the front gate then into the walled yard of flowers and magnolia trees.

An army of bikers, Casey in front of them, appeared on the front porch. Their weapons were concealed but the threat was clear.

'We don't want any trouble,' said the lead cop.

'Good. So fuck off,' replied Casey.

'We need to talk to Maria Chastain,' said the cop.

'I'll give her a message,' said Casey.

'Mate, don't be an arsehole,' said the cop threateningly.

At which the thirteen bikies all took a menacing step towards him. Bikies are the only people on earth who are not intimidated by aggro cops. And cops know it. He took a step backwards. The yard was full of cops and bikies, with the two Algerians looking on, bemused and excited at the same time. One of them pulled out his Samsung and was about to record the event, but the other, his cousin, wisely and gently pushed the phone back into his coat pocket.

While this stand-off was playing out, Maria was sitting upstairs, with Isosceles, staring at the whiteboard, wondering if this investigation was going to lead to a sudden and no doubt inglorious end to her career.

Isosceles had tried to be reassuring by saying, 'Don't worry, Darian always has success,' which was sweet until he then added: 'Except with The Train Rider, of course.'

Darian had outlined the plan to them, well before dawn, and to Casey and the thirteen bikers. 'This is how it will go down,' he had said. 'After I confront Copeland, there will be three possible outcomes, and the most likely is that I'll be arrested and you won't hear from me until it's all over. Then they'll come for you,' he had said, looking at Maria. The acreage of tattoo also looked at her, determined to protect her, come what may. She was a cop, yeah, but she was Casey's girl, and in their primordial minds that meant only one thing: protect at all costs. Loyalty ran deep and Casey, although no longer a runner in their world, was theirs. Till death.

Anvil, or maybe it was Thud, stepped forward and said: 'Let 'em try.'

To which the other bikers all nodded and voiced agreement.

Now the cops had arrived, Casey and the boys seemed to be doing an excellent job of keeping them at bay. Still, there was no doubting that both Maria and Isosceles were very jumpy.

Was this the end of her career? she wondered.

REMEMBER MY NAME

POWER IS BUILT ON FRAGILITY, AND EMPIRES CRUMBLE EASILY. On 17 December 2010, a young Tunisian man who sold oranges from a mobile fruit stall immolated himself during a one-person protest about rising taxes and their effect on his income. Less than four weeks later, the President, Zine El Abidine Ben Ali, who had been in power since 1987, had fled the country, which had risen in anger following the kid's protest.

I'd put my feet up on the interview room table, leaned my chair back against the wall, closed my eyes and hummed the tunes to most of the songs I knew from Bob Dylan. I was on his *Oh Mercy* album when the door opened and Reeve stepped in. He looked ashen. He stared at me a moment without speaking. 'Where's Chastain?' he asked.

'She might be out shopping,' I said. 'She seemed impressed by the fashion outlets in Chapel Street.'

'Get up,' he said.

I'd been in custody for about three hours, and since Racine's brief interlude after I'd arrived there had been nothing until now.

'Found a victim to lay that murder charge on me?' I asked.

'You might say that,' he replied.

—

'COME ON, PROVE it to me.'

'I can't, Dad.'

347

'Yes, you can. You just told me that God doesn't exist because you've learned about Darwin. So, prove it to me.'

'Well, Darwin studied all these species ...'

'Which ones?' he barked.

'Ah ...'

'Don't know, do you?'

'No. No, Dad, I don't.'

'You don't know what you're talking about, do you?'

I didn't mean it, Dad. I'm sorry. I didn't know what I was talking about. It was just something the teacher said in class today and, you know, Dad, it kind of clicked, like, it seemed to make sense.

'What, that we come from fucking apes?'

Jeez, Dad, you were the one who told me that God is a lie and that you'd been an atheist since 1967.

Where are you now, Dad?

Can you tell me?

Did you really die in a Thai brothel, south of Bangkok, in Pattaya? They never showed us a photo of your body. Where are you, Dad? Maybe you're still on the surface of that ocean, like *The Old Man and the Sea*, forever trying to snare the catch and killing it when you do.

I was eleven and Mr Pankridge, who was a great teacher, had introduced the subject of Darwin and creation, a tangled web of religion and argument, but he had said it all came down to one word, one thought, one action.

Survival.

—

REEVE DIDN'T SPEAK as we drove. I was sitting in the front seat of his unmarked car. A change of dynamic from the last time, earlier in the morning, when I'd been thrown in the back seat and taken from one place to another by a uniformed cop.

We pulled up out the front of Copeland's house. I'd been here many times. It was, for a while – a long while, in fact – like home to me. Jan was not a mother but he was a father. Parked in the driveway were three police cruisers.

I counted eight cops standing on the footpath and in the driveway and in the garden as we walked inside.

—

'EXPLAIN THAT,' SAID Reeve.

He was pointing to my Beretta, the very same pistol that Copeland had taken from me some mornings ago, in the backyard of Isobel's house, after I had shot dead a has-been South American hit man employed by the recently deceased Dominic Stone.

The Beretta, which Casey had sourced for me a couple of years earlier, risking a serious conviction for the both of us, was now in Copeland's hand.

The old man had shot himself. Barrel in the mouth, bullet through the brain, smash on the wall behind, body slumped in a chair in his lounge room which was adorned with photos of Jan and, to my surprise, one of him with me, holding a huge fish that we had – he had – caught on a trip to Mount Buller sixteen years ago.

'Explain what?' I said.

'The gun.'

'It looks like a Beretta.'

'It's yours.'

'Is it?'

'Don't fuck with me, Richards. You killed him. That's your gun.'

'Zach, I think you are going to have a ridiculously hard time trying to prove that I killed him.'

'You saying this is suicide?'

'I'm not a police officer anymore; I wouldn't care to speculate.'

He knew it was suicide – anybody who'd seen the body knew it was suicide – but such an event, such a deep shock, requires blame. It's an abrogation, suicide, a betrayal of too much to too many. I would forever be the guy who caused his death.

I didn't care. If there was any grief and remorse, it had hit me the day before. Grief and remorse only belonged to Isobel. Not her killer.

REALLY, IT'S ALL about choice. The decisions we make.

So, he made the only choice I knew he would make. When survival is no longer an option we choose glory.

Of course, there are those who are denied choice. In the city of murder they are the victims, the innocent who are savaged by an ugly choice made by a killer. I speak for them in the aftermath, past that sudden, horrid realisation as they look into their killer's eyes and realise they are powerless and all that awaits them is an abyss.

Maybe Reeve read my mind. After a moment he shrugged and walked out, leaving me free to go.

Copeland was brought down swiftly. He would have imagined a worst-case scenario: me discovering he had killed Isobel. He was prepared to battle me on this, but the hard evidence of DNA, which he couldn't have imagined would haunt him from Jan's grave, was the end of it. And him.

'IS THAT DARIAN Richards?' asked the voice on the phone. It was another new phone; the only people who had the number were Maria, Casey and Isosceles.

'Who's this?' I asked.

'This is the Attorney-General's office. Please hold.'

We were back in Grey Street, packing up, getting ready to haul out of St Kilda, out of Melbourne, my city of murder, and to return …

… where? I hadn't quite figured out that part of the deal yet.

'Richards?' a voice, shrill and prissy, barked.

'Who's this?' I asked.

'It's the Attorney-General – didn't they tell you?' The guy was short on patience. All politicians are short on patience; in fact, they're short on everything.

'Nah. I thought it was the pizza joint calling back to confirm my order.'

'Racine,' he said.

And I waited.

'Racine,' he repeated, this time as if talking to a deaf-mute.

'What about him?' I asked.

'Is he innocent?' asked the Attorney-General.

I paused. There was a complicated answer to a myopic question.

'You were hired to clear his name. The Commissioner is dead and we need to announce his replacement. Today. Is Racine innocent? Yes or no?'

'Define innocence,' I said.

'Oh, good God. They told me you were a problem. Did he kill that girl? That girl, whatever her name was?'

That girl, whatever her name was. I hated this guy. Her name was Isobel, you prick.

'Yes or no. You must have the answer and I certainly hope that it has nothing to do with the Commissioner's death this morning. I was told he had an advanced cancer of some sort. Yes or no; Racine.'

'No,' I said. 'He didn't kill her.'

He hung up without another word. And by three that afternoon Nick Racine had been crowned the next emperor of the kingdom of the strong.

—

IT WAS TWO in the afternoon but Eli had the 'closed' sign on the door of his shop. I squinted inside and saw him sitting at the bench against the back wall, staring back at me. I knocked. He kept staring. I knocked again.

'Is he okay?' asked Maria.

'No. He knows we have the truth and he's scared.'

I knocked again and he finally came to the door, unlocked it and squinted up at us.

'Can we come in?' I asked.

He held the door open, didn't answer and watched as we walked past him.

We stood in the middle of the store. I hadn't noticed it before but there was a strong musty smell to the place.

'Isobel was murdered,' I said. There's no easy way to say this, even years after the fact, so you stick to the basics.

'Her killer was a man who stalked and then attacked her, in her house, at approximately four am on December fifteen, nineteen-ninety. Her attacker was not known to her.'

'It was Stone,' he said.

'Isobel's killer has taken his own life. There will not be a charge, a trial. It's over.'

'It was Stone. And Dunn,' he insisted.

'It's over,' I reiterated.

He stared at me, turned his gaze to Maria, and then, after a rather tense few moments, turned away and walked back to his bench. Twenty-five years of belief could not be shaken, sadly or not, I wasn't sure, by the truth.

—

MARIA AND CASEY farewelled Isosceles. She climbed onto the back of Casey's Harley as the geek promised to send her luggage on via courier. She cast a last glance at me as I pulled my coat tight to ward off an incoming icy gale of sleet and then I watched them roar off down Grey Street, passing the Indian restaurant she never got to eat at.

I caught the late news on Victoria's new Commissioner while sitting in a highway roadside cafe, drinking black coffee and eating chicken soup, staring up at a TV screen, the late bulletin on mute.

Racine was making a speech to the assembled press. Standing beside him was Monahan. I thought I could see Stolly in the crowd. The news bulletin then flashed up an image of the late Commissioner Copeland, followed by a couple of shots of a body, covered and on a trolley, being wheeled out of his house.

It was close to midnight and I was on a road to nowhere. The diner was alive with families and truckers. From behind the counter I could hear Roy Orbison's 'Only the Lonely'. I was a big fan of Roy Orbison. After a huge career in the fifties and sixties he had faded away into an obscurity reserved for guys who no longer mattered, old-school, irrelevant guys whose music belonged to a bygone age. Then, in the late-eighties, he had a massive, unexpected comeback, courtesy of Bono from U2 and the Traveling Wilburys. Suddenly the old guy with weird glasses, the crooner from another time, was hip. It was thrilling to see this sort of return – it was there in his face as he played with cool rockers from the now. He put out a record, the first in ages, and it sold, big-time. He was back.

And then, just as quickly as he'd come back, he died of a heart attack. He had, I guess, a year or two of knowing that his life did matter, that he wasn't going to be left on the scrap heap of obscurity, never remembered, always forgotten.

People would remember his name.

I finished my coffee and walked out, Roy Orbison's voice trailing me into a sinking and unknown night.

ACKNOWLEDGEMENTS

I HAVE A WONDERFUL EDITOR, CLAIRE DE MEDICI, WHO takes my manuscript and elevates it enormously. Additionally Vanessa Radnidge, my publisher, and Kate Stevens from Hachette Australia, made a huge and invaluable contribution to the writing process. As did Elizabeth Cowell, who did the proofread and final edit. Any inconsistencies or weirdness in the text are entirely mine.

We certainly don't do it alone, us writers.

Thanks to everyone at Hachette Australia for their support and for the inspired marketing of the Darian Richards series of novels.

Lucio Rovis gave me wise and considered advice on how an investigation such as the one described in the novel would work.

Claude Minisini also gave me wise and considered advice.

Drawing on many, many years of experience in the hard world that Darian inhabits, both men have been extremely generous with their time. Any mistakes in my description of this crime world are entirely mine.

Dr Simon Lewis was tremendously helpful with the forensic stuff, especially when it came to Isobel's house of dust, left untouched for twenty-five years. Again, any mistakes in the world of forensics are entirely mine.

Great comments and feedback on my early drafts came from Jasin Boland and Ross Macrae. Both Jasin and Ross made a huge difference to the outcome of the narrative. Thanks also to Dean Barker for his comments.

Danielle Binks and Shelleyrae Cusbert made some excellent critical remarks on the characters of Maria and Rose, and I really appreciated this feedback.

Thanks to Bill Waterson and Michael Preece, bad boys from the Ararat West Primary School (a long time ago), for allowing me to use their names. Thanks to Iona Mackenzie for the memories of long ago. Thanks to David Franken and Rachael McGuirk. Thanks also to Jan Soh.

Thanks especially to my wonderful children, Charlie, Delaware and Scarlett, and finally, most importantly as always, thanks to you, the reader, for making the words come alive.

Tony Cavanaugh was nominated for the Victorian Premier's Literary Awards for the screenplay *Father* and the Queensland Premier's Literary Awards for the screenplay *Through My Eyes*. His first novel, *Promise*, was followed in 2013 by *Dead Girl Sing*, and in 2014 by *The Train Rider*. *Kingdom of the Strong* is his fourth novel.

PROMISE

'Chilling and memorable; top-notch Aussie noir
definitely not for the faint-hearted.'
GRAEME BLUNDELL

TONY CAVANAUGH

DEAD
GIRL SING

From the bestselling author of *Promise*

TONY CAVANAUGH

THE
TRAIN RIDER

'As good as Harlan Coben'
WEEKEND AUSTRALIAN

TONY CAVANAUGH

hachette
AUSTRALIA

If you would like to find out more about
Hachette Australia, our authors, upcoming events
and new releases you can visit our website or
follow us on Twitter.

www.hachette.com.au
twitter.com/HachetteAus
facebook.com/HachetteAustralia

Discover more about Tony and his novels by visiting
his Facebook page (www.facebook.com/tonycavanaugh888)
or following him on Twitter (@TonyCavanaugh1).